The Iron Fist

Legacy of the Helping Hands

Kristina Circelli

Book Three in the Helping Hands Series

This is a work of fiction. Names, characters, places and events described herein are products of the author's imagination or are used fictitiously. Any resemblance to actual events, locations, organizations, or persons, living or dead, is entirely coincidental.

The Iron Fist

Author: Kristina Circelli

Edited by Jake George (www.sagewordsservices.com)

Cover design: Jake George

Printed by Sage Words Publishing, (www.sagewordspublishing.com)

ISBN-13: 978-0985918569
ISBN-10: 098591856X

CONTENTS

DEDICATION

For Uncle Louis

A man to whom I owe my inspiration to write; a man who believed in me from the very beginning

PROLOGUE

The crowd rose at the sound of the pianist's harmony, a beautiful woman wearing a flowing ivory dress stepping into view. Her hands clutched a small bouquet of lilies, fingers gripping the flowers nervously. The afternoon sun shone down from a clear blue sky, shimmering amongst the diamond earrings and matching diamond engagement ring that would soon be joined by a sparkling band. Wisps of cool autumn wind gently blew back her thick blonde hair and lifted the veil slightly, but not so much as to uncover her radiant face.

She never moved her dark brown eyes from the man waiting for her at the end of the aisle. The man, the tall, strong, handsome groom she would soon be calling her husband, her perfect match in every way, clasped his hands in front of him, his breath taken away by her beauty, his face a depiction of excitement and anticipation.

An older woman sitting in the first row of seats wiped her eyes with an already-damp cloth as she watched her daughter make her way closer towards her groom. Never had she seen her only little girl so gorgeous, and she was thankful that now her child would have the wedding she was meant to have, the wedding she deserved.

It should have been this way the first time, the mother thought, *a wedding with roses and music and white gowns and tears of happiness*. But her daughter was stubborn, as she always had been, eloping with that half-witted slob who cheated and lied and dared to call himself a man. But she was happy with the man her daughter was marrying today, a kind man with a promising career and a steady income who would care for her daughter and grandchildren.

Two little girls, the bridesmaids of the wedding, exchanged nervous glances with one another when their mother began to say her vows. The older of the two gripped her flowers tightly and swallowed heavily, while the younger looked over at her big sister with apprehension. They didn't smile when the bride and groom placed the rings upon each other's' fingers. They didn't clap when the minister declared them husband and wife, or cheer when the adults kissed and sealed their bond for a lifetime.

Forever.

But they did have a reaction to the moment. As the kiss ended and the bride turned, ready to walk back down the aisle after giving her two beautiful daughters a tearfully happy smile, the groom glanced down. He smiled at them, giving the girls a small, deliberate grin, his eyes darkening for only a second, containing all the disturbing and sinful secrets of his soul.

The little girls could do nothing but step back in fear.

CHAPTER 1

The locker room door slammed into the wall as the raving, tight-fisted teenage boy thrust it open and stalked inside. He punched a locker in a blind, red anger, not noticing the throbbing in his knuckles as he wiped a trail of blood from his bottom lip. He could feel a bruise forming around his left eye, and the pain of it only made him angrier.

He got some good hits in, a blow to the other guy's right eye, a fist to his jaw, another in his gut. Then there was the tight headlock disrupted by his basketball teammates, who were careful of the swinging, potentially lethal fists.

No one would dispute the fact that Robbie Anderson knew how to fight.

The door swung open again with a second crash and a sturdy, middle-aged man wearing a white baseball cap stormed in, his finger already raised in accusation. He gestured to the point guard for the Lakeside High Jaguars basketball team.

"One more fight, Anderson!" Coach Frank Wright yelled at the teenager. "*One* more fight, and you're off the team! I'm sick of this crap!"

"Yeah, well I'm sick of that *bastard* gett'n all up in my face all the time!" Robbie shouted back. "He does it again, I'm gonna break his goddamn face!"

"Robbie, *sit* down and *shut* up!" Wright replied, propping a foot on the bench next to his student. "Now you listen to me. I'm not looking to get fired because I couldn't keep my two best players from bloodying each other's faces! One more fight, and you're off the team," he stated. "Got it?"

Robbie's mouth formed a tight, thin line as he stared at the wall in front of him. His knuckles began to throb and his lip was stinging as his eyes became two furious slits that saw nothing but red. Anger was racing through him, and all he wanted to do was push past his coach and find Coppertone, then literally beat the breath out of him. It wouldn't be the first time he had done so to an enemy.

Robbie took pleasure in the thrill of fighting, in the rush of knocking another person to the ground. He didn't care who he hurt or how badly he hurt them, so long as he won. The lectures from his parents couldn't stop him, nor did the talks from his coach or even his ex-girlfriends. There were no words to change his views.

In his mind, no one was important enough to give up fighting for.

Looking up at Wright, Robbie bit back the bitter words that were on the tip of his tongue and replaced them with ones that his coach would accept. "Yeah, I got it." His words were sharp, with a hint of sarcasm that he didn't bother to try to hide.

Wright nodded. "Good. I swear, Anderson, if you weren't such a good basketball player, and if your father wasn't one of my best friends, your butt would be on the bench every game for all your crap I have to put up with."

Robbie rose to his feet. "So now that we got all this sentimental crap out of the way, can I go back to practice?"

"Not so fast." Wright pulled Robbie back by his jersey as he started to walk away. "You aren't getting off with just a warning this time. I'm giving both you and Coppertone two months of School Service."

"What?!" Robbie cried, stamping his foot. "School Service? Come *on*!"

"Don't 'come on' me. You fight, you get to mop the floors and clean the cafeteria and wash graffiti off the walls."

"Coach," Robbie began again, his voice taking on a more serious tone, "that isn't fair. There's practice every day after school! That means I'll miss three practices a week."

"Good, kid. You can count. School's really paying off for you."

Smirking at his coach's retort, Robbie struggled to keep his middle finger from extending. "You can't give me School Service."

"I can, and I am," Wright replied. "Now if you'll excuse me, I have to go yell at Jason, if Coach Langly hasn't already gotten to him."

When the locker room door shut behind the coach, Robbie let out an angry yell and kicked the bench before heading back to the gym.

Stepping back out onto the court, he glanced around to see Jason Coppertone sitting in the bleachers, watching his team practice. His eye was black, a satisfying sight. Wright pointed to the set of bleachers across the gym from Jason, and with a sigh, Robbie went to them and sat, his arms crossed as he leaned back. He narrowed his eyes at Jason as the other teenager glared over at him with a scowl and a warning nod. Robbie wasn't the least bit fazed.

He was ready to fight, and fully prepared to win.

The tires to Robbie's black Mustang squealed with protest as he peeled out of the driveway of his two-story home and onto the street. It had been two hours since his coach decided to send him and Jason home from practice, and after getting an earful from his mother and father about the chemistry test he had failed and the English homework he refused to do, Robbie decided that it was time to go to Jason's house and finish the fight.

This time with no unnecessary interruptions.

"Damn it!" he cursed when he saw that, three houses down, a moving van was in the middle of the road. Coming to a stop, he sat back for a moment, fingers absently drumming the steering wheel, his mind searching for an alternate course to Coppertone's home. He absently watched a girl of about twelve hobble around on crutches, irritating the movers as she got in their way, giving out orders like she ruled the household.

Shaking his head, Robbie was about to put the car into reverse before a second girl of about his age walked out of the house and over to the dark blue car parked in the driveway. He raised his eyebrows approvingly when she leaned over to pull out a box from the backseat, then threw the car into park and got out, heading up the front walk.

"Hey," Robbie said as he approached the girl, taking in her shoulder-length blonde hair, curving hips, and long, thin legs, "your moving van's blocking the road."

"Nothing I can do about it," the girl answered, barely even looking up at Robbie as she brushed past him.

"Well, I have places I have to be," Robbie pressed, surprised when the girl simply shrugged.

"Not my problem."

Crossing his arms, Robbie leaned against the car. It'd been awhile since anyone had the gall to dismiss him. "So where'd you move here from?"

"Far away."

"You gonna be going to Lakeside?" Robbie tried again.

"Don't know."

"You going into eleventh?"

"Don't care."

"Well, if you are, I could—"

"Leave me alone," she finished for him.

"Okay." Robbie let out a deep breath, staring over at the newcomer. From where he was standing he only had a partial view, but what he could see, he liked. "So anyway, if you want to meet any of the—"

"Look," the girl turned now, facing him squarely, "I just want to get my stuff unpacked. It's late, and I'm tired."

Robbie nodded. "Hey, that's cool. By the way, I'm Robbie. Robbie Anderson." He smiled and leaned back against the car with self-assurance when she faced him again, her arms full with a box marked *Kelly*.

"Kelly Mitchell," she told him.

He grinned at Kelly's back when she disappeared into the house, already thinking of ways to seduce her as he went back to his car and drove in reverse to his driveway.

CHAPTER 2

Mathew Harper smiled and extended his hand as he introduced himself to the new student. "Matt Harper," he told her. "I'll be showing you around Lakeside High." The new girl, Kelly Mitchell, frowned as she looked down at Matt's hand, then back up at him. Momentarily reminded of the woman who had saved his life so many years ago, Matt withdrew his hand casually.

Kelly observed him subtly, taking in his piercing blue eyes that were filled with trust, his sandy blonde hair, and smile that was warm and reassuring. He was cute, but she wasn't interested.

Matt began the tour. "Well, I'm sure Lakeside isn't all that different from your old school. There's the cafeteria, gym across from it. Just walk through the atrium and you can't miss it. Dean's Office is right there," he pointed to his left, "and the majority of your classes will be in these halls. And here's your locker." He stopped and pointed. "Do the whole, spin three times to the right, two to the left thing and you got it."

"I know how to open a locker," Kelly snapped. "I'm not a complete moron."

Matt paused. "I know," he replied after a moment's hesitation. "I was only joking."

"Well your definition of a joke obviously differs from mine."

"Okay." He frowned and his brow furrowed. It seemed to him that the new student was actually *trying* to make him not like her, but the glimmer of anxiety in her eyes told him that it was obviously a defense mechanism. He had seen that look too many times from too many people to not know what it meant.

He still remembered what it was like to be at the Treehouse, to befriend all the kids rescued by Melanie O'Conner and her gang. He was proud to have been the first child ever taken by the Helping Hands, to be the beginning of the legacy. Although the reasons as to why he was actually brought to Treehouse Island still angered him, he was able to get over his abusive past and relish the fact that he was still alive.

Being at the Treehouse had made him a better person. Having been there for four years, he had seen many kids brought in who were battered and beaten, starved and scared. He learned what it meant to be caring, sympathetic, to have empathy for a person even though he had only been eight years old. Those were the qualities Melanie taught him, and they were the ones he cherished the most. It didn't matter if some people teased him or questioned him endlessly about the Treehouse and the Hell Hounds, if they told him he should be angry that he was kidnapped, that the Helping Hands had ruined his life, that being away from home for four years had affected him socially and educationally, resulting in him repeating his senior year. They said he should do all he could to condemn them. They said he should join the fight to bring down all the gangs, but he never, no matter the circumstances, would ever even *consider* doing such a thing.

He knew where his priorities lay.

"So if you ever need anything, don't hesitate to ask me," Matt offered sincerely, only to be hit by a glowering smirk from the girl in front of him.

"You're one of Melanie O'Conner's kids, aren't you?" she asked, and Matt nodded. "It shows."

Matt raised his eyebrows in surprise, unable to think of a reply as Kelly turned on her heel and stalked down the hall.

"Metals," Daniel Fiesk told his chemistry class. "Strong, durable, and many come from compounds." He grinned when his class let out a series of groans. He wasn't always proud of dumbing down his lessons, but these days, he was lucky to get a reaction out of them at all. When it came to chemistry, kids just didn't care. "Now, metals are combined with other metals to form what?"

"Ionic compounds," a girl called out.

"Right, Miss Walker." He gave a smile to the girl he could always count on her to give an answer even if no one else could. Kayla Walker smiled as well at her correct reply, jotting down a note on the sheet of paper on her desk. "And a metal and a nonmetal?"

"Covalent."

"Right again." Turning to the board, the teacher wrote down the two names. "Ionic and covalent. Going to the periodic table, we can see the difference between metals and nonmetals. Now, in the first column, the metals are called alkali metals, the second column the alkaline, and then the transition metals."

As the teacher droned on about things he couldn't care less about, Robbie Anderson glanced to his left at Kelly Mitchell, watching as she ran a pencil through her fingers and stared down at her desk, lost in a world he suspected had nothing to do with chemicals and bonds and skinny, bald teachers.

"Hey," he whispered to her, "you understand any of this crap?" He waited for a reply. "Hey, Kelly."

"Mr. Anderson."

Robbie turned to see his teacher glaring down at him, his hands placed on his hips. "Yeah?"

"Would you mind answering the question?"

"Only if you wouldn't mind repeating it," Robbie replied, getting a few laughs from the class as the teacher sighed.

"I asked, what metal, whether it be natural or a compound, would be the best choice to use to construct a building?"

"Um, copper?" The class laughed again at his response, while Mr. Fiesk shook his head.

"Yes, Robbie. We will construct a building using the same metal that pennies are made from." Robbie shrugged, and Mr. Fiesk turned back to the class. "Anyone? An answer please?" The class was silent, as it usually was when no one cared to answer. He surveyed the students, taking in their blank stares. He saw some that weren't even pretending to think, and in the back corner one of the girls was writing a note to a friend. Shuffling paper and sighs were the only sounds that met his ears, but he waited patiently for someone to take a guess.

"Iron."

The voice was quiet, almost a whisper, coming from the left side of the room. Both Mr. Fiesk and Robbie turned to look over at Kelly as she glanced up from her desk.

"Iron?" Mr. Fiesk repeated, observing the new student carefully to match the name with the face. "Interesting. Why iron?"

Kelly kept her eyes even with those of the teacher. "Because iron is a relentless metal. It's hard, it's durable, and it doesn't break... It's unstoppable."

Mr. Fiesk rubbed his chin. "Why not steel though?" he asked. "Steel is most commonly used. It's durable and efficient as well."

"I said what I said," Kelly replied with a hint of an edge, then dropped her eyes back to her desk. Mr. Fiesk nodded again and went back to talking about steel and what it was composed of. Robbie didn't listen, but continued to stare over at Kelly. Her answer interested him, even if he didn't really know what she was talking about.

The girl was definitely one strange chick.

CHAPTER 3

Salem, Oregon

A socket wrench clanged to the floor as the workbench it was resting on was kicked hard. The mechanic standing next to the workbench jumped back, the wrench barely missing his foot.

"Son-of-a-bitch-piece-of-*shit*, I swear to God..."

With a grin, the mechanic banged gently on the side of the run-down truck. "Yo, what's up?" he called as the person swore again, the string of profanities going unnoticed or ignored by the others. "You okay down there?" Soon the mechanic emerged, covered in a layer of grease and glowering with irritation, as was her way.

"This damn car is unfixable!" Melanie O'Conner threw her rag down and tossed back her hair. "The thing needs to be totaled! I mean, you wrap a car around a pole because you were too damn lazy to learn how to drive stick, you don't deserve to get it back!"

"I feel ya," the mechanic, Hank Garady, replied with a shake of his head. "Welcome to the wonderful world of cars. You'll get used to it."

"Don't give me that shit," Melanie answered, wiping her forehead with a grease-smudged rag as she glared at the grungy, middle-aged man in desperate need of a shower and haircut. "I've been here for almost a year now."

"Never thought you'd last a year," Hank told her honestly, thinking back to her first week when he and the rest of the guys had bets going around as to how long she would last. The only person still in the gamble was Fred Kindle, owner of the shop. "But I'll tell ya, you know your cars."

Melanie shrugged. "It's what I get for hanging around Mel."

"Speaking of Mel, how is he?"

Melanie leaned back against the workbench, crossing her arms and fighting a yawn. She couldn't remember the last time she had gotten a good night's sleep. When she was a teenager, sleep meant always having to keep one eye open in case an enemy was coming for her. As an adult, it meant nightmares of the past and early wake-up calls.

"Mel's good. He—"

"O'Conner!" a voice yelled out from the back of the shop. Melanie turned to see Fred Kindle waving over at her. "I need to speak with you."

"So what else is new?" Melanie called back, looking back over at Hank. "Duty calls," she said, then walked over to Fred Kindle, Tyler Mason's uncle. "Yeah?"

Fred gestured for her to enter, and waited until Melanie had sat down. "Just wanted to tell you that the rent's due in a week."

Melanie nodded, picking at a loose thread on the chair cushion. "Just take it out of my paycheck. I'll get Tyler to repay me his half later."

Writing down a quick note, Fred cleared his throat and squinted in the harsh sunlight pouring through the open blinds. "Sounds good. I went by the house yesterday and I have to say I was a bit disappointed."

"With what?"

"With the fact that you and Mel let my flowers completely die. They look like they belong in the front yard of a haunted house."

Melanie gave an indifferent laugh. "Hey, you're the one who moved out. Don't blame me for not keeping up with all that womanly garden bullshit."

"Frankly, I'm surprised you and Mel haven't burned the place down by now."

"What can I say? We're keeping the place afloat," Melanie replied, sitting back in the chair and remembering the day Fred moved out of his house.

It had been a little over a year since the death of Wess Porter, or Kyle Lindel. The news of his murder and the release of the children he and his gang had taken had quieted down in the media after endless reports and failed investigations. It was a bit amusing for all of the Helping Hands to watch the authorities fumble around and confuse themselves more than they already were.

After returning to Oregon, Melanie started working for Fred at his auto shop, and Tyler, still known as Mel Scotford, graduated from college and began working for Salem Social Services. With the two adults getting themselves on their feet and starting lives of their own, Fred figured that it was time for him to move on. The mansion was far too big for him, but in Fred's opinion, it would be the perfect place for Tyler and Melanie, especially if they were to be alone.

To Fred's way of thinking, if they were alone, they might actually take their relationship to the next level instead of keeping themselves at arm's length. It was frustrating to watch the two people he cared most about in the world dance around one another and avoid the relationship he was positive they both wanted. They deserved to be happy after all the tragedy in their lives, deserved to let themselves enjoy their youth while they still could, and for them both, happiness dwelled in the arms of the one who slept in the room down the hall.

They were just too damn stubborn to admit it.

So Fred moved to Salem, about fifteen miles away, and rented the house to Melanie and Tyler. He still saw them, Melanie nearly every day, so he kept tabs on the two and made sure they were keeping themselves in line. He was especially pleased with Melanie's performance at his shop. She was one of the best mechanics he'd ever had, and did a damn good job proving that a female could hold her own in a workplace of men.

He could still easily recall the day she had come to live with him and Tyler after her prison release. The media told him she was a bloodthirsty bitch with a cold heart and edges so frayed that they were beyond the definition of rough. Tyler told him she was the best thing that ever happened to him. Upon meeting her, Fred had decided that Melanie O'Conner was just the type of person the world needed to have around. She may have had a wild child past and reputation that was shot with the public, but it was his experience that there was nothing Melanie cared for more than the well-being of those she loved.

12

"So if we're all finished here, I got a lot of shit out there that needs to be done and I ain't about to waste the day in here talking about flowers," Melanie cut into Fred's thoughts, and he waved her off while rolling his eyes.

"Yeah, go on," he told her, then grinned when the door slammed shut behind her. "Some things never change."

Melanie yawned as she entered the house, dropping her keys and jacket down onto the table next to the door. Glancing up at the clock, she saw that it was nearly midnight. Staying past shop hours was a common practice for her. Work, to Melanie, was a symbol of the life she was trying so hard to piece back together. And if the only way she could do that was by being a part of the legal crowd of society, then so be it.

She walked past the dining room, stopping long enough to pull her off her thick, rubber-soled boots, the same boots she was wearing when she was arrested. There had been a time when she was about to throw them away, but was unable to make herself toss them in the trash. They were a symbol of her past, of what she had gone through and lived to tell about.

Some things were too precious to toss aside.

"Hungry?"

Melanie turned around to see Tyler standing in the doorway of the kitchen holding a glass of water and chewing on something. "For what?"

"Some chicken and rice," Tyler replied, stepping to the side so Melanie could enter. "Made it myself."

"Yourself?"

At her tone of disbelief, Tyler shrugged. "Well, from a box. It had directions, so I couldn't have done all that bad."

"Sure it won't kill me?" Melanie asked, smiling when Tyler pretended to be offended.

"It's in the microwave," he informed her, watching her rub her eyes. "Long day?"

"You have no idea."

Waiting until Melanie had heated up her dinner, Tyler thought about the phone call he received earlier that night. "Taryn called. They got another kid." Leaning against the counter, he placed the empty cup next to the sink, which was overflowing with dirty dishes. "That's makes the count seventy-nine."

"Yeah, but Randy Harding turns eighteen next month, so he'll be leaving." It was a policy of the Helping Hands for a child to leave whatever hideaway they were at once they reach the age of eighteen. At that age they became an adult, but the gang still helped them out by carefully securing a job and place to stay, usually with the assistance of one of the project benefactors.

It was dangerous to release a Helping Hand child for many different reasons, primarily because the media would eventually get wind of the situation. Whether they were released accidentally or on purpose made no difference if anything about the project was revealed. Melanie wasn't worried about Randy revealing anything. She knew that no child would ever tell.

"Caleb said that the girl lost a lot of blood. Had to get some stitches." Shaking his head, Tyler watched Melanie as she finished off the chicken. "I still can't believe he went to be with Taryn and her gang."

"It's better this way," Melanie replied, putting her plate in the sink with the rest of the dishes. "At least now we're all more together, you know? And Wess's old gang members are doing good, so I kind of like Caleb being with Taryn."

Caleb joined Taryn's gang a few months after Wess's death. Both he and Taryn secured jobs and were living in a small apartment. Taryn, after much deliberation, had decided that living on the streets wasn't as much a thrill as it used to be. All three of the remaining Hell Hounds had been shocked when she agreed to give up the streets, Melanie the most of all. She had even decided to lose the tongue and lip ring, although Caleb still sported his piercings.

It was difficult at first for Taryn to come to a small cubicle of a home every night and sleep in a bed not much softer than the boxes she had on the streets. But she got used to it, and even enjoyed living with Caleb despite their daily arguments, most of which ended up getting physical in one form or another. But in general they got along, and Taryn felt comfortable around him.

Caleb's gang hadn't done much when it broke up. Chris and Sasha left together, and Angie and Kenya had decided to stay with the children of The Fort. They didn't take any more, but simply watched over them. Adam had merely left, to where, Caleb didn't know.

Wess's old gang, however, were doing their parts to keep the Helping Hands alive. Shane and Dylan had gone to Florida and already had benefactors and one child, and another being planned. Bailey had gone to Vermont and had all his benefactors, and Becca was well on her way to getting all of her benefactors in Michigan. And although all of the fifty-seven kids Wess and his gang had taken had been returned back to their parents, relatives, or foster homes, the gang members made sure they were safe before going about their separate ways.

Wess's death had been hard on all the Helping Hands, especially those four who began it all. Had Wess not of been a part of the gang, Melanie didn't think they would have made the impression they did. He had been tough, built, what she thought of as the strong, silent type. Wess had been there for her when she was down, when Tyler had turned her away, and most importantly of all, when Foster attacked.

That attack cost him his life.

Because she didn't want to get lost in depressing memories, Melanie forced herself to think of something else. "So'd you help that co-worker get that little girl away from her foster home?"

"Yeah. Since Benny wasn't brave enough to face the man, I stepped in. He took one look at me and let me in the house. Let's just say, he and his wife won't be in the foster care business anymore." Tyler smiled with self-assurance, lifting his chin cockily.

Melanie shook her head at his display of arrogance. "Don't blame Benny. We can't all have your amazing muscle and bravery." She patted his muscular arm almost indifferently. He started to reply back, but stopped when she yawned for what had to be the fifth time.

14

"Tired?" he asked, tucking her hair back behind her ear in the casual and comforting way that he had, that he'd always had.

"Yeah. I'm going to bed."

"Right behind you." Flicking off the light, Tyler followed Melanie up the stairs. He went to his bedroom, and Melanie went to hers, both closing the doors behind them.

CHAPTER 4

San Francisco, California

Robbie sighed as he pulled a mop out of the janitor's closet and tossed a bucket down onto the floor. He had waited nearly half an hour for the last of the students to leave, and he was ready to serve his punishment and go home. Glancing down the hall, he saw that it was scattered with trash, from paper to plastic bottles to articles of clothing. *All day it's been like this*, Robbie thought as he headed down the hall. *People throwing their shit everywhere for me to clean up*.

Water sloshed across the tile floor as he slid the mop back and forth. A few dark spots refused to budge from the pearl-white tile, and Robbie left them right where they were. It wasn't up to him to peel the dried gum up off the tile. He would leave that for Jason, who was cleaning the bathrooms at that time.

Robbie turned a corner and looked up at the sound of a locker opening. Satisfied in finding the girl who avoided him at all costs, which irritated him to no end, he watched Kelly Mitchell toss a notebook into her locker and pull out another in exchange, her hair falling across her shoulders and into her eyes. He saw her brush it back, and wondered to himself why she was wearing a long-sleeved shirt when even inside the school it felt like it was ninety degrees. She didn't notice him as he walked up, nor did she acknowledge his presence when he stopped right next to her.

"You get detention or something?" Robbie initiated a conversation, wondering why she was at the school so late. An impatient huff from Kelly told him that he was wrong. "So did Harper show you around? He's a pretty cool guy, considering everything he's been through."

Matt Harper was one of the few people at Lakeside that Robbie could actually stand. He hated most of the guys who were into showing off and trying to make a name for themselves. At least when he fought, Robbie considered, it was as much for personal pride as it was to prove to the other guy that he was the tougher of the two. Robbie could remember seeing Matt on television when he was being taken from the Treehouse, and in all the time he had known him, he had never heard Matt talk about it or Melanie O'Conner unless he was praising both. Robbie had to respect him for his loyalty.

Kelly bit her bottom lip, silently wishing that Robbie would leave her alone. It was bad enough that he had come up to her while moving in, because that had resulted in a lecture from her stepfather. Not that it mattered; she didn't want some guy chasing after her, anyway.

16

Turning to him, Kelly kept her eyes slightly narrowed and willed back the sparks in her stomach. "Is there something I can help you with?"

Robbie smiled, a smile that usually got the girls to melt at his feet. "You wanna get out of here? Go grab a bite to eat?"

"Don't you have to mop the floor?"

A bit insulted, Robbie raised his eyebrows and leaned the mop against the lockers, crossing his arms. "And what the hell is that supposed to mean?" When he didn't get a reply, he pressed the subject. "Let me tell you, babe, I got this black eye and busted lip through hard work and the results were well worth it. There ain't a kid in this school who would go up against me."

Kelly gave a disdainful laugh. "I get it. You gotta earn your respect, right?"

"You gonna start telling me that it takes a real man to walk away from a fight?" Robbie shot back. "Well, I'll tell ya something else." He propped his hand up onto her locker. "I know what it's like to take a hit. Obviously, you don't know what it's like to earn *your* respect."

Fury welled, and Kelly's hand clenched the door to her locker until her knuckles turned white. With a breath of rage, she slammed the locker shut, crushing Robbie's fingers. He let out a cry and jerked back his arm, clutching his hand to his stomach. Jabbing pain shot through his veins, gripping his bones with jagged teeth of fury.

"You *bitch*!"

"Did that hurt?" Kelly snarled back. "You don't know *anything*! You *know nothing*!"

Grabbing her backpack from the floor and fighting back a strange and sudden arrival of tears, Kelly fled down the hall, desperate to escape.

"Shit," Robbie muttered, looking down at his fingers, which were red and swollen. He didn't think they were broken, but his middle and ring fingers were bleeding. Snatching the mop up, he headed for the bathroom to wash his hand, cursing the entire way.

Jeffrey Ponder glanced up from the newspaper when he heard the front door open. A frown crossed his face and an aggravated sigh escaped when it slammed. A few seconds later his stepdaughter entered the kitchen, grabbing a can of soda from the refrigerator.

"Where have you been?" Jeffrey demanded. "You should have been home forty-five minutes ago."

"I had some stuff to do after school," Kelly replied honestly, brushing past her stepfather towards the stairs, but was stopped when he grabbed her arm, his fingers digging hard into her flesh.

"Don't give me that attitude," he warned, his dark eyes narrowing. "I won't take that bullshit from you."

"Fine." Kelly yanked her arm from Jeffrey's grip. "Are you done now?"

Anger rising, Jeffrey grabbed Kelly's short blonde hair and pulled her away from the stairs, Kelly crying out in protest. "Don't give me that attitude!" he ordered again. "Now get to your room and start your homework!" Releasing her, Jeffrey shoved Kelly toward the stairs. She tripped over the first step and fell, banging her knee on the banister. "Get your ass up there!" Jeffrey yelled again, shoving a hand in her back, the heel of his hand leaving a swollen red welt.

Reaching the top of the stairs, Kelly wiped a hand across her eyes to erase the angry tears. She pushed open the door to her room with a trembling hand. "Goddamn bastard," she whispered, sitting on the edge of her bed and rolling up her pants leg.

Just another bruise, she thought, rubbing her aching back.

"Kelly? Are you okay?" a voice asked from the doorway, and Kelly stood, turning to see her sister staring over at her.

"I'm fine, Danielle," Kelly replied, trying to calm down. "How was school?"

Danielle shrugged and propped her broken leg up onto the bed, the leg she had broken after tripping over a box while packing for the move to California. "It was okay. Eighth grade sucks. I can't wait to get to high school. Did you have fun?"

Kelly thought of Robbie, slamming his fingers into the locker. "Just another day."

Danielle nodded, her finger tracing the pattern of the bedspread. "I heard Jeffrey yelling," she admitted, her voice quiet and apologetic. "Did he hit you again?"

Kelly gave a small smile. "No. I just fell on the stairs, that's all. Don't worry about it." She hugged her sister, then sat down next to her. "Why don't you finish your homework, and I'll come see you when I'm done with mine, okay?"

CHAPTER 5

San Francisco, California

Eight year-old Ryan Mueller looked down at the floor in shame as his mother yelled. He shuffled his feet when she asked a question, then looked up when she commanded him to. He could barely understand some of the words she was saying, but he knew by the redness of her face and the way she was pointing her finger that she was very, very angry. When his father came in from the kitchen, pulling off his boots, Ryan knew he was *really* in trouble.

"Three times! Three times, Ryan!" Fiona Mueller shouted. "I told you *three* times to clean your room, and did you do it? *No!*"

"Sorry, Mommy," Ryan whispered, a tear falling down his cheek.

Fiona let out a disgusted sigh. "So now you're going to cry? That's great. Now I have a whiny little girl instead of a son. Well, guess what, little girl? Since you didn't clean your room, you don't get to sleep in it for a week! Now get your ass into the living room and go to bed!"

"But the living room's cold, Mommy," Ryan protested, and took a defensive step back when Donald Mueller tossed his boots down onto the floor and came closer.

"Don't you dare back talk your mother!" he ordered, grabbing Ryan's small shoulders. "Now get in there!"

"But I'll clean my room! I promise!" Ryan hated the living room. It was cold, and he was afraid of all the animals that were hanging on the walls, the results of his father's hunting hobby. "Mommy, please let me—"

"Ryan, goddamn it, you do something when I tell you to!" Donald roared, his hand plucking one of his boots up from the floor and swinging it. The boot connected with Ryan's cheek and the child fell back, crying and bleeding from the mouth.

"Now get your ass in the living room!" Donald roared, grabbing the second boot from the floor and lashing out at Ryan again, hitting his knees.

Ryan stumbled to the living room, collapsing on the rug, sobbing along the way.

The night was cold and windy, the sky darkened with black clouds that threatened to release sheets of pouring rain. Frogs and crickets called up to the clouds, and the darkness gave no aiding light to the five figures that crept up behind the Mueller household.

The leader of the gang, clad in black from head to toe, gestured for his gang members to follow close behind as he reached the house. The blinds to the sliding glass door were open, and when he looked inside, he saw a child sleeping in the middle of the room. The boy was shivering, his thin arms wrapped around his body and his knees pulled up to his chest as he slept fitfully.

A second gang member came up to the leader's side, taking a lock pick from his pocket. Months of planning had told him that there wasn't an alarm. The lock snapped open with quiet ease, and the leader gently slid open the door just enough for him to slip through, listening for any and all sounds in the house. Convinced that all was silent, he entered with one of his partners. Outside, one of the figures took a small bottle of shoe polish out from her jacket pocket and began writing a message on the glass door.

Ryan opened his eyes to see two figures standing over him. Instinctively he backed away, and was about to yell when a gloved hand clamped over his mouth. Fear rose like a sickness in his throat and tears burned when he imagined another boot slamming into his face. At the thought, his mouth gave a little twinge of remembered pain and made him freeze in the stranger's grasp.

"Ryan, I know what your mommy and daddy do to you," the person whispered, and Ryan's eyes widened. "I can make it all stop."

"How?" Ryan whispered as the hand was pulled away from his mouth.

"We've been watching you, waiting for a chance to help. We can take you to a place where you will never be hurt again, have lots of friends, and sleep in a nice warm bed, but only if you want to go." He waited patiently as Ryan thought about it. For a moment he was tempted to ask the person if he knew that his daddy punched him one time and had on a really big ring, but he decided not to. Somehow, in some strange way, he had a feeling that the person already knew.

He still remembered that night, when his mommy had made spaghetti, and the sauce tasted funny. She put something in it, and he knew because he watched her do it. It was something from a bottle that she took from under the sink.

Later, he wondered why his parents were eating hamburgers when he had to eat the spaghetti with the funny-tasting sauce, and when he complained, his daddy had reached across the table and hit him so hard that his chair fell over and made him fall on the floor. After that night, he wasn't allowed to eat dinner for a whole week.

"I want to go," Ryan said firmly, and took the stranger's hand.

The leader of the gang led Ryan out of the house and together, he and the rest of the members fled from the residence after closing the sliding glass door. Ryan's parents would see the message as soon as they woke up, the message that would make everyone in San Francisco clutch their children tightly in their arms and make the police and media swarm around the clue like vultures to road kill. He was convinced he was starting something big with his message, something legendary.

It read: *We're Back – The Helping Hands*

CHAPTER 6

When Robbie arrived home from school, his parents were waiting for him.

Brow furrowing at the thought of having to suffer through yet another lecture, he carefully set down his jacket on a bar stool and peered at his mother and father, who were both sitting at the table, hands clasped and resting atop the wood. It was rare for them to both be home before he was and not be holed up in the office or cooking some elaborate dinner, and their lack of activity made him nervous.

"Hey," he said slowly, eyeing them both in turn. "Why the long faces? Did someone die or something?"

"Not yet," his father replied sternly. "We both got a phone call today. At work, no less."

"And guess who it was," his mother continued, lifting her eyebrows expectantly and sighing when her son merely shrugged. "Coach Wright."

Damn, Robbie thought. He thought he'd gotten away with it. "I can explain."

"You better," Adam Anderson said with a nod. "What's all this about fighting and School Service?"

"Which apparently you skipped out on two days in a row," Rachael Anderson added.

Knowing he would have to do some fast and serious talking, Robbie took in a deep breath and prepared himself for the worst. "Look, it was Jason Coppertone. You know, the big guy on the team? He was giving me crap about my shooting and I tried to ignore him but he kept egging me on and—"

"All you had to do was walk away, Robbie." Rachael sighed and rose from the table. "We have talked about this time and time again. You *can't* keep fighting. You're lucky Frank doesn't report this, and the only reason he's not is because we've been friends for so long. But as your coach he has every right to report you, and if he did, you'd be in a lot more trouble then you are now. You know what the principal said."

"I know." He could still hear the principal's stern warning: *you fight again, you face expulsion*.

"Frank tried to save you from expulsion by giving you School Service instead, and you repay him by not doing it? What kind of gratitude is that?"

"God, Dad, it's just some stupid school cleanup. And it was barely even a fight!"

"I don't care how big or little a fight it was because it was still a *fight*!" Adam yelled, also rising. "You want to get expelled? Is that it?"

"Damn it, Dad—"

"Watch your mouth with me! I'm not done with you. If you get expelled, then it's all over. You can kiss any career, basketball or otherwise, goodbye. Is that the direction you want to take? Is it?"

"You're overreact—"

"Overreacting?" Adam cut him off. "You call this overreacting? I call this being a father! You want to blow your shot at going to college on a basketball scholarship just because you can't control your temper?"

"I don't even *want* to go to college!"

Oh, shit, Robbie thought instantly as soon as the words left his mouth. He knew he had dug his own grave when he saw the change in his parents' expressions.

"Robert Samuel Anderson, you—"

"No," Adam interrupted, putting a hand on his wife's arm. "We're not even going to argue about this. You are going to college, and that's that. Now get your butt up to your room, do your homework, and prepare yourself for another three months of School Service!"

Blood boiling and tongue threatening to release a string of profanity, Robbie spun around on his heel and stomped to his room.

Haston, Oregon

Tyler sat back on the white-cushioned couch, a couch that he and Melanie had effectively ruined one night during a particularly physical, harmless, yet amusing fight involving scissors and baked beans, and took the remote control from the armrest. Flicking on the television, he turned the channel to the news station with Stephanie Mathews.

At precisely eleven, the anchorman station appeared and greeted the viewers. Tyler listened, bored by the report on a convicted murderer and another of a coverage of health regulation violations in the local restaurants. When Stephanie Mathews came on the screen, he directed his attention to the television. He still hated her with a deep passion that would never fade, yet could endure her reports more than any other self-interested reporter, provided that she stayed the hell away from him and his girl.

Stephanie began to talk about the kidnapping of a little boy named Ryan Mueller, and Tyler leaned back, half-listening to what she had to say. The thought of Stephanie Mathews covering the kidnapping of a child annoyed him.

"Ryan Mueller of San Francisco, California was kidnapped last night between ten o'clock P.M. and seven o'clock A.M. Parents Donald and Fiona Mueller woke to find their son missing from his room, and were shocked to find this message scrolled across their sliding glass door."

Tyler bolted straight up when the home of Ryan Mueller came on the screen and he saw the words written on the glass.

"The message, written in shoe polish and reading, 'We're back, the Helping Hands', has left the police angry and flabbergasted. They are yet to determine whether this is another copycat act, or if San Francisco is about to see yet another branch of the Helping Hands."

Tyler leapt to his feet, his hands tugging his hair. "Oh, shit," he said to himself as a picture of Ryan Mueller was shown. He didn't recognize the child, or the parents. Worse, he knew nothing of the kidnapping. Dread began to form a knot in his stomach as the panic of an unknown gang running around taking kids started to burn like fire in his gut. There had been copycat gangs before, ones that posed as the life-saving groups but were really criminals who took kids for ransom or mere pleasure. All but two of those gangs, the real Helping Hand members had taken care of silently. The cops took care of the rest, but only because they got to the copycat gangs first. Now it seemed that another group of psychotic freaks was rearing its ugly head.

"Goddamn it!" Tyler cursed as he ran up the stairs and into Melanie's room. He didn't bother knocking as he entered. He never did anyway, and he didn't waste time by turning on the light. The moonlight was good enough, as was the orange glow that came through the window from the light that shone from her bedroom balcony.

"Melanie," Tyler whispered, gently shaking her shoulder. Her back was facing him, and her breathing was heavy, telling him that she was in a deep sleep. That surprised him a little, for she had always been a light sleeper, always on full alert, always ready and sharp. It was one of the things he admired most about her, something most people learned to respect rather quickly.

Shaking her shoulder harder, Tyler disregarded his surprise by telling himself that it was just because she didn't have to worry about Jerry Hunter anymore that she was able to sleep better. "Mel, wake up!" he said louder, leaning closer to her ear. "Melan—whoa, *shit*!"

Tyler stumbled back as Melanie spun around suddenly, seizing him by the arm and pressing the biting blade of a six-inch kitchen knife up to his throat as they both tumbled to the floor, Tyler on his back and Melanie hovering over him. Her eyes, no trace of sleep among them, were filled with fury and he recognized the expression on her face. It was the look she always got before getting ready to fight, when her eyes were glazed with the instinct to kill and her jaw was set firm and hard, prepared to take a hit. But when she saw who she was holding the knife against, Melanie's eyes widened and she let out a quick gasp.

"Tyler, what the hell are you doing? I could've killed you," she spat, and her voice trembled slightly because she nearly had. It wasn't often that she hesitated to attack, and Tyler sensed a touch of relief in her voice.

"Um, can you take the knife away from my throat?" he replied carefully, hands out to his sides in surrender, and Melanie did so after muttering an apology. "What the hell are you doing with a knife in your bed?" he asked after rising to a sitting position, taking it from her hands, having to pry it from her tense fingers. She released the knife somewhat reluctantly, and he set it down on the floor, making a mental note to himself about being more careful the next time he entered her room without knocking first.

Melanie lifted herself to the bed, pushing back her hair and swallowing hard. "Just... just for safety. After everything that happened last year..."

Tyler licked his lips, tossing a glance down at the knife and sitting down next to Melanie as she rubbed her eyes. "Mel, all that shit's over with. You're safe here."

"I know." Melanie sighed and shook her head. "But I thought I was safe with Wess, and then—"

"Hey, hey," Tyler cut her off. "That's in the past. It was over a year ago. You don't have anything to worry about." He smiled softly, searching for her gaze with gentle eyes and expecting her to agree with him. His smile dropped into a frown when Melanie let out a shaky breath and shook her hands as though trying to rid herself of the quakes.

"Melanie, what's wrong? What is it?" Melanie shook her head, swallowing heavily, curling her fingers into her palms as horror spread through her. Tyler, worried now, took her hands in his own, holding them tightly. "Mel, what is it?"

Melanie swallowed again, peering through the darkness at the man before her. Letting out a deep breath, she lifted her eyes to meet his. "It's just that... I almost didn't hesitate. I almost... Tyler, you don't realize how close..."

"Melanie, it's fine. Everything's fine. I'm fine. Don't worry about it."

"Don't worry about almost killing you?" Her voice got stronger now, and it cracked with worry. "Tyler, what would I do if-" she stopped herself there, because what she was about to say next was far too impossible to think about.

"It just... scared me for a second, that's all."

"Well, you hesitated, so there's nothing to be scared of," he assured her, waiting until she nodded to continue. "No hard feelings, no bloodshed, so we're all good. And I hate to break it to you, babe, but right now we have a much bigger problem than you almost slicing my throat."

Melanie frowned and turned to stare at Tyler, catching the worried glint in his eyes. "What exactly do you mean by that?"

CHAPTER 7

Federal Bureau Investigator Zack Corwin and his partner, Agent Jay Neilson, stood on the front porch of Mel Scotford's two-story home, their hands clutching their badges. The house was dark, but Corwin didn't care. He wasn't going to waste any time waiting around for a couple of criminals to drag themselves out of bed. They were there for one reason and one reason alone.

He wanted answers, and he wanted them fast. Corwin, an F.B.I. agent for nearly half his life, knew how to get what he wanted out of people.

Agent Corwin rang the doorbell and rapped on the wooden door, waited a minute while swaying from foot to foot impatiently, then knocked again.

"Maybe they're not home," Neilson offered, but Corwin shook his head.

"Two cars in the driveway, somebody has to be here," he replied, knocking for the third time. He went right on knocking as loudly and obnoxiously as he could until he heard the lock to the door being turned. Soon after, a tall, well-built man wearing nothing but a pair of baggy gray sweatpants pulled the heavy door open. Corwin was slightly taken aback by his muscled six-two frame, but didn't show his surprise as he stared at the man, whose messy blonde hair was slightly tousled and his eyes tired from a night of little or no sleep.

Tyler Mason stared back at the stranger and the other man next to him without saying a word. He knew instantly that they were cops. He kept his hand on the doorknob, ready to close the door in their faces, but when the taller of the two men held up a badge and announced who he was, Tyler changed his mind and decided to hear him out just for the hell of it.

"Agent Zack Corwin, F. B.I. I was hoping I could ask Melanie O'Conner a few questions," Zack said as he showed Tyler his. Jay Neilson did the same.

"A few questions about what?" Tyler crossed his arms across his muscular chest, a move that usually made his opponents take at least two steps back.

"About the Mueller kidnapping two nights ago," Zack replied, not the least bit daunted.

Tyler raised his eyebrows. "Since when does the F.B.I. go door to door questioning people about kidnappings that have nothing to do with them?"

"Since the kidnapping became labeled with a message written by the Helping Hands, that's when," Neilson replied hotly.

"Oh, right. The whole Helping Hands thing." Tyler rolled his eyes and gestured to the gate the agents had left open. "You do realize that you're trespassing, right? Unless you got a warrant or something—"

"You want to get technical with us I can easily haul you in for insubordination, and you can file all the complaints you want after we're done with what I promise will be hours of questioning," Corwin cut in, aggravated. "Now, is Melanie O'Conner here or not?"

Running his tongue over his teeth and forcing down the instant hatred that came with the sight of a cop, Tyler observed the two men before nodding slightly. "Yeah. She's here." Closing the door, he called for Melanie. A few minutes later, she appeared before the F.B.I. agents.

Zack Corwin raised his own eyebrows when the door was opened again and Melanie O'Conner stared out at him. Her long hair was slightly jumbled from sleep, and Zack found himself observing her for a moment before questioning. He'd been expecting some rough-and-tough delinquent bearing a leather jacket and a heavy attitude, much like she was portrayed in the media, but here he saw a thin woman, toned in all the right places, wearing a white tank top and a pair of gym shorts standing next to a powerfully built male, the man hovering close as if protecting her. Both were barefoot, both stood with a confidence acquired through years of hardships, and neither felt the least bit of distrust for the other. That much could be seen in the obvious bond they had with one another that enabled man and woman to stand mere inches apart yet still hold their own.

It seems so... normal, Zack thought.

"Melanie O'Conner, I'm Agent Zack Corwin, F.B.I." He showed her his badge. "Mind if I ask you a few questions?"

Melanie stared at the agent, challenging his gaze the same way Tyler did just moments ago, tucking her hair behind her ears. "Yeah, sure. Whatever," she replied, stepping back and gesturing for the two agents to enter. They did, with some amount of caution as if they were being set up, and she led them to the kitchen, Tyler trailing close behind Neilson. "What's this about?"

"The kidnapping of Ryan Mueller." Corwin didn't sit at the table like Melanie did, but instead leaned against it, his palms on the top of the wood to give him the advantage of looking down on his suspect. "I assume you saw the news?"

"Assuming is a dangerous thing," Melanie answered coolly, not the least bit affected by his obvious methods of questioning. "Yeah, I saw it. And let me spare you the time and breath. I didn't do it."

"I don't think you did," Corwin told her sincerely, leaning closely to her. Out of the corner of his eye he saw Tyler make a move, as if to warn him of the dangers of getting too close to the woman, but one glance from Melanie had him stopping in his tracks. "We've already talked to a few people who all confirmed where were you the night of the kidnapping."

"Then if I have the alibi, why are you here?"

Neilson came up to Zack's side. "Because while you may not have done it firsthand, we have reason to believe you may have been a part of it."

"A part of it?" Tyler repeated. "Why? Because she was a Helping Hand herself?"

"Exactly." Zack nodded, glancing up at Tyler. "So, is there anything you want to tell me about Ryan Mueller's kidnapping? Anything you know?"

Melanie shook her head. "Agent Corwin, I can honestly say that I had nothing to do with Ryan Mueller's kidnapping. I've never seen the kid before, I know nothing of his family, and I didn't even *know* there was a branch of Helping Hands in San Francisco."

Then she gave a small and surprising laugh, glancing up at Tyler. "Huh. That's the first time I didn't lie to a cop."

"But you know of the others," Corwin pressed. "Do you associate with them?"

Tyler started to protest, but Melanie held up a hand. "Officer, I've done my time and all I want is to get my life back. I'm not about to screw it up by associating with the other branches that may be out there. Are they copycats? They must be, because I'm not the leader of any of the gangs. I know of them because of the media. But I know nothing of Ryan Mueller." Melanie was somewhat relieved that she didn't know about him or his kidnapping at that particular time, and didn't feel the least bit ashamed for lying about the rest of what she said. She did, however, hope to find out soon who the new Helping Hands were. Having an unknown gang running around kidnapping kids was a danger not only to her project but to the children as well, and was something she refused to stand for.

Zack's eyes searched Melanie's face as she spoke. She looked and sounded honest, but he knew that she excelled in the art of lying. She had to, since she was once a Helping Hand, and the entire nation had seen her skills of deceit during her first court trial when she was seventeen. But he couldn't accuse her of something he couldn't prove she knew or did concerning the Helping Hands. That fact burned him right down to the core.

Finally, Corwin nodded. "Alright. But keep in mind, I'll have my eye on you."

"Dually noted." Melanie sat back, then rose to her feet when the agents headed towards the door. She gestured for Tyler to stay where he was, then followed their unwanted guests.

"Hey, Corwin," she said as he stepped out onto the porch. Corwin turned, and Melanie moved closer to him. "About Ryan Mueller. I don't know if the people who took him actually took him due to child abuse or because of some other reason," Melanie paused to take in a deep breath, "but the message was written in shoe polish, and that can mean one of two things. One, it means absolutely nothing because they are just copycats, or two, Ryan was hit with some kind of a shoe."

Zack crossed his arms while Neilson frowned. "And why would you say that?" he pursued curiously, and Melanie shrugged.

"Because if I were taking the kid and I knew that his mom or dad beat him with a shoe of some kind, that's what I'd write the message in. It's a clue, and I don't know if I'm way off base or not, but it's something you may want to look in to. For Ryan's sake."

Zack nodded, taking in the seriousness of Melanie's voice. Her eyes told him that she was genuinely concerned for the child, and he began to doubt that she had had anything to do with his kidnapping. "Alright. I'll keep that in mind," he promised, then went to his car.

Melanie closed the door behind the officers, seeing Tyler waiting for her in the hall. "So what do you think?" she asked him, and he shrugged.

"I think you're right about the shoe thing. But we still don't know who the kidnappers are."

"I know. And that worries me." Sighing, Melanie grabbed the phone. "Do you think it could be another copycat gang?"

Tyler thought about it, about the style, the message, the fact that no ransom had been made or no body found. "I don't know," he answered dejectedly. "I mean, the last copycat was busted in less than a week. All of them screw up eventually because they don't really know how we work. But there's something about this kidnapping that seems…"

"Real," Melanie answered for him, and he agreed.

"Yeah, real. The message is so Helping Hand style, you know? We should call around, see if any of the gangs know anything."

Melanie agreed, wondering who would be the most likely to know. One name came to mind, not because the person would have the answers to her questions, but because it was he who she thought of the most when it came to her project. "I'm gonna call Harper. All this Helping Hands shit always makes me think of him."

"Tell 'em I said hey," Tyler said, then started for the upstairs bathroom to take a shower.

Melanie nodded and dialed Matt Harper's number. It was early, so she hoped to catch him before he went off to school. She smiled when he answered the phone after the third ring.

"Hello?"

"Hey kid, what's up?"

"Miss Melanie?" Matt's voice sounded hesitant, and when Melanie confirmed whom she was, his tone changed. "Oh, hey! How's it going?"

"Not bad, Matt. I just wanted to call and see how you were."

"Just getting ready for school."

Toying with an apple that was left on the counter, Melanie listened to the familiar voice of the first child of the Treehouse, feeing a surge of warmth course through her. The kid had always held a special place in her heart. "So did you hear about the kidnapping of Ryan Mueller?"

"Yeah, I did. A reporter was talking about it on the news," Matt replied.

"Town's probably going nuts right about now, huh?"

"It's pretty wild. Another branch of Helping Hands right here in San Francisco. I didn't know a gang had moved out here."

"Neither did I." Melanie shook her head and tossed the apple into the sink for no apparent reason other than to get rid of it. "But I'll find out sooner or later. So where were you that night?"

"At a concert with Leighann." He briefly told her about it, and some band she'd never heard of.

Nodding, Melanie rose to her feet. "That's cool. Well, I'll let you get ready. Just wanted to say hey."

"Okay."

"Bye, kid," Melanie said, then turned off the phone after Matt had told her good-bye. Hanging up the phone and heading for the stairs, the former Helping Hand frowned. "Weird. The kid's usually never short-winded."

San Francisco, California

Danielle Mitchell hesitated in front of the bathroom door, leaning heavily on her crutches. The door was open a crack, and she could just barely see her older sister leaning over the sink, peering into the mirror as she held a damp towel above her eye. Kelly's face was stained with tears, and the cut on her forehead was still bleeding slightly. For the millionth time, Danielle found herself wishing that she didn't have brittle bone disease so that Kelly wouldn't be the only one being hit all the time. Danielle was grateful for Kelly's defense, but at the same time, she felt an incredible amount of guilt that, at times, was physically painful.

It wasn't always like this, Danielle thought as she watched Kelly throw the towel in the hamper. *It only started when Mom began dating Jeffrey*. Danielle thought back to the time when she was much younger and it had just been her, her mom, and Kelly. Even without their father, who Danielle didn't even remember, she had been happier. When Jeffrey came into the picture, the yelling and hitting began, even before they got married. Danielle remembered the wedding clearly, neither she nor her sister shedding a single tear of happiness. Everyone else smiled happily and told their mother that she was lucky to find such a great man.

That's because everyone thinks Jeffrey is an amazing guy, Danielle told herself bitterly. *No one knows him like we do. Even Mom thinks he's only looking out for our best interest.*

"Danielle?" Kelly asked as she left the bathroom, catching her sister off-guard. "You need something?"

Danielle bit her bottom lip, her eyes tracing over the gash. It was in the process of swelling up and was still red and dimly bleeding. "No. I um, just wanted to see how you were doing."

Kelly gave a small smile and rubbed her sister's arm. "I'm fine. It's just a little cut. Nothing I can't handle. So," she headed for the stairs, "when's the cast come off?"

"Next Monday," Danielle answered. "I can't wait. You can have my crutches if you want."

"Why would I want them?" Kelly stopped at the top of the stairs, ready to help Danielle descend them.

Danielle grinned and shrugged. "You know, if you wanna knock Jeffrey over the head or something."

Kelly laughed. "Yeah, then you could punch him with your brute strength," she teased, and her smile dropped in a flash when she heard the familiar thumping of Jeffrey's heavy boots on the stairs. Both she and Danielle fell silent as Jeffrey approached them, and Kelly began to fear that he had heard their conversation. But Jeffrey simply looked at Kelly, roughly brushing past her and keeping his eyes level with hers. Kelly narrowed her eyes, challenging him, and as he turned into his room, she heard him muttering something under his breath that made her blood run cold.

"What'd he say?" Danielle whispered, and Kelly shook her head.

"I don't know," she lied, then wrapped her arms around herself as Danielle began to hobble down the stairs. Dread caused goosebumps to rise on her flesh, fear of the future, for she had heard him loud and clear.

One of these days.

CHAPTER 8

Haston, Oregon

"Fred, what the hell do you want? This is the third time you've called me in here, and I have a lot of work to do," Melanie complained as she entered Fred Kindle's office. She wiped her hands on the rag hanging from her waist and stood in front of her boss.

Fred hung up the phone after signaling for Melanie to wait a moment, then stared up at her. "That was a friend of mine from Florida," he informed her. "She moved down there last year and wants me to come and visit her."

Melanie raised her eyebrows. "She?" she repeated, grinning slyly. "Not bad, Fred. So why should I care, just out of curiosity?"

"Well," Fred moved a few papers off his desk and into the trashcan, "she wants me to come down the same week I had planned to go out to the beach house. You know, the one down in California?" Melanie nodded, thinking about the house. She had seen pictures of it before in albums that were lying around the house. It sat right on the shore of the Pacific Ocean in Northern California. Fred rented it out when he wasn't using it. "Well, I've decided to go to Florida, and since it'll be vacant for about a week, I was wondering if you wanted to take that week out there. I'll pay you for your time off if you want."

Melanie thought about the offer. "That'd be great, but I don't know if Tyler can take a week off."

"Oh, I'm sure he can find a way," Fred assured, knowing that Tyler would do whatever it took to get Melanie off somewhere by themselves. "Also, invite Johnny and Carrie along. Spend some time with the old gang. I'll be happy to pay for their tickets."

"Yeah, I haven't seen them in a while." Melanie wondered why Fred still called Taryn and Caleb by their new names since he knew everything about the Helping Hands and Hell Hounds. "I'll call them when I get home. Thanks, Fred."

Tyler shoved a stack of papers into a manila folder, wrote out an address on the front, and stood up from his desk. He brushed past a man pushing a tray filled with mail, ignoring the activity around him, the laughs and conversations, the people that called out his name. He was there for the kids, not to socialize.

Coming up behind a woman who was typing furiously on her computer, he plopped the file down in front of her, disturbing her flow of words.

"File for Dustin Huber," he told Sharon Summers, who turned to face Tyler.

"I heard about him," she told Tyler before he could walk away, opening the folder and glancing through it to make sure all the necessary items had been included. "Heard that some big guy went to the house and threatened the foster father with his life."

Tyler shrugged innocently. "You're kidding."

Sharon nodded. "Also heard that this big guy, he slammed the father up against the wall and nearly knocked him out, then walked straight through the house and took Dustin Huber right from the foster mother's arms."

"No way."

"And on the way out," Sharon continued, "this guy grabbed the father by the neck and threatened him yet again."

Tyler sighed and crossed his arms. "It's a shame how violent people can be these days," he said to her, grinning when she smirked.

"You better watch yourself, Mel. You're going to get yourself in trouble one of these days." Turning back to her desk, she picked up another file. "Here's the report on Jessica Hollings. She was just adopted by the Whites. And by the way," she added as Tyler started back to his desk, "you don't want to cross that line between do-gooder humanitarian and vigilante."

"Yeah, Sharon. I'll keep that in mind."

Tyler had only been working at the agency for a year, but in that short time he had managed to make himself known as the enforcer of the company. He had acknowledged from the beginning that being a social worker would mean coming up against children who were abused and foster parents who neglected to care for their kids properly. Feeling as though it was his job to make sure no child was put into a home filled with neglect and beatings, he did all that he could to help each and every kid.

And sometimes that involved getting physical.

In an odd way he had earned the respect from his co-workers, and even from his boss, from his hard-hitting antics. But Tyler didn't want or need their respect. He cared only for the children. It had taken Melanie a long time to accept his decision of being a social worker, despite the fact that she knew he would be just the type of person the system needed. He understood her anger and hesitance, but she eventually came around.

"Hey, Mel!" Sharon called over from her desk, interrupting his thoughts. "Phone call! Line two! It's your wife!"

Tyler gave Sharon a nasty look, though he was amused. Most of his coworkers liked to tease him about Melanie. They had all seen her at one time or another, and he couldn't even count the number of times he'd been asked if they were dating. But he quickly put an end to the sometimes playful, other times serious comments that were said about Melanie and her bedroom potential.

Tyler answered the phone, pleased to hear Melanie's voice on the other end. In the background he heard all the sounds of the auto shop. Brief memories of him with Caleb and Wess came to mind, the three of them arguing, fighting, having a good time. For a moment he was filled with a brush of nostalgia for the past, a place he could never go again but one that would define his life for the rest of his days to come.

Leaning back, he smiled at the sounds. "Hey, honey. I'll be a little late for dinner tonight, so don't slave over a hot stove for me."

"Screw you, Mason," Melanie replied, getting a laugh out of Tyler. "The day I cook for you is the day you admit you're an annoying, self-assured pig."

"Well then, I guess I'm going hungry tonight." As harsh as she was, Tyler liked hearing Melanie's callous and ruthless words. "So what's up? Everything okay?"

"Everything's fine. Just wanted to ask you something," Melanie replied. "You wanna take a week off of work?"

"A week?" Tyler raised his eyebrows, holding up the file he had just received. "I don't know. Why? We going somewhere?"

"That depends. Can you get a week off or do you have a lot of upcoming cases?"

Tyler glanced through Jessica Hollings' file, mentally judging the time it would take to visit the house and write up the report. "Just one, but there may be more. A week's a long time. Where would we be going?"

"Your uncle's beach house."

"Just the two of us?" Tyler grinned and sat up straighter.

"And possibly Carrie and Johnny."

But I can get them to leave for a night or two, Tyler thought slyly. "We're going."

CHAPTER 9

Gregson, Oklahoma

Randy Harding sighed as he grudgingly packed the last of his things into the black duffel bag Carrie and Johnny had given him. He picked up an old T-shirt, the shirt he had been wearing when Carrie Baggard and the Helping Hands had taken him away from the beatings of his father so many years ago. It still had bloodstains on it.

Randy remembered that night like it was yesterday. His father had come home after a late night at his favorite bar, drunk and barely able to stand. He was angry because he lost a bet on a football game and was out three hundred dollars, and so he decided to get the money from Randy. Randy, a thirteen year-old boy with no job or money, told his father he didn't have the cash and received two black eyes and a bloody nose as a result.

That night, Randy had awoken to see a dark figure hovering over him, gently shaking his shoulder. He had been taken to a place called The Ranch, and he loved it. He had friends, got to ride horses, and do all the things his father had never let him do before. He even had the special distinction of being the first kid ever taken by Carrie's branch of Helping Hands, and he took that role seriously. Being one of the oldest at The Ranch, he had taken it upon himself to help the younger ones, whether it be playing cards with them or listening to them tell an outrageous story or simply being a shoulder to cry on. Not once had he ever regretted his kidnapping, for this was the life he deemed perfect.

But now, he was turning eighteen, and it was time for him to leave. Carrie had planned it all for him, where he would go, what he would say. She had found him an apartment about fifteen miles from his old home, since he had informed her, much to her surprise, that he would like to return to his hometown. She told him that he could talk about his time at The Ranch so long as he didn't mention where he was or who he was with. Never use names, she said, never be specific, but Randy knew he would never give up the location of The Ranch or members of the gang. It was all too precious, too important, for him to ever do anything that may jeopardize the project. Besides that, he really had no idea where he was. He was brought to The Ranch blindfolded, and would be leaving the same way. He wouldn't be able to give directions even if he wanted to.

"Randy? You almost packed?" Taryn Jones, also known as Carrie Baggard, asked, entering the room. Randy nodded, placing the bloodstained shirt in the bag. She recognized it, not having to ask to understand why he kept it. "Tomorrow's the big day. Excited? Scared?"

Randy glanced over at Taryn and shrugged. "Both, I guess," he answered, then sighed and shook his head. "No, that's a lie. I'm not at all excited. It sucks that I have to leave. This totally sucks. I mean, this place has been my home for like six or seven years. I love it here."

Taryn smiled and rubbed Randy's shoulder comfortingly. "You're an adult now. You have the chance to start a whole new life and live it just the way you want to. This is your time, Randy. This is your time to go out and do great things, experience a whole new life in a whole new world. You deserve the chance to do all that."

"I guess," he said softly. "My time."

"Your time," Taryn agreed. "What do you think you will do?"

"Well, after I get myself away from all the reporters, I think I'll get my GED and go to college." Randy nodded to himself and bit his lip, thinking about what he would have to go through when his story hit the press. All the interviews he would have to give or decline, all the questions, all the frustrations.

But it was worth it, he thought. *All of it.* He had survived his father, the abuse. He had overcome childhood trauma to become a man who knew the true meaning of loyalty, love, happiness, life. So what were a few reporters compared to the privilege of living his life?

Taryn took in a deep breath. "Just remember, Randy. Don't tell anyone where we are, or who we are. That's the most important thing."

"I won't," Randy assured her. "This place means too much to me for me to say or do something that might shut it down."

"And what about your parents? Will you see them?"

Sitting down on one of the three beds in the room, Randy ran a hand through his hair. "I'll see my mom," he answered. "She deserves to know what happened. But I won't see my father." His voice went cold suddenly. "I will never see my father."

Taryn sat down next to Randy. She was happy to have watched him grow up, like she was with all the children, but Randy was different. He was the first child ever taken by her gang, and the first to leave. She knew he would do great. He was smart and had done well in his studies during tutoring, and had turned into a fine young man.

In a way she looked at Randy as a little brother. She was only seven years older than him, so there were times when it seemed she was looking out not only for a Helping Hand child, but for a family member. They got along great, and despite the small age difference he saw her as a mother figure.

"Carrie?" Taryn glanced up to see Caleb Brinson in the doorway, gesturing over to her. "I need to talk to you."

"About what?"

"O'Conner called." It was all he had to say, and Taryn was on her feet instantly.

"We'll talk later," she promised Randy, then followed Caleb out into the hall. "So what's up?"

Caleb started for the kitchen. "O'Conner and Tyler are going out to Fred's beach house in a couple of weeks, for like seven or eight days. They want to know if we want to go with them."

Taryn smiled and waved to a little girl as she ran past, her hands filled with toys from the playroom. "The big house that Fred owns?" Caleb nodded. "Yeah, let's go. It'd be nice to get away for a week."

Opening the back door, the two Helping Hands stepped out into the afternoon sun, heading for the coral. There they saw three children riding horses with the ranch owner. He was teaching them how to trot, the children squealing and laughing in delight. Taryn smiled while she watched them, leaning against Caleb as he put his arm across her shoulders.

San Francisco, California

Kelly pulled her chemistry notebook from her locker and took out a pencil from her jacket pocket. She briefly wondered if she had had any homework from the night before that she either didn't do or just forgot, then decided that it didn't really matter. School was school, and she wasn't going to waste any more time on it than necessary.

In the small oval mirror hung on the locker door, she could see that the cut above her eye was healing quickly, but was still fairly noticeable. She wished she could have put a Band-Aid on it, but because of its location, it would have been both difficult and uncomfortable, not to mention attention grabbing. People had believed her when she said she tripped over one of the boxes she hadn't unpacked yet and hit her head on the table.

"That's quite a battle wound," a voice said from behind, and Kelly turned to see Robbie coming to a stop behind her. "Thought you didn't fight."

Kelly rolled her eyes and slammed her locker shut. Robbie winced at the sound, his fingers throbbing slightly as he remembered the pain that same locker had caused him. She noticed the way his eyes narrowed at the sound, and for a moment she was tempted to smirk. "Who says I fought anyone?"

"What'd you do, run into the wall?" Robbie asked, falling into step next to Kelly when she turned to walk away. "You don't look like the klutzy type, someone who would trip over, say, an unpacked box. Me, I'd say I've had my fair share of trips and falls."

She rolled her eyes again. "The things you learn about people. Why are you following me?" She stopped and faced Robbie, who pointed down to her notebook.

"We got the same chem class. Figured you could use the company."

"I don't need company."

"Well then, I do. Hey, can I ask you something?"

"No."

"Please?"

"No."

"Pretty please?"

She nearly smiled at that, despite her intention to hate him. "Fine. What?"

"Well, it's not all that cold outside, and you got on a long-sleeved shirt. Actually, I don't think I've ever seen you wear like a tank top or anything. You always cold or something? I'll bet you got some really sexy arms." Robbie raised his eyebrows suggestively, then took a step back when Kelly's expression changed suddenly to almost scared. Scared or worried, he couldn't tell.

"I just, I don't like tank tops. I get cold easily, so leave me the hell alone about it," she replied, holding her books tight against her chest. The warning bell rang and the halls began to empty, so Kelly turned away quickly in hopes of dropping the subject.

"Hey, wait." Robbie stopped her by grabbing her arm. He jumped when Kelly let out a painful cry, her books falling from her arms as she pulled back. "What's wrong?" he asked, concerned, taking her wrist and not letting her get away. A sharp bite of dread gnawed at the pit of his stomach when he sensed her fear and need to hide what had caused her pain.

"Let me go. Robbie, let go!" Kelly ordered, trying to pull her wrist from Robbie's grasp. "No, Robbie, don't!" she protested when Robbie took the end of her sleeve and pulled it up.

"Shit." Robbie's eyes widened when he saw the ugly black and blue welts on her forearm. "What the hell happened to you?"

"Nothing. I fell and hit my arm on a chair. That's all." She tried to sound convincing.

"If that's all, why did you try to hide it? Kelly, I've been in a lot of fights. I know bruises. Those are from somebody's fingers. No chair could have done that." He let Kelly pull her arm away, and she yanked her sleeve down angrily. "What's going on?"

Kelly raised a hand to her forehead, covering the cut above her eye without realizing it. "Please don't tell anyone," she pleaded quietly. "Just forget you ever saw anything."

Robbie sighed in disbelief, throwing out his arms as the final bell rang. "Kelly, how can I forget that? Just tell me who did that to you and I swear I'll kick his goddamn ass !"

"No, fighting isn't the answer." Kelly shook her head. "Just forget it. It's nothing." He was about to press the subject, but was stopped when a pair of hands shoved him hard in the back. His head slammed up against a locker, the metal resonance ringing through his ears. Kelly saw his blue eyes go dark with a combination of pain and hatred, as well as a bit of fury, and for a moment she felt a twinge of fear of him and what he was capable of doing.

"Let's finish this," Jason Coppertone snarled as Robbie picked himself up from the floor, lightly touching the fresh cut on his cheekbone. "You and me, right now. Or maybe I should settle it with your little bitch."

Robbie stepped in front of Kelly. "This is between us. Leave her out of it." Reaching out with his fist, Robbie punched Jason hard in the jaw. Jason fell back, then lunged for Robbie, knocking him off his feet. They both fell to the floor, struggling against one another before two campus advisors ran over, pulling the two teenagers off each other.

"That's enough!" one yelled to Robbie as he dragged him off of Jason. "What are you doing, Anderson! You're in enough trouble as it is!"

Robbie didn't reply, but as he was being pushed towards the office, he caught Kelly's eye. He saw a glint of anger and another of fear, but also one of disappointment. That punch hit him the hardest.

CHAPTER 10

Northern California

Taryn smiled gratefully as she entered Fred Kindle's two-story beach house. The plane ride had been long and tiring, as had the cab drive to the house. She was ready to relax and get something to eat. Melanie came up behind her, also ready to kick back and do absolutely nothing.

Melanie gazed around the beach house. She had never actually been to it, but had only seen pictures. It was interesting in design, and everywhere she looked she saw the tastes of Fred Kindle. Rugs and expensive statues were positioned strategically around the place, and paintings of surfers and beach scenes hung on the walls. Every lamp was made of collections of seashells, and on one oak table she saw a glass bottle with a small ship trapped inside it.

Corny, but cute, she considered.

The windows were tall and domed, with sky-blue curtains held back by mermaid-shaped ribbons that wrapped around the bottom of the fabric with dark green tails. Streams of sunlight caught the shine of the oak floors, casting a glow around the white walls and filling the rooms with radiance.

The downstairs served as the living room area. It was one big room with a few separate areas for a bathroom and office space, and another section for storage. Two matching sofas were in the center of the room, along with a big-screen television and sound system. A small refrigerator was in the corner, stocked with drinks. A winding staircase with a banister painted in the design of a red-and-blue-scaled fish twisted from the floor to the balcony.

Upstairs were the living quarters. There they found two bedrooms, two bathrooms, a small den, and a modest kitchen. An outside balcony extended from the kitchen to halfway around the upstairs, accompanying both bedrooms with a lookout view. As they stopped at the top of the stairs, which left them standing in a small yet cozy loft, the four former Hell Hounds dropped their bags and looked about themselves.

"So what do we have, two rooms?" Caleb asked as he stretched.

"Yup." Tyler picked up both his bag and Melanie's. "Me and Melanie in one room, you two can decide the rest." He walked off into the master bedroom. Taryn and Caleb exchanged amused grins while Melanie shook her head and followed Tyler into the room.

"You do realize that this doesn't mean anything," she told him, crossing her arms while watching her new roommate place their bags at the foot of the bed.

Tyler held out his hands innocently. "All I want is to have a bed to sleep in."

"Yeah, okay. Whatever."

"So what are we doing tonight?" Caleb asked, entering the room and flopping down on the bed.

"Let's go out," Taryn offered. "We haven't done that in years. There's got to be some clubs or bars around here."

Melanie didn't reply at first, thinking that a club wasn't really the number one place she wanted to spend her time. She had never been one for the social scene, for people in general tended to make her day dark and depressing. She couldn't go anywhere without getting disgusted stares and grimaces because of who she was or how she looked. But as she glanced around at her friends, she saw that both Taryn and Caleb looked hopeful at the idea of going out, and Tyler didn't seem too disdainful either.

With a shrug, Melanie forced a smile. "Let's do it."

The music to Styles Rock Club was thundering, nearly causing the sidewalk to quake as the four friends walked up to it. The line was long, but they waited only about twenty minutes before getting in. After showing the bouncer their IDs, for once doing things the legal way, the Helping Hands entered with no problem.

Inside, lights of all different colors were flashing every which way, the DJ standing on a high platform to the right of the stage, moving and dancing along with the beat of the music. Dancers were placed around the club, some in cages suspended from the ceiling and others attached to poles, and every now and then men and women were pulled up from the floor to dance on the stage.

In one corner, a blast of smoke that was colored red engulfed a group of people, who cheered and held up their arms as they disappeared in the glow. Black lights picked up the white in the club and created a brilliance of pallid flecks among the floor. At the bar, waitresses waited for orders while bartenders expertly flipped bottles in the air and filled shot glasses with vodka and whiskey. A few drunken men and women were escorted from the club by oversized bouncers dressed in black and dark blue.

Melanie found herself staring around in wonder at all the sights before her. She had never gone to a club before, never had any interest to. A quick glance over at the bar had her unimpressed. Momentarily, and much to her own personal disgust, she pictured Tyler at a club with Sara, knowing that they used to go on the weekends. At that thought, a part of her wondered if Taryn and Caleb ever went out.

"I'm gonna go get us some drinks!" Taryn yelled over the music, and Caleb nodded.

"I'll get a table!" he replied in the same loud tone, and Melanie followed him as he wove through the crowd. She was shoved to the side as a trio of women brushed past her, and she was about to grab one of them in retaliation when Caleb pulled her back.

"I wouldn't fight here, O'Conner," he said seriously. "You never know who's backing up who."

Melanie pulled her arm from Caleb's grip, no longer wondering if Caleb had been to a club before. "I take it you're speaking from personal experience?"

"A little," Caleb admitted, glancing up at Tyler as he sat down at the table. "What about you? You dig the whole club thing?"

Tyler shrugged. "I used to. Sara would drag me out every weekend. She—" He cut his sentence short when he saw Melanie's eyes darken and she glanced down at her hands, her jaw set firmly. Nervously speechless, Tyler cleared his throat and sucked in a deep breath. "I'm gonna go find Taryn." He rose from the table and left, eager to avoid any confrontation he may have with Melanie about Sara Wiles.

Taryn waited patiently at the bar while the bartender got her drinks. Her foot tapped along with the rock music, and she sang quietly to herself while pushing back her hair. Leaning against the counter, she looked around the club, observing the people. She saw couples dancing, kissing, fighting. She watched two girls argue over something, and a man try to hit on a woman who clearly wasn't going to give him an easy score. For a moment she found herself wishing that Wess could be there with her, joking about the lonely hand that would be working that man tonight. He had always been quick with wit, and she missed that. Sometimes she felt guilty doing the things she did, going out to clubs, eating at a restaurant, grocery shopping, because she *could* do all those things. And Wess...

"So, come here often?" a man asked as he came up to Taryn's side. Shaking herself from her thoughts, Taryn shrugged, indifferent. "I'm here every weekend," the man continued.

"A real party man," Taryn replied dryly, not sparing him a glance. "How can I be anything other than impressed?"

The man shrugged, not realizing that Taryn was mocking him. "I'm Billy. And you are?"

Taryn thanked the bartender as he arrived with her drink order. She paid him, then turned back to Billy. "Not interested," she answered. "Hey!" She glared at him when he grabbed her arm.

"I'm still talking to you," Billy told her, pulling her closer to him. Taryn, smelling the alcohol on his breath, set her jaw angrily as she balanced the tray of drinks while thinking of how she could hit him without dropping it.

"Like I said before, what's your name?"

"You got our drinks, babe?" Tyler asked as he came up behind Taryn, sliding his arm across her shoulders and staring over at Billy.

Taryn smiled and looked up at Tyler. "Yep. I got 'em."

"Good. This guy giving you a hard time?" He never moved his steely eyes from Billy's.

Billy, taking in the tall and muscular man who was obviously the woman's boyfriend, held up a hand. "Hey, I was just talking."

Tyler nodded. "Right. Now you're just leaving." He raised his eyebrows, and after a moment of staring Billy down, he looked at Taryn while the other man stalked away. "Don't worry about it. You just gotta know how to handle a man."

Taryn shrugged Tyler's arm off her shoulders and pushed him with her free hand. "You just had to go and ruin the moment, Mason," she said as they started towards the table. "Here I was, ready to thank you for saving the day, then you start with those egotistical comments."

"Oh, Taryn, you know you love me anyway." Tyler grinned, taking the tray from his friend. He surveyed the club quickly, a reflexive habit he had gained from being a Hell Hound and Helping Hand, then went to join his friends.

CHAPTER 11

It was nearly three in the morning when the four friends entered the beach house. The place was dark, the only light coming from the moon that shone through the open windows and bounced off the floors. Silently, they headed upstairs and into the bedrooms after muttering good-night to each other. Caleb, who was originally going to sleep on the bed that pulled out from the couch, decided he was too tired, as well as too wasted, to go through the hassle of making the bed and instead went in with Taryn.

After changing, Melanie sat down and rubbed her eyes, more exhausted now that she was sitting on the bed. Unconsciously, she ran her fingers over the long, thin scar across her forehead before pulling her long brown hair off her shoulders. It had been an interesting night, she thought. An enjoyable one, but strange nonetheless. She wasn't used to being around so many people, but sitting at the table and observing everyone had given her a new perspective on them.

Because it would have been all too easy to, she hadn't drank much, and therefore arrived home nowhere near as drunk as Caleb and Taryn. Even Tyler had managed to stay sober, and Melanie wasn't sure if that was because he didn't care to drink all that much anymore or because he was with her. She hadn't put one foot out on the dance floor, and probably never would for the remainder of her life, but that hadn't stopped Caleb and Taryn. Melanie recalled feeling more than mildly surprised when she watched them dancing together, their bodies pressed up against one another in a manner that would suggest that they were a whole lot more than just friends.

There had only been one time that left her feeling unsettled. She guessed that because she and Tyler weren't dancing, it hadn't seemed like they were together. When the woman, the tall, slender, blonde woman with long legs and a tight miniskirt had come up and asked Tyler to dance, Melanie felt the anger.

Not anger, she corrected herself, *jealousy*. It had been jealousy that raced through her blood when the woman asked in her sweet and sexy voice, her hand on Tyler's shoulder. But even with her long legs and blonde hair and flat, tight stomach, Tyler barely even glanced at her while declining her offer. Although she had done her best to ignore the scene, Melanie hadn't been able to help looking over at Tyler, who had been staring over at her. He'd simply shrugged, and she hid a smile, all the while wondering why she had gotten angry.

After all, it wasn't like her to care so much about the romantic antics of her best friend.

Lifting the heavy blanket, Melanie got into bed, resting her head on the pillow as the night replayed through her mind. A few minutes later Tyler emerged from the bathroom, wearing only a pair of sweats. He refrained from grinning when he saw Melanie already in bed, and felt an odd sensation of warmth run through him.

"We're only here to sleep," Melanie warned him as he got into bed next to her.

"Don't worry, Melanie. I'm too tired to do anything anyway," Tyler told her, pulling the blanket up to his chest and vaguely recalling that the last time he had been in the same bed with her he wound up making a comment that ended the relationship before it even begun.

Melanie turned on her side, her back facing Tyler. The room was silent, a comfortable silence, and after a few minutes, Tyler rolled onto his side as well. Melanie opened her eyes when she felt him shift and put his arm around her stomach slowly, as if he were nervous, and for some reason she found the nerves endearing. He moved closer to her, until she could feel his steady breathing and the rippled muscle of his chest against her back. It felt right, as if this was where she belonged, as if this were normal, or as close to normal as she would ever know.

Melanie smiled to herself, and Tyler did the same. Neither said a word as they both closed their eyes and fell into a deep sleep.

Tyler opened his eyes in the early dawn light, slowly stretching and reaching over to find that Melanie was no longer beside him. He paused, remembering the previous night, the way he had slept by her side, holding her to him like he'd always wanted to do. And this time, she hadn't pulled away. Whether that had been due to exhaustion or consent, he didn't know. But in his eyes, he was making progress.

He sat up, looking over at the balcony to see her leaning against the rail, staring out at the ocean and golden sky. He watched her for a moment, the way one leg was bent at the knee and how her tousled hair was lifted from her shoulders as the wind blew in gently from the sea. Even though her pants were baggy, Tyler could still make out her figure, the muscle and tautness of her curves, the strength of her limbs. He could also just barely see the black tattoo on the small of her back of the number thirteen. It was a reminder of the age she had been when she started her project, a symbol of her past.

Getting out of bed, Tyler walked out onto the balcony. Melanie glanced over her shoulder briefly before looking back at the sea, at the pink and orange clouds that were spread across the morning sky. He came up behind her, wrapping his arms tightly around her waist, wondering what her reaction would be. After a moment's hesitation, Melanie placed her hands over his arms and leaned her head back against his shoulder.

From the kitchen table, Taryn and Caleb watched through the glass door leading to the balcony as Tyler came up behind Melanie. Taryn sipped her coffee as Tyler put his arms around her, and Caleb grinned when Melanie accepted the gesture.

Taryn propped her feet up on a chair, pulling her knees up to her chest and adjusting the blanket that was around her shoulders. "About time, huh?" she said quietly to Caleb, who nodded in response.

"It's the way it should be."

Taking another sip, Taryn gazed fondly at her friends and grinned when Tyler leaned over and kissed Melanie's neck, slowly moving his lips down to her shoulder. "Finally," she remarked, "it's Tyler and Melanie."

CHAPTER 12

San Francisco, California

It was late, and Kelly tossed and turned in her bed, not wanting to sleep because she was still angry with her mom for sending her to bed early, a whole hour before her bedtime. She could hear the TV downstairs as the people on the screen laughed. A small line of light came from under her closed door. Her window was cracked open, and a cool breeze came in from outside, causing the child to pull her covers up tighter to her chin.

Kelly sighed and stared up at the ceiling, her eyes tracing the swirls of white paint. She thought about the wedding. It hadn't been that long ago, only a few months. Her mom still talked about it, still got all sappy when she looked at her ring. Then she had to go and find her new husband and give him a big kiss so he would know how much she loved him.

But she doesn't really know him, Kelly thought. She doesn't know Jeffrey. She only dated him for six months before she wanted to marry him. Kelly thought about her real father, who had left not long after Danielle was born. It was better after he left and before Jeffrey, Kelly decided, crossing her arms beneath the blanket. At least then she didn't have to listen to her parents argue or have to be hit every time she came home barely five minutes late from school, even if it was the bus's fault.

Kelly looked over at the door when she heard footsteps in the hall. With terror rising in her belly, her breath caught in her throat when a shadow appeared beneath her door. Kelly knew who it was, and she knew exactly what would happen next. As if on cue with her thoughts, the doorknob twisted and the door opened a crack. Jeffrey stood in the doorway, his shadow outlined by the hallway light. Kelly tried to shrink back into her bed, but it was useless.

"Thought you'd get away with back-talking your mother, didn't you?" Jeffrey questioned as he came closer. "It's time you learned to respect your elders."

Kelly took in a deep, quivering breath as Jeffrey grabbed her shirt. She saw a glimmer of silver in her stepfather's fist as he raised it high, and she could smell the alcohol he liked to drink at night when he breathed in her face.

With fear in her eyes, Kelly stared up at the wrench in Jeffrey's hand. She remembered the tool well. It had been a wedding gift from one of Jeffrey's old high school friends.

"Solid iron, that one," the friend had boasted when Jeffrey opened the gift.

44

Kelly didn't think that the gift had been given with the intentions that Jeffrey was using it for now, and as his fist swung down, she squeezed her eyes shut and waited for the pain.

Kelly shot up in bed, her hair and body drenched in sweat and the sheets tangled around her feet. Reflexively, she looked over at the door, seeing that it was closed and there was neither light nor shadow beneath it. Her breath came out in raspy sobs, and her hand went immediately to her left temple, where her fingers hit a jagged scar.

The first scar she had ever received from a fist filled with iron.

Her nightmare was still fresh in her mind, and the memories of the pain and confusion she felt that night were overwhelming. She had only been seven, but even a seven year-old knew what it was like to not be loved. That night had never come so clearly to her in a dream before, and Kelly began to search her sheets for blood frantically, still sobbing.

Leaping out of her bed when she found nothing but sweat-soaked sheets, Kelly pulled on a pair of pants and grabbed her jacket from the floor. She had to leave, had to get out of the house with that haunting figure. She remembered that there was a trellis right next to her bedroom window.

Stepping out onto the ledge, she quietly headed over for the trellis and climbed down quickly. Her feet hitting the grass, Kelly ran from the house.

The crowd leapt to their feet, screaming for the Lakeside High Jaguars as the game came to an end and the victory assured. Coach Wright punched the air with his fist, slapping hands with some of his team members, and congratulating the other coach for a great game when the two teams started for the locker rooms.

Robbie grabbed a water bottle from the bench and took a long gulp. His final three-point shot had won them the game, and he was damn proud of himself. He wiped sweat from his face as he and his team went into the locker room.

"Great game, guys!" Wright told his team. "Way to play defense! And Robbie, that was a killer last shot."

Robbie grinned as a few of his team members slapped him on the back. Jason Coppertone glared over at him without envy or gratitude, and Robbie ignored the look. After taking a quick shower, he dressed and started out for his car, not bothering to chat with his teammates about the game. His parents had already left and were expecting him to go straight home after the game for dinner, so he didn't have much time.

He made it home in ten minutes, and as he pulled into his driveway, he saw two squad cars parked in front of Kelly Mitchell's house. The lights were flashing on one of them, and a few of his neighbors had emerged from inside to their front doors to see what the commotion was about. His parents were two of them.

"What's going on?" Robbie asked as he reached his parents, who were standing on the front porch. His mother was wearing an apron and holding a wooden spoon in her hand.

"Seems the Mitchell girl ran away last night," Adam Anderson answered, staring over at the police cars.

"Kelly ran away?" Robbie asked, and Rachael Anderson nodded.

"Yeah, last night," she repeated. "Do you happen to know anything about it?"

Robbie looked down at the ground before staring back over at the Mitchell household. He thought back to the previous night, when he watched Kelly climb out of her window, climb down the trellis, and run as fast as she could.

As if something had been chasing her, he remembered thinking.

"No. Don't know a thing," he lied, and his parents accepted it, turning back inside with Rachael informing Robbie that dinner was in ten minutes.

Robbie crossed his arms thoughtfully as a third squad car pulled into the driveway. The officers from the first two came out of the house, Jeffrey and Monica Ponder at their heels. Through slightly narrowed eyes, Robbie watched as the back door to the police car was opened and Kelly was pulled out by her arm. He saw her flinch in pain, and her mother ran over to her, wrapping her daughter in a tearful hug while Jeffrey hung back. When she passed him, Kelly turned her head to shoot him a glare filled with hate, and in the lowering sun, with shadows forming around her tired eyes, the girl looked downright murderous.

A theory forming in his brain, Robbie turned away from the scene and headed inside for dinner.

"Yo Harper."

Matt Harper looked up from his locker. "Hey, Robbie," he replied cautiously. "What's up?"

Robbie shifted from foot to foot, looking everywhere except at Matt. He hated having serious conversations. They were worse than facing his coach after a bad game.

"I uh, wanted to talk to you about something," he told Matt, somewhat nervous. "Well, ask you something, actually."

Matt closed his locker after taking out his homework. "Sure. What about?" He frowned as Robbie sighed, knowing it must be serious. Matt had known Robbie since he was a sophomore, and Robbie a freshman. They hadn't really gotten along at first, being competitors in gym class and having an overall distaste for one another in general for reasons neither could name. Their interactions now didn't expand any further than a casual nod or wave when they passed in the halls.

"I, well, this may be way too personal for me to ask you about, but I have to ask because, well, I figure you're the only one who'll be able to help." Robbie took in a deep breath before continuing. "How do you... how do you know when someone is being abused? Like, by a parent, or boyfriend, or something."

Biting back a heavy sigh, Matt hesitated and stared down at the floor. The question rang through his mind as he thought about it. He remembered standing on the fresh green grass of the Treehouse, watching as Melanie O'Conner and the Helping Hands brought another child they had helped, a child who would soon become one of his best friends. In every child, he recalled, there had been a darkness to his or her eyes, an emptiness, a void. Each child had been quiet, withdrawn, afraid to be touched by anyone or anything.

Looking back up at Robbie, Matt pushed his memories aside. "You're asking me about Kelly Mitchell, aren't you?"

Nodding in surprise, Robbie crossed his arms curiously. "Yeah. How'd you know?"

"Because I suspected the same thing when I met her," Matt replied. "And I've been watching you two. I've seen you guys talking."

"More like me talking, her shooting me down," Robbie corrected with annoyance. "But seriously though, do you think she is?"

Matt thought about the possibility. "Maybe. She could just be clumsy, or like to get into fights. Hell, she could just be shy or quiet or something. I don't really know. But I'd advise you to try and find out."

"Oh, I will." Robbie's eyes narrowed as the thought of someone hitting Kelly crossed his mind. "You can count on it."

CHAPTER 13

Northern California

A cool breeze drifted in from the rising tide, blowing across the back deck of Fred Kindle's beach house. A light creak sounded from an old wicker chair as Caleb rocked back and forth in it, his hands filled with a bottle of beer. Tyler, sitting across from him in a matching lounge chair, tossed the newspaper he was holding over to his friend and picked up another section.

To any passing person it would have seemed like a casual evening between two friends as they relaxed after a long day at the beach, but to Tyler and Caleb, it was much more. It had been nearly four months since they'd seen each other, and it was a rare moment when they got the opportunity to talk or merely just sit around in comfortable silence. Now, since Melanie and Taryn had left for a walk on the beach, Caleb could finally ease into the subject he had wanted to talk to Tyler about for so long.

"So," Caleb began, "Wess's birthday is coming up, you know?"

Tyler nodded and placed the paper on the table next to him. "Yeah, next month," he replied quietly. "Me and Melanie are going out to the cabin."

"You gonna go see his grave?"

"Yeah. Melanie really wants to go, so I told her I'd take her out there."

Swallowing a mouthful of beer, Caleb thought about Wess, remembered his friend when he had been in the hospital, and recalled what had happened between Wess and Melanie. Their relationship, those months after Tyler let Melanie go, had come as a surprise to Caleb, for he had always seen Melanie as someone who wouldn't ever even *think* of being with anyone besides Tyler. Not that he had cared though, for Wess had been his best friend and therefore he was happy for him. After all, Melanie was one hell of a woman and Wess was the best of men, so as far as Caleb was concerned, they were a good match.

But that didn't change the fact that Melanie and Tyler were meant to be together.

Glancing up at Tyler, he could tell that his friend was thinking about the same thing. For a few months after Wess's death Caleb had wondered if Tyler resented Wess or felt any sort of anger for Melanie because of the relationship, but all he had to do to answer his question was see the way Tyler looked at Melanie, and any doubts as to his friend's heart were blown away with the wind.

"You know," Caleb began cautiously, "if you had asked Wess to, he would have convinced O'Conner to go back home. To you," he added when Tyler gave him a cautionary stare. "I mean—"

"I know what you mean," Tyler cut in quietly with a wave of his hand. Sighing, he sat back and rubbed his eyes. "And I know that Melanie and Wess were... together. She told me. But it's not something we talk about, you know?"

Caleb nodded in understanding. "Like you and Sara," he compared the relationships, and when Tyler winced slightly, Caleb laughed in disbelief and sat forward. "What? You mean you haven't told O'Conner about that?"

"What's to tell?" Tyler tried to play off Caleb's question. "It meant nothing to me."

"Yeah, but O'Conner might see things differently, considering how she feels about Sara and all. You may want to tell her before someone else does." Seeing that his friend was about to get annoyed, and knowing that when Tyler got seriously irritated bad things tended to happen, Caleb changed the subject. "So, did you and O'Conner do anything last night that you should have been doing for at least a year now?" He smiled suggestively, getting a small laugh from Tyler.

"Nah, man. We just slept."

"Together?"

Tyler shook his head. "Together, in the same bed. Other than that, we just slept."

"Come *on*, Mason. You finally get her in your bed and what do you do? Nothing. You've gone an entire year without getting her in bed, without getting laid is what I'm saying. Now, O'Conner going celibate I can understand, because, well, she's... O'Conner," he said cautiously when Tyler sent him a warning glare. "But what about you? How the hell have you gone a whole year? I'm not sure I can believe the fact that you haven't gone elsewhere." He raised his eyebrows and pointed at his friend with his beer when Tyler merely shrugged. "Whatever, man. You, I just don't get. I mean, what went wrong with you two? I thought for sure that when she went back to live with you that you guys would hook up."

Tyler let out a heavy breath and thought about the night he and Melanie had sat by the fountain, over a year ago now. At the time, it had seemed like a turning point in their relationship, when he truly believed that he could fix all the things that had been broken. Yet somehow, without him realizing it, an entire year had passed and no progress had been made.

"I really don't know what went wrong," he answered truthfully. "I guess with all that happened, with Wess dying, the whole Foster thing, both me and Melanie getting jobs, we've just been distracted. Busy."

"Busy making excuses," Caleb corrected. "Give it up, man. You want her, and you know it."

"I do know it," Tyler confirmed, rising from the wicker chair and leaning against the railing. "I have no problem admitting it. I've wanted her for as long as I can remember."

"Then what's the problem?"

Tyler stared out at the sea and lowering sun, shaking his head when the truth hit home. "I don't really know if that's what she wants."

He was quiet for a moment, leaning over the wooden railing and peering out at the ocean, watching the foam-crested waves crash against the shore. A few seagulls hovered above the water, scanning the clear glass sea for their dinner. A couple walked along the shoreline, their hands clasped, the woman's light brown hair wisping away from her shoulders as the breeze drifted among the strands. He found himself sighing as he watched them walk away.

"I made a promise to Wess one time when he was in the hospital." Tyler turned and faced Caleb, leaning back against the rail. "He told me to never let Melanie go, and I promised him I wouldn't. And I'm not about to break a promise to a best friend."

Caleb leaned back against the cushion of the chair as he set the paper on the porch floor. "Then what's stopping you?" he asked curiously, watching as Tyler gestured out to the beach.

"She is," he answered. "She won't let me get close or personal about anything. It's always about the project, or work, or you guys. She avoids anything that has to do with just us."

"Maybe she's afraid," Caleb suggested, shrugging when Tyler frowned. "I know it sounds weird, O'Conner being afraid of something, but you never know. I mean, she's been through a lot, with her father, jail, Wess, and now she's starting to rebuild her life. Maybe she's scared that if she gets too close, something will happen and she'll lose it all. It's not really a matter of you not being able to talk to her, but you not giving up."

"I'm not giving up." Tyler shook his head and crossed his arms with a wry grin. "She's just so goddamn frustrating. I'm about ready to just say screw the talking and drag her up to bed whether she's holding my hand or clawing my back after I throw her over my shoulder."

"I'd kind of like to see that," Caleb muttered with a grin as he pictured the scene. "She'd be so pissed."

"She's always pissed."

"Yeah, but that's what's so fun about her."

Tyler laughed. "She wouldn't be the same without that temper, that's for sure."

Caleb started to reply, but stopped when he saw Melanie and Taryn heading up to the house, holding their shoes and the legs of their pants rolled up to the knees. Tyler straightened and wiped the low-spirited expression from his face, smiling when Melanie glanced briefly at him from the bottom of the stairs. Caleb met Taryn at the top of the steps and pulled her back down, dragging her out to the beach before she could ask what he was doing.

Melanie dropped her shoes on the porch floor as she reached the top of the stairs and greeted Tyler. She started for the door, but Tyler stopped her suddenly by grabbing her arm. He did want her, and it was that fact that made him pull Melanie tight against him and lower his mouth to hers. He didn't give her a chance to protest or pull away as he held the back of her neck with one hand while the other gripped her arm. Melanie was surprised, but she didn't fight him. Instead, she consented to the kiss, raising her hands to Tyler's broad shoulders as he ran his own through her hair.

It was a moment neither of them had ever experienced before, one that brought forth sparks deep in their beings that shone through the brush of lips, the dance of tongue and mouth. There was a degree of need in their embrace, and both were breathless by the moment's end.

"Melanie," Tyler pulled back and swallowed heavily, "can I ask you something?"

Licking her lips, the former Hell Hound nodded. "Sure."

Tyler took in her eyes for a moment, seeing that the usual fierce, mad-at-the-world glare had been temporarily replaced with one of tranquility. It threw him off a bit, for it was something he wasn't used to at all.

"I... We..." It was harder than he'd thought it would be, having a deeply intimate moment and facing it with complete seriousness. "I... Look, I don't want to have to throw you over my shoulder."

A quiet laugh escaped. "Well that's good to know."

"Yeah, because the last thing I need right now are scratch marks down my back. The last ones you gave me finally healed." And that had been quite an incident, he briefly recalled, one in which he learned quite a lesson: never grab an angry woman by the shoulders because that left her hands free and his arms vulnerable.

"So I figure that this time you have a choice,' he continued. "Take my hand or start scratching."

Eyeing him carefully, Melanie crossed her arms and shifted to a position that he recognized as being both defensive and playful. "And you have a choice as well. Wake up in the beach house or in a hospital bed?"

"Depends on why we're requiring an emergency room. I might enjoy a little bit of hurt here and there."

Curious now, Melanie narrowed her eyes pensively while stifling a smile. "Are you trying to tell me something, or is this just some weird casual talk?"

Tyler pushed any and all doubts from his mind. "What would you say if I asked you if you wanted to go to bed a little earlier tonight?" He tried to keep from smiling, although he was being entirely serious. He felt his hopes rising when Melanie seemed to consider the question with a small smirk on her lips.

"Well, that depends," she replied, cocking her head to the side thoughtfully. "*Are* you asking me if I want to?"

"Yes." Tyler sounded confident, but inside his nerves were jumbling about. It looked as though Melanie was about to agree with him, but he knew better. He knew that she could easily hide her feelings with her notorious smirks and glares.

She's so damn hard to read, he thought as Melanie took his hand slowly.

"Then I say I'm getting a little tired." She bit down on her bottom lip, suppressing a grin as Tyler guided her to the stairs on the far side of the deck that led to the upstairs balcony, his hands already pulling at her leather jacket as he kissed her neck gently, lovingly, yet with all the passion he had stored up from deep within.

CHAPTER 14

San Francisco, California

A twinge of nervousness ran through Robbie as he walked up the three steps that led to the Mitchells' front door. He stood on the welcome mat for a moment, his hands in his pockets as he silently worded his invitation. Finally, after lifting a hand, he knocked loudly, having to wait at least two minutes before it was answered.

"Yes?" Monica Mitchell-Ponder said after she pulled the door open, seeing a young, strange face peering at her through the screen.

"Um, hi," Robbie greeted with a small smile. "I'm Robbie Anderson. I live a few houses down." He pointed to his house. Monica nodded but didn't reply, staring at the teenager while waiting for him to tell her what he wanted. "Well, my parents and I were wondering if you and your family would like to come over for dinner tonight. Sort of like a welcome to the neighborhood, even though you've been here for like three weeks."

Thinking about the offer, Monica smiled and pushed open the screen door. "I would love to," she answered, thrilled at the offer to meet some of her neighbors. "Would you like to come in? Meet the family?"

Robbie started to enter, then changed his mind because he wasn't in the right mood to face the man he suspected was laying his hands on the girl he had a serious thing for. "No, I have to get back home. Told my mom I'd help her with dinner."

"Oh, that's nice," Monica answered, wishing her own two daughters cared enough to spend time with their mother instead of always being holed up in their bedrooms. "We will definitely be there. What time?"

"Six-thirty."

"See you then." As her neighbor turned and jumped down the three steps, Monica closed the door with a happy smile. She'd been hoping to meet some of her neighbors. Since she didn't work, it got lonely when her daughters were at school and her husband was out. There were times when she wished she had a career to call her own, but if she had a job she wouldn't be able to have dinner on the table when her husband wanted, and nothing good would result from that. Monica didn't like to displease him, for he would only be irritable for the remainder of the night and unpleasant to be around.

"Who was that?" Jeffrey asked as he came out of the den, a beer bottle in hand.

"A boy named Robbie Anderson," Monica informed him. "He invited us to dinner at his house tonight."

"You told him we couldn't make it, right?"

"Um, no." Monica shook her head, getting a baleful glare from her husband. "I thought it would be nice if—"

"If what?" Jeffrey cut in angrily. "If we got buddy-buddy with the neighbors, and you'd have someone to talk to? How many times do I have to tell you that if you get lonely or bored during the day, get a damn job!"

Monica stepped back at the harsh snap. She swallowed, not knowing what to say, but knowing enough not to remind him that he didn't want her to have a job. But Jeffrey was right, of course. He was always right, always knew what was best, and she should have known what to do. She should have known what to say to the Anderson boy, but she had been selfish, doing what she had wanted instead of thinking of the well-being of others and of what her husband would have wanted.

"You're right, Jeffrey. I'll go over and tell them we can't come."

"No. That would make me look bad, and I won't have that. We will go, and we will make the best of it, as long as your children behave."

Her children, Monica said in her head as she headed for the bedroom. There had been a time when Jeffrey thought of them as his own, and loved them as much as she did. He would have done anything for them, bragged to his friends about how smart they were, always told her he would do whatever he had to do to help them.

But now, now he saw them only as a burden.

Robbie frowned as he stared across the table at Kelly, toying with the fork in his hand. He glanced over at Danielle, who was sitting next to her sister. Both were quiet, hardly having said ten words between the both of them. The adults kept a steady flow of conversation, with his father at one end of the table and Jeffrey Ponder at the other, and the two women on either side of Robbie.

But it was different with the girls, Robbie noted. They didn't talk, not even to each other. Every now and then Kelly would glance over at Danielle, who would nod or shake her head slightly in response. He was surprised that Kelly was so quiet. He knew from experience that she always had something to say, and wasn't usually reserved when it came to expressing her opinion.

Her chance came towards the end of dinner, when the conversation between the adults began to wind down and make room for small talk amongst the rest of the table's inhabitants.

"So, Kelly," Rachael Anderson turned to Kelly while buttering a slice of bread, "do you like it here in San Francisco?"

Kelly looked up from her plate, her hair falling across her eyes. She pushed it back, giving a small smile. "Yeah, it's not bad," she replied. "I miss it back in Florida though. It's—" She glanced over at Jeffrey, who was staring at her through slightly narrowed eyes. "It's nice here, though," she finished quietly, turning her eyes back to her plate.

Pausing with his fork in mid-air, Robbie frowned and looked back from Kelly to Jeffrey. He saw the glare Jeffrey gave her, quick as it was, and also saw the way Kelly shook her head at her sister. His parents didn't seem to notice, however, and continued about with their conversation.

An hour later, after dessert had been served and the table cleared, the four adults headed into the living room, Adam offering his guests a drink before they headed home. Robbie, Kelly, and Danielle were left alone in the dining room. Danielle, always nervous around new people, kept her head down and ran a finger along the white lace pattern of the tablecloth.

Lifting her eyes, Kelly looked across the table at Robbie, who was staring back at her with his dark brown eyes. "Dinner was great," she told him. "Your mom's a good cook."

Robbie nodded. "Yeah, she is. You mind if I ask you something?" Kelly shrugged tiredly and Danielle listened intently. "Where'd you get that scar on your temple?"

Kelly frowned at the unexpected question, taking a quick look at Danielle before waving her hand with a forced smile. "It was nothing. I fell out of a tree as a kid and hit my head on a rock. Just a few stitches."

"I don't believe you," Robbie challenged, raising his eyebrows as Kelly sighed. "Try again."

"Fine," Kelly spat out. "I got into a fight at my old school and the kid hit me. Satisfied?"

Robbie shook his head. "Nope, still not working."

"Danielle, will you excuse us?" Kelly asked her sister, who nodded and rose from the table. She disappeared into the kitchen, and Kelly turned back to Robbie,. "What the hell do you want from me?"

Shrugging, Robbie sat back. "I want to know why you didn't talk tonight, and why every time you looked at your stepfather you looked down at your plate."

"What are you, a cop?" Kelly asked scornfully.

"No, and normally I wouldn't care about this. But it wasn't only you. Your sister was the same way."

"Stay out of my life, Robbie," Kelly warned, rubbing her eyes and letting out a deep breath.

"I can help you."

"No, you can't, because you don't know what you're talking about."

"Kelly—"

"You kids ready to go?" Jeffrey asked as he came out of the living room, Monica trailing behind him, a big smile on her red-painted lips. Kelly nodded, rising to her feet as Danielle came back from kitchen. Adam showed them to the door, Kelly giving Robbie a look that he guessed meant that she didn't want him to say anything to his parents.

As the door shut behind the Mitchells, Adam turned to his wife and son. "Strange family, aren't they?" he asked. "The girls hardly talked at all."

"Danielle looked nervous, probably because she doesn't know us. Kelly seemed reserved too. I think they were just too shy to talk," Rachael replied, pulling Adam into the kitchen so they could start the dishes.

"Or were just too scared to," Robbie muttered under his breath, then fell back down into the dining room chair.

Kristina Circelli

CHAPTER 15

Salem, Oregon

Brian Hawkins sidestepped a mechanic as the man rolled out from under a Corvette, grabbing a tool from a pile next to the tire and disappearing beneath the car again. Looking around the large shop, he noted its atmosphere. It was hot, crowded, and filled with the sounds of tools clanging and crude banter circling among the mechanics, just the type of environment a person would have to be able to endure for what he was looking for.

"Can I help you?" a man asked as he came out of an office on the far side of the fairly large workspace. He looked the exact opposite of everyone in the shop. His face was clean, he wore a pair of nice black slacks and a white shirt, and his hair was neatly combed, but there was a certain paleness to him that had Hawkins wondering if the man ever went out into the sun at all. Hawkins was the type of person who spent as much time as possible outdoors, and didn't understand those who preferred being within the confines of four walls and a roof.

"Yes. I'm Brian Hawkins. We spoke a few days ago on the phone." Hawkins shook Fred Kindle's hand, his voice deep and demanding.

"I remember," Fred replied with a nod, looking the man up and down. He was tall, built, and carried himself with an air of authority that matched his close-cropped hair and military-like stance. "Well, I don't know where O'Conner is, so you'll have to go find her. I'd like to help, but I have an appointment to get to. Try the back. That's where she usually is. Just listen for a female voice shouting a bunch of curses and nonsense. Good luck."

Hawkins headed for the back of the shop, making his way around workbenches and automobiles. His thick black boots made dull thumps against the concrete floor, and he kept his stride steady and even, making sure to avoid the spots of oil despite the fact that they were nothing more than stains.

Once in the back of the shop, he saw racks and racks of tools lining the floor like a library, and to the far right sat three old and battered cars that he wasn't sure were up and running. Hawkins looked about himself, searching for the one person he had come for. He didn't have to search for long before he was led to his objective through a verbal map.

"You good for nothing piece of *shit*!" he heard a female voice shout, loud and clear. "Get the hell out of my face!"

"What're you gonna do about it, O'Conner?" a deep male voice yelled back in response, sounding both annoyed and challenging. "What, huh? Yeah, yeah I dare you to hit me with that, you—"

Hawkins winced when he heard a crash and a grunt of pain from the male voice, then a series of laughter and catcalls from the spectators. Both curious and hesitant, he walked further into the back, stopping sharply when a figure came out from behind a rack of tools and nearly ran into him.

"Watch it," Melanie told him sharply, her face red with anger as she stepped back and took in the unfamiliar face. She stopped, examining the man, the tall, obviously well-disciplined man who didn't belong in any auto shop as she clutched a heavy steel rod in her right hand. Her eyes strayed briefly from his when she caught movement to her left and glanced over to see the man she had hit holding his head with a grimace. For a moment she felt sorry for him, but that sympathy diminished when she remembered why she had attacked him in the first place.

No one talked trash about Tyler and walked away without a bruise.

Looking over her shoulder at the crowd that had gathered, she gestured with her head at them. "Get lost." The sharpness of her order had the group laughing as they parted and Melanie turned back to the stranger.

"Can I help you with something?"

"Yes, actually," Hawkins answered, his eyes on the rod. He should have told her instantly why he was there, but curiosity quickly overtook any other thoughts. "Mind telling me what that man did to deserve being slapped upside the head with that?"

"He forgot how to think before he spoke," Melanie replied, still annoyed. "And I didn't slap him upside the head."

"No?"

"No. I shoved it against his forehead, like this."

Despite himself, Hawkins flinched and pulled back when she lashed out with the rod, aiming for his head like she had done to the mechanic. This time, she stopped before actually connecting with flesh. Immediately embarrassed at being shown up by a woman, especially considering that that same woman was now staring over at him with an expression that oozed satisfaction, Hawkins regained his composure and lifted his chin with arrogance.

"Well, Miss O'Conner, now that we've got that out of the way, let's get down to business."

"I have no business with you."

At her indifferent dismissal, Hawkins straightened. He would have his way no matter how bored she seemed to be with him. "I'm here to offer you a job."

Melanie gave a small, sarcastic laugh, crossing her arms and leaning back against the tool rack. "You're kidding, right?"

Hawkins held out his hand and pulled it back when the woman in front of him didn't move. "Brian Hawkins, South Bay Juvenile Detention Camp."

"South Bay?" Melanie repeated, thinking of the place with disgust. She'd heard of South Bay before, once when she was living in Sacramento, and later on when living in Knoxport. Her foster father in Knoxport, Jerry Hunter, had often threatened to send her there, and even started to make the call to the camp at least a dozen times when he was staggering drunk. It was known as one of the toughest juvenile camps in the country, the most disciplined along the western coast. The drill instructors showed no mercy, and rumor had it that at least ninety-three percent of the kids who came out after serving their sentence were too scared by the thought of having to go back to ever do anything illegal again. Melanie had always been eager to test that theory, so every time Jerry had dealt out the threat she had only made him all the more furious with her reply of "bring it on."

As a result, her beatings had been all the worse.

She'd never been afraid of going to South Bay, and had always wondered how she would have handled herself out there with all the sand and obstacle courses and supposedly bad-ass instructors, but that didn't mean she wanted to work there.

"So why are you here?"

Hawkins smiled and handed Melanie a small stack of papers. "Here's some information on the camp. There's an opening for a drill instructor and counselor. I'm here to ask if you would like the job."

Melanie skimmed an article about South Bay, then glanced through the rest of the papers somewhat scornfully before lifting her eyes, cynical and disinterested as they were, back up to his. "Look man, I *got* a job. I got a life here, and I don't need you coming up to where I work and handing me this shit. Sorry." She held out the papers, but Hawkins didn't take them. Instead, he stared down at her evenly.

"As an employee at South Bay, I know what it's like to have to work not against, but with the kids who come. I'm a drill instructor. Sergeant, in fact."

Melanie gave Hawkins an indifferent, unimpressed stare. "Well, I'm sorry, but you'll have to forgive me for not quivering with fear," she said, rolling her eyes as Hawkins smiled and nodded.

"Yes, there's the famous Melanie O'Conner attitude I've heard so much about." He caught her attention again with his comment, as he hoped he would. "As a drill sergeant, I know that you have what it takes to whip these kids into shape. You're perfect for the job."

Melanie took in a deep breath. "You *do* know that I went to prison for kidnapping kids, right? And that pretty much the entire public hates me?" Brain nodded. "And that I didn't even finish high school and have no qualifications as a counselor? Now you want me to work with them? What's wrong with your boss?"

"You have what it takes," Hawkins repeated. "You've lived through a lot of what these kids have, experienced what they've experienced, lived to tell the tale, gone straight. That's what we want. South Bay has a lot you would be interested in."

As Hawkins talked, Melanie found herself actually considering the job offer. It didn't seem so ridiculous when she really, seriously thought about it. A drill instructor, a counselor. Not two things she had ever pictured herself becoming, but she would get to work with kids, get to help them again.

And this time, that help would be legal.

"Tell you what," the former Hell Hound held up a hand, "let me think about it, talk it over with some people, and I'll let you know. I can't just pack up and leave."

Hawkins nodded in understanding. "I know. And if you decide to take the job, you can choose a house, apartment, whatever, and South Bay will help with the relocation. Also, I was provided a few things to give to you. Kind of like incentives for you to take the job, catered to your personality. Well, what we could figure without having met you, of course."

Melanie took the envelope from Hawkins as he offered it, setting the rod aside. "I'll think about it," she told him, glancing through the items in the envelope as Hawkins turned to walk away. She flipped past a few gift certificates that she knew Tyler would like to a hardware store, pizza joint, and some kind of bar, among other places. Along with them, she saw two concert tickets that made her hesitate.

"Hawkins!" she called out, and he turned. She held up the tickets. "Why'd you guys give me these? The concert's already happened."

Hawkins frowned, a thin line forming on his forehead as he went back to Melanie and peered at the tickets. "No, it's next Saturday. See?" He pointed to the date.

"Yeah, but this band has already been to San Francisco," Melanie protested as she thought back to her conversation with Matt Harper, getting another confused expression from Hawkins.

"What are you talking about?"

Shaking her head in consternation as she began to put the pieces together, Melanie didn't know whether to be angry or pleased or both at once. "Nothing," she replied quietly, staring down at the tickets, crumpling them with an incensed fist. "My mistake."

Melanie went straight to the phone when she got home from work, having left early for the sole purpose of making the one phone call that she was sure would leave her more furious and more disappointed than anything else she had ever managed to come across. She dropped the information about South Bay onto the counter and flicked on the kitchen light, wondering if Tyler was home. She hadn't bothered to see if his car was in the garage.

As quickly as she could, Melanie dialed the number she was most familiar with, waiting impatiently while listening to the ringing on the other end.

"Hello?"

"Matt? That you?" Melanie asked, already knowing it was.

"Yeah. Miss Melanie?"

"What's up?"

"Not much."

Melanie knew without a doubt that Matt was hiding something, and didn't waste time digging into his secrets. "I wanted to ask you about that concert you went to a few nights ago. I was telling a friend of mine that you went, and she asked me some questions." Melanie didn't feel the least bit guilty about lying, even though it did feel like a bit of a betrayal using her skills against the teen she still remembered as a little boy with huge smiles and extravagant dreams.

"Okay."

"Where was it again?"

"Here."

"Oh yeah." Melanie nodded, looking at her tickets that said the concert would, indeed, be in San Francisco, but not for another week. "Was it inside or outside?"

"Outside," Matt replied after a pause.

"Really? I saw on the news that it's been raining a lot down there for like the past month. Was it raining for the concert?"

"Um, not really." Melanie could picture Matt's face as he struggled to think of a good lie. "Well, yeah it rained a little, but not bad."

Contradicting himself, Melanie thought. "So it was crappy weather for a concert?" She waited for a moment, the line silent as she tapped her fingers on the countertop.

"Yeah, it was pretty crappy."

Melanie felt the sudden urge to laugh and went in for the kill. "So it was crappy weather for a concert, but perfect for a kidnapping, right?"

"Not really. The grass was wet, and—oh shit," Matt cursed as he stopped mid-sentence, realizing what he said. "Wait, I didn't—"

"What the hell were you *thinking*, Matt?!" Melanie yelled. Fury welled up from within, and she was perfectly willing to unleash it. "Do you have any *idea* what you've done!"

"I know what I'm doing!" Matt protested. "I learned everything from you!"

"Don't you dare try to give me that bullshit. You are putting yourself in danger! And what are you going to do with Ryan? Who are your benefactors? Do you even have any?" Melanie was furious with the first child of the Treehouse, and had no problem letting him know it. "Who are your benefactors, if you were even smart enough to get any?"

Matt was quiet for a moment. "Um, Mickey is one of them. He was happy to get back into the project after you guys left."

With a sigh that came out as more of a grunt, Melanie squeezed the bridge of her nose and pictured the man among her jumbled thoughts. There was no doubt in her mind that Mickey Wraling would have jumped at the chance to be a part of the project again. He had been one of her best contributors, hiring Tyler, Caleb, and Wess at their young ages, giving them monthly bonuses of three or four hundred dollars so they could buy gear for the kidnappings or pay for medicine when one of the kids of the Treehouse was sick. He also, what Melanie considered to be the most important of all, allowed them to store all their gear and data in the safe in his office when there was no more room at the apartment. Without his help, all of the original Helping Hands knew that they wouldn't have made it as far as they had.

Even when the Helping Hands had been ripped apart by the reporters and Melanie had no choice but to call an end to her project, Mickey had been there. The reports had come out on the news about the police getting more and more leads on whom the Helping Hands were, and Melanie had been forced to sit helplessly and accept the fact that all her benefactors had backed out, all saying that they didn't want to go to jail and lose their businesses. But Mickey had been there until the end, never thinking twice about his loyalty to the Helping Hands.

Melanie knew he loved the project, which was why she wasn't surprised that he had agreed to help support Matt. For a moment she wondered how Matt found out that Mickey had been a benefactor, but quickly figured that he heard her or one of the guys talking about him at one point or another at the Treehouse.

Even so, she felt that with Mickey's aid or not, Mathew Harper should never be a part of any of the Helping Hands gangs.

"So you got Mickey to help you." Melanie fought to keep from yelling again, and the restraint, for her, was nearly painful. "Am I to assume that he's your only one?"

"I have others too!" Matt replied hastily. "And Ryan is in a safe place, I swear. We call it The Lake, because, well, it's on a lake."

"We?" Melanie repeated, only a little comforted by the fact that Mickey was a benefactor. "Who else do you have for your gang?"

"Um, Carry Valentine," Matt answered. "And, um, Jimmy Fencles and Isaac Davidson."

Closing her eyes, Melanie ran a hand through her hair as she sat down on a stool and leaned against the counter. They were all children of the Treehouse. Carry Valentine had been one of the last kids ever helped by the Hell Hound branch of Helping Hands, the very last, in fact. Jimmy Fencles nearly died on Treehouse Island due to the starvation he endured. Isaac Davidson had been one of the first kids ever taken. He had been subject to terrible neglect and beatings, and was one of the toughest kids of the Treehouse. It had taken a long time to teach him how to control his violent temper.

The fact that the gang was made up of Treehouse kids made Melanie somewhat proud despite her anger. They had all gotten together again after being ripped apart and were working for a common cause, the Helping Hand cause. But that didn't change the fact that they hadn't informed Melanie or any other Helping Hand of their plans.

"So that's four of you," Melanie said after thinking of the names. "I'm going to go out on a limb here and assume you have a fifth member that you don't want to tell me about." She figured she was right when Matt didn't reply right away. "So who is it?"

"It's um... a girl," Matt answered. "You, well, you know her."

Taking a moment to consider a girl whom they both knew, Melanie made a fist when she realized who it had to be. Matt would know better than to bring a complete stranger into the project, so that left only one person. "Oh, no," she said to herself. She knew who it was. There was only one other person that Matt would ask to be a Helping Hand, a girl who thought of Melanie as a hero, who fought for people to see the Helping Hands as saviors. And not only that, there was also the fact that she and Matt were somewhat involved with one another.

"Leighann Cross, right?"

"Yeah."

Melanie punched the countertop. "Mathew Taylor Harper." Her words were short and strict. "Why the *hell* would you bring her into this? She has *nothing* to do with the Helping Hands! She's been getting her life back on track after her mother, and you're dragging her into the project? She's not strong enough to be a part of the gang!"

"Yes, she is!" Matt protested. "We all are! And we're good at it!"

"Matt, you've done *one* kidnapping!" Melanie yelled, her anger rising again. "One! You have absolutely *no* idea what you're doing! Every branch of the Helping Hands has been started by someone who knew what they were doing! A veteran, someone who had *experience* in a Helping Hand gang! You are being *totally* irresponsible!"

"Look, I spent four years at the Treehouse, and I always heard you and Tyler and everyone else talking about the project and how it worked. I know what I'm doing! And we're careful! I know you're mad at me, but just try to understand! I can't have you mad at me because I know I'll need your help." Matt's voice was sincere and nervous.

Melanie sighed and rubbed her forehead, squeezing her eyes shut as a headache began to throb. She was silent for a moment while she calmed herself down, not wanting to yell anymore. "Matt, I understand why you did this, and I'm not mad at the fact that you want to be a Helping Hand. But you took a kid without telling anyone, and when I heard about it on the news, do you have any idea how worried I was? I mean, there's a gang out there calling themselves the Helping Hands, and I had *no* idea who they were! And worse, I had two F.B.I. agents come to my house trying to figure out who you guys are. And they'll be back, I know it. You just, Matt, you don't know what you're getting yourself in to."

"I do." Matt was quiet. "I can do it. I know I can. I learned from the best, and if anything goes wrong, I swear I'll end the whole thing. I'm gonna make you and the others proud of me. You've done so much for me and I'll never forget it. I want to help some kid the way you helped me."

Melanie shook her head at Matt's words. He always knew how to soften her, she thought with a small smile, always knew just what to say. "You're really gonna do this, aren't you?" she asked, nodding when Matt affirmed her question. "Well then, kid, I got just one thing to tell you."

"What?"

"Being a Helping Hand is a lifetime commitment, and I hope you realize that. Once you're in, you can never get out, no matter how far away you move, no matter what kind of new job you take, no matter how many people agree to keep silent. If anyone *ever* traces you to a kidnapping, they'll talk. So don't get caught." She wasn't going to tell him anything else. It was his decision, and if he screwed up, it would be his mistake.

"Thanks for understanding, Miss Melanie," Matt said, and Melanie smiled at the title. Even as a seventeen year-old senior, he still respected her enough to call her what he had when he was only eight.

"Be careful, Matt. I mean it," Melanie replied, then hung up. She sat with her head in her hands for a moment, listening as she heard footsteps heading for the kitchen.

"Is it safe to come in?" Tyler asked, coming up next to Melanie, who sighed in response. "Heard a lot of yelling in here. It was Harper, wasn't it?"

"And Carry, Jimmy, Isaac, and Leighann." Her voice was muffled by her hands. "Damn kids are crazy."

"If they're crazy, we must have been downright insane," Tyler offered. "I mean, we were only thirteen when we started our gang. At least Harper's seventeen. And at least he has us and all the other gangs who'll be there for him."

Leaning her head on her hand, Melanie thought about the newest Helping Hand branch. "I just don't want anything to happen to them. They don't realize how dangerous it is."

Tyler went behind Melanie and wrapped his arms around her neck, having to lean over further when she attempted to bury her head in her arms. "Neither did we. Maybe they'll learn from our mistakes."

"I hope so."

The two were silent while they thought about the newest addition to the Helping Hands. Melanie toyed with a pencil that was lying on the counter, feeling Tyler rubbing her shoulders comfortingly. It was a soothing moment, one that she cherished.

"What's this?" Tyler stood up suddenly and reached across the counter, picking up the small stack of papers that caught his eye. He glanced through them, surprised at the information. "South Bay? Isn't that the detention camp somewhere near Sacramento?"

"Yeah." Melanie rose from the stool and took the papers. "It's like four hours from Knoxport." Briefly, she informed Tyler about Brian Hawkins and the job offer. "But I don't think I'll take it," she finished as she tossed the papers back onto the counter.

"Why not?" Tyler frowned and crossed his arms. "You'd be really good at it. And you'd get to work with kids again. That's what you've always wanted."

"I know." Melanie ran her hands through her hair. "But I have a good job, a good house, and you have your job. I don't really want to go alone, and I would never ask you to leave your work. Besides, I don't think I really want this job."

Tyler observed Melanie silently, biting his bottom lip thoughtfully. He didn't need anyone to tell him that she wasn't being honest. He was, and always had been, the only person she had never been able to successfully lie to. The truth was, she wanted the job, but was hesitant about taking the next step in her life. She never was good with change. It irritated her, made her uncomfortable, and was something she didn't like dealing with.

"Melanie," he began, rubbing her arms, "this job is perfect for you. You have to take it. So we'll have to move." He held up a hand when Melanie started to protest. "No, hear me out. I can be a social worker anywhere, but this isn't an offer you'll ever get again. So you're going to take it. When it comes down to it, I'm going wherever you go."

Melanie lifted her head until she was staring into Tyler's deep blue eyes. In them, she saw nothing but honesty and affection. She didn't doubt what he said. He had given up his gang to be with her, and although he wouldn't admit it aloud, he was happy to have a life outside the Helping Hands.

His gang had scattered, with Mia heading for New Jersey. Jared stayed in Oregon, continuing to attend college while Sara had left, to where, Tyler didn't know. Keith decided to stay with the children, and he and three other adults cared for them.

Tyler didn't regret breaking up his gang, especially when it meant that he now had the privilege of coming home every day from a job he loved to a woman he loved even more. And to him, even if they weren't officially together, he was confident that one day he would be able to break through Melanie's shell. He had made some progress in the last year, and he knew all her soft spots.

He brushed back her hair with a gentle hand, giving her a small and comforting smile. "I'd never let you walk away from a job opportunity like this, even if it means having to pack up every goddamn knickknack in this place that Fred had managed to stow away over the years."

"You mean that?" Melanie asked softly, feeling reassurance and comfort as he lifted her head by placing a finger beneath her chin and kissing her softly.

"Of course I do."

She couldn't help but smile. "Then I guess I'll give Hawkins a call."

Gregson, Oklahoma

Taryn smiled to herself as she read the daily newspaper, glancing across the table at Caleb after finishing the article on the eighteen year-old who was 'back in society' after spending the better part of his childhood in the hands of 'America's vigilantes.'

"Says that Randy got reunited with his mother," she informed her partner-in-crime. "He enrolled in college, just like he said he was going to."

"That's great," Caleb replied, taking the paper from Taryn and observing the photo that had been included with the article. "I kinda feel bad for him though. I mean, he's had reporters down his back for the past month. He's bound to be sick of it by now. I know I was when that damn Mathews chick was in our faces."

"Yeah, but she proved herself worthy of our time after she helped O'Conner." Taryn pointed out. "She definitely took her job to the next level with us."

"Speaking of jobs," Caleb remembered his conversation with Tyler the previous night on the phone, "O'Conner got a job offer to be a counselor at South Bay. She took it. Already gave Fred her two weeks' notice. They're going to be moving back to California in about three weeks or so."

"South Bay? That's where Jerry always threatened to send her." Taryn was surprised by the news, considering that South Bay had been a reason for Melanie's father to hit her when she was younger. "It would be a great job for O'Conner though. Besides working with the kids, she's a hell of a bitch. She can definitely whip anyone into shape."

"She did it with us." Caleb nodded, his thoughts going back to the years when he had been a Hell Hound. "Many times."

"Johnny, Carrie, I'm glad I found you."

Taryn looked over her shoulder to see Brayden Collins, a member of her gang, entering her and Caleb's small apartment. "What's up, Brayden?"

"I just got this from the scout." Brayden handed Taryn a slip of paper. "Emily Livingston, eight years old. Suffers from starvation and neglect."

"Cute kid," Caleb said as he rose from the table, walking around and peering over Taryn's shoulder. "Where's she live?"

"In The Villages."

"The Villages?" Taryn repeated, her eyes widening at the name. "That's where all those rich bastards from the restaurant live." She spoke of Hannigans, the restaurant she served as waitress and hostess for the past year. "It's like Security City in there."

"I know. It's gonna be tough." Brayden sat down next to the leader of his gang, taking another square of paper from his pocket and tossing it on the table. "Two-story house, brick, three dogs. One pit bull and two Dobermans. Motion sensor lights all around the house, steel gate, patrolling night guard."

"In other words, the best security possible, and most unworkable environment for us." Caleb sighed, glancing at the picture of Emily Livingston again. "It would be a hell of a long night, careful and tedious planning. We'd have about ten minutes, if even, to get in, take the kid, leave the message, and get out, all without setting off any lights or alarms and without being seen by the dogs or the guards. It's impossible. No sane person would even *think* of attempting it."

Brayden nodded in agreement and started to rise from the table, frowning when he saw Taryn's lips curve up into a mischievous grin. She licked her lips excitedly, holding up the notes from her scout and turning her eyes to meet Caleb's. "So we doing it, or what?"

"You bet your ass we are."

CHAPTER 16

San Francisco, California

The lunch bell at Lakeside High School sounded at precisely eleven-fifteen, reverberating off the hallway walls as the students poured from the classrooms. Lockers clanged, voices rose into shouts and laughter, and friends met up at their usual lunch locations. Some stood in the food lines, some had brought their own lunch, and others headed off-campus to the local fast-food joint, or for their houses if close enough.

The media center was always a quiet place during lunch, located on the third floor of the high school. Not many students ever ventured to the considerably large archive of books, except for the one particular student who found her way upstairs every day at lunch for the past few weeks.

Kelly chose to spend her lunch period alone in the silence of the library. It was a safe haven, a place where she was never bothered, never had to talk to anyone, and could for once be by herself and enjoy the privacy.

She sat in the back of the library at a small round table with only two chairs, surrounded by rows and rows of books. She loved to read, to get lost in a story about love and mystery and defeating the odds. At home, she didn't get to read a whole lot, for most of her time was spent defending herself and her sister from her stepfather, and sometimes refereeing between her mother and Jeffrey.

Chewing on an apple slice, Kelly picked up Steinbeck's *Of Mice and Men*, which she had started the previous day. Opening the book to the last page she'd read, Kelly leaned forward on the table and opened the bottle of water in front of her. The story intrigued her, the characters fascinating with their undying devotion to one another despite the obvious differences that at times seemed to wage wars against them and the people around. She had just finished reading a conversation between George and Lennie concerning a puppy when her ears picked up the slight thumping of footsteps. She glanced over her shoulder, rolling her eyes when she saw Robbie Anderson standing behind her, his hands in his pockets.

"Pretty quiet in here," he observed, his voice like a shout among the books and silence.

"Yeah, it is," Kelly answered with a smirk. "Or at least, it was."

Robbie pulled out the other chair and sat down next to her. "*Of Mice and Men*," he read the book title. "So you like to read?"

"How very observant of you."

"One of my better qualities." Robbie shrugged. "I never was much of a reader."

Resigning to the fact that she wasn't going to get to read that day, Kelly marked her spot in the book and placed it down on the table. There was always tomorrow, so long as she watched herself around Jeffery. "Then why are you here?"

"I wanted to talk to you."

"Look," Kelly sat back and crossed her arms, "if this is about the other night at your house, you can—"

"It's about me and Coppertone," Robbie interrupted. He lifted a shoulder when Kelly replied with a questioning look. "You remember a couple weeks ago when we were in the hall and me and Josh started fighting?"

"Yeah. So?"

"Well, I want to know why you got offended by us fighting."

Kelly laughed sarcastically, tucking her hair behind her ears. "What makes you think I was offended?"

Robbie paused long enough to help himself to a piece of apple from in front of Kelly. "Because when I looked at you, you looked like you were disappointed, or scared, or something. Maybe you weren't offended, but you were definitely something else."

"Maybe I just don't like people fighting."

"I thought that's how you got that scar on your temple, from fighting," Robbie challenged, but when Kelly set her jaw and glared back at him, he held up his hands in surrender. "Okay, fine. Bad example. But I still want to know what you were thinking."

With a frown crossing her face, Kelly shook her head and stared down at the book in her hands. She knew what Robbie was doing. She knew what he was leading into, what he was trying to get her to admit. But she also knew that it wouldn't work, not with her, and she didn't understand why he wouldn't just let it go.

"I was thinking about what you told me before, about how it takes a real man to fight," Kelly replied. "I was thinking that you were wrong when you said that. I mean, it's not the fight that makes the man, but the man that makes the fight."

Robbie thought about the comment. He was sure it meant something deep and profound, and was convinced that Kelly was trying to tell him something, but he wasn't that insightful. "So what are you saying? That I have to be big and tough in order to take a blow? That I have to be smart enough to know when I can or can't win a fight? Trust me, I know my limits, and I can definitely dish it out when the time calls for it."

"Robbie." Kelly rubbed her eyes, exasperated. "When are you going to realize that it's not *who* you fight, but *how* you fight that really matters. I know that people fight to prove something to themselves and to other people, but tell me, what could you possibly have to prove?" She was tired of trying to make him see things from her point of view. He obviously was not the type of person who cared enough about others to open his mind to their thoughts.

Robbie was silent for a moment, drumming his fingers on the tabletop. He didn't have a good reply to Kelly's question, and what she had said made him think. What did he want to prove to others? That he was tough? That he could take a hit and get back up? That people had better leave him alone or he would draw blood? It didn't sound so appealing when he broke it all down and started to analyze himself. In fact, it all seemed a bit childish.

Finally, he shrugged and met her eyes with his. "I don't know," he answered honestly, and when she shook her head in disgust, he leaned forward thoughtfully and with a hint of impatience. "Kelly, why don't you like me?"

His question caught her off-guard. Of all the things he could have asked, she hadn't been expecting that one, and all she could do was be completely honest with him. He deserved at least that much.

"I don't really know you," she replied tiredly. "And to be honest, I don't think I want to. I mean, you take pleasure in hurting others, in physically hurting them and making them bleed or bruise. You give them scars outside *and* inside." She peered up at him with lines of worry and sadness creasing her forehead. "How could I possibly like a guy like that?"

"Kelly, I'm not like that," he argued, trying to convince the both of them. "It's not... I'm not..."

With a sigh of discouragement, Kelly shook her head. "It's all a game with you guys, isn't it?" she asked, wringing her hands together. "Fighting, seeing how long you can go before your opponent breaks down, before you win and the other guy loses. It's all a goddamn game."

Hearing the anger in her voice, Robbie frowned. "What? Who are you talking about? I never said it was a game."

"I never said you did. But you know what?" Kelly's voice got stronger. "I won't lose. If this is all some stupid game of strength and stamina, then I will *not* lose."

Robbie leaned back when Kelly slammed her palm down on the table. He saw tears in her eyes and all over again felt confused. He never understood her, and on that level he was disappointed, because he really wanted to. "Um, Kelly, I don't think of it like that. And as far as the game goes, you can only lose if you let yourself lose. So don't let the other guy win." He had a pretty good idea of who her 'opponent' was, but she wouldn't want to go into that subject. "But, in all seriousness, what were you really thinking that day when me and Coppertone fought?"

Her breath came out in a heavy wind of labored air as she rose from the table, grabbing her books along the way. Robbie watched from his seat while Kelly stood in front of him. "I was thinking about how unfair life can be. You know. Some people spend their entire lives trying to get away from a fist, while others just can't wait for an excuse to use theirs."

Kelly turned on her heel and left the media center quickly, and Robbie stared after her, unconsciously clasping his hands together. He glanced down at his right hand, clenching it into a fist, running the fingers of his left hand over his knuckles. Small scars covered them, battle wounds from his years of fighting. Teeth had been broken, lips spilt wide open, eyes bruised, all with his two hands.

With a sigh and shake of his head, Robbie uncurled his fingers and made the fist disappear.

Haston, Oregon

"No. I don't want that one."

"Why not?"

"Because it doesn't have a two-car garage."

Melanie looked up from the newspaper she was holding and gave Tyler an annoyed glare. "Why do we need a two-car garage? One can easily fit in a driveway."

"I don't care about the cars. I want a place to work in," Tyler replied.

"You are such a guy." Melanie went back to the paper. She was getting tired of talking about houses with Tyler. The decision to move had been easy enough, and the choice of buying a house instead of an apartment hadn't been much more difficult. But deciding on which one to buy wasn't at all the leisure time Melanie had been hoping for.

"Well, what about this one? Two bedrooms, two bathrooms, a fireplace, and a manly garage." Tyler grinned and puffed out his chest.

"Big enough for you *and* your ego?" Melanie shot back, frowning thoughtfully. "Is that what we need? Two rooms? What if Taryn or Caleb or someone comes to visit?"

"Then... they'll sleep in the second room," Tyler answered slowly, unsure of what Melanie was getting at as she chewed her bottom lip uncertainly.

"Oh," she said quietly. "Then wouldn't we need three rooms?"

"Why?"

"One for you, one for me, and the other—"

"Why wouldn't we share a room?" Tyler cut in, holding up a hand. "Do we really need to sleep in separate rooms?"

Melanie sighed as a headache began to form. She rubbed her forehead and shrugged. "I don't know," she answered, her voice dull.

Tyler stared at Melanie, waiting for a good reply though he didn't really expect to get one. When he got no such luck, he ran a hand through his hair, preparing his thoughts for the conversation they'd been needing, but avoiding.

"Melanie, where are we?" He raised his eyebrows when she simply glanced up at him. "I mean, are we together, or are we just friends who occasionally sleep together?"

"Tyler, I don't want to talk about this right now." Melanie rose from her chair, and Tyler did as well.

"Well, I do."

"No, I have a headache, and I just want to go to bed." Brushing past Tyler, she left the room.

CHAPTER 17

Melanie's thick, rubber-soled boots clumped noisily on the stairs as she ran down them the next morning, throwing her leather jacket over her shoulders and shoving her arms into the sleeves at the same time. She pulled her hair out from under the collar while jumping down the last three steps, patting the pockets of her baggy jeans.

"Shit. Where are they?" she muttered, rummaging through her jacket. Irritation surged through her. She was tired, pissed, and didn't want to go in to work. She'd had a hard enough time getting to sleep the previous night, thinking about Tyler's question and wondering why she was so worked up over it. And only adding to the frustration, she couldn't find her keys, which she could have sworn she left on the dining room table.

"Tyler, have you seen my keys?" she asked as she entered the kitchen, seeing Tyler standing in front of the refrigerator, staring into it while holding the door wide open. He didn't reply or even move, which, as Melanie had discovered after a year of living under the same roof with a member of the opposite sex, was apparently a typical man thing to do. Or a typical Tyler thing, at least.

"Tyler? Have you seen my keys?" she repeated.

"Well, that depends," Tyler replied without turning, eyeing some leftover Chinese takeout on the shelf and trying to decide if that was what he was really in the mood for. "Are we going to finish the conversation we started last night?"

Melanie crossed her arms. "Tyler, I don't have time for this. Do you have my keys?"

"Do you have an answer to my question?"

"Tyler!" Melanie yelled, aggravated, stomping her foot on the tile. "Have you seen my goddamn keys or not?"

Pulling out a carton of rice and setting it on the counter, Tyler turned and faced Melanie. He held out a hand, allowing a key ring with three keys on it to show. "These them?"

"Yes. What are you doing?" Melanie asked as she reached for them, only to have Tyler pull his arm back and close his fist.

"You want 'em, come and get 'em." He held his arm above Melanie's head.

Melanie glanced up at his closed fist, considering her options. She'd never get them by jumping. He was too tall and too fast. And, she wasn't going to humor him by jumping up and down like an idiot.

But, strong and tall as he was, she did know his weakness.

Tyler was caught by surprise when Melanie reached up and wrapped her arms around his neck, touching her lips firmly to his. She ran her hands through his hair, having to rise to her toes to reach him. Tyler lowered his arms until both were around her waist. With his free hand he held the back of her head, his skin tingling when she ran her fingers down his arms. He didn't think anything of it when she took his hands, didn't find it strange that she was making the first move, didn't realize what was happening until she had already pried the keys from his fingers and pulled away sharply.

"Thank you," Melanie mocked with a playful grin, backing away.

"Ah, you conniving bitch!" Tyler cried, the familiar and acceptable sign of affection getting another mischievous smile from Melanie. He reached out for her, grabbing for her waist, but she twisted and ran for the front door with a laugh. Chasing after her, he caught up in the living room.

"No, Tyler, let go! I have to get to work!" Melanie protested as he came up from behind, wrapping his arms around her stomach. "I'm going to be late!"

"I'm sure Fred will understand." Tyler held onto her wrists.

"Damn it, you're such an asshole!" Melanie laughed out as she fought to get away, her hand still clutching the keys as she spun around, trying to untangle herself from Tyler's grasp.

Tyler tightened his grip on her wrist, pressing her against him with the other hand. "You know, we have to find a more appropriate way to show our affection for each other."

"Screw affection. You're a buffed-up bastard."

"And you're a teasing vixen with a cold heart." Tyler tackled Melanie as she kicked at him, throwing her down onto the couch and landing on top of her. "But you're still mine, so I forgive you."

Melanie struggled beneath him and found it was useless. Instead, she let her head fall back against the cushions and relented, an uncustomary act for her. "If I didn't know any better, I'd say you planned that."

"Maybe I did." Tyler shrugged with fake innocence. "What are you gonna do about it?"

"Go along with whatever you have planned. It's not like I have much of a choice."

"Why not?"

Melanie struggled again, but Tyler simply raised his eyebrows, humored by her attempts. "Because even if I wanted to, I wouldn't be able to get up."

Tyler smiled, surprised to see humor in her expression. Kissing her lightly and pulling his head back, he worded his thoughts carefully. "So what do you say? Can we share a room?"

Her breath became heavier as her eyes closed for a moment. She had known that the question would arise again sometime soon, but she didn't want it to be now, not when her thoughts were jumbled and nothing made sense anymore.

"Tyler, I honestly don't know if I'm ready for that. After all that's happened..."

"I know you're scared. I am too," Tyler admitted.

"I'm not scared," Melanie protested.

"I know you've had a lot of bad shit in your life. With Jerry, and Foster, and Wess, but Mel, this is right. I know it is."

Melanie didn't know what would happen by opening up to him, *really* opening herself up, but she did know one thing. "I know it is too," she confessed, more to herself than to Tyler. She *was* scared, scared of the consequences if she let someone, particularly a man, into her life to where he would always be there.

But, she thought silently, *Tyler already* was *there*. He knew all her secrets, all her thoughts.

"You know, that week at the beach house, that was the best time of my life," Tyler told her. "And it really got me thinking."

"About what?"

"About the fact that I want you sleeping in my room every night, in my bed, not having to say good-night to you before watching you walk into another room and shut the door."

Dropping the keys onto the floor, Melanie stared up at her best friend. "Tyler, what exactly are you saying?"

"I'm saying that I've wanted you ever since I can remember, but I've never been able to tell you. And when you and Wess were together, I swear if I didn't have to save face in front of my gang, I think it would have been the end of me. I still think that, when I think of losing you again."

"Tyler, I'm not going anywhere. Why are you so worried?" Melanie frowned. "I've never heard you talk like this before."

Tyler kissed Melanie again and pushed back her hair, then took her hand as he slipped his free arm beneath her back, between her and the couch. "I love you, Melanie. I always have, and I always will. Even if you're a crackhead, or all pissy knocked up with the second of our three kids."

"Oh, so it's three?" Melanie gave a small laugh. "Why not four?"

"As many as you want," Tyler replied with a grin, linking his fingers with hers. "As long as one of them looks like me and has my amazing good looks and charm."

"Well, of course." Melanie rolled her eyes. "And—"

She stopped, her breath catching in her throat when she felt the cool sensation of metal gently slide down her left ring finger. She stared at Tyler, into his blue eyes, seeing love and affection, along with a glimmer of hope challenged by one of confidence.

"Marry me, Melanie," he said in a voice that was nearly a whisper. He took in a deep breath when she pulled her hand from his.

Melanie ran her eyes over the sapphire that Tyler had placed on her finger. The white gold band gleamed up at her, and the small gem that was embedded into it shimmered beneath the ceiling lights. It wasn't a big show, and a big show was exactly what she wouldn't want. She hated big rings, always had, and never wore gold. The fact that Tyler knew that made the insides of her stomach clutch together.

Marriage. Family. A future without solitude. A life with some semblance of normalcy after so many years of chaos. Such things she had never thought possible for herself.

A smile forming on her lips, Melanie lifted her eyes to meet Tyler's. "You must be the only guy in the world who would know that I like sapphires, not diamonds."

Nerves, anticipation, and excitement were creeping around his gut all at the same time. "Is that a yes?"

"Yes." Melanie pulled Tyler's head down to meet hers, her hand on his heart as he smiled against her lips.

CHAPTER 18

Sacramento, California

Isaac Davidson pulled up against the curb and put the car into park, glancing around to see nothing but the clouded night sky shadowing them in darkness, the perfect weather conditions. Next to him, Mathew Harper pulled out a small drawing.

"Okay, this is the house. We've been over this a million times. Jimmy, you're going to turn off the alarm and me and Leighann will get Holly. Carry, you'll take care of the locks and get back to the car. Everybody clear?"

They were fighting nerves when they got out of the car. It was only their second kidnapping, and this one was more dangerous. The house was guarded with both an alarm and a family dog, and it was bigger than Ryan's home. But more than that, their gang was new. They had a long way to go before they could consider themselves experienced Helping Hands.

It hadn't been a hard decision to put together a Helping Hands gang. Ever since he was taken from the Treehouse, Matt had been filled with a longing to be a part of the project, a part that could be labeled as 'member' rather than the media's favorite term of 'captive.' He wanted to save lives, sacrifice everything for one life.

He was more than willing to put his own life on the line for the children, as Melanie and her gang had once done for him.

When it came to finding gang members, he never doubted who they would be. The Treehouse kids had that special bond and knew the most about being a part of the project. Matt had chosen Isaac Davidson because, while he was the most aggressive and volatile child of the Treehouse, he knew how to defend himself and better, he was strong and tough. He was the perfect enforcer of the group, much like Caleb had been for the original gang.

Jimmy Fencles had been another easy choice since he and Matt were best friends on the Island, and Jimmy had the heart they needed, much like Wess. The sickness his parents were responsible for made him want to help other kids even more, and tolerate abuse all the less.

Matt asked Carry Valentine to join simply because he knew she would do a good job. He didn't know her as well as he did the others since she was one of the last kids taken before Melanie O'Conner was arrested, but it was obvious that she was smart, had all the sharp wisdom and soft compassion they needed and more to be a success. She reminded him of Taryn.

Although Leighann Cross wasn't a child of the Treehouse, Matt had gone to her because he knew that she followed the Helping Hands. She knew everything about the project, how it worked, what was done before a child was taken. Plus, they were sort of, unofficially, dating.

Besides the fact that every member of the gang had been subject to child abuse at one point in their lives, there was another feature that bonded them together, a symbol of what they stood for. Whereas the Hell Hounds tattooed their hands with the bold, black, symbolic HH, the members of Matt's gang was united by their facial scars. Matt received his from a ring on his father's hand, Carry's from hitting a table after being thrown into it, but Isaac's scar was the worst of them all. It started at his temple, trailing down to the corner of his mouth, an ugly, dark red line of flesh that made him seem even more menacing and prone to violence.

Holly Jessup, the child they were taking that night, was an eight year-old girl with a brute for a father and a pushover as a mother. Her entire life had been filled with fists, and as a result, she was deaf. Her parents told the doctors that she had fallen off a horse, but Matt and his gang knew better.

Matt spent a month investigating the Jessups and was convinced that he knew everything there was to know about the family. He knew the house, the adults' and child's routines; he knew their entire background. Now all that was left was getting Holly out and somewhere where she would be safe.

Creeping up to the back of the house, the four Helping Hands kept low to the ground, their feet moving silently upon the midnight-dewed grass. Holly's bedroom window was right above them when they leaned back against the wall of the residence, waiting for Jimmy to disarm the security system.

Jimmy peered through the darkness at the power box that was next to the side door. He pried open the cover with a screwdriver, then took in the wires and switches. He had spent many hours studying the system, and he was sure, ninety percent sure anyway, that he could shut it off. This was his first time disarming a system outside of practice at The Lake.

Reaching for the first wire, he squinted through the night air to determine the color. "Blue," he muttered as quietly as he could, "leads to the... no, shit that's the green." He took a pair of wire cutters from his pocket and snapped the green wire in two, hands shaking all the while, and stepped back to wait to see if the alarm went off. When he heard nothing, he took a red wire in his hands and gently, carefully, cut off the outer coating until he could peel it back. The copper-colored wire inside told him he had made the right decision.

"Bingo," he whispered, then cut the blue wire and flicked a switch next to it. Closing the box quietly, he went back to his gang and nodded.

Carry rose to her feet and went to work on the window. She slipped the screwdriver into the crack between the windowsill and screen, hoping that Jimmy was as good as he thought he was. Pulling off the screen, Carry slipped a thin wire through the small crack between the two halves of the window and grasped the lock with the looped end of the wire after her third try. The lock turned and Carry smiled down at Matt, satisfied with herself.

"Your turn."

Matt and Leighann rose to their feet, sliding open the window and stepping inside. A jingle sounded when Leighann came in after Matt, but she didn't worry. Pulling out a treat, she tossed it to the small terrier lying next to Holly's bed and headed for the child.

Leighann shook Holly gently, waiting for her to open her eyes. When she did, Matt snapped on a dim flashlight so she could see their faces. Holly's eyes went wide as she tried to shrink back against her mattress, and Leighann quickly began to sign to her.

"We're here to help you." She spoke the words quietly as well as signed them so Matt would know what she was saying. "We're good people."

Holly stared at Leighann's hands, then looked up at her with both fear and hope. She knew what the stranger was saying, and she was surprised that the person knew how to sign her words. Her own parents couldn't even talk to her, so Holly had given up hope that she would ever be able to talk to anyone ever again, unless she was at her school. And it didn't matter that the girl was a stranger because as far as Holly was concerned, people who knew sign language were people who could help her, whether it be sharpening a pencil or being allowed to eat a big lunch since dinner wasn't something she ate very often.

"I don't like my dad," Holly signed back with a frown, tears forming in her eyes as Matt knelt down beside her. "He hurts me."

"Do you want to come with us?" Matt asked, gesturing to him and Leighann. "We'll take care of you and be your friends, and you'll never be hurt." He took the smile Holly gave him to be a yes.

Five minutes later, after putting a leash on the terrier and hoisting both it and the child out the window, the newest branch of Helping Hands fled the scene, leaving nothing but their single, trademark message behind.

It was nearly three in the morning when Isaac parked the car behind an old cabin lodge and got out. His friends and fellow gang members followed, taking Holly and the dog, Sunny, along with them. Carry held a large bag packed with as many of Holly's things that they could grab. Jimmy took charge of the dog, feeding the terrier treats to keep the barking to a minimum.

The only sounds coming from the lake were those emitted by the frogs and crickets calling up to the clouds for rain. Trees and shrubbery surrounded the area, blocking The Lake from probing eyes for miles. Because The Lake and most of the land around it was owned by an extremely wealthy man by the name of Patrick Gandy, it was fenced off and closed to anyone other than those involved with the Helping Hand project.

"And who do have we here?" Patrick asked from the front porch of the cabin as Matt and his gang approached, gesturing to the sleeping child in Matt's arms.

"This is Holly."

"The deaf child?"

"Yeah." Matt entered the cabin, Patrick holding the door open for him while he stepped through. "Did you get her room ready?"

"Sure did." Patrick, whose wife minored in interior design and loved children, nodded as the rest of the gang members went to the living room to start a fire and destroy the evidence. "She's the first little girl of The Lake. Gets the whole room to herself."

Matt went to the room and gently laid Holly down on the bottom of one of the four bunk beds. He didn't know how many kids his gang would help, but was sure that the two-story cabin would be fine for the time being, as they currently had only one child of each gender. He smiled as Holly rolled over in her sleep, tightly clutching the blanket he draped over her.

"We explained who we were and everything in the car, so when she wakes up, she shouldn't be too afraid." It had been hard signing to Holly everything that he wanted to say, but somehow he'd managed, and had all the books he bought on sign language to thank for it. "So where's Ryan?"

"He's in his room playing some video game. He knew you guys were coming tonight, and he was so excited he couldn't sleep, so I told him he could stay up and wait for you. Looked a little bored today, so at least he'll have a friend now." Patrick trailed behind Matt as he headed for Ryan's room. "I guess it's harder for the first kid, waiting for more to come."

"Yeah," Matt replied, thinking back to when it had just been him on the island. It got old real quick having only the adults to talk to, and even though they were eager to play with him it wasn't the same as being with kids his own age. Adults just didn't understand the same things kids did. "We'll have to teach him how to sign," Matt added, pushing the bedroom door open and walking inside.

"Matt!" Ryan jumped to his feet, abandoning the game as he ran over. "I just make it to the next level on my game and I get to battle the evil emperor! Did you bring another kid?"

Matt smiled at his excitement. "Yes, but she's different from you." He squatted down in front of the child. "She's deaf, which means that she can't hear. I'm going to teach you sign language. Do you know what that is?" Ryan nodded solemnly. "When you learn it, you'll be able to talk to her. Her name's Holly. And we brought her dog, Sunny."

"A puppy?" Ryan's grin returned as he jumped up and down. "Can I see?"

"Tell you what," Matt picked Ryan up with ease and plopped him down onto his bed. "You lay right here and I'll bring in Sunny, as long as you go to sleep afterwards."

"I will. I'll go to sleep. I promise." As if to assure Matt that he really would go to bed, Ryan crawled beneath the covers and closed his eyes, peeking out through one carefully.

"Okay. I'll be right back." Matt and Patrick went to find the dog, which was in the kitchen, lying peacefully on its side. He rose eagerly when Matt entered, thumping its tail against the floor. Matt shook his head disdainfully. He had never been a big fan of dogs, but the kids loved them.

And that, he thought while watching Ryan hug the terrier, *is all that matters.*

CHAPTER 19

Tulsa, Oklahoma

The night was dark and still, the sky clouded and starless. Few cars covered the streets at the late hour, and the heavy brush of trees and shrubs shadowed the two quick-moving figures as they made their way around the tree trunks and potholes.

The Villages, a wealthy neighborhood where popular, prosperous doctors, lawyers, professors, and stockbrokers dwelled, was calm and quiet. Cameras were stationed around the fence that surrounded the complex, as were motion sensor lights that shone bright as day. A few security officers patrolled the streets every hour, and the guard at the front gate stopped all from entering the vicinity.

Stopped all, that is, except the Helping Hands.

Caleb hoisted himself up onto a tree branch, leaning down and helping Taryn up next to him. Together, they jumped from the tree onto the other side of the six-foot wall that surrounded The Villages, making sure to avoid the cameras. They were clothed in black, their hair tucked securely beneath black ski hats. Taryn didn't bother to stop to gaze in wonder at the size of the homes. She'd seen mansions before, and they never managed to impress her.

The two Helping Hands were silent as they crept through the edge of the woods, keeping their eyes peeled for guards and local residents. It took them nearly ten minutes to reach their destination, and when they finally did, they were disappointed to see that their view was blocked by a thick wooden fence.

They didn't speak as they looked about themselves, and Caleb turned when Taryn grabbed his arm, pointing to a tree a few feet away. Nodding, Caleb went over to it, finding a way up. He placed his foot on a small bump in the trunk, grabbing hold of a limb above his head. Leaves rustled slightly as the two gang members positioned themselves on a thick, solid limb that branched out over the fence. They didn't drop down into the backyard, but instead observed the mansion closely from the confines of the tree. The lights were dim and the curtains ajar, allowing Taryn to see directly into the living room.

"Check out the motion sensor lights," Caleb whispered, handing a pair of binoculars to Taryn. She peered through them, seeing a set of lights at every corner of the house. "What do you think? Fifteen foot range?"

"No," Taryn whispered back. "More like twenty, if not more. Can you see what brand they are?"

Caleb took the binoculars back, shaking his head. "I can't tell. But if we can remember what they look like we can get another set for ourselves."

Taryn nodded, her eyes straining as she stared into the living room. She saw the edge of a couch and a solid oak table, and in the far corner, a man as he entered the room. He walked over to the window, grabbing hold of the curtains and pulling them across the glass. At the sight of his face, Taryn's lips parted in both surprise and dread, and her heart, she swore, skipped a beat.

"Oh my God," she whispered, and Caleb looked over at her. "Why didn't I see the connection? Do you know who that is?"

Caleb looked back at the window, seeing the closed curtains. "No. Who?"

"George Livingston," Taryn replied. "That's the goddamn mayor of Tulsa! We're about to take the kid of the most important man in the entire damn city!"

"Which means he's gonna do whatever it takes to get his kid back," Caleb thought aloud, holding the binoculars up when the light to the living room snapped off. "Check that. One-thirty-five, he goes to bed. We'll have to come back a few more times to confirm that."

Taryn sighed and shook her head, the costs of failing running through her head. "This is gonna be so hard."

"Well, I'm up for it." Caleb shrugged confidently. "We can do it."

San Francisco, California

The basketball rebounded off the wall as Robbie threw it hard, catching it as it flew back at him. He bounced it between his legs a few times, spinning around and thumping it against the wall again. He tossed the ball up, caught it, then grabbed his bag from the locker room floor and headed out into the halls. He nodded to a few remaining people that were still at the school, not bothering to stop and talk. He wanted to get home and eat a quick dinner before heading back to the gym for his game that night.

"Anderson!" Jason Coppertone's deep voice cut through Robbie's ears as he came up from behind, his eyes narrow and his right hand curled in a fist.

Robbie spun around, face-to-face with Jason. He tucked the basketball under his arm, biting back a few choice words. "What?"

"You and me, right now. No teachers, no bullshit," Jason challenged, holding out his arms. "I heard you told that Mitchell bitch you could take me. Well, here's your chance."

Robbie glared up at him, his eyes narrow as his fist clenched. He felt his blood burning, and his fist longed to wipe the smug expression off of his opponent's face.

Suddenly, Kelly appeared in his mind, the day when he had talked to her in the library. He remembered staring down at his fist as her words rang through his mind, when she made him think twice about ever hitting someone again.

It's not the fight that makes the man, but the man that makes the fight.

It's not who you fight, it's how you fight that really matters.

He had never backed away from a fight, never walked away from a challenge. His pride, his ego, never let him do such a thing. Suspensions, bloody knuckles, stitches, he lived for them. He basked in the fear of his peers, paraded down the halls where paths were cleared for him.

What could you possibly have to prove?

Robbie held up his hand, which was no longer balled into a fist. "You know what, Coppertone? This is bullshit. I'm not gonna fight you."

"What? You all of a sudden too chickenshit to fight?" Jason challenged as Robbie turned his back on him.

"I'm not fighting you, Coppertone," Robbie said over his shoulder. "See you at the game." Pushing open the door, he left Jason behind.

As Jason punched the wall in anger and stalked off and Robbie disappeared behind the large double doors, Kelly Mitchell stepped out from around the corner, her arms crossed, a smile forming on her lips.

CHAPTER 20

"Anderson! Watch number three! *Watch* him, damn it!" Coach Wright yelled out, flinging up his arms in frustration as the opposing team shot for the hoop. "Get the rebound! Yes!" he shouted when Robbie leapt up and grabbed the ball from the air, landing and passing it to Mike Chany, who ran down the court and scored. The crowd roared in response, flags, signs, and posters waving from the stands.

Robbie slapped Mike's back as he passed him at center court. "Nice shot, man," he complimented.

"Nice pass," Mike returned, grinning up at the crowd as they cheered for him. Some people held up signs sporting the number of their favorite players, others wielded small banners and flags flying the blue-and-gold Lakeside colors. The girlfriends had the numbers of their boyfriends painted on their cheeks, and the friends of the players shouted through funnels while shaking empty water jugs filled with coins. Everyone who was considered to be anyone was at the game, cheering for the team, packing the bleachers, deafening themselves with the noise that thundered through the gym of wall-to-wall bodies.

This game, to top it all off, had one more person sitting in the stands.

Kelly made her way through the crowd, standing in one of the few empty spots left as she peered down at the court. She gave a small smile and slight wave to Robbie, who gestured back with a nod, his expression either somber or determined, she couldn't tell. Sitting, she pulled the cuffs of her jacket down over her hands, although it was extremely warm in the gym, resting her chin on her hands as she watched the game, not really interested.

Robbie took a quick swig of water, keeping his eyes on Kelly.

"Yo Anderson! You got a girl up there or something?" Wright asked after Robbie looked up at the stands for the third time, his attention obviously not on the game.

Robbie shrugged, not able to wipe the small grin off his face. "Dunno," he replied honestly. "Maybe."

"Well, maybe ain't a sure thing," Wright retorted, but had to laugh at the fact that there actually was something in the world that could faze Robbie Anderson. "So get your butt out there and try to impress her."

"Will do, Coach." Tossing the water bottle onto the bench, Robbie ran back onto the court.

The game ended with the Lakeside Jaguars defeating the Carson High Hawks sixty-three to forty-seven. Coach Wright congratulated them on an outstanding win in the locker room, and after, Robbie slung his bag over his shoulder, ran a hand through his wet hair, and wondered if Kelly had already left. His question was answered when he left the locker room, hoping to see her standing there along with the girlfriends of his teammates only to find empty air waiting for him. Heaving a sigh, he walked down the sidewalk to where he was parked.

"Nice game," a voice said from behind.

With a smile, he turned slowly, hoping he didn't seem too excited or eager. "We had some really good luck."

"You played good. Lots of baskets."

"I had some pretty nice motivation." Robbie stepped closer to Kelly, who was leaning against the wall, her hands grasping her arms as if chilled. "I didn't know you like basketball."

"I don't." Kelly shook her head, unconsciously starting to wring her hands together. She glanced down at the ground, clearing her throat. "Actually, I wanted to tell you something."

Robbie glanced down at her hands, and she caught the movement and shoved them in her jacket pockets. "Something good or bad?"

Kelly breathed deeply, her eyes searching the ground. "I wanted to tell you that I think what you did today was really cool."

"What, the game?" Robbie gestured back towards the gym. "That was nothing. A few lay-ups and three-pointers. I could show you if—"

"No, no," Kelly interrupted, a bit irritated. "I mean when you turned down the fight with Jason Coppertone."

"You saw that?"

"The entire thing." Kelly nodded, pushing herself up from the wall. "It took a lot of guts to do that. And I want you to know that I really respect you a lot for doing it."

Robbie closed the gap between them, moving his head closer to her, but she pulled back, closing her eyes and swallowing heavily. "Kelly, I'm not going to hurt you," he said quietly, almost whispering. "You can trust me."

Taking a second attempt, he moved closer again, and she didn't pull away, nor did she respond. Robbie took it as a good sign, considering that she didn't hit him or bristle at his touch.

"You know, you're stronger that you think you are," he told her, and she swallowed heavily while tears formed at the corners of her eyes. "Come on, I'll give you a ride home."

Haston, Oregon

Jared Haus laughed as he bumped into a table covered with plastic cups, sloshing beer over the carpet as he fought to keep his balance. The room around him blurred and spun, colors and objects swirling together. He steadied himself, blinking a few times, then made his way through the house until he found Tyler.

"Yo Scotford, awesome party!" he yelled over the music, taking a swig of beer and nearly knocking himself off his feet. "Can't believe you're actually leaving this place! It's a damn mansion!"

Tyler shrugged, thinking that some people never really grow up, and excused himself from the couple he was talking to so he could find his former gang member a place to sit down. "I think you've had enough to drink," he told his friend, taking the bottle from Jared and making sure he would remain seated before weaving through the crowd in search of Melanie.

One hell of a good-bye party, he thought while tossing the beer bottle into the trash. Fred had taken it upon himself to host the farewell party, eager to show the two how much they were loved, and had harassed Tyler into giving him the names and numbers of all the people who would be interested in attending. Tyler saw some of his co-workers, mechanics from Fred's shop, friends from his college, various people they had met around town, and members of his old gang, with the exception of Sara Wiles. Most of the people were Tyler's friends and met Melanie through him, though the ones from the garage, who'd known Tyler longer, were closer to Melanie.

Entering the kitchen, empty except for two, Tyler found Melanie standing next to the counter talking to Taryn, apparently deep in conversation. Taryn was nodding, her eyes trained on the floor as she concentrated on Melanie's words. He figured by the serious expression on Melanie's face that they were talking about the Helping Hands, and he watched as she gestured vividly with her hands, the light reflecting off the ring on her finger. Fighting the urge to take Melanie in his arms and drag her away from the party, he started for her, knowing that if he were to do what his mind was telling him to do, he would most likely end up with either a black eye or an earful of curses.

Both possibilities thrilled him.

"Having a good time?" he asked, coming up behind Melanie and taking her left hand in his as if to admire the ring.

"Well, well, Mason." Taryn nodded at Tyler. "Finally got up enough balls to pop the question?" She gestured with her head to Melanie's hand. "Took you long enough."

"Better late than never," Tyler replied with a shrug. "Besides, I don't see anyone lining up to get you in the sack full time, now do I?" He raised his eyebrows mockingly as Melanie punched his shoulder.

"Nice to know I'm wearing this ring as a sign that now you get to screw me whenever you want," she told him, crossing her arms. "You think marriage gives you some kind of sex benefit?"

"Well, it's got to count for something."

"And you think that something is a sex guarantee?"

"Of course he does, babe. Now he won't have to go scrounging around town to get any," Caleb put in, half-drunk as he came up from behind and swung an arm around Melanie's shoulders.

Tyler huffed and shook his head defiantly. "I *never* had to scrounge around town."

"No? What about that chick from the convenience store? Jenny? No, Jackie. No—"

"Jodi," Taryn offered with a grin. "And I seem to remember a Colleen from the strip club."

"And Bridget from that same club," Caleb reminded them all, and despite herself Melanie had to say her part.

"Don't forget Sara." She was smiling, mainly due to the look of shock that passed Tyler's face.

"Melanie—"

"Don't worry, Tyler, I'm only kidding."

"Now, you see, that's what it's all about," Caleb said with a nod, and by the slur in his voice the three knew he was well on his way to being completely trashed. "Good old O'Conner here can deal with the fact that Mason's slept around town and can still joke around about the one who never got her way." Taryn's smile slowly dropped and Tyler was starting to wonder what his friend was getting at while at the same time getting a bit angry with Caleb's exaggeration of his sex life, which wasn't nearly so noteworthy.

With a slight sway, Caleb pointed at Tyler, having to lean slightly on Melanie, who planted her feet firmly against his weight, to keep his balance. "But the real question is, can Mason deal with the mere three men in O'Conner's life?"

His words sliced through Melanie and made her blood run cold as her mouth parted slightly with unease. Confused, Tyler stared at her, ignoring the drunken chuckle that came from Caleb. "Three?" he asked, knowing only of two, himself and Wess. "Who's the third?"

Taryn, sensing the obvious need for a private moment, took hold of Caleb's arm. "Okay, Brinson, I think your work here is done. No, shut up," she said harshly when he tried to convince her to let go.

Alone in the kitchen, Tyler watched Melanie lower her head, and by the action, he saw the nerves. "Mel, it's okay. I don't really care. I was just surprised when he said…" A thought occurred to him suddenly that made him change his tone. "Wait a second. Why does Caleb know about the third guy and not me? It's not Brinson, is it?"

"Hell, no. Give me more credit than that."

"Well then who is it?"

"Why is it such a big deal?"

Tyler met her challenging glare with one of his own. "Because there must be a reason why you never told me. You knew about my other… times. I thought we told each other everything."

"Then why don't you tell me about Sara."

"God, Melanie, it always comes back to this." Frustrated and hating Caleb for ruining what had been a pleasant moment, he punched a fist on the counter. "Mel, we were just friends! Damn it, how many times are we going to go over this?"

"Okay, okay. No more cheap shots with the Sara thing." Melanie held up her hands. The only reason she'd brought it up was because she was stalling, but there was really no point in doing so. Tyler would badger her until she caved. "You're right. Normally I would have told you. I just… you won't like it."

Seeing that she was weakening, he took advantage of the moment. "Who was it? Someone from high school?"

"Not quite."

"It wasn't… Evan, was it?" Thinking about the man who had been murdered because of the Helping Hands gave him chills, as it did with Melanie at times. He was glad when she shook her head. "Someone from Taps or Fred's garage?"

"Gross, Mason."

He hid a smile at her tone of disgust. "Then who?"

Giving a small laugh in disbelief of the truth herself, and knowing she would be kicking herself later for revealing the name, Melanie ran a hand through her hair. "Um… well… Casper."

"*Casper*?" Tyler spat out the name incredulously, lines of shock forming along his forehead as his eyes widened. "When? Why? And more importantly, how totally *stoned* were you that you would sleep with that crackhead? He's so… Casper." There was no other accurate way to describe him and do the man justice. "God, Melanie, that is *so* wrong." Because it was something he never would have guessed and was, in addition, completely bizarre in his mind, he found himself laughing at the news while shuddering at the same time.

Melanie was relieved when Tyler started to laugh, and she knew that he wasn't mad. There was some amount of comfort in knowing that they could talk about such things without letting them get too personal. "Tyler, I was like sixteen and yes, I was totally *stoned*," she mocked. "Casper, for once, wasn't all junked up, and as we both know, Casper sober is like a normal person stoned. It just happened. And it was only once. Brinson only knows because he overheard us joking about it like almost a year after it happened and I warned him that if he ever told anyone, especially you, I would cut off his balls and feed them to a mangy dog for breakfast."

And Tyler knew she would do it without so much as a second thought. "Ah, babe, this is too much." Moving closer and taking her in his arms, he peered down at her. "At least tell me that I'm better than he was."

Laughing and tipping back her head so she could look up at him, Melanie kissed Tyler firmly. "Trust me, you are *much* better. A little overconfident in certain aspects pertaining to the lower region of the body, considering—"

"Yeah, yeah, yeah." He silenced her with another kiss. "You just remember who's the stronger of this pair."

"Oh, go bench press your ego." She pushed him towards the door. "And send Taryn back in here while you're at it." When he had disappeared she let out the breath of nerves and trepidation she had been holding back. So he wasn't angry or annoyed or disgusted with her. He could accept her, as she could with him, just as she was with all her flaws, and it warmed her to know that she had found someone with whom she could be so close with, close on so many levels.

Taryn smiled when she entered and saw the contented expression on her friend's face. "So Caleb didn't screw things up too badly, I suppose?"

"Not this time." Melanie shook her head, glancing over her shoulder as if Tyler were standing right behind her. "What?" she asked when she saw Taryn grinning at her.

"You got it bad," Taryn teased. "But it's all right. I always knew it would end up like this. He's a great guy."

"Yeah, he is." Melanie smiled. "But anyway, back to the job we were talking about before Brinson opened his big mouth." She began to discuss the security issues that Taryn would run into during the kidnapping, and they forgot about Tyler and the party as they discussed the dangers of the job.

Tyler sang along with the song that was playing, making his way into the living room and all but forgetting about the kitchen scene. The truth was, he didn't care who Melanie had slept with in the past. It didn't matter who she had spent the night with or who she had confided in during her teenage years, because now, she was all his.

In the end, she chose him.

His eyes widened slightly when he saw the mess the people made, but he didn't worry a whole lot about it. They had a maid, and he was sure Melanie would make him help clean it up with the both of them the next morning anyway. He nodded to Keith Bradley, another of his former gang members, and was about to turn away when Keith gestured him over.

"Hey Keith, what's up? How are the kids doing?"

"Great. We had a couple fights break out last week. You know Scotti?" When Tyler nodded, Keith pictured the boy and continued. "Well some of the kids started calling him 'Snotty Scotti' because he's always being a pain-in-the-ass and when they called him that he started pushing and shoving. Went through about three days of that."

Tyler frowned, remembering his days with the children. "So how is Scotti doing now?"

"He's fine." Keith waved a dismissive hand. "I talked to him and said he couldn't be so bossy all the time and we came to an understanding. So, I've been meaning to ask you all night, have you seen her yet?" he asked, shouting over the music.

"Seen who?"

"You know, *her*. Is O'Conner cool with her being here?"

"Keith, I have no idea who you're talking about," Tyler answered, then paused when a pair of hands covered his eyes from behind. He frowned, knowing that it wasn't Melanie when he felt the person's lips brush up against his ear.

"My father still doesn't know," a raspy, familiar voice whispered seductively into his ear, and Tyler knew at once who it was when he felt a pair of soft lips and teeth gently bite at his ear. Grabbing her hands, he spun around and saw Sara Wiles smiling up at him, her eyes shining.

"Sara. How's it going?" he asked, giving her a small and strained hug.

"How's it going? I don't see you for over a year and all I get's a lousy how's it going?" Sara pretended to pout. "What about a kiss?" She nodded in understanding when Tyler looked over his shoulder, his deep blue eyes scanning the crowd. "Oh I get it, *she* might be watching. Silly me."

"What are you doing here?" Tyler asked. "Why didn't you call?"

"Can I talk to you?" Sara deliberately changed the subject. Tyler stared at her for a moment, watching as she dragged her fingers through her dirty-blonde hair in a manner he recognized as being both inviting and teasing, then nodded, leading her out onto the back porch. It was empty, which both surprised and disappointed him as he sat down on one of the three lawn chairs. Sara sat in front of him, a serious expression on her pretty face and desire set in her dark brown eyes. "So I hear you're moving."

"Yeah. Three days," Tyler affirmed. "But something tells me you're here to try and change that."

"Come home with me," Sara said abruptly. "You don't want to be with her. We had a great time when we were together."

"Sara, we were never together." Tyler ran a nervous hand through his hair. "We've always been just friends."

"But we can be more than that," Sara pushed. "She's not right for you. Trust me. Mel, I want to be with you. Don't you remember what it was like when we were a gang?"

He did remember. He remembered going out to clubs with her, dancing with her, having a great time while Melanie was trapped behind the steel bars of prison. He also recalled feeling guilty every time he kissed Sara, and he knew that that feeling would never change, whether Melanie left him or vice versa. He and Sara had shared some good times, some bad. They had had their fair share of both laughs and fights, and Tyler always felt comfortable around her. But comfort was as far as it went, and no matter how hard he tried, even when she left for Wess, he had always wished for Melanie.

And it was time Sara accepted that.

"Sara," he began seriously, "we were a great gang, and we had some good times together, but I lost Melanie once, and I'm not going to lose her again."

Sighing inwardly, Sara pushed back her hair. "Not even to me?" Her voice was nearly a whisper.

"Especially not to you." Tyler nodded, feeling bad about the harsh comment, but Sara didn't seem to hear it.

"Mel, we were meant to be together," she tried to convince him, pulling back when Tyler laughed in disbelief, a heated and determined expression overcoming her face.

"Sara, get the picture. I—"

Tyler was cut off when Sara leaned forward suddenly and placed her mouth on his, grabbing the back of his neck and holding his head to hers in an attempt to overpower his love for Melanie with a promise of passion and pleasure. After the initial shock wore off, Tyler pulled away. He was about to yell at her when he caught a movement out of the corner of his eye, and turned to see Melanie standing on the edge of the porch, just outside the house with her arms crossed.

"And it always comes back to this," she said, her voice steady but with a hint of an edge. It was a tone Tyler recognized as being calm and cool, yet with an underlying angry and dangerous rage. "Keith said I'd find you out here. He didn't happen to mention who you were with."

"Melanie, it's not what you think." Tyler rose and tried to explain, but Melanie simply shook her head.

"No Tyler, don't. Just don't." She started to turn away, but Sara rose and walked over to her.

Sara gave a small, deceiving grin as she stared at Melanie, at her competition. She didn't know what Tyler saw in the woman. Melanie's face was covered in scars, some more noticeable than others. There was one long, jagged mark across the top of her forehead, and another along her jawline. A thin line went from her right eyebrow to the top of her cheekbone, causing her eye to slope down slightly, and at her eyebrow there was a dark line from where the piercing she had as a teenager had been torn from her skin. A light red scar trailed across her neck, and her arms and shoulders were sprinkled with marks. Even her hands had red and white lines running across them, as well as calluses, looking as though Melanie was some sort of farmer who was prone to injury from the tools of the field.

She looks... deformed, Sara thought to herself, sneering at the notion as she let out a disgusted sigh.

"Must be nice," she told Melanie. "Getting to sleep in the same bed as Mel. It's great, isn't it?" She flicked her eyebrows, and Melanie frowned while Tyler's eyes widened.

"What exactly do you mean by that?" Melanie asked firmly, her jaw set. She glared over at Tyler when he took in a deep breath.

"I mean, I guess it doesn't take long for Mel to move on from an attractive and talented woman to some burned-out prison junkie," Sara scoffed, her eyes narrow as Melanie realized what she was saying.

Melanie turned to Tyler, who was looking at her nervously. "So you did sleep with her," she accused, her voice surprisingly calm. "You told me nothing happened. You *just* told me you were only friends."

"It wasn't what you think," Tyler defended himself. "It only happened like maybe five or six times, maybe less."

"Five or six times?" Melanie was taken aback, not catching the smile on Sara's face, when the realization of the dishonesty hit her. "No, don't touch me!" she yelled when Tyler reached for her. "You *lied* to me, Tyler!"

"Melanie, I'm sorry." He wanted to kick himself for not telling her the truth sooner, because now she had found out in the most difficult way imaginable. He reached for her, but she pulled back.

"Get away from me!" she yelled again when he stepped closer. "No, Tyler, let me go!" When he grabbed her arms, she pulled back and struck him hard in the stomach. He released her with a grunt, and she turned and ran into the house.

Recovering from the blow, Tyler straightened himself and faced Sara, fury rising in his chest. "Get the fuck of my house," he ordered her, his teeth clenched. "If I ever see you again, I swear to *God* I'll kill you." He didn't bother to care as Sara's face went pale with shock. He ran after Melanie.

"Melanie, wait! Let me explain!" he shouted after her as she stalked through the living room, heading for the front door. He caught up with her outside on the front lawn, ignoring the stares from his guests. He grabbed her arm, pulling her over to him. "Melanie, listen! It meant *nothing*!"

Melanie replied by sending her fist directly into his jaw, satisfied when he released her, cursing and rubbing his face with an angry scowl. It only made her more furious when he merely wiped away the blood carelessly, for she knew that no matter what she did, it would be nearly impossible for her to physically hurt him, and that *really* pissed her off.

"I don't care *what* it meant! You lied to me! You looked me right in the eye just ten minutes ago and said you were only friends! I don't give a damn about any other chick you screwed, but you *know* how I feel about *her*!" Melanie had never before screamed at Tyler with such anger and hatred, and her emotions created tears of misery that she refused to let fall.

"Of course I know how you feel!" Tyler cried, throwing out his arms. "Why the hell do you think I didn't tell you the truth? I knew you'd react just like this!"

"How the hell else am I supposed to react? You slept with her, and you said nothing happened! I *knew* something was going on when I met her! I knew you guys shared more than just some stupid sex joke! What was it like, Tyler? Did you think,

88

oh Melanie's in prison so it's okay for me to go screw some other chick until she gets out?"

"We weren't together when you were in jail!" Tyler yelled back, starting to feel frustrated as his chin throbbed. "What? Did you think that I was just supposed to stop my life because you didn't want me but didn't want anyone else to have me either? And you were with Wess, so what's the difference?"

"The difference is that I was honest about it! I told you the *truth*!" Melanie shouted, her hair flying across her eyes. "Me and Wess weren't together when I was in prison. It wasn't until *after* you treated me like shit that I went to him!"

"And you want to know why?" Tyler spat out, taking her arm again as rage rose from within. "Because you were too much of a bitchy, goddamn coward to admit your feelings for me, and you *still* are!"

Melanie's lips parted in surprise at his words, but she recovered quickly as she yanked her arm from his grasp. "Better to be a bitchy coward than a back-stabbing, insensitive asshole," she said coldly. "Get away from me."

Tyler watched helplessly as Melanie ran away from him, through the gate and onto the street. He didn't go after her, didn't try to get her back and make her listen to him, not realizing that he was making the same mistake he had made just over a year ago.

CHAPTER 21

San Francisco, California

Matt checked his bag for the fourth time, making sure that the plans he had written for the next kidnapping were safely stored between his math book and English folder. He grabbed a hat, then pounded down the stairs in a dash for the front door.

"Matt!"

He stumbled to a halt at the door, silently cursing. Apparently his plan to race out of the house so quickly that his mother wouldn't have time to stop him wasn't as hitch-free as he originally thought.

Hoisting his backpack across his shoulder, he trudged into the living room. "Yeah?" He raised his eyebrows and tried to act like he wasn't in a hurry while waiting for his mother, who was sitting on the couch watching her favorite sitcom.

"Where are you going? It's almost ten."

"I'm going to Leighann's."

"I thought you were over there earlier."

"I was. She had company for dinner so I came home and now I'm going back. We're gonna get some of our homework done together." *Of all the people to lie to*, he thought, *it had to be Mom*. He couldn't shake the guilt, the remorse.

Janet Harper eyed her son, letting the tension fill the air. She wondered if he actually thought he was fooling her. "It's a school night."

"It's Friday," Matt argued, shifting from foot to foot. "Come on, Mom, Leighann's waiting for me. I won't be out long."

Acquiescing to her son's request, Janet leaned back against the cushions and picked up the shirt she had been sewing, the shirt her son had mysteriously torn at school. "Fine, go. But don't think you have me wrapped around your finger, you hear me?" She smiled when he gave her a confused and somewhat worried frown. "I'm kidding, Matt. Go see your girlfriend."

"Well, she's not really… Thanks, Mom." Matt kissed his mother on the cheek quickly, then ran for the door, all the while thinking that if Melanie had witnessed the living room scene she would have smacked him upside the head.

Unlike his idol, Matt still had a lot to learn about the art of deception.

Haston, Oregon

Caleb stood outside Melanie's bathroom, leaning against the frame as he rested his head on the wooden door. He could hear Melanie on the other side, banging and rummaging around. He glanced around her bedroom, not seeing much of anything, which didn't surprise him. She had never cared much for personal possessions, although a picture of Tyler and Melanie sitting by the fountain in the backyard did catch his eye. They were close together and smiling, obviously delighted to be in one another's presence.

Frowning, Caleb thought about where Tyler had gone. He briefly heard the fight at the party the previous night, as had everyone else, but no one really knew what was going on. All he knew was that Tyler had stormed out not long after Melanie and was still gone, and Melanie had come home in the morning only to lock herself in the bathroom.

"O'Conner, come on," Caleb said through the door. "What the hell are you locking yourself in the bathroom for? It can't be very much fun in there."

"Go away, Brinson," Melanie's voice came back hard and tough. "This has nothing to do with you."

Caleb sighed and rolled his eyes. "O'Conner, give me a break. I'm not going away until you tell me why you won't come out." When the air went silent again, he knocked once more. "Why won't you come out?"

"Because I got into a fight!" Inside the bathroom, Melanie slammed her palm down onto the sink, ignoring the stinging pain as she glared at her battle wounds in the mirror. On her lip was a patch of dried blood and her right eye was practically black with an unattractive bruise. Her left cheek was swollen and above her eyebrow was a small gash. She hadn't meant to fight, but she had been so angry that her rage pushed her to do it.

She remembered walking down the street, heading down an empty road that she knew was rarely used. Her hands had been clenched, her thoughts jumbled, her body torn between the need to cry, tremble, or beat the living hell out of something.

Tyler lied to her, and it wasn't a small lie that could be easily forgiven. She could handle the fact that he slept with Sara, and had always known the truth despite never admitting it to herself, but what infuriated, disappointed, and made her question everything they had together was that he stared her straight in the eye and told her nothing happened.

Just as her anger over the entire situation had finally started to calm, a man had stepped out of the shadows, bumping into her and knocking her against the wall with an order to stay out of his way. For her state of mind, that was all it took. She walked away with her wounds, as did he.

Outside the bathroom, Caleb took in a breath and held it for a moment, wondering to himself what the other guy must look like. Sighing heavily, he shoved his hands in his pockets and leaned his head against the door. "What kind of fight was it? Fist or verbal?"

"What the hell do you think?"

"Fist." Caleb nodded to himself. "Come on, how bad can it be?"

"Brinson, I went for more than an entire year without fighting, and now I slip up because I was pissed off. I don't give a shit about my face."

Caleb scratched his head, his foot tapping the floor patiently. "So what happened between you and Tyler?"

"Piss off."

"Fair enough. So will you come out?" He waited a moment, then stepped back when the click of the lock being unlatched met his ears. He peered at Melanie as she opened the door, staring at him almost as though she were ashamed of herself. His eyes widened when he saw her face, but he tried not to show much emotion.

Melanie, catching the surprise that he tried unsuccessfully to hide, shrugged and frowned. "Sadly enough, I'm pretty sure I won," she told him quietly, and he gave a small smile.

"Don't worry about it." Caleb pulled her against him in a tight, reassuring hug, and she sighed into his shoulder.

CHAPTER 22

San Francisco, California

A heavy weight of trepidation and apprehension dropped on Kelly's shoulders as Robbie pulled into her driveway, stopped, and turned to look at her. Kelly stared up at her house, not moving from the passenger seat. The early morning light seemed to make her house darker, and she was afraid to enter. She would be punished for what she had done, sneaking out in the middle of the night to meet with Robbie, then going off to a party.

She needed the night though, just one night without worries. It had been so long since she had been able to just let go and for once smile and laugh without it being nothing more than an act.

It all began in Florida, the running away, the rebelling. She had gotten used to sneaking out in the middle of the night only to return to her bedroom minutes before her alarm went off or her mother entered to tell her to rise and shine. Usually she would head to a party, or a friend's house, or sometimes the beach if she could get a ride. It wasn't a surprise if she ended up wasted, but it had been when she started experimenting with drugs that she got caught. Arrested, in fact.

And so they moved to San Francisco, her mother's hometown. They didn't speak of what happened in Florida, what had caused them to move away. Kelly was watched now, night and day, and she didn't care for it one bit. It had taken a lot of careful planning to get out of the house with Robbie, and she knew what the consequences would be. But it was worth it, she told herself as she took off her seatbelt, the night of dancing, the drinks, the laughs. He had been kind, not pressuring her to do anything, lending an ear when she wanted to talk.

He would be the perfect boyfriend, Kelly thought wistfully with a saddened frown. If only she could have one.

"You know, you can always come to my house," Robbie offered when Kelly didn't move from the front seat, but she shook her head. "I can help you."

"I'm fine. Thanks for the ride." She unlocked her door. "I don't know what's wrong with my car. It just won't work for some reason." It pissed her off that Jeffrey wouldn't let her bring it to an auto shop to be fixed. "I've had to use Jeffrey's."

"Bet you love doing that," Robbie muttered.

"Well it sucks, but the funny thing is, his car got stolen yesterday." She laughed to herself, shaking her head, remembering how mad her stepfather had been when he walked out of the house, intending to go to work. Instead, he came barreling back inside, yelling out curses and accusations while dialing the police.

"Isn't that his car over there?" Robbie pointed to his left, and Kelly peered through the driver's side window, seeing Jeffrey's black Nissan parked against the curb.

"Oh, yeah, it is. I guess he got it back. Well, I really have to go." She thanked him for the ride home again, then walked up to her front door as he pulled out of the driveway.

She didn't see anyone as she headed further into the house. Walking up the stairs, Kelly approached her room, pushing open the door to find Jeffrey and her mother standing by her bed with two men dressed in dark uniforms. All four glanced over when she entered.

"You have some explaining to do," Monica said harshly, jabbing a finger at her daughter.

"Why?" Kelly's brow furrowed in confusion. "What did I do?"

"Well, stealing my car for one thing!" Jeffrey cried. "And sneaking out in the middle of the night! And not to mention the dent you put on the passenger side!"

"What are you talking about?" Kelly yelled back. "I didn't take your car! It was stolen!"

One of the men dressed in a suit stepped forward. "You mind telling me where you were last night?" His voice, deep and demanding, chilled Kelly to the bone.

"I was at a party."

"How did you get there?"

Kelly hesitated. She didn't want to get Robbie in trouble, yet knew that if she told them she walked or got a ride, they wouldn't believe her. So instead she was silent, setting her jaw angrily.

"Silence means only one thing," the man informed her, and Monica stepped forward.

"And how do you explain this? A keepsake from your party days in Florida?" She grabbed a bag from the bed, and Kelly stared down, her mouth dropping open at the pills.

"Those aren't mine," she defended herself. "I don't know where you got those, but they aren't mine. And I didn't steal the car!"

"We found your fingerprints on the car, Kelly," the man in the uniform said.

"Yeah, because my car was broken, and—" Kelly stopped short when she realized what was happening. Her car was broken, so she had had to use Jeffrey's. She went out last night, and had no one to vouch for her if she wanted to keep everyone out of her problems, which meant that if Jeffrey reported a stolen car, she would be the prime suspect.

One of these days.

The phrase rang through her mind. She pictured Jeffrey on the stairs, threatening her under his breath. She had known then that the time would come, and now here it was, and that fact terrified her to the core, made her want to turn and flee as far and fast as she could.

So don't let the other guy win.

For Robbie, for Danielle, for herself, she wasn't going to let him win.

Crossing her arms, Kelly stared defiantly at the adults in her bedroom. "So what are you going to do about it?"

Monica took in a quivering breath. "We've discussed it, and with the trouble you've had lately, with the running away and now all this, we're going to send you away."

"To where?"

"South Bay Juvenile Detention Camp."

F.B.I. Headquarters, California

Jay Neilson hurriedly pushed past a woman carrying a stack of files, muttering an apology as he thrust open the door to his partner's office. He tossed a newspaper down onto Zack Corwin's desk.

"What's this about?"

"The new Helping Hands got another kid."

"I know." Zack gestured to his own copy of the paper, and Jay sat down in front of the desk. "We were informed of that earlier."

Jay took a file from Zack's desk, opening it and sifting through the papers. He saw the message, a picture of the little girl, of the family, the house, and everything else that could have possibly been recorded. "So do you think this new branch is just a copycat act?"

Zack rubbed his chin, leaning back in his chair. "I don't think so. Everything is too perfect, too careful. These people know what they're doing. Someone who didn't know how the project worked wouldn't be able to pull it off so well. I mean, there've been, what, two or three copycats busted by the F.B.I., and the others mysteriously disappeared after the first kidnapping, with the child returned. My guess is that they disappeared because the real Helping Hands got a hold of them, so if this San Francisco gang wasn't legit, I think it already would have been put to an end."

"Yeah, but all any copycat gang would have to do is find out how the project works."

"Jay, *we* don't even know how it works, and we're the goddamn F.B.I. Melanie O'Conner has never said anything, and the only other known Helping Hand is dead. Seeing as how we can't make O'Conner talk and we can't conjure up the dead, we officially have nothing to work with."

"What about the man O'Conner lives with? Mel Scotford? Something tells me he knows more about the Helping Hands than he's letting on. Who's to say he's not one himself? He's got the tattoo, lives with O'Conner, protects her when we come to the house. Not to mention he lives in the same place as the Helping Hand branch that appeared not long after O'Conner's arrest."

"You think I don't know that?" Irritated by Jay's spiel, Zack glared up at his partner. "You think I'm so blind that I can't see the connection? Mel Scotford fits the profile of Tyler Mason to the T." He had carefully read the descriptions of the Hell Hound gang given to him by the Knoxport police department. Kyle Lindel was the pseudo-identity of Wess Porter, and that left two males who were a part of the Hell Hounds. Though the remaining two were very close in description, Tyler Mason was, according to the files, the one who was essentially O'Conner's partner, from confidant to fellow junkie to possible love interest.

"The fact is, I'm not concerned with the original gang. Melanie O'Conner was caught, arrested, put in jail. She did her time, she served her sentence, and she is now living her life. Whether or not Mel Scotford was a Hell Hound is irrelevant, one because we could only indict him based on circumstantial evidence, and two because O'Conner took the heat for the entire gang. Our focus is on the new San Francisco branch, and how we can catch them."

Jay read a small note on Ryan Mueller's parents, regretfully putting Mel Scotford to the back of his mind. His partner was right, of course, but it still irked him to know that they couldn't put the man in prison. "So what do you think Melanie O'Conner is hiding?"

"She's got to have something to do with the Helping Hands." Zack was convinced of that much, if not anything else. "I think she knows who every other branch is, but whether or not she's helping them, I don't know. But I do think she was surprised by this California branch. She seemed honest."

"But if she doesn't know about it, and she does know about the others, wouldn't that lead us to believe that it's a copycat act?" Jay suggested carefully. "I mean, the copycat gangs we've busted in the past five years had nothing to do with her either. What makes this one any different?"

Narrowing his eyes thoughtfully, Zack Corwin rested his elbows on his desk and tapped his thumbs together. "Because Melanie O'Conner knows more than she's letting on, and she knows that we know that. She also knows that we can't bust her without any evidence or without getting her to admit to it. So we can't do anything about her not telling us. But this new gang, like I said, it's too perfect. Sneaking into the house in the middle of the night, dealing with a dog, disarming a difficult alarm system, knowing the parents' schedules, these people have had some kind of inside training. I wouldn't be surprised if they contact Melanie O'Conner soon, if they haven't already."

"And when they do, we'll go for what O'Conner knows," Jay finished, understanding his partner.

"Exactly. It's all a matter of time."

Shortly after his partner left for a quick lunch break, Corwin leaned back against the soft cushion of his office chair and studied the file of Holly Jessup. Eight years old, deaf since the age of five, daughter to Dan and Chrissy Jessup. Attended the Orsen Academy for the Deaf, was a good student according to teachers, and was a quiet and reserved little girl. Nothing seemed out of the ordinary to Corwin about the child.

Picking up the black telephone on his desk, he punched the number for Melanie O'Conner, who was still at her home in Haston, although he had heard that she wouldn't be there much longer. A day, two at the most. He waited a few minutes, impatiently tapping his fingers on his desk until he heard the phone being picked up.

"Yeah?" Melanie's voice came on the line, sounded distracted.

"Miss O'Conner, this is Agent Zack Corwin. We met a few weeks ago."

"I know who you are. What do you want?"

Zack wasn't the least bit taken aback by her attitude. He was used to dealing with people like her. "I want to talk to you about Holly Jessup."

"Who?"

"Don't play dumb with me, Miss O'Conner. Think really hard. Holly Jessup, eight years old. Kidnapped by the Helping Hands of San Francisco two nights ago." Zack rose to his feet with annoyance.

"Corwin, I don't know what the hell you're talking about. I have work to do. I'm in the middle of loading the truck right now, and—"

Zack didn't hesitate to interrupt. "If you don't cooperate with me, Miss O'Conner, you won't have to worry about moving. That's a promise."

"And if you interrupt me again, Agent Corwin, you can forget about me cooperating with you at all," Melanie replied just as harshly. "So what do you want?"

With a sigh, Zack slammed his fist down onto his desk. "Listen to me very carefully. I will catch these good-for-nothing thugs, even if it kills me. And you *will* help, I don't care what you say or do. And if you—"

"What did the message say?" Melanie cut in suddenly, catching the agent off-guard.

Zack picked up a copy of the message that had been left behind. "It said, 'Holly's been taken. We'll let you know if we hear anything.' "

"So she's deaf," Melanie concluded.

"Yes, she's deaf. How convenient that you would know. Now, I'll ask you one more time. Do you know anything about this?"

"No, I don't. But since the child's deaf, I can tell you that chances are it's because of her parents hitting her so often. Severe blows to the head will damage hearing after so long, and the parents came up with some elaborate story about the girl hitting her head on something and that's how she lost her hearing, like she was pushed into a brick wall or she fell or something. That's all I know." Taking the final word along with her, Melanie hung up on Corwin.

"Bitch," Corwin cursed, slamming down the phone. Shaking his head and staring down at Holly Jessup's picture again, he made up his mind. "Looks like I'll be paying you another visit, Miss O'Conner," he murmured, then stalked out of his office.

CHAPTER 23

Collinsville, California

The sun shone down brightly as afternoon slowly began to drift into evening, creating a layer of humid heat that was impossible to avoid. Sprinklers were on in front and backyards, and children ran through them gleefully with squeals of happy laughter. Pools were overflowing with a mass of people, the park was crowded with a thicket of parents watching the final inning of a pee-wee baseball game, and the local grocery store was filled with individuals all doing their afternoon shopping.

Radford Lane, a street located on the outskirts of town, was quiet and slow moving, the only bustling activity coming from a few children playing in the distance. Along both sides of the street were five fence-wrapped houses, spaced far apart with large acres filled with greenery between each home, creating plenty of room for privacy.

And privacy was exactly what Melanie O'Conner wanted.

She stood on a ladder in the afternoon fever, her long hair pulled back into a tight braid and her skin and clothes covered in pearl-white paint. She squinted in the sun as she painted her new house, feeling a twinge of satisfaction as she finished the small patch of wall she had been working on. Part of her wished Tyler was there to share the whole moving-in process, but they were still not talking and he had left for a job interview with no desire to join in. In a way, she was glad for his absence.

Once settled into the house, Tyler had approached Melanie with the intent of smoothing things out, but when she accused him of being a liar and a cheat, he had replied with an equally harsh retort. They parted on bad terms, and even when Melanie later said she was willing to forgive and forget, Tyler turned his back on her.

It was how things always went with them, she figured. Fighting for weeks at a time because of one argument or one misunderstanding, each one attempting an apology at least once. It had been that way since they were kids. They just weren't very good at admitting when they were wrong. Though in this case, Melanie was certain it was Tyler who was at fault.

"So when do you start the new job?" Taryn asked from the base of the ladder. She and Caleb had decided to go with Melanie and Tyler to help with the move. Both noticed the obvious tension between the newly engaged couple, though they weren't too concerned about it. They too knew of the cycle, and were sure it would all blow over soon.

"Monday," Melanie replied. "Two days."

"You nervous?" Caleb wiped a trail of sweat from his forehead and pulled off his shirt, which prompted a teasing catcall from Taryn. He grinned and snapped his shirt at her, hitting her skin with a satisfying smack.

"Not really," Melanie answered, dragging the paintbrush across the wall. "It's not like I can't handle myself around a bunch of unruly teenagers, *Caleb*," she added pointedly when Caleb snapped at Taryn again.

A comfortable silence followed, although Melanie could tell that her two friends had something on their minds.

"So O'Conner," Taryn began cautiously, pausing before continuing, "what, um, what happened between you and Tyler?"

Melanie hesitated, the paintbrush hovering on the wall. Caleb stopped as well, moving over next to the ladder so he could listen. He peered up at his friend, seeing that the remnants of the brawl she had gotten into were healing slowly but surely.

"We just had a fight," Melanie replied quietly, turning her eyes away. "He called me a coward, I called him an asshole, and we haven't really spoken since."

"All because of Sara?" Caleb asked, and Melanie shrugged.

"That and more. Just things that should have been brought to attention a long time ago. Look guys, I appreciate you trying to help and all, but I really just want to not talk about it. It's kinda frustrating." With a sigh, Melanie dropped the brush onto the tray of paint that was balancing on the edge of the ladder.

Before she could catch it, the tray tipped over, falling and hitting the top of Caleb's head with a dull thud. Pearl-white paint splattered through his hair and down his face. He wiped his eyes and spit a mouthful of paint while glaring up at Melanie.

Melanie, her lips parting in surprise then curving into a grin, quickly covered her mouth with one hand as a snort burst from her. Her shoulders shook as she tried to hold it in, watching Caleb run a hand across his face and flick paint-matted hair from his eyes.

"You are so paying for that," he told her. "Taryn!"

Melanie cried out in protest as Caleb grabbed her waist and pulled her down from the ladder, holding onto her shoulders tightly while spinning her around. "Taryn, don't you dare!" she warned as Taryn came at her with a paintbrush, wiping it down the center of her face. Melanie let out a cry, not out of anger but fun, and grabbed the brush that had fallen from her tray as Caleb released her. She went at him, dropping the brush and instead tossing wet paint at him with her hands. It sprayed across his bare chest. She pushed him, creating two white handprints on his flesh as Taryn laughed.

"Damn, Caleb, you look like you just got your ass whipped by a snowman!" she teased, laughing and pointing. Caleb and Melanie paused, looking at one another with knowing grins, then turned in unison and lunged for Taryn. She squealed as Melanie ran a paintbrush through her hair and Caleb held her arms so she couldn't move. Taryn kicked Caleb's foot hard, and he stepped back in pain. She reached into the tray of paint, covering her hand with it, then smeared it in Melanie's face. Melanie turned to retaliate, stopping when she heard a car door slam.

The three friends all turned to the end of the long driveway, where Tyler had parked to avoid the painting mess. He took in the scene before him through slightly narrowed eyes, not laughing at the sight of his friends covered from head-to-toe in paint. Instead, he walked up the drive and didn't stop until he reached Melanie.

Melanie stared at Tyler as he approached her with a steady, determined stride. She didn't recognize the expression on his face, the set, serious look with no traces of humor or anger. He kept his eyes trained on hers, never saying a word until he reached her.

"It's always only been you." Tyler pulled her against him as he kissed her passionately, ignoring the bitter taste of paint as it hit his tongue. He ran his hands over her face, through her hair, held her as tightly as he could against him. Taryn and Caleb exchanged a satisfied grin as they watched.

Melanie drew back after giving in to his apology, laughing when she saw the paint that surrounded Tyler's mouth. He lifted his hands to her face, his fingers spotted white. "Can we not fight anymore?" he asked, his eyes soft. "It's way too exhausting."

"That's because you know you'll never win," Melanie retorted with a grin.

"So am I forgiven?"

"Well, that depends." Melanie cocked her head to the side. "You gonna help us paint?"

Tyler glanced up and down Melanie's body, then glanced over at Taryn and Caleb, who looked pretty much the same. "Am I painting you or the house?"

"Whatever you want, man," Caleb piped up. "Grab a brush."

CHAPTER 24

South Bay Juvenile Detention Camp

Dirt rose from the hard-packed ground as it was kicked up by a pair of feet. Voices rang out from drill sergeants shouting at teenagers, who were carrying out their daily chores, some hoisting heavy bags of sand, others pushing carts with sheets and utensils towards the bunks or cafeteria. Most followed the orders that were barked out to them by the drill sergeants, but there was one who dared to defy them.

Kelly Mitchell resisted against the two guards who were holding her arms in a tight, relentless grasp. She grunted against their embrace, her feet kicking against the ground as she was pulled into a small, dark, windowless room furnished with a mattress and small bucket.

The guards dropped her down onto the dirt floor, non-sympathetic when she gave a small cry of pain. A shadow fell across her, and she jumped to her feet when she saw Sergeant Hawkins standing in the doorway. Her eyes narrowed as she set her jaw, determined not to look scared or nervous.

Her attitude had changed upon arriving at South Bay. Once she saw what it would take to survive the tough, relentless, and dangerous girls in her bunk, she knew she had to be just as fierce. Everyone thought she was there because of drugs and a stolen car, which labeled her one of the hardcore girls that most left alone, and she wasn't about to tell the truth, the real, embarrassing truth.

No one was to know about that.

"Kelly Mitchell," Drill Sergeant Brian Hawkins said sternly as he entered the room that served as solitary confinement. "Second time this month you've been put in here. Slow learner, are you?"

Kelly shrugged. "Maybe you just don't know how to teach."

Sergeant Hawkins stared at Kelly, knowing from experience that yelling merely resulted in rolled eyes and bored shrugs. After several encounters, he found that she became the most unsure and self-conscious when he spoke quietly and calmly.

"You will be meeting with a counselor tomorrow," he informed Kelly, who crossed her arms and smirked. "A new one. You won't be speaking with Sergeant Aims anymore."

"Why not? She couldn't handle me?" Kelly shot back. She hated counseling, had been the same difficult patient with her shrink in Florida.

Hawkins shook his head once, keeping his eyes level on hers. "No, Sergeant Aims simply got sick of all your bullshit. She wanted more of a challenge." He figured Kelly would fall silent at the comment, and she did. For a moment, anyway.

"So who is it?"

"You'll find out tomorrow. Enjoy your night." Stepping out into the afternoon air, Hawkins pulled the heavy door shut and locked it tight, closing Kelly into complete darkness.

Melanie sat behind her new desk, taking in the heavy oak of the wood, flicking the small lamp on and off, swiveling around in her new chair. She glanced around the office, not seeing much of anything because she knew it was up to her to decorate it. She wasn't one much for adornments, so if she were going to put anything in the room at all it would be a couple of pictures, maybe something practical, like a pencil sharpener or trashcan. Other than that, she couldn't care less about what the office looked like.

Rising from her chair, she went to the window, staring out at the teenagers all working hard and steady. She had a good view of the girls' camp and a slight one of the boys' from where she stood in her office.

Her office. The phrase had an odd ring to it, one she never thought she would find herself saying. Never in her life would she have imagined having a steady job that required her to do any sort of work that was actually legal.

"Miss O'Conner," Hawkins said as he entered her office. Melanie turned, giving him a small nod as he walked up to her desk and stood in front of it, hands clasped behind him and his back straight in a manner so formal and rigid that it nearly ticked her off. "I take it you've already spoken with the superior?"

Melanie nodded again. "Yeah, I have. He got me squared away for the most part and said you'd take care of the rest. So what exactly am I supposed to be doing?"

Brian handed her a file. "Your first case will be Kelly Mitchell, San Francisco. Seventeen years old, junior at Lakeside High School."

"Lakeside?" Melanie repeated. "That's where Matt goes," she mumbled under her breath, staring down at a picture of the girl, a pretty blonde with a menacing frown. Figures, she thought, that her first case would be a girl who probably knew the leader of the newest branch of Helping Hands.

It was either a small world after all, or a twist of fate that couldn't be ignored.

"So what's her story?"

"Runaway, auto theft, drugs," Hawkins rattled off the offenses. "She's a real stubborn hard-ass. You two might actually get along. You know, trying to be rogues and all. "

Melanie's head shot up at his words. "Go screw yourself, Hawkins," she told him.

"Hey, I'm just preparing you. You're going to hear a lot worse from the kids here when you actually get out there and work with them one-on-one."

"So what am I doing?" Melanie closed the file. "Am I finding out why she did what she did, getting her to admit some deep dark secret, what?"

Hawkins shifted his weight, thinking about the question and the best way to word the answer. "You're trying to guide her, trying to get her to change her attitude. If you can make her see the wrong she's done, she can go home."

"So basically, I'm trying to break her down." She smiled when Hawkins confirmed her deduction. "Shouldn't be a problem. I've made grown men cry. A teenage girl with an attitude problem is a piece of cake."

CHAPTER 25

Gregson, Oklahoma

The night was quiet, the wind light as a pair of feet worked its way carefully and methodically across the grass. The figure slipped on the dew that covered the blades, not saying anything as it picked itself up and continued on. Above, the leaves rustled slightly as crickets and frogs held quiet conversations with one another, and sight was nearly impossible as the shadow crept closer to its destination—a window set within a home that harbored two vicious blackguards.

A light flashed on without warning, spreading a pool of yellow illumination across the grass and casting the figure that stood upon it in brightness, fully and dangerously exposed as the man looked about himself. The silence of the night air was disturbed by a high-pitched, beeping alarm. A steady stream of curses was heard, and from behind, the second figure that had been watching from the sidelines sighed and crossed her arms.

"I told you to get closer to the ground," Taryn scolded Caleb, who turned to face his friend.

"And I told you I wanted to see if it worked this way," he replied, pulling his black ski hat down further over his forehead. Taryn shook her head, her own hair covered by a black hat as she tugged on the collar of her jacket. She glared at her fellow Helping Hand, her partner, who was clad in the black gear used for every kidnapping.

Caleb still stood bathed in light as he observed the models of the motion sensor lights he and Taryn had purchased. After buying the lights, Caleb and Taryn had brought them to The Ranch and built a makeshift structure practically identical to the back wall of Mayor Livingston's home. Then they set up the lights and began practicing, figuring out which was the best way to get around the sensors without setting them off.

His hands on his hips, Caleb stalked over to Taryn. "If my way doesn't work, then what do you suggest we do?"

Taryn paced in front of the lights, her eyes raising slightly when the light that caught Caleb flashed off. Her mind raced with thoughts and strategies, picturing her plan. "The Livingstons' lights have approximately a twenty-foot range. That means we can be in the backyard without the lights flashing on. Maybe if we go in between them just right..." her voice trailed off as she positioned herself between the lights and began walking towards the artificial wall, keeping low to the ground. She groaned when both lights flashed on.

"And you're caught. Sent to jail by the mayor of Tulsa," Caleb sighed. "Do not pass go, do not collect two hundred dollars."

"Eat me, asshole."

"Been there, done that."

Ignoring the smirk Taryn shot his way, Caleb scanned the structure in front of him. It would have been much easier, under normal circumstances, to get the girl when she was going to or from school, but the mayor made sure Mary had a personal bodyguard at all times.

A possibility began to form in his mind, and he pieced together his thoughts carefully. He moved his eyes along the wall, the roof, the lawn. "What if we don't go in from the ground?"

"What?"

"What if we go in from the top? From the roof?"

Taryn laughed sarcastically. "Brinson, we aren't in some Hollywood movie with green screens and special effects. We're real, pal. We ain't got helicopters and bungee ropes."

"I wasn't thinking helicopters and ropes." Caleb shoved Taryn, pushing her up against a tree as she scoffed at him. "If I remember right, there's a big oak right next to the house." He walked over and pointed. "It's right behind the first light. If we can get to the tree without triggering a light, we could reach that balcony that overlooks the backyard."

"That balcony goes into the master bedroom," Taryn reminded Caleb. "What are we going to do? Go through their room while they're sleeping?"

"We could, but that would be risky," Caleb thought aloud. "They'd hear us for sure."

Taryn nodded, scratching her head. The she broke out into a grin. "But not if they're passed out cold."

"What do you mean?"

"Mayor Livingston has this banquet thing to go to next month. I heard some guys in the restaurant talking about it. It's a big fancy function for some charity but it's mainly going to be a gathering of rich bigwigs who drink and party and feel good about themselves because they donate a grand or so a year. Apparently there's going to be the whole big-shot party things there, champagne, wine, the works."

"And everyone knows how the mayor is prone to knock back a few from time to time." Caleb remembered reading an article about George Livingston and his past on alcohol usage. It never failed to amaze him how a man known to be an alcoholic managed to garner enough votes to take the win.

Apparently, with enough money, anything was possible.

"If we took the chance that Livingston and his wife get drunk that night, which is a pretty good possibility, we could go through their bedroom," Taryn continued, playing off Caleb's idea. "We know how to be silent in a house." She thought about the consequences to herself. "We just might be able to pull this thing off."

CHAPTER 26

South Bay Juvenile Detention Camp

A blinding pain seared through Kelly's eyes when the door to her dark, black, solitary room was thrust open. She squinted, holding a hand in front of her face to block the light as she sat up on the bed, staring through one eye at Sergeant Brian Hawkins.

"Let's go, Mitchell," he ordered, pulling her up when she didn't move.

"Where am I going?" Kelly asked, trying to gain her footing as she was yanked out of the room.

"To speak with your new counselor."

"Can't wait. We'll have some serious bonding time," she said sarcastically. "Who is it?"

"You'll see."

Kelly ignored her nerves as Hawkins led her to the counseling office. She had been there practically every day since her arrival at the camp and would be for the remainder of her sentence, which was in her opinion unnecessarily lengthy, and she knew the building well. She frowned when she was led to a room that wasn't the one she was normally in.

When the door opened and Hawkins pushed her inside, she gazed in surprise at the sight of her new counselor. The face, the scars, the attitude, all she recognized from past media exposures, and all caused chills to grip her bones.

"I know you," Kelly said, more to herself.

"No, you don't," Melanie replied plainly, leaning against her desk with her arms crossed.

"Kelly Mitchell, meet your new counselor, Melanie O'Conner." With the introduction out of the way, Brian Hawkins left the office, pulling the door shut behind him.

"Have a seat." Melanie gestured to the chair in front of her as she observed Kelly. She had spent most of the night reviewing the girl's file, reading about her offenses, her past, her present, and her attitude at the camp. As a former Hell Hound, Melanie hadn't been the least bit impressed.

"You're the Helping Hand, aren't you?" Kelly asked as she sat down, leaning back and crossing her arms. "Talk about a failure."

Melanie didn't react to the jibe. She wasn't interested in giving the girl the pleasure of being insulted. Her job was to help, not to encourage a teenager's angry offenses. "So why are you here?"

"My parents sent me."

"You know what I mean."

Kelly sighed and flicked her hair from her eyes, staring out the window. "You read my file?" Melanie nodded. "Then I guess you know."

"You're right." Melanie nodded again and pushed herself up off the desk. "I know that you stole a car and that drugs were found in your room. I know that you ran away last month, and that you ran away when you were living in Florida while consuming a significant amount of drugs and alcohol. I know that you've moved four times in the past five years, that you get good grades in school, and that you used to have a dog named Candy." She raised her eyebrows when Kelly's expression changed from angry to surprised, then back to angry. "I also know that I'm going to find out why you stole that car, inevitably screwing up your future."

"Maybe I just wanted to steal it," Kelly challenged

Melanie returned the menacing glare, narrowing her eyes at the teenager. "Nobody steals a car just because they want to. Believe me, I know."

When the girl merely lifted a shoulder and stared out the window, Melanie bit back a sigh. She could tell it was going to be a long day.

Melanie ran a hand through her damp hair as she padded through the hall of her new home, not caring as she dripped water onto the floor. She glanced around as she walked, hardly noticing the bare walls and furnishings. She and Tyler had only taken a few things from Fred Kindle's home, some lamps, furniture, and other household necessities, so the rest of the decorating was up to them.

Glancing at the clock, she saw that it was nearly ten in the morning. After over a week at her new job, she was happy to have a day off. Even better, Tyler didn't have to be at work for another hour.

"Morning," Melanie said as she entered the kitchen, seeing Tyler standing at the sink, the faucet running.

"Morning, babe," Tyler greeted back. "Haven't unpacked the brush yet, have you?" he asked as Melanie combed her damp hair with her fingers.

"No. Too many boxes for me. It'll get done eventually." Melanie glanced over her shoulder at the stack of unpacked boxes piled by the front door. She had no idea what was in most of them, and wasn't looking forward to sorting through them. As long as she had clothes to wear and food to eat, she was perfectly content.

"Hey," Tyler said suddenly, "you know how neither of us cook, so we don't spend a whole lot of time in the kitchen?"

"Yeah. So?"

"Well, I was exploring, so to speak, the kitchen this morning, and you want to know what I found?"

Melanie yawned and sat down on one of the few chairs they had in the house while Tyler turned back to the sink. "Sure. What'd you find?"

Tyler spun back around, a spray hose that connected to the sink gripped in his hand. "I found a removable sink faucet." He grinned a mischievous grin and cocked his head to the side as Melanie rose from the chair.

"Don't you dare," she warned, holding up a hand when Tyler crept closer to her. She took a step back, eyeing him threateningly. "Tyler, don't do it. Tyler!' she yelled when he pressed the nozzle and a stream of water shot out of the hose, hitting her directly in the stomach, soaking her shirt. "Damn you!"

"Hey, I got a question for you." Tyler, loving the aggravated glare that was being directed his way, lowered the hose. "When we getting married?"

"What? I don't know."

"Wrong answer." Tyler raised his hand again and sprayed Melanie in the face, laughing as she spit the water out. "How about next month?"

"How about you shove that hose up your ass?" Melanie responded, her eyes dark as she turned her back on Tyler. He watched while she yanked the front door open and stepped outside, slamming the door behind her.

"Ah, shit," Tyler cursed. "Take a damn joke." He followed her path, opening the door again while thinking about what he could say to prevent the argument he was sure was about to take place. "Mel, come on!" he called as he stepped out onto the front porch. "Take a joke!"

"Hey!" Melanie yelled from behind, and he turned only to get hit with a shower of water. He stumbled back, his head drenched and his hair dripping cold liquid down his neck, soaking the collar of his shirt. He looked up to see Melanie standing a few feet away from him, her arms crossed and a hose clutched in her hand as she raised her eyebrows with satisfaction. The hose was cinched to stop the water flow, but her fingers were loose on the grip, a wicked gleam in her eye.

Sensing that he was about to be sprayed again, Tyler quickly held up a hand. "Okay, okay. Truce." He wiped his face with his shirt. "Damn, girl. At least *my* attack was for a good purpose. Yours was out of spite."

Melanie dropped the hose after turning it off and walked over to Tyler. "Now that we're even, let's talk about that purpose you mentioned." With a grin, she took hold of Tyler's shirt and pulled him into the house. She started for the living room, stopping in her tracks when the doorbell rang. Tyler sighed as Melanie turned to answer it and took a step back in surprise when he saw the person standing outside his new home. He watched Melanie greet the figure with a frown and an annoyed backward glance.

Tyler shook his head and crossed his arms. "Man, I hate reporters," he mumbled, then grudgingly walked up to Melanie's side.

CHAPTER 27

"It will be the wedding of the century. Melanie O'Conner, the rough and tough outcasted rogue of society, settling down from her past of narcotics and bloody mischief and starting a family of her own. It'll be huge!"

Melanie sighed and rubbed her eyes. "Well, thank you for that... vivid portrayal of my life," she said sarcastically to Stephanie Mathews. Already, though the woman with big blonde hair had been in her home for less than twenty minutes, Melanie was starting to feel the same loathing annoyance for the certain individual who had all but ruined her life so long ago. It was no surprise to Melanie that the reporter would show up at her house unannounced, and she wasn't about to let it go by unnoticed that she was more than just a little bit pissed off.

Stephanie nodded excitedly, caught up in the idea of her captivating story. "Imagine what people will say! They'll see that you really have changed your ways, that you're starting a new life!"

Melanie rubbed her eyes with an exasperated huff. "Stephanie, that's just it. It's *my* life, and I don't need to prove anything to anyone. Who I marry, and *how* I marry, is nobody's business but my own." She glanced over at Tyler, who nodded back, keeping silent. Melanie didn't think he would say much. She knew that he blamed Stephanie for most of the things that had happened in the past, if not all of it, and with good reason.

"Look, I know that you just started with this new magazine deal and everything, and you're looking for some hot new story to really get your name out there, but I can promise you this." Melanie took a step back and gestured to herself. "There's no story here."

"O'Conner," Stephanie, determined not to take no for an answer, only crossed her slim legs and gestured to Melanie, gold bracelets sliding on her wrist. The gold matched the bright red of her pencil skirt and white, freshly pressed blouse. "You're starting over. New job, new home, new husband." She pointed towards Tyler. "You could be famous instead of infamous. People could know that you're starting a whole new life!"

"Exactly, Stephanie!" Melanie threw out her arms. "I'm starting a new life, without all that bullshit of the past getting in the way! I don't want to be famous. I don't want everyone knowing that I'm starting a whole new life! I just want to get over everything that's happened and move on, and here you are, trying to get me to prove myself to the world. I don't have to prove anything. Not to anyone."

"In other words," Tyler stood next to Melanie, his voice deep, "she's starting a new life that doesn't include you or your bullshit reports."

Melanie shook her head. "No, Tyler, that's not what I meant."

"Well I'll tell you what *I* meant." He focused on Stephanie, disgusted by her painted face, red lips, diamond earrings. "I'm sick of you showing up wherever Melanie is, whether it's at prison, or a goddamn cabin in the mountains, and *especially* at her new house, where I happened to live as well. You screwed us both over once before, and I don't give a *shit* if you helped Melanie get out of jail. She would have found a way to do so with or without you. You only helped her because you were trying to cover up your *own* goddamn mistake. There is no way in hell I'm going to let someone like you anywhere near Melanie, so it would be in your best interest to keep your goddamn distance. *That* is what *I* meant."

Stephanie hesitated before replying, taking a good look into Tyler's deep blue, furious eyes. *If looks could kill*, she thought, a bit intimidated. She had seen those eyes before, been unnerved by them. The first time she met the Hell Hound gang, it had been those piercing eyes that she remembered the most.

"Mel, listen to me," she began cautiously, but Tyler wouldn't have it.

"No, you listen to me, you self-righteous twat," he spat out, stepping in front of Melanie. "You are *not* welcome here, and if it weren't for the fact that you actually got Melanie a second trial, I would deck your pampered ass right here. I don't give a shit if you *are* a chick. So why don't you go home, go back to your rich husband. I'm sure he'll be willing to aid and abet in whatever plot you have to fuck up another person's life."

Finishing, Tyler swallowed heavily. It felt good to finally tell the reporter what had been on his mind since Melanie's arrest. He stole a quick glance at Melanie, seeing a surprised yet somewhat pleased expression on her face.

Stephanie, not wanting to show her fear of the former Hell Hound, nodded and took a step back. "I can see I'm not wanted here," she stated firmly, and stalked to the front door.

Melanie followed her. "I'm sorry, Stephanie," she said as the woman pulled the door open. The reporter turned back around, her lips pursed as Melanie shrugged. "I just don't want what you want."

"Then you're just fooling yourself," Stephanie replied quietly, and hurried to her car.

Tyler crossed his arms when Melanie closed the door behind the reporter and turned to face him, her eyebrows raised and jaw set accusingly. "What?"

"What the hell was that all about?"

"She had it coming," Tyler defended himself, relaxing a little when he saw that Melanie wasn't mad. "I really hate that woman."

"I know." Melanie rested her head on his chest, feeling the ripple of muscle, a bit tense from confrontation. "And as much as I'd like to talk about your hatred for her, you have to get to work or you'll be late. Plus, you're still wet, so you have to change."

"You're right." Tyler kissed the top of Melanie's head and stepped back. "What are you going to do today?"

Melanie glanced over at the phone. "A little research," she replied vaguely.

"Have fun. I really do have to go." He kissed her again, heading for the stairs to grab a dry shirt while Melanie headed back for the kitchen. He paused at the base of the stairs with a sly grin, calling out to his future bride, "Feel like making me a sandwich to get me though a hard day at the office, my lovely wife-to-be?"

"Feel like having that sandwich shoved up your ass, my dear ex-fiancé?"

Tyler grinned at her retort. "That's my girl," he said to himself, and jogged up the stairs to change.

San Francisco, California

Janet Harper knocked lightly on her son's bedroom door, waiting patiently until she heard the doorknob being turned. She held out the phone when Matt opened the door, a pencil behind his ear and a book in hand. Her breath caught in her throat, as it always did when she saw her son involved with school, with sports, with friends, but she tried not to let him see her emotion.

Even after all these years, she still felt the fear of it all being taken away again.

She remembered the day of his kidnapping clearly. She had arrived home late from work, and went to his bedroom only to discover that it was empty, his clothes gone, his backpack nowhere in sight, a message left behind indicating that her only child had been kidnapped. After the police had been informed and there was nothing left to do but worry and cry, she started interpreting the message, desperate to figure out its meaning. In the back of her mind she supposed she had known all along that Matt had been taken because of the abuse.

So many beating. So many bruises, cuts, scars. She herself had plenty, a victim as well, afraid to go to the police because of the death threats her husband had lashed out at her.

She'd felt guilty in her happiness that Matt was no longer at the house. Somehow she had known that he was safe, a mother's intuition perhaps, but that didn't take away her sorrow for her lost son. Never would he enjoy the thrills of a teenage life. Never would she watch him graduate, live a normal life. Such things she feared the most, not knowing if Matt would come back to her, if he would be gone forever, lost without ever being told good-bye or that he was loved just once more.

When he returned, and her husband was locked away, she held on as tightly as she could, even if only through long talks at dinner and taking an active interest in his life. What pleased her even more was that Matt was letting her hold on. In fact, he even took the time to ask her, every day, what they should talk about next.

Janet knew that Melanie O'Conner taught Matt more on the values of life than any mother ever could, and for that she was eternally grateful. The first time she met Melanie, the then-teenager had been behind bars, full of fire and spitting flames. Even so, Janet had never respected anyone more than that girl, and now, years later, not a single feeling had changed. A part of her wished the Treehouse was still alive, still filled with children. But the Treehouse was the past, and the present was with Matt, standing in the doorway to his bedroom, staring at his mother with his eyebrows raised as he waited for her to talk.

"Telephone," she told her son, and Matt took the phone.

"Hello?" He closed his bedroom door as his mother turned to head back down the stairs.

"Hey, Harper," Melanie's voice came through the line. "You busy?"

"No. Just doing some homework." Matt fell back on his bed.

"On a Saturday? Damn kid, that's dedication." On the other side of the line, Melanie laughed to herself. "Well listen, I have a few things to ask."

"Okay." Matt tossed the pencil onto the desk and closed his book, sitting up on his bed and leaning back against the headboard. "Ask me about what?"

Melanie opened a file on her table. "Do you know a girl named Kelly Mitchell? She's a junior at your school. Blonde hair, pretty, a bit of a bitch."

"Yeah, I know her." Matt rose to his feet. "How do you know her? She got sent to South Bay a few weeks ago."

"I know. Long story short, I'm working there now," Melanie replied. "I've been meeting with her for a about a week now, and I saw that she went to your school, so I thought you might know her."

Matt started to pace on his floor. "So you called just to ask if I knew her?"

"Well, no," Melanie admitted. "The girl's got a real attitude on her."

"Yeah, I know all about it," Matt said dryly.

"Anyway, I can't get anything out of her just yet, but I do have my suspicions."

"Suspicions about what?"

"She's got scars," Melanie said bluntly. "Bad ones, on her face, her neck, and I saw a couple on her left arm. Every time I ask about them, she changes the subject real casually, as if she's used to doing so. And when I talk about her stealing the car, she just gives me this weird look. I've never gotten her to actually admit to taking the car."

Pulling out the chair to his desk, Matt nodded to himself. "So what are you asking me exactly?"

"I'm asking you what you know about her."

Matt hesitated before replying. He didn't want to say something that may not have been true, no matter how sure he was. "I think she's abused," he finally confessed.

"That's what I was thinking too. Why do you say that?"

Matt pictured Kelly in his thoughts. "Because I could see it in her eyes, that look of fear and pain. It was the same look that every kid at the Treehouse had when they first arrived. Plus, this guy that lives down the street from her, Robbie Anderson, is friends with her and he told me he saw big bruises on her arms. He also met her stepfather and said he was a real dick."

"Did Kelly admit to anything?"

"No, Robbie said that she never really said anything, but kind of hinted at it." Matt remembered their conversation at his locker. "Has she said anything to you?"

"Nothing." Melanie picked up a sheet of paper in the file. "Look Matt, I need you to do something for me. I want you to watch the Mitchells. Kelly's got a sister, Danielle, who has brittle bone disease. I don't want her in danger, so watch carefully. If you find anything out, I'll have Tyler investigate further."

Matt tried to hide a smile, although he knew Melanie wouldn't be able to see it. "So you're asking me to investigate the Mitchells. I thought you didn't want me doing this."

"I don't," Melanie replied harshly. "To tell you the truth, I think you're too young, and so is everyone else. And I would have told you that if you had come to me. But the fact is, Matt, you didn't. So if you're going to go off and get all high and mighty about me asking you to help out, then forget it. I'll ask someone else."

"No! No, I'll do it." Matt was slightly taken aback. Melanie had never spoken to him so harshly. At the Treehouse, she was the perfect companion, always nice to him, always a friend. She had never spoken a harsh word, and even her scoldings were used in a tone that was more encouraging than threatening. But in becoming a Helping Hand, things were different. Melanie wasn't considering him a child anymore, as a little boy in need of love and smiles. Instead, she was frowning, she was reprimanding.

She was treating him like an equal.

CHAPTER 28

Tulsa, Oklahoma

Taryn felt nothing but nerves and anxiety racing around in her stomach, nearly making her sick as she fought to gain control of her emotions. Her head was spinning with possibilities, with consequences, strategies. She was doing her best to focus on the car ride to The Villages as her eyes scanned the floor, her mind taking a mental run-though of the kidnapping.

Next to her, Caleb sat calm and ready. He was confident that their plan would work. It had to work, for the life of a child depended on it. Sure, the mayor would do all he could to catch the people who took his daughter, but he wasn't worried about that. His main concern at the moment was the motion sensor lights.

"It's a good plan," he said to Taryn, unsure whether he was saying it to comfort her or himself. She turned to glance at him briefly before averting her eyes back down. He knew she was preparing herself for the job, like she always did. Psyching herself up, calming her frayed nerves. It was a long and tedious process, planning a kidnapping, and it put everyone on edge.

Brayden stopped the car two blocks from The Villages. Only three of the Helping Hands had come on this kidnapping. Taryn and Caleb could get the job done alone, but still needed a driver.

"If we're not back in forty minutes, leave without us," Caleb ordered, and shut the door as quietly as he could.

It took nearly ten minutes to reach the same wall of The Villages that they had jumped about a month ago. There was no light except for the moon and the dim glows from the homes they passed. Shadows from the trees hid the Helping Hands well.

They came to the home of George Livingston, stopping in the backyard. Taryn was no longer feeling her nerves or anxiety as she stood straight and still. Now all she was thinking about was the child and the job. She was focused; she was ready.

She was pumped with pure adrenaline and fear.

Caleb climbed the tree first, turning around to help Taryn up. They waited there for a full three minutes, making sure all the lights were off in the Livingston household. They had watched the mayor and his wife arrive home a little after midnight from their party. George had been leaning heavily on his wife, stumbling up the massive stone steps that led to the front porch. His wife had been staggering a bit herself, though not nearly as bad.

Caleb crept out onto the limb of the tree that hung over the roof. The drop to the roof was about six feet. Swinging down, his gloved hands grasping the limb, he touched his feet down silently. He grabbed Taryn as she too came down, settling her on the shingles without a sound. Crouched low, they made their way across the roof.

They came to the roof that was just above the balcony of the master bedroom. On her stomach, Taryn leaned over until she was bent at the waist, upside-down, her head and shoulders hanging over the edge. In her hands were a dim, very dim, flashlight and a pair of wire-cutters. Careful observation through powerful Army-designed binoculars, bought off the streets thanks to a black-market contact Taryn met a few years ago, had informed her and Caleb of the alarm wires that ran along the top of the French doors leading out to the balcony.

The flashlight in her mouth, she examined the wires closely. She could feel Caleb's hands gripping her ankles, and she could imagine an impatient glower on his face as she snapped the green wire in two, paused for a second, then got up when she was convinced she hadn't tripped an alarm. Both had already thought of the possibility of a silent alarm being set off, but they had done as much research as possible and were confident in taking the risk.

Quickly and quietly, the two slipped down onto the balcony, breathing fear and apprehension. But there was no turning back now, and with that in mind, Caleb snapped the lock on the doors as if he had done so all his life. Breaking into homes had never been a problem for him.

Taryn opened the door a crack, peering in and seeing nothing but blackness. She could hear the loud, steady snores of the mayor, and hoped his wife was sleeping just as soundly. Slowly, she crawled in on her hands and knees, Caleb doing the same. He closed the door behind them, and soon they were cloaked in darkness. They crept past the bed, freezing when they heard a slight rustling, then breathed out silent sighs when all went quiet again. Despite shaking hands, the two managed to creep silently, keeping their breathing to a minimum until they reached the hall.

Luckily, the door to their bedroom was open, and the Helping Hands went out into the hall. There wasn't one of the three dogs in sight, and for that they felt extremely fortunate. They knew that the pit bull was in the garage, where it always slept at night, but as for the other two, their whereabouts were unknown. In a place as big as the mayor's, it was next to impossible to locate the whereabouts of an animal that never made noise except when indicating an intruder.

Two doors down the hall was Mary's bedroom, and they went in without acknowledging the fancy décor and expensive knickknacks. The child was asleep, as they had figured she would be.

Switching on the dim flashlight, Taryn went to the bed and gently shook Mary's shoulders. The little girl stirred, and after a moment, she woke to see two strange faces peering down at her. Fear caught in her throat, her chest tightening with terror, and before Taryn could speak, Mary bolted upright in her bed.

"*Mommy!*"

The shout could have shattered the silence had it been made of glass. The little girl's high-pitched squeal caused Caleb to jump and pull back, while Taryn took her arm quickly yet gently.

"No, no, don't yell!" she whispered loudly. "We're here to help you!"

Mary struggled, her arms flinging out wildly. One of her fists connected with Taryn's jaw. Despite the child's small size, her fear made her strong. "*No!* No, no, *no!*" she shouted as fiercely as she could, resisting as best she could against her kidnappers.

"We know your daddy hits you!" Taryn whispered urgently, and at the comment, Mary went still. "We can help you so you'll never get hurt ever again." Taryn spun around when she heard footsteps in the hall. The sound tore the breath from her lungs, short rasps of air escaping to reveal the panic that was churning in her gut. With fear in her eyes, she looked back at Mary. "Don't tell anyone we're here. Pretend you had a nightmare."

As quickly as they could, fretting over whether or not the child would keep her mouth shut, Taryn and Caleb fell back into the bathroom. It was pure luck that the girl had her own. They had no sooner disappeared into the shadows when Denise Livingston appeared, tired and annoyed.

"What are you screaming about?" she demanded, a bothered glint in her eyes.

Mary didn't look over at the bathroom, where the strangers were hiding. Should she tell her mother about the people? They were strangers, after all, and they were in her room late at night. But, they knew about her father hitting her, something she had never told anyone before. They could be her guardian angels, like the man in the black suit talked about at church on Sundays. Angels who had come to help her and heal her when she got hurt, and she didn't think God would like it very much if she told on two of his angels and got them in trouble.

Her mother stared at her with her hands on her hips, waiting impatiently, her foot tapping against the floor. Mary could smell alcohol. She knew the smell well.

"I had a bad dream," she finally said after remembering the last time her father had smelled like that. "About a monster." In the bathroom, Taryn refrained from sighing in relief.

Denise let out a huff of air. "Monsters? Mary, you're old enough to know that monsters aren't real. You know that nightmares are only dreams and you don't have to go screaming every time you have one."

"I know," Mary replied quietly. "But I got scared."

Denise pushed back her hair. "Do you want a glass of water to help you sleep? I'll get you one," she said, despite Mary's protest. Heading into the bathroom, she flicked on the light and went to the sink.

Behind the bathroom door, Taryn and Caleb could do nothing but hold their breaths and wait. They couldn't see Denise, but could hear the water running and the mother muttering beneath her breath, something about enough being enough. Dread ran through Taryn's stomach, and Caleb wanted to look over at her, assure her that they were safe, but was afraid to move. The ten seconds that the light was on seemed like ten hours, with both their eyes wide and their bodies shaking. Taryn had the distinct impression that *this* was what Melanie had felt like just before the cops caught her, with terror racing among icy blood like fire with bone-splitting claws. Caleb, his eyes filled with alarm as he bit his bottom lip, tried to shrink back against the wall as he gripped Taryn's hand tightly.

Mary was relieved when her mother finally came out from the bathroom and handed her the water after shutting off the light.

"Now that you've ruined my sleep, I'll be downstairs reading a book," she told her daughter. "Don't you come down if you have another nightmare, you hear?" When Mary nodded, she turned and left the room.

Taryn and Caleb came out of the bathroom and went straight to Mary. They didn't take the time to laugh in relief or exchange their gratitude with the child. Instead, they explained who they were and where they could take her. When Mary agreed to go, saying something about angels and heaven, they slipped out of her bedroom. With Denise gone and George still snoring away, they walked through the room easily and hoisted one another onto the roof. The climb across the limb and down the tree was difficult, but they made it. It wasn't until they had reached Brayden that Taryn and Caleb dared to even consider their nerves.

"I was about to leave. What took you guys so long?" Brayden accused when they got into the car and he pulled out onto the street. "What happened in there?"

Taryn and Caleb didn't reply, but instead looked at one another and burst into laughter, hysterical laughter brought on only by fear and relief.

As far as they were concerned, they had just pulled off the greatest kidnapping in Helping Hand history.

CHAPTER 29

South Bay Juvenile Detention Camp.

"You know, Kelly, we've been meeting almost every day for over three weeks now, and I am yet to find out why you're actually here."

"I guess that makes you a crappy counselor."

Melanie huffed. "Keep trying, Kelly. Maybe one day you'll have the tough-guy thing down." She stared across her desk as Kelly Mitchell crossed her arms defiantly. "But for now, let's drop the bullshit. I can see right through it."

"I don't know why you find my attitude so offensive," Kelly said indifferently. "I'm no more a bitch than you."

"I'm going to excuse that last remark, simply because I know you're only pretending to hate me." Melanie rose and walked around her desk, leaning against it when she stood in front of Kelly. "You wanna know the difference between me and you?"

"No, but you're going to tell me anyway."

"Right. I am." Melanie wasn't the least bit affected by Kelly's harsh replies. "You see, we both have a bit of an attitude problem. Let's start with mine. I grew up on the streets. That's where *my* attitude came from. You think I put on some hard-hitting face just to impress a few junkies and scare away reporters? Hell no. And do you think all these scars came from my father?" She gestured to her face. "No, these are because of *my* attitude, because I thought I was brave and dangerous, some hard line chick from the streets. And I was, Kelly." Pushing herself from the desk, Melanie started to pace. "The things I say and do are said and done because they're the only way I've ever known. You say things to push people away, and you do certain things to make sure those people stay away. My attitude is real, yours is a cover-up for something you don't want people to see."

"What could I—"

"Now I don't know what that thing is," Melanie continued, "but I can promise you that one way or another I will find out. Now, *I* think you're acting like this because you don't want to go home. So, you can do one of two things. One, you can tell me why you stole that car and save us a bunch of time and energy, or two, you can stay silent. Which, in a nutshell, means I'm going to have to spend more time talking to your friend Robbie Anderson." Melanie knew the name would cause a reaction from Kelly, and she was proved correct when Kelly leapt to her feet.

118

"What?" she cried, her face flushed with anger. "You talked to him! Why? He's got nothing to do with this! He knows *nothing* about me!"

"Why get so defensive then?" Melanie asked calmly as she stopped pacing. "You have something to hide?"

"Why are you so convinced I have something to hide?" Kelly yelled, throwing out her arms in frustration. She was so over it, so tired of having to meet with some counselor who always thought there was something wrong with her.

"You know what I think? I think you want me to admit to something so you can keep me here forever! You want to *torment* me, not help me!"

"Sit down." The order was crisp and demanding. Kelly sat, afraid not to obey the command, and Melanie crossed her arms with deliberate slowness, making it obvious that she wouldn't tolerate such an outburst. She walked back in front of Kelly, who was breathing hard. "You want to know what else I think? I think that you didn't steal that car and that those drugs weren't yours."

Kelly started to reply, then changed her mind and instead closed her mouth. She had been expecting Melanie to yell and scold, but the calm confession took her by surprise. "You... you don't think I did all that stuff?"

"Well, I believe that you ran away. My guess is that you were running from something, but I can't be sure of that unless you tell me." Melanie felt that she was getting closer to Kelly admitting the truth, so she kept on pushing. "All I know is what Robbie told me, what I read in your file, what you've told me, and some of what you haven't. I can see those scars on your face just as plainly as you can see mine. Kelly, if you trust me, I can help you. And I don't mean just in here."

Kelly lifted her eyes to meet Melanie's, a tear threatening to slip down her cheek. "You mean... the Helping Hands?" she asked, her voice wavering slightly. Melanie didn't move, but something in her eyes affirmed her question. "How can the Helping Hands help me? I'm not a little kid anymore."

"Let's play a game." Melanie held up a hand and began her offer. "I'm going to ask you a series of questions. If I think your answers are honest, then you get a Helping Hand. When you get five Helping Hands, you have a gang. With a gang, I can guarantee that you and your sister will be safe. What do you say?"

Kelly thought about the proposition. She was about to disagree until she pictured Danielle, all alone with Jeffrey and his iron fist. "Fine."

Melanie smiled, knowing that Kelly cared more about her sister than she did herself, and therefore would do what it took to keep her safe. "Okay, question one. Where are your scars from?"

Kelly was surprised by the bluntness of the question. She'd expected something less personal, like where she grew up. She cleared her throat nervously, hesitating before replying. "Um, the one on my temple is from a wrench, and on my nose is from a piece of glass. The one on my arm is from a ring."

Melanie looked down at the floor before continuing, shuffling her feet a little. "Who gave them to you?"

"Jeffrey," Kelly whispered. "My stepfather."

Melanie remembered the picture of Jeffrey Ponder that had been in the file. He looked like a decent family man, but apparently looks were deceiving. "We've established the fact that you didn't steal a car. So why are you really here?"

"Jeffrey set me up. My car broke down so he told me to drive his. I should have known he was up to something." Kelly's voice went cold. "He probably broke my car himself just so he could get my prints on his. And I know he planted the drugs. He wanted to get rid of me. He told me he would."

And he did, Melanie thought grimly. "Kelly, do you trust me enough to help you?"

Kelly considered the question, thinking back to all the articles she had read on Melanie O'Conner, most of the reporters claiming that the woman was nothing more than a deceitful scoundrel who deserved to rot in prison. The photos confirmed any suspicions of her being a rough-around-the-edges bitch from Hell, and Kelly recalled getting chilled by the narrow green eyes. Everyone said she was a criminal, someone who would stab her best friend in the back if the money was right, yet here she was, claiming that she was only interested in helping. Suddenly those eyes didn't seem so scary. Now it was just the question of whether or not the media knew what it was talking about.

"I don't know," Kelly replied honestly. "No one can ever really trust anyone." She lowered her eyes to her hands, which she was wringing together.

"That's not true," Melanie said quietly, honestly. "I used to think that, when I was younger. That's why I kept things hidden. But you want to know something? I found someone I can trust."

"Who?"

"At the time, he was my best friend. Now, for some weird reason I agreed to marry him." She gave a small smile when Kelly's eyes widened.

"Really? Who is he?"

"His name's... Mel." Melanie caught herself before saying Tyler.

"Mel and Melanie?"

"It's a long story." Melanie waved a hand. "But the point is, there are people who you can trust with your secrets. Mel was the person I could trust, and I still can. And you seem to trust your friend Robbie," she pointed out, and Kelly nodded.

"He was nice to me for some reason," she remembered. "I told him stuff. I don't know why. It just sort of happened, you know? One day I was slamming his fingers in my locker and the next I was calling him to sneak out in the middle of the night."

Melanie crossed her arms and observed the ceiling, deciding to ask her final question. "So why didn't you ever tell anyone?"

Shrugging, Kelly dropped her shoulders with a sigh. "It's embarrassing," she answered. "You know how it is." Melanie nodded in understanding. "And I didn't want to be taken away to some foster home or something because then me and Danielle would be separated. I always put myself in front of her, pissed him off whenever he was drunk so he wouldn't go after her. I mean, one hit from Jeffrey and Danielle could break every bone in her face. Mom always takes his side."

"So it's all up to you," Melanie concluded, and Kelly conceded by lowering her eyes dejectedly. "You know, Kelly, sometimes it's okay to care more about yourself than about others. I understand what you say about Danielle, and I understand that you're doing this whole attitude thing because you don't want to go home, but by not telling anyone, you still put her at risk because you never really know if he's going to go after her. And now, you're stuck in here while she's alone."

"I know." Kelly buried her head in her hands. "If anything happens to her, I'll never forgive myself."

"It's not up to you," Melanie tried to comfort her. "But I can promise you that as we speak, she is being watched. If anything happens, they will get her out of there."

"Do you promise?" Her voice was muffled by her hands.

Melanie nodded. "I swear. And in the meantime, I want you to get rid of this attitude bullshit and straighten up. Be nice, follow the rules, and I'll see what I can do about getting you out of here."

"How? I thought my sentence was like a year or something."

"Or something. But technically since you didn't do any of the things you were accused of doing, except for sneaking out, you really have no reason to be here. Like I said, I'll see what I can do."

Kelly nodded and rose from the chair. As Kelly left, a guard appeared at her side while she wiped her eyes and led her out of the office. Sergeant Brian Hawkins watched the scene from down the hall, staring after Kelly as she passed. He turned to Melanie, his eyebrows lifted as he stepped closer to the new counselor.

"You made her cry." His voice was flabbergasted. "I spent over a month, day in and day out, trying to break that girl down and nothing worked. Two hours a day with you and she's crying. You broke her."

"Tears mean someone's been defeated," Melanie said quietly, and Hawkins nodded with a smile.

"Exactly. You've won."

Wondering how he could possibly applaud the tears of a tortured girl, Melanie fell into her chair behind her desk and lowered her head. "No, Hawkins, I haven't."

F.B.I. Headquarters, California

Zack Corwin tossed a file down disgustedly onto Jay Neilson's desk, jabbing a finger down upon it to draw attention to the name. "Mary Livingston. Mary Livingston, daughter of the goddamn *mayor* of Tulsa, Oklahoma."

"I thought we were only covering the San Francisco gang," Jay said carefully with a frown, observing the photo of the girl.

"We are, but if the Oklahoma branch is capable of taking the mayor's kid, then our branch can't be too far behind!" Zack threw out his arms. "Which means, we're going to have to work harder."

Jay opened the file, taking in the information, the picture of the child, scanning an article for a note on the message left behind. When he didn't find one, or even a single mention of the Helping Hand name, he started to question his partner's sanity.

"Wait a second, boss. This doesn't say anything about any Helping Hand gang. It just says the girl was kidnapped. What makes you think it wasn't done by someone else?"

"Because," Corwin snapped, hands on his hips, "there's a gang that surfaced not twenty miles from Tulsa about a year after O'Conner's arrest. And this kidnapping, it was done in the middle of the night. They got through a state-of-the-art alarm system, and hell, they walked right through the master bedroom twice to get the girl! There is no way in Hell that this was anything other than a Helping Hand job."

"Then why didn't the mayor hand over the message?"

Corwin sighed and wondered just what exactly his superiors had been thinking when they thought Neilson had what it took to be his partner. "Think about it, Jay. If you were the mayor of Tulsa, would you want everyone to know that you're a child abuser?"

"No," Neilson answered when he saw things from his partner's point of view. "So what do you propose we do?"

Zack's smile was slow and determined, and his eyes narrowed. "We're going to pay our friend Melanie O'Conner a little visit."

CHAPTER 30

Collinsville, California

It was a hot day in California, muggy and filled with buzzing insects that swarmed together in the stiff air. There was a light wind, a warm wind that wasn't the least bit comforting to the surrounding sweltering atmosphere.

Safe from the heat and afternoon insects, Melanie stood in the bathroom of her new home, staring at her stomach as she stared at it with a frown. She had put on weight in the last year, since Foster's attack, Wess's death, her new job. She wasn't really one to worry about her appearance, but some things weren't easily ignored. There was so much stressing her out that she could feel the anvil on her shoulders, constantly pushing her down.

She and stress had never really gotten along, and she wasn't one who dealt with it easily. Apparently, the strain that had been put on her life for the past few years had gotten to her, and she wasn't the least bit happy about it. Even being in prison hadn't been as bad as living a so-called 'normal' life. At least in jail there wasn't the constant hassle of work and bills and earning a decent living in order to be deemed a respectable member of society.

It was so much easier being a criminal.

She turned to the side, lifting her shirt to observe her stomach in the mirror and grimacing. That was how Tyler saw her when he entered the bathroom, standing with her shirt lifted and a glower on her face.

"Mind if I ask what's up?" he asked casually while biting back a laugh, causing Melanie to lower her shirt and glare up at him with a scowl.

"I've gained weight, that's what," she replied, crossing her arms.

"Really?" Tyler peered at her toned stomach through narrowed, searching eyes, then moved his head as though taking in the rest of her body. "Where?"

"Everywhere. And I blame it on you."

"Me?" Tyler repeated incredulously, silently wondering why she was so concerned with how she looked. She never cared about her appearance before, and couldn't have weighed more than one-twenty had she of been dunked in a pit of mud. And what weight she had was pure muscle. "How is you gaining weight my fault?"

"Because you insisted that I come live with you and Fred and a maid who cooks for an army of ten thousand. That's how." She brushed past him, but Tyler knew that her sharp comment was in fun. With a sly grin, he followed her as she pulled on her shoes.

"Hey, maybe you're pregnant."

He fully expected the fierce scowl that she threw at him, narrowing her eyes as she shook her head. "Yeah right, Mason. I already have an aggravating and stubborn Mel Scotford on my hands. Why the hell would I want an aggravating and stubborn Mel Scotford junior?"

Tyler gave a small laugh and shrugged, walking closer to Melanie as she stood up straight, the top of her head not even reaching his chin. He looked like a giant next to her, with his height and well-developed muscle, but there was no doubt in his mind that she could wipe his slate clean if she wanted to.

He crossed his arms and stared at her defiantly, deliberately picking a fight. "Oh yeah?" he challenged. "It could just as easily go the other way. Maybe I don't want to have to go chase'n after another know-it-all junkie running the streets in the middle of the night."

Melanie hid a smile as she set her jaw. She knew exactly what he was doing. He loved to get her all riled up so he could go after her and engage in some form of adolescent and very hands-on wrestling match. He always used bits from her past to throw back at her, but she didn't mind it coming from him, or from Taryn and Caleb. In a way, she was proud of her past. Sure, she had done some things that weren't exactly honorable or admirable, but she wouldn't trade her life for anything.

Instead of walking away, Melanie stared at Tyler for a long moment, then caught him off guard by lightly sending her right fist directly into his gut. Tyler jumped more out of surprise than pain, then caught Melanie as she stepped around him. She pulled her arm, but he tightened his hold and pushed her out of the bathroom and into the bedroom they shared.

"Come on. Let go." Struggling was useless. She despised the bitter reality that Tyler was so much stronger, because it meant she was helpless when he took hold of her.

Tyler fell back with Melanie onto the bed, holding her arms above her head. He started to kiss her, but pulled back when she turned her head to the side. He had expected her to do so, which was why he didn't let that stop him and went for her neck instead, going for the spots he knew would have her melting beneath his mouth and hands.

"Tyler," Melanie managed to free one of her wrists and put her hand on his shoulder, trying her hardest to ignore the fact that her thoughts were starting to cloud, "as much as I'd like to continue with this little plan of yours—"

"Don't talk." He kissed her before she could reply, feeling her fingers curl around his shirt. He ran his own down the arm he still had extended above her head, down the side of her neck, her side, until they reached the bottom of her shirt. She gave herself to him for a moment, allowing them both a brief but cherished time of tenderness and passion.

When she grudgingly forced herself to pull away, Melanie attempted to push Tyler off of her and hating the fact that he knew just what to do to keep her silent and willing.

"Tyler, seriously… seriously, we should get downstairs."

"Why?"

"Because we're about to have company."

Tyler paused with his lips on Melanie's shoulder, refusing to move and not allowing Melanie to rise either. "How do you know we're gonna have company?" he asked, lifting his head enough so that he could mumble his muffled response against her flesh.

Melanie gestured to the window. "A car just pulled up." She was vaguely surprised that Tyler hadn't heard the car as well.

Then again, she considered, *he* is *particularly busy at the moment.*

Stealing a final kiss and taking a moment to collect himself, Tyler headed over to the window, stepping around the bags that were packed for the Denver trip they were making the next morning. He was impressed to see that a car had in fact pulled up in front of their house. Turning to Melanie, he nodded and raised his eyebrows. "I knew I wanted to marry you for a reason."

"You mean other than the sex guarantee?"

"Sex? What sex?" He put his hands on his hips and stared at her frankly. "No, I was referring to another reason."

"And what reason is that?"

Tyler shrugged and fought a grin. "Well, I always wanted a dog."

Letting out a small snarl of provoked annoyance, Melanie lunged at him and attempted a shove before he caught her in a tight hug, pressing his mouth to hers. Then they headed down the stairs to meet their company.

Zack Corwin and Jay Neilson stepped from their car and out onto the curb of Melanie and Tyler's new home. They glanced over at one another, nodding once before heading up the front walk in silent unison. Zack was positive that both Melanie and Tyler would be there, for it was Sunday, Melanie's official day off and the day when Tyler went in later in the afternoon, if he went in at all. He had done his research on the couple, finding out every possible detail of their daily and personal lives, and had done a good job at that.

Reaching the front door, Corwin twisted the doorknob only to find that it was locked. He knocked loud and hard, not taking a step back when he heard the locks being turned. As the door opened and Melanie's face appeared, Zack brushed by her, holding up his badge and the search warrant he had obtained while entering the house.

"Hey!" Melanie cried when the agent shoved her back as he swept by. "What the hell do you think you're doing? Corwin! Get the hell out of my house!"

"You won't tell us what we want to know, so we'll have to find out our own way." Zack began sifting through a stack of papers on the table, ignoring the footsteps he heard coming quickly down the stairs as Jay started investigating one of the guest bedrooms.

"Who the hell do you think you are coming into my house?" Tyler's deep and booming voice demanded. He came up next to Melanie, arms crossed threateningly. "You have no right being here!"

"Mr. Scotford, we're the F.B.I., meaning that we have the right to serve warrants, carry firearms, and make arrests, the last of which there may be a very good possibility of us doing." Finding nothing in the papers, Zack faced the two. He held out a folder that contained the information, retracting his hand and shrugging when Melanie simply glared at him. "We can do this the easy way or the hard way. Either tell me what I want to know, or I'll search the house top to bottom. I have the warrant right here and therefore I am granted the right to search every goddamn nook and cranny, every locked cabinet and what's the most fun for me, every sealed-shut safe."

Melanie wasn't the least bit intimidated when he shoved the warrant in her face. She didn't care what they poked their noses into, because the agents wouldn't find anything in the house. Neither she nor Tyler kept anything that had to do with the Helping Hands anywhere in any cranny, cabinet, or safe. "You can search the house, but you won't find anything you're looking for, Corwin," she told him defiantly.

"I'll be the judge of that."

"This is bullshit," Tyler put in, stepping forward. "You have no reason to think Melanie is involved with the Helping Hands anymore. Why the hell don't you just leave her alone?"

Zack whirled around from the table, facing Melanie with squared shoulders and narrowed eyes. "We have task forces everywhere working on the kidnappings by the Helping Hands. Each kidnapping is being picked apart piece by piece, getting us that much closer to discovering identities. Every gang will be caught. It's only a matter of time."

"Well, if and when they're caught, it won't be my problem," Melanie replied coolly.

"Did you know that the D.E.A. was about to investigate you for all your drug crimes when you were arrested?" Zack asked while pointing at Melanie. "That's right, the D.E.A. You could have gotten the death penalty, especially if they had found anything out about you, what you used to do on the streets."

Melanie couldn't help the smile that crossed her face. "The D.E.A.?" she repeated. "The Drug Enforcement Administration was going to try and take a stab at my past. Damn," she laughed, "I didn't realize I was so popular." Uncrossing her arms and placing her hands on her hips, she smirked at the agent. "And besides that, I *did* nearly receive the death penalty, in part to my drug past, when I was arrested, before I had the second trial. Don't you watch the news?"

"Downstairs is clean, from what I've searched so far," Jay announced, cutting off Corwin as he started to reply. "You want me to start the upstairs or finish down here?"

"Neither." Zack's answer was short and crypt. "We're done here. We're done," he repeated when Jay started to argue. Zack stepped closer to Melanie, noting that she so much as a bat an eye. "Consider this a warning. I'll catch you in the end, and I won't be as lenient as the court system was to you."

"Fair enough." Melanie pointed to the door. "Now get the fuck out of my house."

Chapter 31

Denver, Colorado

A light snow fell from the gray, clouded afternoon sky that hovered over the white-peaked Rocky Mountains. The wind blew in a chilly breeze, lifting and twirling them about the air. White, camouflaged rabbits nibbled on what little plant life they could find, playing among the valleys of snow like children on a day off from school.

Among the surrounding environment, bordered by trees and encircled by the rabbits, stood a lone cabin, windows crusted with the frost of winter. The narrow dirt path that led to the driveway was blanketed in white, and only someone with extensive knowledge of its existence would know where to find it.

Such was the case with Melanie O'Conner. With Tyler following close behind, they hiked up the mountain, cheeks and noses red from the cold.

"How much longer?" Tyler panted out, trudging along in her footsteps. "I think I have icicles in my lungs."

"We're almost there," Melanie insisted, keeping her eyes forward.

"That's what you said a half-hour ago."

"No, a half-hour ago I said we'll be there soon. There's a difference."

Tyler rolled his eyes and kept up the steady pace, not arguing because he could hear the strain in her voice that wasn't caused by the cold or hike.

As Melanie promised, they reached the cabin soon. For a moment Tyler merely stared at it, imagining his departed friend. He had visited the cabin only once before, when Wess's ashes were brought up to be buried in the mountains.

Melanie took in a nervous breath as she pushed the door open. The familiar sight of the cabin rushed to her eyes, bringing to them an instant pool of water. She dropped her bag onto the floor and entered the cabin, Tyler doing the same. Although he didn't have the same connection to the cabin as Melanie did, he still got a powerful sense of his deceased friend.

"He never was one much for tidiness," Tyler joked lightly as he glanced around at the mess, likely the result of squatters and wildlife that found their way in. He looked over at Melanie, who was standing with her back to him, her arms wrapped around herself as she shivered slightly. She didn't reply, but instead turned suddenly and walked down the hall.

Melanie peered into her old bedroom, seeing the heavy quilt, the rumpled pillows, and hearing the shutters banging against the wall, still loose. She didn't enter the room; she didn't have to, nor did she want to.

As she walked slowly down the hall, she pictured herself padding across the carpet, chilly in the late-night air as she headed for Wess's room, trembling from a nightmare about Evan. As they did then, her feet guided her to his room, his former bedroom. The door was closed, and Melanie hesitated before opening it.

The door swung open easily, and Melanie was slammed with a flood of memories. It had been in this room where they became more than friends, shared more than a common interest of just the Helping Hands. It was here that Melanie had allowed herself to trust another person, to let someone else into her life after Tyler pushed her away. This room was the former home of someone so close to her heart.

Melanie swallowed heavily as she pictured Wess sitting at the small table in his room, writing down plans for a kidnapping. She could hear his deep and soothing voice as he scolded Dylan for calling early in the morning. If she tried hard enough, she could catch a whiff of his scent in the air. As she scanned the room, she saw one of Wess's old shirts thrown across the back of a chair. She took in a wavering breath, a sob nearly escaping her as she closed her eyes, picturing the two of them strolling down the street, arm-in-arm. They were laughing, smiling, for once enjoying a night free of worries. She jumped when the sound of a gunshot exploded in her ears, and her eyes flew open to see the bedroom blur as the memory sliced through her heart.

Melanie rubbed her arms, shivering and walking over to the bed. She ran a hand over the thick blanket. She was overwhelmed by the recollections, by the pain and despair she felt for her departed friend. Wess had been one of her best friends, had always been there for her. He had been quick to back her up, had given up his life in order to save hers.

She loved him still, as much as she could ever possibly love a friend. She'd never been *in* love with him, that much she knew. She had a feeling Wess knew that as well, but none of it mattered anymore. He was gone, and the only person she could blame was herself. It was her project, her arrogance, that led to this.

Pulling back the blanket, Melanie lowered herself onto the bed, lying down and resting her head onto the pillow. The scent of Wess, his cologne, his very self, filled her, though she wasn't sure if it was real or imagined. Pulling the blanket up to her chin and curling herself into a ball, Melanie allowed the tears to overcome her and she cried quietly into the pillow.

Tyler stood in the doorway, peering across the room at Melanie. He had watched the entire scene. It would be useless, he could plainly see, to try and comfort her. There wasn't anything he could say or do to help. She had never let herself grieve in the past, fighting to remain strong and proud. This was her time to let it all go, to forgive herself for Wess's death, to try to forget. He wasn't sure if Melanie would ever be able to forgive herself.

Turning from the sight, Tyler lowered his eyes sadly and headed into the second bedroom, exhausted and defeated.

The next morning was bright, clear, and crisp. White-peaked mountains decorated the horizon, but Melanie hardly noticed them as she sat before Wess's grave, her hands clasped around her knees.

It hadn't taken her any time at all to find his grave. Even with the wind and cold, she pushed the fallen snow away from the makeshift headstone and sat down upon the ground, not caring as her pants soaked up the snow. Her eyes scanned the words etched into the stone. His names stretched across, his birth name of Josh Tucker, teenage identity of Wess Porter, and his last pseudonym, Kyle Lindel. Three different identities for three different lives of one person. She ran her fingers over his name, then down to her own. She, Tyler, Taryn, and Caleb had all scratched their names into the headstone.

"It's been a long ride, Wess," Melanie said quietly. "Full of all those goddamn bumps." She picked at a tuft of grass she had unburied. "Matt Harper started a new gang. Can you believe it? With Isaac, Jimmy, and Carrie. And Leighann Cross, but you never met her. They're doing a good job, I guess, but I still don't want them being a gang. I don't know what I'd do if something happened to them, you know?" She shrugged and pushed the thought of them failing from her mind. "And I got a new job. Counselor at South Bay. Never would have seen that one coming, huh?" She looked up at the stone, wishing it were Wess instead.

"Me and Tyler, we, um, we're getting married." She rubbed the ring on her finger. "But I guess you always knew that would happen. Hell, everyone else did." She laughed and shook her head, her eyes watering. She swallowed hard, reaching out to run her fingers over Wess's name again.

"I miss you, Wess," she whispered. "So much. So does everyone else. It's so different without you… What happened, you know? We had it all figured out, and it was all going great. Then… this." She gestured to the tombstone. "It's down to four now… Your gang's doing an amazing job, by the way. They're really pulling it all off. You'd be proud of them."

Her attempts to keep back what was really bothering her were failing as she stared at Wess's name. "I'm so sorry, Wess," she whispered hoarsely. "I am so sorry. This is all my fault. It wasn't meant for you." The bullet should have ripped through her chest instead of his, and everyone knew it.

"I wish I could take it all back, you know? Go back and change what… what happened." Her throat clutched with sobs. "I'm—no, I'm not going to cry. You once said that Melanie O'Conner doesn't cry. You wanted me to be strong, so I will." She sniffed back her tears and wiped her eyes, rising to her knees.

"Happy birthday, Wess." Her voice was quiet and filled with tears as she rose to her feet. "I'll be back. I promise." She looked up to see Tyler heading over to her, and she offered a small smile once he approached.

"Are you okay?" he asked, gently taking her arm when he saw the redness of her eyes. He ran a finger down her cheek to wipe away a lone tear.

"I'm fine. I just want to be alone for a little while," Melanie replied, and Tyler nodded. She walked away, and he went to Wess's grave.

"Hey man, how's it going? You look good. Strong, well-rested." He smiled and squatted down in front of the grave. "I guess Melanie just talked to you. Bet you got an earful from that girl, huh?" He smiled, wondering to himself what Melanie had said. He was sure he would never find out because he would never ask and she would never tell.

"Yeah, she's been wanting to come up here. This place really means a lot to her, in more ways than one." He peered around for a moment with a frown, feeling slightly foolish to be talking to air. "She probably told you we're getting married. Finally, you know?"

He shook his head, his smile dropping. "I swear, man. I don't know what I'm getting myself into. Right now, it's just like it was when we were teenagers. You know, having the love-hate relationship, not really depending on one another for a whole lot, being with each other but not really *with* each other, you know? Even though we're engaged, it still feels that way. The only difference is that now we're sleeping together." He shrugged and ran his fingers through his hair, wondering what Wess would have said had he been alive. He had always been the best at giving advice.

"Marriage, though, man it's a big step. But it'll all work out. I mean, we fight a lot and all, but I love her. She's worth everything, you know? Well, I guess you do." He lowered his head and toyed with his shoelaces.

"I um, wanted to tell you something." Tyler didn't look up. "Melanie, she... she blames herself for your death. She can't forgive herself. She told me last year that she should have been strong enough to fight her own battle. I know as well as you do that what happened wasn't anybody's fault but William Foster's, but she can't accept that. I don't know if I believe in the whole spirit and ghost thing, but if by some chance you can hear me and you are, like, with us or something, maybe you help her out. It's not a burden she should have to carry."

"Happy birthday, man," Tyler said, standing and staring down at the grave. "I'll talk to you later."

Chapter 32

South Bay Juvenile Detention Camp

Kelly grimaced as she swallowed a mouthful of mashed potatoes. Never had she eaten such disgusting food than at South Bay. Things that were supposed to be soft were crunchy, crunchy things were disturbingly soft, and the meat seemed almost watery. Oddly enough, as she stared down at her plate, she found herself wishing she could go home.

Even if that meant facing Jeffrey.

"So I hear you're meet'n with Melanie O'Conner," Jessica Baily said as she sat down next to Kelly. "She a real bitch or what?"

Kelly glanced over at Jessica, who had been sent to the camp after punching a teacher. She shrugged. "Kinda. She thinks she knows everything there is to know and she's always telling me that I'd never make it on the streets. She tries to act all bad-ass about everything, but she ain't bad once you really start talking to her."

"You actually talk to your counselor?" Jessica asked incredulously. "Why?"

"Because it gets me out of here faster than not talking, that's why," Kelly replied quickly and callously, and Jessica held up her hands.

"Okay, jeez."

With a sigh, Kelly rose from the table and threw away the rest of her lunch. She started for the restrooms that she had to clean for her daily chores, ignoring the shouts and everyday arguments from the girls around her, but stopped when her name was called out. She turned to see Sergeant Hawkins heading over to her, his stride steady and filled with a haughty confidence that she was learning to despise. It didn't matter that she was supposed to be respectful in order to go home, because the fact of the matter was, she hated the man.

Kelly sighed, rolled her eyes, and faced the Sergeant with her hands on her hips. "I have a lot of chores to do, *Sergeant.*"

"Miss Mitchell, come with me." He ignored her mocking tone and led her to his office silently, and Kelly followed without a single question or protest. It wasn't worth fighting him anymore. "I have some good news for you," Hawkins informed her as he closed the door to his office, gesturing for Kelly to sit.

"What kind of good news?"

"You're being released," Hawkins said, and Kelly fell silent as she struggled to remember if her counselor had said anything about her release. "Two days, you're going home. You will be on probation, more or less, for six months. If you screw up in that time, you're coming back."

Kelly shook her head, rising from the chair. "How am I able to go home?"

"I spoke with your counselor, Miss O'Conner, and she did a lot of smooth and fast talking and luckily for you that's something she's good at. We came to an agreement that you would be released on the account that she serves as your probation officer herself."

"And where is she now?" She hadn't had a meeting with her counselor in a few days. Not that it bothered her, but did arouse a little curiosity.

"She took a few days off for personal reasons. Now, if you'll have a seat, we'll discuss your release."

The Lake, California

"Guess what." Matt sat down at the kitchen table, tossing a newspaper in front of Leighann. "Taryn and Caleb got the mayor's kid. The *mayor*. Can you believe that?"

At Leighann's blank stare, Isaac reached over and took the paper. "Taryn and Caleb, you know. Part of the original gang," he said to her meanly. With a shake if his head, he turned his eyes to the paper, ignoring the glare from Matt. She may be Matt's girlfriend, or friend with benefits, or whatever the hell she was, but that didn't mean he had to like her.

In fact, he hadn't liked her since the moment he met her. A dirty-blonde-haired girl with an alcoholic mother and a father who treated her like a princess, gave her anything she could ever possibly want, and let her get away with everything. She didn't know anything about fear, about pain. He knew what it was like to be on the verge of death, then to be saved by people who were watching over him like five guardian angels. Leighann had lived with the drunken temper of her mother for less than two years. He had known what a fist was since he was a year old.

Isaac could still remember every detail of his father, his face, his eyes that burned with cold fury, his mouth that always seemed to be shouting curses and threats. He could still see his blood smeared across his fingers, dripping down onto the floor, could feel it scabbing across his lip. More importantly, he could still remember that night when he had been taken away, when hope conquered death and he had trusted his life in the hands of strangers. Maybe it was his youth and naivety that made him trust the Helping Hands, at the time people who were complete strangers. Maybe it was simply the fact that he didn't care if he died.

Either way, he owed Melanie O'Conner and her gang more than he could ever even begin to offer.

Which was the exactly the reason why he didn't want Leighann Cross in his gang. She hadn't been a child of the Treehouse. She didn't have that special bond that he and the others shared. But she and Matt had a thing for each other, and Matt was the leader of the gang, and it would be useless to argue. Although he was two years older than Matt and a good deal stronger, not to mention meaner, he still respected the first child of the Treehouse and would therefore tolerate Leighann. After all, Matt had taken the time to come to him, to track him down, and for the first time since Melanie had been taken away from them all, he wasn't ignored or cast aside.

Upon his return home after leaving the Treehouse, Isaac lived with an alcoholic mother who hid her habit well. The social workers who came to investigate never caught on, and even when Melanie contacted him after being released from prison he never said a word. He didn't tell her anything because he knew what she would do, and he refused to allow his savior to get into any more trouble on his behalf. Besides, his mother never laid a hand on him. He could deal with one parent who was never there emotionally rather than one who was always there physically.

Once he hit seventeen he walked away and never looked back, working odd jobs here and there to pay for his rides to whatever destination he had chosen for the time being. Finally he settled in upstate California and was working at a scrap yard when one day Matt Harper walked in with the same friendly smile he'd always had. It had been a quick and easy conversation, Isaac remembered. No beating around the bush, no bullshit.

"*I'm starting a gang in San Francisco,*" Matt had said plainly. "*I was wondering if you wanted to be a part of it.*"

Less than two minutes later, Isaac was an official member of the Helping Hands.

"So, Mayor Livingston," he said, skimming the article. "Says here the kidnappers must have gone in from the roof since none of the lights or alarms went off, and they walked right through the master bedroom." With a grin, he looked up at Matt. "Caleb always was one brave bastard."

"So what'd the message say that they left behind?" Carry Valentine asked, taking a banana from the bowl on the center of the table and peeling back the outer coating.

Isaac read further down the article, then shook his head. "It doesn't say. Actually, the article doesn't even mention that the Helping Hands were the ones who took the kid."

"What?" Matt took the paper back, rereading it. He knew that Caleb and Taryn were the ones because he had talked to Melanie a few days earlier. But he saw that Isaac was right.

"How could they not know?" Carry inquired. "The only way the media wouldn't find out is if—"

"He didn't tell anyone," Isaac finished, then sighed. "The arrogant son-if-a-bitch didn't tell anyone because he knew he'd go to jail. He must have hidden the message. But hey, that's cool. I talked to Caleb. It said, 'That was way too easy, The Helping Hands.' Bastards," he added, more to himself as he laughed.

"Leave it to them to say something like that." Matt wasn't really bothered by the fact that Livingston hid the note from the police. It wasn't unusual for a guardian to lie about their child being taken by a Helping Hand, especially now that people knew the reason why children were taken.

"So what does the paper say she suffered from?" Leighann asked, getting a stare from Isaac that told her he thought she was an idiot. She bit her bottom lip and lowered her eyes as he answered in the bitter tone that he always used with her.

"It doesn't say here, in a newspaper article written by a reporter who knows nothing about a little girl suffering from child abuse, Leighann," he answered coolly, getting another glare from Matt. Sighing, he shrugged and dropped the attitude. "But when I talked to Caleb a few days ago he said it was starvation and neglect."

In unison, Matt, Carry, and Isaac turned to glance at Jimmy Fencles, who was sitting silently at the end of the table. He let out a quiet breath of air when he heard the word *starvation*. His heart went out to the child.

He knew what that was like, not having food or water, living each day with a pain in his stomach that felt as though thousands of tiny chainsaws were cutting up his guts. He could remember throwing up a green, sticky liquid, and there had been times when he went days without going to the bathroom. If he tried hard enough, he could still feel the way his skin had to stretch over his bones, and how every day he was dizzy, tired, and sick.

Then there had been that one night when he had been lying in bed, all but passed out from the pain in his belly and head. His vision had been blurry, his limbs weak, and the only thing he could think about was food. Suddenly, two shadows appeared from the darkness. He hadn't had the energy to scream or fight when they simply picked him up and carried him out his bedroom window, through his backyard, and finally, across the water to an island.

He could barely remember those six months when he was dying, literally on his deathbed. He had been told that Melanie O'Conner came to see him every day, fed him, talked to him. He didn't remember any of that, but he did recall that hers was the first face he saw when he woke up one morning, strong enough to ask who she was and what he was doing in that strange place. She had smiled, and in a voice calm and soothing, explained what happened.

And, he thought with a half-smile, he had lived for practically three years on that island, playing with his friends, going to school, being allowed to eat whenever he was hungry. It had been hard for him to get strong again, to be able to eat large amounts of food without getting sick or having a bad stomachache, but with the aid of the Helping Hands, he was now healthy.

Turning his attention back to his friends, he smiled. "At least they got to her in time," he said to them, taking Carry's hand when she came around the table to hug him. "Starvation is a hard thing to live through."

"Yes, it is," Carry agreed, sitting down on his lap. "We should know," she said it more to Jimmy than to the others, for the two of them had something in common with one another than with the rest of the gang. Both had been subject to starvation, and like Jimmy, Carry could remember those pains of hunger.

A silence fell upon the gang as they thought about why they had been brought to the Treehouse, and about that night when they had been taken. Leighann, although never having gone, knew what it was like to be hurt by someone who was supposed to love her. She may not have been a child of the Treehouse, but she too could relate to the pain and fear of a fist.

Chapter 33

Collinsville, California

The afternoon was gray, overcast with unpromising clouds that hung drearily within the bleak sky. A heavy wind blew, running its fingers through the leaves and bringing with it soft whispers that told all that rain was on its way. The streets that traveled the town were empty of liveliness, but the local movie theater and pizza joint were packed with bodies.

Despite the impending storm, Edna Waller stood on her front lawn, a light green garden hose in her hands as she ignored the thunder that rolled across the sky. She smiled while watching the water shower out on her flowers, creating little drops of crystal color that bounced vivaciously on the petals. Her limbs moved as fast as her seventy-six years would allow, but she didn't mind, for her flowers were her pride and joy, her only company now that her Albert was gone.

She spoke to them while she stood beneath the dark sky, telling them about her day and laughing when they answered back. She loved hearing their little stories about the bees visiting and the earthworms tickling their roots beneath the soil. The white hair that framed her face in tight curls blew back from her eyes as the wind breezed by, but she gave it no thought.

Edna was so caught up in her conversation with the flowers that she didn't hear the approaching footsteps until they were right behind her. Turning slowly, she smiled at the two men who were standing on her lawn, holding the hose in her right hand.

Zack Corwin nodded at the old woman, returning her cheerful smile as he held out his badge. "Good afternoon, ma'am. My name is Zack Corwin; this is Jay Neilson. We're with the F.B.I."

Edna's smile grew larger as she flashed her teeth. "F.B.I.? Why, what are you big city boys doing in my little California town? You heard about my beautiful flowers, didn't you?"

Zack shook his head, although he had to grin when he saw that she was serious. "Actually, I wanted to ask you something about one of your neighbors."

"Did you know that sometimes, if you're real quiet and you listen real close, they'll talk to you," she went on, her face a combination of honesty and mischief, as if she were telling a secret she wasn't supposed to tell. "If you're lucky, they might even ask for a drink of water."

Neilson stepped forward, gesturing to the dark clouds. "Well, ma'am, I'd advise that you try to hurry. It looks like we're going to have a storm pretty soon."

"Ah." Edna waved a hand at the sky. "Those clouds won't start all their racket for another half-hour or so. But my flowers, they were thirsty now, so I wasn't going to make them wait. Waiting is bad for flowers, you know, because they get impatient and stubborn and say they won't grow anymore. And sometimes they won't, just because you ignored them."

Getting tired of talking about flowers, Zack shoved his badge into the inner pocket of his coat and pointed to a house down the street. "Ma'am—"

"Oh, quit it with all that ma'am nonsense. You're making me sound like an old woman. My name is Edna. Edna Waller."

"Ms. Waller," Zack repeated with a nod, "do you know who lives in that house right over there?" He pointed again, and Edna barely glanced over.

"I've known everyone on this street for years," she told him, turning the hose back to her flowers. "They all come to see my garden. When my Albert died, all my nice neighbors gave me a flower. See those?" She gestured to a little square patch of soil filled with an assortment of flora, colored red and white and yellow. "I put them all right there. Such nice people."

Corwin fought not to let frustration get the better of him. "Ms. Waller, have you met Melanie O'Conner yet, or her fiancé, Mel Scotford?"

Edna paused, her back to the agents. When she turned, she looked over at the house, which was set back far from the road among trees and other vegetation. Her expression was calm and pleasant.

"She came to see my flowers," she told the two men quietly. "She said they were gorgeous, and she even helped me put one in the ground. Such a nice woman."

Annoyed, Neilson pushed past Corwin. "Ms. Waller, have you seen anything unusual about Melanie O'Conner? Do you know if she is associating with any suspicious characters? Any information you could give us concerning her would be very helpful. She may be connected with a series of kidnappings."

Edna cocked her head to the side, considering the questions. "I remember," she began slowly, her voice dreamy with a touch of amusement, "when they first moved in. Such a nice couple. I was sitting on my porch, talking to my little petunia, it's purple, you know, and I saw that Melanie come running out onto her front porch."

"So what happened?" Neilson pressed when Edna paused, lost in her thoughts.

"Well, then a very handsome young man came out after her, and well, that little lady just squirted him right smack dab in the face with a hose." Letting out a laugh, Edna shook her head. "I was sure that young man would be mad, but he just kissed her and smiled like they did that kind of stuff all the time. Why, I just love watching them together. Reminds me of when my Albert was alive."

"So you've never seen her do anything illegal, or have any suspicions as to anything she might be doing that's against the law?" Neilson didn't give a damn what Melanie and Mel Scotford did together in their spare time unless it had something to do with the Helping Hands.

Edna faced Neilson with a frown. "Now why would you want my new neighbor to do anything illegal?" she asked haughtily. "Now, I know she's had some troubles in the past because I watch the news, but I can promise you that—"

"She's a convicted criminal, Ms. Waller," Corwin cut in, holding up a hand. "We just want to make sure you're safe, living on the same street as her and all."

"That little lady over there told me my flowers were gorgeous," Edna argued. "And it sounds to me like you just want to get her in trouble. Why, if my Albert were alive he'd skin your behinds for trying to get some poor woman put in jail. If I weren't standing here in front of my baby petunias, I'd skin you both myself. You should be ashamed of yourselves."

"I understand that you like her, Ms. Waller, but—"

"Now you two scat. Good day to you, gentlemen." Edna waved a hand at them, and when they didn't move, she lifted the hose until they had to jump back to avoid being sprayed with water. "Run along, and let me get back to my flowers."

Consenting to her sharp orders, Corwin began to back away. "Thank you for your assistance, Ms. Waller. Don't get caught in the rain."

"What a waste of time," Neilson said as he strapped on his seatbelt. "Fifteen minutes of listening to some old hag go off on a tangent about flowers and her dead husband."

Corwin didn't reply, for he was thinking the opposite. Whereas Edna Waller may very well have been undeniably crazy, it seemed to him like she spent a lot of time observing her neighbors. He never really thought Melanie would be stupid enough to do any Helping Hand business right out of her own home, but he had to cover all his bases. Edna had proved that he didn't have to worry about Melanie O'Conner getting in his way.

Edna watched the black car until the back end turned the corner. Her old eyes, bordered by deep wrinkles, narrowed as she shook her head. *Those men*, she thought as she turned back to her flowers with disgust. She cared deeply for her new neighbor, and although she knew exactly who and what Melanie O'Conner was, it didn't bother her at all. The Melanie she met was kind, sincere, and not in the least bit a criminal.

Of course, she considered while watching the water sprinkle out over the soil, the young woman did look quite threatening, with the scars all over her arms and face, and the tattoos. Even the way she walked, with a sort of assured strut that Edna normally would have scoffed at, demanded respect and wariness from the person on the outside. The woman was obviously dangerous, and Edna didn't doubt that for a single moment.

Thunder began its threats of rain and storms. Before she turned to go inside, Edna glanced over at her new neighbor's home, or what she could see of it among the trees. She recalled a couple of weeks earlier, when Melanie's friends had come to visit, the two who came frequently. They had been there the entire day, and when they finally left, Melanie had run out to the car to catch them before they drove off. Edna watched Melanie hand an envelope to the woman, then whisper something to the male. Then, when the car pulled out of the driveway, Melanie instantly dialed a number on her cell phone while walking back inside the house.

Edna didn't need anyone to tell her what the secrecy was all about. She may have been old, but she was wise. And she was happy knowing there were still Helping Hands out there saving abused children.

"I know, I know," she said suddenly, exasperated as she shook her head at the flowerbed. "I can smell the rain too." Dropping the hose onto the ground and forgetting to turn it off, Edna put the agents' visit out of her mind, stepping inside the house just before the thick sheets of water began to fall.

Denver, Colorado

The cabin was satiated with warm air, the glow from fire filling the living room. Outside, the blackness of night hid the rest of the world. Windows were crusted in halos of ice, but the bitter cold couldn't touch them inside.

Melanie leaned back against Tyler's chest and smiled, stretching her legs out in front of her as she sat before the fire, a blanket across her lap. Tyler, sitting with his arms wrapped around her from behind, rested his chin on her shoulder and stared into the fire.

She felt safe in the cabin, and yet, disheartened. It was painful seeing the remnants of her departed friend, especially his personal belongings. She had packed away a few of Wess's old shirts the night before, storing them in her luggage without informing Tyler. It was something she needed to do, to have something other than a memory of her friend. It was a kind of weakness, needed that connection, but storing the clothes had somehow given her a sense of freedom from that pain. She didn't want Tyler to know, didn't want him to see that weakness.

Tyler, unaware of the thoughts running through his fiancée's mind, smiled to himself as he tightened his hold on Melanie. "It's quiet up here," he noted. "Almost too quiet."

"You're just used to hearing kids yelling and playing. Or those deafening college parties."

"Speaking of kids," Tyler kissed Melanie's neck, pulling her hair out of the way, "we just had a foster mother arrested for starving one of her foster kids."

"That sucks," Melanie replied with a frown, immediately remembering the six months she had spent by Jimmy Fencles's side. "So what'd you do to her?"

Tyler shrugged. "There were kids watching, so I just leaned real close to her and threatened to have her sliced apart piece by piece for what she was doing to the kids."

Melanie smiled despite the seriousness of the threat. "How very noble of you," she teased. "So where are the kids?"

"Back at the group home." Tyler sighed. "One of them, a little boy named Tommy, was really sad about having to go back."

"Well, yeah. Who'd want to go to some big lonely house with hundreds of kids and no parents? Not to mention crappy food, poor living standards, kids who want to fight you, abusive foster parents—"

"I get the picture," Tyler interrupted. "And you're right. But what got me was this kid, Tommy, he asked me to adopt him."

Melanie let out a deep breath, her heart breaking for the child. Every kid she had ever met loved Tyler, which amused her since adults tended to cower in his presence. "So what'd you say back?"

"I told him that I wished I could adopt him, but just couldn't. He said he guesses he understood, and I told him that one day he would have an amazing family with lots of brothers and sisters, and maybe even a pet dog. He seemed pretty happy when I said that."

Melanie nodded, gripping Tyler's hand. "It's every foster kid's dream," she thought aloud. "I never wanted a dog, but I would have taken one if I had to."

"Oh, shut up." Tyler teasingly pulled Melanie's hair. "I wouldn't have minded adopting him, you know? Having a kid around the house would be great, but I'd rather have one of my own running around and getting into trouble first." He laughed, but Melanie was quiet, her eyes scanning the warm fire in front of her as she tightened her grip on Tyler's hands.

"Do you mean that?" she asked, taking in a deep breath.

"Of course I do," Tyler replied, frowning as Melanie turned around and faced him, sitting on her knees. "I mean, I wish we did have a kid running around. Why?"

Melanie took in a breath, her stomach a bundle of nerves. "Well, um, you know what they say…Be careful what you wish for." She watched as Tyler's face went blank, then the realization set in.

"You mean you're—we're gonna—you're pregnant?" He gasped out a breath when Melanie smiled and nodded, leaping to his feet and pulling her up with him. "That's incredible!" He grabbed Melanie in a hug, swinging her off her feet and in a circle. "Why didn't you tell me sooner? How long have you known?"

"Not long," Melanie replied. "At first I wasn't sure, but I took a test the other day. Well, three, actually. I wanted to wait for the perfect moment."

"Any moment would have been the perfect moment, Melanie." Tyler couldn't keep the grin off his face. "You know what this means, don't you?" He laughed when she shook her head. "We're going to have to get married, like, now."

"You just keep on pushing that damn marriage thing, don't you?"

"Sure. It's proof that someone in this crazy world was man enough to wear down the famous Melanie O'Conner."

"Too bad that man's gonna be sleeping on the couch for the rest of his life."

With mock pain and insult, Tyler clutched a hand to his chest. "Would it help if I said I was marrying a woman who was much smarter than me?"

"And stronger."

"Right. And stronger."

She considered it, then nodded. "Alright then, we'll get married."

"When?"

"Soon," Melanie replied, hugging Tyler hard. "Very soon."

Chapter 34

San Francisco, California

Hesitation and anxiety racked her bones as Kelly stared up at her house, her mother by her side and Danielle waiting on the front porch. The open door seemed like an invitation to death, a dark passageway leading to nightmares of iron fists and broken bones. She stepped through anyway, a weight of trepidation falling onto her shoulders.

"I'm so glad you're home." Danielle hugged her sister, smiling happily.

"Me too. Are you okay?"

"Not so much as a mean look," Danielle assured her, her voice low so that only her sister could hear.

"Think of this as your second chance, Kelly," Monica told her daughter, hanging her coat on the rack by the door. "Only six months. You can do it, right?"

Kelly nodded and pressed her lips together, observing her mother. Her hair was perfect, her cheeks colored with a thick rosy powder. Dark red lipstick painted her lips, matching the burgundy that lined her eyelids. There had been a time, Kelly remembered, when her mother wouldn't think twice about going out to the store in a sweat suit and her hair up in a messy ponytail. It wasn't until she met Jeffrey that things started to change. He liked his women to be neat, and Monica was happy to oblige.

"Why don't you go on up to your room and rest while I make dinner," Monica suggested and Kelly agreed, eager to get away from the woman who had long since become a stranger. Danielle followed her up the stairs and to her room.

"So what was it like?" she asked as Kelly fell back onto her bed. "Was it scary?"

"Not really," Kelly replied, rubbing her eyes. "There was a lot of yelling, a lot of chores and stuff that I had to do, but it wasn't really scary. Just boring."

"Did you have to go to counseling?"

"Yeah. Four times a week. I met Melanie O'Conner."

Danielle's eyes widened. "The Helping Hand? And you didn't write a letter to tell me? What was she like? Was she mean?"

"No, actually, she wasn't." Kelly had been surprised to find out that Melanie O'Conner was, in fact, a very kind and caring person. "She was... understanding. She promised to help us out with Jeffrey."

"Really? I met this guy the other day who promised the same thing." Danielle struggled to remember his name as she pictured his face in her mind. "He was really cute. He said his name was Mark something. No, it was Matt. Matt... Harper, maybe?"

Kelly's ears pricked up at the name. "Matt Harper? He said he was going to help?" Danielle nodded, and Kelly laughed to herself at the new information. It made sense that a former child of the Treehouse, the first in fact, would begin his own branch of the life-saving project. "Son-of-a-bitch is a Helping Hand." Now she felt bad about how she'd treated him in the past.

"Kelly! Someone's here to see you!" Monica's voice traveled up the stairs. "I'll send him up to your room!"

Kelly turned to the door when she heard footsteps on the stairs, excitement bubbling up at the thought of the only person it could possibly be. A moment later Robbie appeared, his hands in his pockets as he smiled over at her.

"I heard you were back." He entered the room, greeting Danielle with a nod. "He set you up, didn't he?"

"Yeah." Kelly nodded. "He got me good."

"Well, I'm glad you're back."

"I'm going to my room," Danielle cut in, understanding that this was a time that her sister needed to spend with Robbie. "I'll talk to you later, Kelly." She disappeared around the corner, and Robbie watched her go before turning back to Kelly.

"It was weird. One day, I'm dropping you off at your house, the next, you're gone." He sat down next to her on the bed. "Rumor had it you were taken away because of drugs and stealing a car. Some people were saying that they thought you had an accomplice. They said it wasn't fair that you had to take all the blame. I know this really probably means nothing to you considering the crap you had to go through, but for what it's worth, thanks for not telling the cops you were out with me."

"Don't worry about it. Thanks for not giving up on me," Kelly replied, looking down at her hands.

Robbie took her chin, raising her head so he could look into her eyes. "I don't give up on anything I like." He reached out and pushed back her hair, then leaned closer until he was kissing her. This time, Kelly responded and kissed him back, gently holding his neck.

"You really are glad I'm back, aren't you?" Kelly smiled as she pulled away. The grin dropped when she imagined what the consequences would be if anyone, a certain man in particular, were to walk in to see the two of them leaning close together with their hands linked and their mouths practically touching. She lowered her head and cleared her throat. "As much as I hate to do this, you'd better go. Jeffrey will probably be home from work soon, and if he catches you here, I'll get major shit for it."

"Right." Robbie rose to his feet, pulling Kelly up with him. He hugged her tight. "Come down with me." He led her into the hall, down the stairs, and out the front door. When they reached the sidewalk, he turned and faced her. "I just wanted you to know that if you need anything, I'm only a few houses away."

"Thanks, Robbie." Kelly reached up and kissed him, then took a few steps back. "But you really better go." She waved as Robbie nodded and turned, jogging to his house. He looked over his shoulder before entering, giving her a brief yet affectionate wave.

Kelly laughed and hugged herself, rubbing her arms in the chilly evening. She all but skipped up the driveway, her grin never fading. She never had a boyfriend before, and hoped that Robbie would want the position.

Completely unaware of the shadowed figure that had been watching her every move, Kelly gasped when a pair of hands grabbed her by the hair and thrust her head back. She tried to cry out as the figure dragged her to the side of the house, throwing her onto the ground. She winced as her head connected with a rock.

"Where'd you come from?" she asked timidly when she saw Jeffrey hovering over her, his eyes angry. Her mouth parted in surprise when he lifted his hand and swung down, connecting with her ribs. She knew by the clang of metal and the amount of pain that she was hit with more than just a fist, and her eye caught a glint of silver as he lifted his hand again, a shimmer of iron of a tool that had been meant as a wedding gift.

"Who'd you tell?" Jeffrey rasped out, grabbing Kelly by the neck and squeezing hard. She struggled beneath his grasp, sucking in breaths as best she could. "I had some people come to investigate me, Kelly. Now tell me, why would they come?"

"I don't know!" Kelly gasped out, her hands clutching Jeffrey's wrist. "I didn't tell anyone!" She couldn't even cry out when Jeffrey hit her hard on the side of the face. A trail of blood oozed from the gash as Jeffrey released her, rising to his feet.

"We'll see if you're telling the truth or not," he warned, pointing down at her with the wrench. She saw a wild, homicidal glare in his eyes that terrified her. "Let's go see what Danielle has to say."

"No! Jeffrey, leave her alone!" Kelly scrambled to her feet, falling against the wall as a wave of dizziness rushed through her head. The ground blurred and the trees began to spin as she gripped her forehead. Her throat burned with sickness, but she forced it down and tasted blood in her mouth. For a moment she forgot who and where she was.

The sound of the front door slamming snapped her out of her daze, and Kelly raced for the house.

Collinsville, California

Tyler thrust the key into the lock and twisted it quickly, shoving the front door open. He ran inside, reaching the telephone on its fourth and final ring.

"Hello?"

"Tyler?"

"Matt? That you?" Tyler asked with a smile. "How you doing, kid? Everything okay?"

"Um, I need to speak with Miss Melanie." He sounded urgent.

"Okay. Hold on. Mel." Tyler waited until Melanie had set her bags by the front door. He held up the phone. "Harper."

"Oh, good." Melanie took the phone in a hurry, and Tyler stepped back. He sensed something was going on with the two, something he wasn't supposed to know about and probably should find out, but thought it best to stay out of it. "What's up, Matt?"

142

"I've been watching the Mitchell family," Matt began. "And I talked to Danielle a bit."

"So what'd you find out?"

"Well, we were right about everything. Their stepfather, Jeffrey Ponder, hits Kelly. He's hit her with a wrench, sticks, belts, you name it, he's done it. Ever since Kelly was young."

"What about Danielle?" Melanie grabbed a pen and slip of paper and began writing notes. It was safe to record such observations, for she could always justify her cause as being a work case.

"Danielle said that she's never been hit, but that's because Kelly always gets in front of her. You know, because of her disease. And when they sent Kelly to South Bay, apparently you or somebody told the cops that he abused Kelly, and they started investigating him."

"*What*?" Melanie leapt to her feet. "Social Services began investigating him?"

"Yeah. You didn't tell anyone?"

"The only person I told was Sergeant Hawkins. Shit! That means when Kelly goes home he'll be pissed. Who knows what he'll do." When Matt didn't say anything, Melanie knew that something was wrong, terribly wrong. "Matt? What's happened?"

"Well… um, I thought you knew. Kelly came home today."

The blood drained from Melanie's face as her knees buckled and she fell back down onto her chair. Tyler rushed over to her, but she brushed him away. "Matt, what do you mean, she's home? She wasn't supposed to go home until I came back from Colorado and supervised her return."

"Well, I don't know how she did it, but she's back. I watched her arrive. She got home, went inside, and her friend Robbie came over. Then I left to call you."

Melanie jumped up again. "Matt, I want you to get her and Danielle out of that house. I don't care how you do it, but get them out. I've been doing research on Jeffrey Ponder. He's been arrested for assault and battery when he was younger, and got fired from his last job because of blackmail, and was almost put in jail a few times but got off because he's got money. Kelly and Danielle aren't safe there, and if she's home with Jeffrey pissed about being investigated, a lot of bad shit is about to happen. Get her out."

"I will. Don't worry, Miss Melanie, I'll get her out."

Chapter 35

San Francisco, California

"No! Jeffrey, leave her alone!" Kelly shouted, pulling open the front door and racing inside. She staggered, catching herself on the dining room table as her feet stumbled and her eyes wildly searched for her stepfather.

Her mother came out from the kitchen, wiping her hands on a rag. "Kelly! Stop that yelling!" She stopped short when she saw the blood on her daughter's face. "What happened to you?"

"He's gonna *kill* her, Mom! He's fucking snapped! You have to stop him!" Kelly was in tears as she ran for the stairs, Monica following, unsure of what was happening.

Kelly heard Jeffrey in the hall, banging on a door. She prayed that Danielle wouldn't unlock it, prayed that she would know better, but the sound of the door being busted from its hinges caused terror to pulse through her veins.

"Ow! Jeffrey, stop! You're hurting me!" Danielle cried as Jeffrey grabbed her arm and dragged her off her bed and out of the bedroom.

"*Don't hurt her!*" Kelly screamed, reaching the top of the stairs to see Jeffrey holding Danielle against him, one hand on her arm and the other at the back of her neck. Dizziness threatened to overcome her, but when she saw her sister's terrified face, the petrified tears in her eyes, Kelly fought through it. She didn't care about her own injuries.

"Jeffrey, please. Let her go," Kelly pleaded. "Your fight is with me, not her. Everything is my fault, not Danielle's."

"Who's your sister been talking to, Danielle?" Jeffrey asked, his voice rough as he leaned over and spoke directly into her ear.

Danielle cringed when she felt Jeffrey's breath against her skin, smelling alcohol on his breath. "I-I don't know."

"Don't lie to me, you useless invalid!" Jeffrey roared, grabbing Danielle by the shoulder and throwing her across the floor. Kelly ran for her sister, hearing the loud snap and crack as two bones were shattered in Danielle's body.

Danielle's cheeks were stained with tears, and she cried out when she turned over onto her back and saw a bone protruding from her leg. She started to grab for her leg only to see that her wrist was twisted at an odd, unnatural angle.

"Oh, Danielle," Monica whimpered as she came up the stairs. "Jeffrey, what have you done?" She glared at her husband, an unusual defiance in her eyes.

"You goddamn bastard! *I'll kill you!*" Kelly screamed, leaping at her stepfather. She punched him squarely in the jaw, surprised that her fist actually connected, but he hardly flinched. Reaching back with his arm, he lunged for her, hitting her in the side of the head. Kelly jerked to the side, crimson blood splattering across the walls.

Kelly staggered and fell back, barely hearing her mother's screams as Jeffrey lashed out again, shouting curses and threats that she couldn't comprehend. Her vision blurred and her limbs weakened as she was hit again, and again. Pain ransacked her every bone, every inch of flesh.

With a final burst of strength and courage, she ran for Jeffrey, burying her head in his gut, her neck jamming into her tense shoulders. Jeffrey staggered back, then regained his footing and shoved her hard on her shoulders, landing his fist on her chin. Kelly was spun completely around by the force of the blow, and as she stepped down, her foot twisted harshly on the edge of the stairs. Her hand, wet with her own blood, slipped from the banister as she grabbed for it. Her knee connected with the top step, and she was unable to catch herself as she fell.

Kelly barely felt the steps as she banged against them. She could feel her ribs crack as she watched the ceiling become the floor. The fall seemed like a dream, painless and fast. Hitting the base of the stairs, she landed hard onto her back. The white paint of the ceiling streaked red, and soon was painted black as her eyes closed.

Matt stumbled to a stop, his gang members narrowly avoiding running in to him as he ducked behind a tall tree next to the road. He peered around the trunk, silently praying to find all to be well within the Mitchell household.

"Oh no," he sighed when he saw the police cars and ambulance parked outside Kelly Mitchell's house, lights flashing. He watched as paramedics rushed out of the house, pulling two stretchers along with them. Danielle seemed to be awake, merely lying down, her head twisting to the side as she desperately searched for her sister. The second figure was less fortunate, covered with braces and tubes and lay perfectly still, deathly immobile.

"Get off me!" a man, who Matt assumed to be Jeffrey Ponder, shouted as he was led out of the house in handcuffs. His face was smeared with blood, most of which wasn't his. It was spread across his forehead and cheeks, and the front of his shirt was stained red, as was the skin on his arms.

"Shit," Leighann panted, leaning over to catch her breath as a tear fell down her cheek. "We didn't make it."

Matt watched the ambulances until they had disappeared around the corner. "We're too late." His voice was choked with grief as he fought with the decision to call Melanie or not. "We're too late."

Chapter 36

South Bay Juvenile Detention Camp

Melanie stormed into Brian Hawkins's office, her feet pounding on the green-tiled floor and her hands already in fists as she slammed the door closed. Her breath was heavy and her eyes were narrow, glaring with accusation. Hawkins looked up sharply from his desk, seeing the anger in her eyes.

"O'Conner?" he asked, slowly rising from his chair. He already knew what she had come about, and he had a lot to tell her before he could let her go off on a furious tangent. "I had a feeling you would want to talk to—"

That was as far as he got before Melanie crossed the room in quick, angry strides and planted her fist squarely in his jaw.

"Damn right I want to talk to you!" Melanie spat out. She didn't bother to consider the consequences of hitting not only a sergeant, but also her boss. "You sent Kelly Mitchell home without my consent or supervision! I told you I wanted to be there upon her return home and that I wanted to bring her there myself! You *deliberately* went against my requests!"

"Now O'Conner," Brian began, holding up one hand in defense and the other against his aching jaw. The woman may be small, but she packed one hell of a right cross, and was a lot quicker than he had expected. He had to admire her bravery to assault him, although he wouldn't press charges since he figured the punch was a little, if not entirely, deserved.

"I told you that there was a chance she would be going home early, and you said that was fine."

"I also said I wanted to know the exact date that she would be released, and you *agreed* to that!"

"You can't control when we let someone out of here, Miss O'Conner. Now, I know you're upset—"

"You bet your ass I'm upset." Melanie shoved back her hair and flung out her hands in anger. Her right hand throbbed mildly. "Do you have any idea of the danger you're putting that girl in? Do you know what's going to happen when her stepfather finds out we've been investigating him, if he doesn't know already? She's in serious danger!"

Shit, Hawkins thought with a frown, *she doesn't know..*

"O'Conner, there's something I need to tell you. You may want to take a seat."

"I'll stand." Her words were bitter.

146

Hawkins worded his thoughts carefully, taking a few cautious steps back from his newest South Bay counselor. "Upon her return home, Kelly was.. .attacked by her stepfather." He watched as Melanie's eyes widened. "He broke a couple of Danielle's bones, one in her leg and the other in her wrist. Then he beat Kelly with a wrench and all but threw her down the stairs."

Melanie raised a hand to her mouth. Guilt, sympathy, and fury welled up inside her chest at once. In the back of her mind, she wondered why Matt hadn't informed her of the attack. "How bad is she," she asked, her voice muffled

Brian took in a deep breath and cleared his throat. "She's… she's in a coma. She lost a lot of blood, broke her arm and two ribs, and had well over a hundred stitches with all the wounds. I'm sorry, O'Conner," he added the last part when Melanie didn't reply. "Her mother called the police and both she and Jeffrey Ponder were arrested. The sister is staying with some neighbors. The Andersons, I believe."

"Robbie Anderson," Melanie replied quietly, raising her eyes to Brian. "What have you done?"

"I did nothing, O'Conner. If you want someone to blame, blame Jeffrey Ponder."

"I'll blame who I damn well please." The arrogance of the man made her blood boil. "You didn't have enough respect for me to listen to what I had to say, and now this happens." Fists clenching and unclenching as she fought for control, Melanie shook her head. "I'm going to see her," she informed Hawkins. "I'll be back when I'm back, and you better hope to God that she lives or I swear you'll be next." She turned away and pulled open the door, stepping out into the hall and slamming it shut as hard as she could.

She felt only the mildest pangs of satisfaction when the window in the door cracked and shattered to the floor.

San Francisco, California

Pierson Memorial Hospital was bustling with activity as morning flowed into afternoon. Paramedics wheeled victims into the ER, surgeons performed life-saving operations, family members anxiously gathered in waiting rooms.

Four stories up, in Room 415, a light whisper of strained voices could be heard. Robbie Anderson and Danielle Mitchell sat on either side of Kelly's still body. Danielle's eyes were wet with tears as she gripped her sister's hand, and Robbie had his head braced in his arms. His parents had gone off to get something to eat, promising to bring back dinner for the two who refused to leave Kelly's side.

But at the moment, food was the last thing on either of their minds.

Robbie raised his eyes to Kelly's face. He no longer cringed at the sight of the ugly bruises, which had turned from a dark purple to a sickening yellow. He didn't squeeze his eyes shut in sorrow anymore when he saw the tube that was sticking out of her mouth. And his breath no longer caught in his throat when the doctors and nurses told him that there was still no change in her condition. He didn't react anymore to such things; he was used to them by now.

Danielle couldn't keep the sight of Kelly's bloody body lying at a twisted angle at the bottom of the stairs from her mind. Every time she closed her eyes the picture came back, and every time she felt more and more guilty.

It meant a lot to her when Robbie and his family offered to care for her while Kelly was in the hospital. They wanted to help Kelly get better, and they both knew that Danielle needed them. Since both her mother and stepfather had been arrested and were awaiting arraignments, Danielle wasn't left with a lot of options for a home. Her grandfather would have taken her if she had asked, but he lived in Florida and she wanted to be close to Kelly.

"Do you think she'll wake up?" Robbie asked, his voice muffled by his hands

Danielle wiped her eyes. "She better," she whispered in reply. "I need her."

So do I, Robbie thought with a sigh, glancing up at Danielle. She wasn't looking at him. He started to respond, but when a knock sounded behind him, he closed his mouth and looked over his shoulder towards the door. "Can we help you?" he asked the unfamiliar figure standing in the doorway.

"I'm here to see Kelly."

"Who are you?"

Melanie entered the small hospital room, gazing through the dim light at the two teenagers sitting by the bed. She suppressed memories of Wess in the hospital, his four closest friends gathered around his bedside. "My name's Melanie O'Conner. I was Kelly's counselor at South Bay." She waited until the information registered, and was surprised when they both simply turned back to Kelly as though they hadn't really heard. The tense silence that passed after her declaration made her slightly uncomfortable.

"Kelly told me about you when she got home," Danielle said dully. She normally would have been honored to meet the former Helping Hand, or maybe even a little frightened, but now she was just defeated.

"Why are you here?" Robbie asked. He barely spared her a second's glance.

Melanie pulled a chair up next to Danielle and sat, leaning forward with her arms resting on her knees. "Kelly told me about her home life. I tried to help her, but some things happened, and she was released without my permission. I'm here to keep my promise to her."

"And what promise is that?" Danielle asked, never taking her eyes off of Kelly.

"I told her I would do all I could to get her away from her stepfather, and now I'm going to make him pay."

Robbie stared across the bed at Melanie. In the dim light her face was shadowed, but he could still see the scars strewn across her face. He had seen pictures of her before on television and magazines, but being up close was completely different. Seated across from her, talking to her, made her seem almost like a normal person, not some kidnapping criminal with a cold heart and bloody intentions, as he once read in the newspaper. She was just another person, worried about the well-being of someone she barely knew.

For that, he could find it in him to trust her.

"The doctor doesn't know if she'll wake up," he told her.

"She will."

"How do you know?"

"Because Kelly is strong." Melanie looked over at Robbie. "She's tougher than she thinks. She's brave."

"She's my sister," Danielle whispered, her choked voice quiet, "and my hero. She saved my life." She turned her head to look at Melanie through the gloomy atmosphere of the room. "Please, help me save hers."

Tyler frowned as Melanie got into the car, slamming the door. He was silent for a moment, clearing his throat as a precaution. "How bad is she?"

"A coma," Melanie replied, picturing Kelly lying on the bed, cruelly decorated with tubes and wires, along with more than her share of cuts and bruises. "She's bad, Tyler. Real bad."

Tyler started the car and pulled out of the hospital parking lot. He thought about how to comfort her, but wasn't sure he had the right words to do so. He'd never met Kelly Mitchell and didn't know much about her situation, nor did he know if she would be okay.

They drove in silence for a while, Melanie staring out the window. As San Francisco disappeared behind them, Melanie looked down at her hands and decided that she needed to talk to Tyler about Kelly's situation or else it would eat at her for weeks.

"You know what Danielle asked me?"

"What?"

"To help her save Kelly." Melanie looked over at Tyler. "To save her sister."

Tyler hesitated before replying. "What did you tell her?"

"I said I'd do all that I could. God, Tyler, her voice was so desperate. Kelly means the world to her. She saved Danielle's life so many times, and now she's in a coma, and Danielle is looking to me to make everything better again. I told her I would make Jeffrey suffer for what he did, and I will. But this, not knowing if Kelly will be okay, I don't know. Wess was in a coma, and he died when he woke up. I can't tell that to Danielle. I can't say that there's a chance she won't be okay. She's depending on me. I just don't know what to do."

Tyler looked over at Melanie as she buried her face in her hands. He felt a deep tug of sympathy for Danielle, but at the same time, he didn't want Melanie to get too involved. He knew how she got when she wasn't able to help someone. She got angry, furious even, and did what it took to get her way.

Even, he thought grimly, *if it meant putting her own life on the line.*

"Melanie, maybe you should just take a step back from all this," he said carefully, not at all surprised by the harsh glare she gave him in return.

"What do you mean? I can't just turn my back on them!"

"I know." Tyler held up a hand. "I'm not talking about turning your back. I'm just saying that you have no control over this, so you shouldn't get all worked up over it. I mean, you're almost three months pregnant. You don't need that kind of stress right now."

Melanie crossed her arms defiantly. "And Kelly doesn't need to be in a coma right now, but I guess that's not my problem, right? After all, I was only her counselor and I only promised that I would do what I could to help. But that doesn't mean anything." She huffed with disgust. "How can you tell me to stay out of this?"

"I'm not telling you to stay out—"

"Yes you are!" Melanie interrupted. "You want me to leave this whole thing alone and let them figure it out on their own! I can't turn my back on Kelly or her sister. They both need me right now."

"It's not your fight, Mel!" Tyler argued, slamming his hand down on the steering wheel. "Danielle is dragging you into this! I'm sorry that this happened to Kelly. You know I am. But shit happens, and when you can't help someone, it drives you crazy. I just don't want you to get hurt when all this is over."

"Kelly was *abused*, Tyler! You don't know what it's like to live in fear of someone every day of your life, never knowing when he's coming after you, when he's going to kill you!" Melanie would have smacked Tyler if she could have gotten into a good position to do so. She knew he didn't understand. He never would, because he never lived through what she and Kelly had. It both infuriated and disappointed her that he didn't even try to understand her position.

Melanie punched the dashboard instead of Tyler when he sighed. "I can help her because I *know*. And if I can help her, even if it's only giving her a shoulder to cry on, I will, because helping her will mean saving her life."

Tyler set his jaw and refrained from shaking his head. Anger was racing through his blood, but he didn't reply to Melanie's shouts. He wasn't dumb enough to start an argument about her father. The past still affected her, despite her claims otherwise.

It did some damage to his pride that the woman he was going to marry thought they were so far apart that he wasn't able to relate to her pain. So he was never abused, he thought, but damn it, his parents *abandoned* him in some dumpy alley to fend for himself. He was a goddamn kid with no food and no money, no place to go and absolutely no idea why he had to be alone when all the other boys got to go to the park with their dads and toss around a baseball. At least Melanie had the luxury of being able to say that she ran away from home. He had to admit to being left behind.

So who the hell was she to say that he didn't understand?

Instead of continuing an argument he would never win, Tyler gripped the steering wheel tighter and kept his eyes on the road, wishing every moment that Melanie had never met Kelly Mitchell.

150

Chapter 37

Melanie ran to answer her cell phone, dodging a pile of unpacked boxes and grabbing the phone on the fourth ring, banging her elbow against the counter while doing so. "Yeah?"

"Hey, O'Conner. You sound out of breath. You a bit busy over there?" The voice was teasing.

"Real busy," she replied, rubbing her sore elbow with a scowl, "trying to find you a man so you can have your own sex life and stop worrying about mine." She smiled, jumping up and sitting on the counter after shoving a pile of newspapers aside. "What's up?"

"Not much," Taryn answered. "Just the usual, kids being kids, you know. So how are things with the Mitchell girl?"

"Still no change," Melanie sighed. "Doctors say it doesn't look good."

"Oh. I'm sorry, O'Conner." Taryn was genuinely concerned for the girl she had never met. "But if it helps, that's what the doctor said about you when Foster stabbed you. He said that with all the internal wounds, there was a good chance you wouldn't make it, and now look at you. We just never thought you dying was possible, so we refused to believe it."

That was something neither Caleb nor Taryn had ever admitted to Melanie. Taryn could remember sitting next to Melanie, knowing for the first time what it felt like to lose it all. She had never felt so defeated, seeing Melanie O'Conner, the toughest, bravest, most strong-willed person she'd ever known, lying in a hospital bed with a doctor saying she probably wouldn't live past the next three days.

Melanie had to admit that the confession surprised her. The new information of an almost certain demise made her feel a bit strange, like she cheated death and got away with it. She rubbed a hand over the scar just below her shoulder, thinking about Kelly. They were two different people with two different ways of handling pain and trauma.

"I'm not sure it works that way," she said to Taryn. "Just because I got better doesn't mean she will. Kelly's not as physically tough as she thinks she is. Her strengths are in other areas."

"She'll be fine, O'Conner. Just don't believe anything else." In an attempt to change the dreary conversation, Taryn switched gears quickly. "By the way, Johnny says to tell you again that he's sorry for causing the rift at the party. He still feels bad about it." Melanie shook her head with a smile. Caleb had already apologized five times. "So what's going on over there? You and Tyler still mad at one another?"

Melanie sighed and looked up at the ceiling, thinking back to their fight on the way home from the hospital. "Seems like we're always mad at each other. But yeah, things haven't blown over yet."

"Of course not. It's only been a week," Taryn replied. "You guys hold grudges longer than anyone I've ever met."

"Yeah, well..." her voice trailed to an end. "He's been acting kinda weird lately. Kind of... distant, or something. Like he's mad at me but doesn't really care. I don't know. But I do know that this time it's not my fault. I thought he'd at least *try* to understand why I need to help Kelly and Danielle. He just doesn't get it, and so he's all pissy."

Taryn thought about it, about what Tyler had once told Caleb in confidence. Of course, Caleb had in turn told her, that there were times when Tyler was a bit hurt that Melanie often said he couldn't understand where she was coming from. It wasn't her place to let Melanie know about that conversation, and Taryn didn't want to butt in, but there was a part of her that hated to see her friends fight and wanted them to have their happily ever after.

"Maybe he's just... trying... Damn it, I don't know. You're the one who thinks you know everything about him."

Melanie frowned, hearing Taryn swear to herself on the other end of the phone, something about so much for staying out of it. "What do you mean by thinking I know everything about him?"

Taryn sighed and wished she could kick herself in the ass. "Just that... O'Conner, there's things that Tyler feels too, bad stuff about his own past. And when you..." she stopped, reminding herself that it wasn't her place to talk. "It's something you have to discuss with him is all I'm saying." She paused, and when Melanie was silent, she knew she had to do something quick. "So how's the court stuff going?"

Still comprehending what Taryn had told her, and wondering what the hell her friend was talking about, Melanie replied vaguely, staring out the window at her husband-to-be. "Um, the trials for Jeffrey and Monica are in about three weeks, if not longer, and I have to go to San Francisco to testify. Hawkins told me to take the week off to cool down." At the mention of Hawkins her temper flared. "In other words, he knows that if I'm still pissed when I go back to work, I'll kick his ass."

"Well, you could do it," Taryn agreed. "So what's Tyler doing? I hear a lot of noise."

"He's cutting down a tree limb in the backyard. Jared came down for a few days and they're out there." She glanced out the kitchen window again and saw Tyler standing on top of a ten-foot ladder, a chainsaw running in his hands as he peered up at the limb and said something to Jared, who was standing at the base of the ladder. "Well, actually, Tyler's cutting down the limb. Jared's just kind of standing there looking lost."

"Well, we all know what a genius Jared is when it comes to tools," Taryn said sarcastically. "Anyway... I called to tell you something. Ask you, actually. I wanted to ask in person, but I don't know when I'll see you next."

152

"What's on your mind?" Melanie turned away from the window and heard Taryn take in a deep breath. The sound caused Melanie to feel a tug of worry run through her stomach.

"Well, we got like what, a good six projects going on right now, with others on their way, right?"

"Yeah. So?"

"Well, spread out mine, and you got four more, right?"

"Very good, Taryn. You can count." Melanie rolled her eyes. "What are you getting at?"

"Me and Johnny, we're thinking about… you know, retiring," Taryn admitted. "Like you and Tyler. We've been doing this for a long time, and we both just want to have a normal life, you know? Of course, we'd still take care of everything we need to, but—"

"Taryn," Melanie cut in, "if you guys want to retire, I'm not going to stop you. You're right, you have been doing this a long time. And we have a lot of projects out there. It's not my choice, it's yours." She turned her head at the sound of the two men outside yelling at one another, seeing Tyler's angry and frustrated expression, then went back to her conversation, inquiring with her friend as to what she planned to do after retiring.

Outside, Tyler glared down at Jared. "I told you to hold the rope, damn it!" he yelled. "You aren't doing jack to help!"

"Well, you ain't much for telling me what to do with this damn rope!" Jared shouted back over the roar of the chainsaw. "Just cut the goddamn branch!"

Tyler lifted his arms over his head, feeling the heavy vibration as the blade cut into the bark of the tree. Sawdust flew across his face and bare chest, sticking to his skin. Sweat poured down his forehead, but was blocked from his eyes by his safety glasses. He rose to the next step of the ladder to reach the branch better, not feeling it wobble.

It happened before he had a chance to react. The branch snapped unexpectedly with a loud crack, crashing down and slamming into the ladder. The rope was yanked from Jared's hands, tearing across his skin, and Tyler lost his footing and swung backwards. The chainsaw slipped around in his hands and a sharp slap of pain raced through his right cheek when the running blade slashed through flesh.

He saw the sky, blue and blurred, as he fell, feeling as though he was in slow motion. His only thought was that this must have been how Melanie felt when she had fallen off the roof of William Foster's house. He could barely register the pain as fear overcame all other senses.

Tyler hit the ground hard after his back bounced off the ladder. The breath exploded out of his chest and his head connected to the soil with a loud thump as his ribs cracked beneath the muscle of his bare chest. The tree branch smashed against the ground a few feet from him, sending a shower of leaves and small branches across the lawn.

Jared raced over to Tyler, ignoring his bleeding palms. He fell down next to his friend, gasping at the sight of the gash. Blood poured down Tyler's face and formed a pool of scarlet liquid on the ground. Jared could see, with eyes filled with frantic worry, that his cheek was split open, the two flaps of town skin revealing the insides of his mouth.

"Mel? Mel! Come on, man! Mel!" he shouted, leaning over his friend. Tyler groaned and opened his eyes, barely able to see through the red glaze until they closed again. Jared shot up to his feet and ran to the back door, where Melanie was already running out.

"O'Conner, get a towel, or ice, or something!" he yelled frantically.

Melanie stepped back inside the house long enough to grab a towel from the counter before running to reach Tyler. Her heart pounded in her throat and she felt sick when she saw him lying on the ground, his cheek slit open and blood gushing from the wound.

"Tyler! Tyler, wake up!" she shouted, falling to her knees and shaking his shoulders as Jared held the towel over his face. Melanie pushed back her hair, smearing a streak of blood across her forehead. She leaned over him. "Goddamn it, Mason, don't do this to me. Wake up! No, don't move him! Jared, call an ambulance!" she yelled and grabbed the towel, wiping away blood to see the wound. She had seen hundreds of cuts and lacerations in her life, many being her own, but the one on Tyler's face was by far one of the worst.

Despite her panic, natural instinct took over, the control she had to have when in situations of life and death. She knew what to do, what she *had* to do, and so taking in a deep breath she pressed the towel down firmly over the gash. The blood poured down his neck and his breathing became shaky. Melanie felt the tears in her eyes and barely realized that she was crying as she knelt over the man she loved, the unconscious, bleeding man who had been her best friend for thirteen years.

Jared ran back out of the house after calling for an ambulance with a fresh towel and switched it with the used one. Melanie threw the bloody rag to the ground and felt for the first time completely useless as she gripped Tyler's hand and silently begged to see his bright blue eyes again.

Chapter 38

San Francisco, California

Matt yawned and blinked a few times to keep from falling asleep. He tapped his pencil on his desk, glancing up at his English teacher, who was busy writing down quotes from the book he was supposed to be reading, *One Flew Over* some kind of nest. English had never been his favorite topic. In fact, he despised it, and had thoroughly annoyed Melanie when she tried to teach him at the Treehouse.

Of course, he thought with a wry grin, he'd quickly learned upon re-attending school that she taught according to her own rules and by what she deemed important enough to learn. So he learned about anagrams and reading between the lines, and knew nothing of subjects and predicates and suffixes and whatever else his teacher droned on about.

A knock sounded at the classroom door, and most of the students looked over as it opened. Mrs. Clayton set down the piece of chalk she was holding and headed over to the door, stopping when the principal walked in, looking a bit nervous.

"Mrs. Clayton, I need to speak with one of your students. I'm afraid it's very important."

The gravity on Edward Elliot's face made Mrs. Clayton nervous as well. She'd known the principal for over ten years, and he was never anything but composed.

"Who do you need?" she asked quietly.

"Mathew Harper," Elliot answered in a brisk tone.

Matt raised his head sharply at his name, everyone else in the classroom turning to stare at him. Dread curled in his stomach as he rose, knowing that everyone who was ever summoned by the principal himself was always someone who was in a whole lot of trouble - and trouble was never a good thing for someone involved with the Helping Hand project. For some reason he had a feeling he wasn't being called upon to be accused of cheating on a final or partaking in the latest school prank.

"What did I do?" he asked, his voice steady although inside he was a bundle of twitching nerves.

"I'll need you to come with me," Elliot answered, gesturing to the door.

"So what did I do?" he asked again when he had stepped out into the hall and the door shut behind him. He trailed behind the Elliot, who didn't answer as he led the way to his office. Worry and paranoia continued to grow along the way. "Am I in some kind of trouble?"

"That's not for me to decide," Elliot answered, opening the door to his office to reveal two men dressed in dark suits, eyes narrowed as they watched Matt enter. "I'll leave him to you," the principle said to the two, and walked back into the hall, closing the door behind him.

Matt faced the agents, placing his hands in his pockets so he wouldn't wring them nervously. "I hope there's a good reason I'm here. I'm missing important notes in class."

Corwin stared at the teenager. "This won't take long. I'm Agent Corwin, this is Agent Neilson. We're with the F.B.I."

"The F.B.I.?" Matt repeated, willing himself to sound tough.

"Exactly. Why don't you have a seat and we'll begin."

"I… I'd rather stand." Matt crossed his arms and remained by the closed door, while the agents kept their spots in front of the desk. "What do you want with me?"

"I want to talk to you about an old friend of yours, Melanie O'Conner."

"Don't I have the right to an attorney?"

"Sure, but if you want to be a smart-ass with me I'll just go ahead and arrest you right here and now." It was easy to scare a kid, that much Corwin was sure of. His threat seemed to have an effect when Matt fell silent, so he pushed ahead. "Now, about Melanie O'Conner."

"What about her?"

"We have reason to believe that she is associated with the new San Francisco branch of Helping Hands." Corwin kept his eyes on Matt, noting the way his mouth twitched just a bit. "You being the first child of the Treehouse means you had the most time with her. I know you still associate with her, and I know she's been to see you a few times at your home. I'm not going to ask why she does that, or what she tells you when she comes."

"Then what the hell do you want to know?" Matt didn't mean for the question to come out so harshly. He supposed it was nerves rather than anger that gave his voice the edge.

Corwin wasn't the least bit fazed. He had been dealing with criminals for the better portion of his life, and some high-school brat with a bad attitude wasn't at all any sort of challenge. Stepping closer, he backed Matt against the wall. "I want to know if Melanie O'Conner is a partner with this new branch, if she's helping them. I want to know all you know about her."

Matt stared at the agent, swallowing heavily and keeping his eyes level with Corwin's. "I don't know anything about O'Conner and that gang. If she associates with them, then that's her business, not mine. And even if she did tell me anything about the project, I sure as hell wouldn't tell you because you'd put her back in prison, where she doesn't belong."

"Prison is for people who steal, who murder, who deal narcotics, who commit crimes against children. Seems to me that your good friend O'Conner's done, let's see, all of those things. And yet she doesn't belong? Someone who has repeatedly committed crimes?"

"She committed a crime to stop a crime. Is it just me or are you siding with the abusive parents on this one?"

Noting that he was wrong and that the teenager would be more of a challenge than he originally thought, Corwin just smiled. "You don't get it, do you, kid? The more children she takes, the more gangs she helps, the longer she gets to go to prison. She's on *thin* ice with the law. One word from you, and we can stop all this before it goes too far. But whether or not you tell me, I can promise you this. I *will* catch her, and I *will* catch the members of this new gang. And when I do, every last one of them will be put in prison with no hope whatsoever of ever seeing daylight again."

Matt took in a breath, not letting Corwin's words affect him. He knew what cops were capable of doing. They had already taken Melanie away from him once and brought him back to the home he had been so afraid of as a child. They had broken up a legacy, let a crazy man out of prison so he could murder a Hell Hound in cold blood, and were a general pain-in-the-ass for all Helping Hands.

But for all they could do merely through the use of their job title, Matt also knew that cops would lie to get their way, would exaggerate punishments to scare their opponents. Melanie had taught him that much and more, and for that, their attempts to frighten him wouldn't work.

He narrowed his eyes. "What do you have against the Helping Hands?" he asked coolly. "You pissed because you were beaten as a kid and nobody would help you?"

"Listen to me, kid," Neilson piped up when Corwin simply laughed. "Melanie O'Conner's messing with the wrong side of the law. She doesn't realize who she's dealing with."

"No, I think she does," Matt replied quietly, keeping his eyes smug and his stare even. "But the fact is, she's smarter than you guys. She knows the laws and how to get around them. You can't touch her. And this new gang? I don't know if she's helping them, but whether she is or isn't, it doesn't really matter."

"And why not?"

Matt turned his eyes back to Corwin's steely glare. "Because they've already got two kids, and you guys can't catch them. If you can't get them after two kids, then you sure as hell aren't going to get anything out of me. You want Melanie O'Conner, you catch her on your own time, and stop wasting mine."

"Let him go," Corwin ordered as Matt stormed out of the office and Neilson made a move to stop him. "We'll be back, and he knows it. The kid is scared."

Chapter 39

Collinsville, California

Melanie stood in the doorway of her room, staring dejectedly at the bed with her arms crossed. The room was dimly lit, and she preferred the darkness. She felt completely drained of energy, of emotion, of strength. Her eyes were dark and her mouth in a thin line, and she felt as though she hadn't slept in years as she rubbed her arms with cold and unsteady hands.

It had been four days since Tyler's fall, four long days filled with tears, worry, and more tears. Melanie had never known that she was capable of crying so much. For the first time, *she* was the one who had needed a shoulder to cry on, *she* was the one who everyone was helping. She was so used to being strong, to being the one everyone looked to for advice, that for a moment she didn't know what to do with the support. Caleb and Taryn had come from Oklahoma, and been there every step of the way. Melanie was barely able to tell them what had happened without starting to cry, and so Jared had taken over with the accident report.

She couldn't think straight, felt scared, as she had during the bloody and terrifying ride to the emergency room and by Tyler's side in the small, suffocating hospital room. Taryn had been right at the hospital, Melanie thought, when she said that her fear reflected her love for Tyler.

She ran a hand over her stomach as she walked into the room slowly, feeling a small swelling from where she was beginning to show. Her mind wandered to her unborn child, a child she had never imagined would be possible, never a gift granted to her after a lifetime of wrongdoings. The thought of her baby not having a father made miserable tears come to her eyes. Melanie never knew how it felt to have a family, as did no other former Hell Hound.

The only family we ever had was one another, Melanie reflected.

When she had discovered she was pregnant, she promised both herself that her child would have a family, two parents who loved one another as much as they loved their son or daughter. And it was because of that promise that she was so determined to fix the bond that had been broken between her and Tyler.

She crawled into bed, exhausted and drained, and laid next to Tyler's sleeping body. She peered down at him, at his wounds. A trail of stitches ran from the top of his right cheek to his bottom lip, the lesion still swollen. A dried scab of blood above his left eye was slightly red from where his safety glasses had broken and shattered against his skin. His forehead was bruised from hitting the ground, as was a good portion of the rest of his body. A dark contusion on his back was covered by a bandage, and three of his ribs had been cracked as a result of the fall.

Because of his injuries, he lost a lot of blood and went into shock. Even when being released from the hospital, he could barely walk, much less move. It took all three of them, Melanie, Caleb, and Taryn, to lift him from the car, into the house, and up the stairs to their bedroom.

Melanie pulled back a little when Tyler's eyes opened and he peered up at her tiredly. He didn't, couldn't, smile. His mouth wouldn't let him. But Melanie knew by the gleam in his eye that he wanted to, and that was enough. He moved his hand a little, but Melanie shook her head.

"Don't move," she ordered in a hushed voice, frowning as he winced in pain. She gnawed the inside of her lip for a moment, swallowing down the sudden tears that were threatening to surface. "You really scared me, Tyler," she told him, her voice shaky, and he moved his shoulders a bit.

"Sorry." He could barely speak the word as he gazed up at Melanie in the dusky light of the bedroom.

Melanie reached out and pushed back his hair, running her fingers through the messy blonde strands. She had to tell him now. He had waited long enough.

"Tyler, I know that you think I don't think you understand me," she said quietly, "but you're wrong. Sometimes I say stuff like that because I just get caught up in the moment, and I get so angry about everything that I just say it even if I don't mean it." Melanie swallowed hard, willing back tears. "But I want you to know that I'm sorry. I don't... I don't want you to think that I don't care about what you went through as a kid, because I know how hard it is for you to think about your parents. And..." she trailed off as she shook her head, not knowing what to say next.

"Mel—"

"No, don't talk. You'll mess up your stitches," Melanie ordered softly, gently running a finger down the cheek that wasn't swollen. "I love you, Tyler."

Tyler felt a twinge of warmth run through his chest and he desperately wanted to take Melanie in his arms. He hated not being able to move, but he knew that he was lucky he didn't die. The fall could have easily killed him. But he didn't care about his injuries, because he survived, lived through the chainsaw-split cheek, the cracked ribs, the terrifying fall.

And, he thought, *if this is what I had to go through to get Melanie to say those words, then so be it.*

"I love you too," he whispered, ignoring the pain. He gripped Melanie's hand as she took his.

Melanie lay down next to Tyler, resting her head against his arm and careful not to disturb any of his wounds. "Let's not fight anymore," she whispered, pulling the blanket up to her waist as she closed her eyes.

Tyler tightened his grip of her hand, feeling the warm silver ring on her finger, and together the two fell into a long, deep sleep.

Chapter 40

San Francisco, California

Danielle tossed an empty can of soda into the trashcan by Kelly's bed and rose from her chair. She hobbled across the room, a numbing pain running through the healing ankle. She was used to it though, to the bites of curing bone, to the chafing of crutches beneath her arms. It was hard to grip the crutch with her cast, but she made do the best she could.

Heading out into the hall, she went to the vending machine that was a few feet away from the room. She wasn't really hungry, but she hadn't eaten much since Kelly had been admitted into the hospital and the Andersons were beginning to hound her about getting food in her stomach. Quite frankly, they were getting on her nerves.

"Hello, Danielle," Rachael Anderson said as she and her husband approached. "How are you, dear?"

"I'm fine." Danielle managed a smile. "How are you?"

"We're good." Rachael noted the darkness beneath the teenager's eyes. "Have you seen Robbie?"

Danielle nodded. "Yeah. He went to the cafeteria to get something to eat. He should be back any minute. Did you need him for something?"

"Oh, no. We just wanted to see him and find out how he's doing." The Andersons fell into step behind Danielle as she headed back into Kelly's room.

"You two have barely left the hospital for the past month," Adam said. "Are you sure you don't want to come home with us for a few days? Just to relax or something? You both have to go to school sometime or another. You can't keep having people bring you your homework."

Danielle resumed her place. "I know. I'll go back soon. I promise." She looked up at the Andersons and nodded, pleasing them with her reply even though it was a lie told straight through her teeth. She felt a little guilty about lying, since they were doing so much for her and Kelly.

Danielle started to thank them for all the help and support when a movement in front of her caught her eye. She snapped her attention back to Kelly in time to see her sister's head moving slightly on the pillow.

"Mrs. Anderson, look!" she cried, rising to her feet and taking Kelly's hand. "Kelly? Can you hear me?"

"What's going on?" Robbie asked from the doorway, his hands filled with a tray of food.

"She's waking up," Adam told his son excitedly, and at the information, Robbie dropped the tray at the door and rushed to the bed. He touched Kelly's cheek, seeing a crease in her forehead that formed as she shuffled her body among the sheets.

"Come on, Kelly. You can do it," he whispered. "Come on, Kelly."

The four people that stood hovering over Kelly watched in a jumble of apprehension, disbelief, and joy as the sleeping girl in front of them slowly awoke from her five-week slumber. Danielle took in a deep breath as Kelly's eyes fluttered open, becoming wide with fear and bewilderment.

"Kelly?" Danielle asked, leaning closer to her sister. Kelly shrank back against the pillow, a fearful expression crossing her bruised face. "Kelly, what's wrong?"

"Who are you?" Kelly said in return, her brow furrowing as she took in a deep breath, observing the strange face hovering over her. Her eyes scanned the room, taking in the dim light and yellow walls, none of which looked familiar. A wave of nausea and drowsiness flowed through her, along with a strange sense of insecurity. "Where am I? What am I doing here?"

"Kelly, it's me. It's Danielle." Danielle and Robbie exchanged worried glances and looked back down at Kelly. "Don't you know who I am?"

"Kelly, you know me. It's Robbie."

Kelly pulled her hand from Danielle's grasp, not knowing if she should scream in panic or believe the girl in front of her. "I don't know you people. Who are you and why are you here? Why am I here?" She struggled to sit up, wincing as pain raced through her limbs. She looked down at her body to see her leg and arm in casts. "What—what happened to me?"

Robbie backed away from Kelly while Danielle shook her head with tears in her eyes. A nurse rushed in and began to examine Kelly, asking questions to the Andersons all the while.

"When did she wake up?"

"A few minutes ago."

"What did she say?"

"She doesn't know who we are."

The nurse straightened at Danielle's tear-filled reply. She faced Kelly's sister, her eyes sad, and then glanced at Rachael, who nodded to confirm the information. "What's your name, dear?" she asked softly.

Kelly opened her mouth at what should have been a simple question with a simple answer and closed it again when the reply didn't come to her. She searched her brain for her name, for any name. She couldn't even recognize the people in front of her, not even the slightest hint of recognition, although for some reason, they seemed to know her.

"I—I don't know," she admitted, raising her eyes to the nurse. "What's happened to me?"

Chapter 41

"Amnesia," Doctor Nathaniel Banks said as he sat before the Andersons and Danielle. "She suffered severe head trauma, most likely from the fall down the stairs, and as we had predicted, the damage to the brain gave her amnesia."

How freak'n insightful, Danielle thought sarcastically, rolling her eyes and wondering how the man had ever become a licensed doctor.

"How long will it last?" Rachael Anderson asked, taking Robbie's hand as he sighed. "Is it temporary?"

Dr. Banks looked down at his hands and leaned forward, resting his elbows on his knees. All the medical statistics and vocabulary terms came flooding to mind, frontal and parietal lobes, consolidation, but it had been his experience that using them only led to an earful of frustrated, angry-yet-terrified snaps of bitter words. Sometime, laymen terms had to be used.

"To be honest, I don't know. Sometimes it's temporary, sometimes it's permanent. It's different with every person. Some people remember things from their childhood, while others can only remember things that happened a week ago. Some experience anterograde amnesia, in which case they remember everything before the incident but cannot form new memories of anything that happens afterwards. And then there are those who don't remember anything at all, such as Kelly."

Danielle pulled her hair from her face. "But, Kelly's going to be fine, right? Why wouldn't she?" she added when Dr. Banks sighed and sat back, rubbing his eyes.

"In Kelly's case, I would hesitate to say that she will regain her memory right away. She took a bad hit to the head, and that caused some definite damage. More specifically, to the frontal and temporal lobes, which control the ability to form a memory, to store them, and to basically make a short-term memory a long-term one. There's a lot more to it, but it's all just medical talk and not any more helpful than what I just said. From this point, I have to admit that I don't honestly know what will happen with her case. But I do know, unfortunately, that the odds are not in her favor."

Adam bit his bottom lip, taking a quick glance over at Robbie as he lowered his head with a deep sigh. "What would you suggest we do?"

Dr. Banks fiddled with a pen, running it through his fingers as he thought about Kelly. "I would suggest getting her back to her normal schedule. Have her spend time with her friends, her family. Get her back into her old routine, do the same things she used to do for fun, and so on. Putting her in the same environment she was in may help her memory return, even if it is only a few memories that she gets back."

162

As Adam and Rachael nodded, Dr. Banks rose. "I'll leave you to discuss this amongst yourselves. If you have any further questions, please don't hesitate to ask."

"So what are we going to do?" Danielle asked as she left the doctor's office and back out into the hall. "The only lifestyle Kelly has ever known was with Jeffrey." She shuddered at the nightmare of ever having to live with him again.

"You and Kelly can stay with us, of course," Adam offered. "But I would suggest not telling Kelly what happened right now. She just woke from a coma and remembers absolutely nothing, and hitting her with the truth may be too much for her to handle."

"I agree." Rachael nodded.

"But Kelly's going to want to know what happened," Danielle said. "What are we supposed to say when she asks?"

Robbie cocked his head thoughtfully. "We could lie," he offered his opinion, getting three blank stares. "The doctor said that her memory will probably never return, right? So what if we give her new memories, fake memories. Positive memories."

"You mean give her a past that never really happened," Danielle realized what he was saying. "How exactly do you plan on doing that?"

Kelly offered a small smile when she looked up to see the same four people entering her room who had been by her side when she awoke from her coma. None of them looked familiar, no matter how hard she tried to remember them. It was a hard concept for her to accept, not having any recollection of who she was. What she really didn't understand was the fact that she had a complete grasp of the English language, she could count as high as she wanted and distinguish one color from another, yet she couldn't even remember who she was.

What happened to her?

"Kelly? How are you feeling?" Danielle asked as she sat down on the bed next to her sister.

"I'm fine," Kelly answered, a bit tired. She scanned the faces of the people in front of her. "Please, I want to know why I'm here. What happened to me?"

"You were in a car crash," Robbie answered before anyone else could say anything, and Kelly didn't notice the way Danielle's eyes closed at the reply. "It was real bad. You got some broken bones and went into a coma. Danielle broke her leg and wrist from the crash as well." He pointed to Danielle, who remained silent.

Kelly's eyes widened slightly as she struggled to remember any sort of crash, but found her mind blank. "What... how did I crash?"

"It was raining out, and another car lost control and slammed into you."

"Oh." Toying with a strand of her shoulder-length blonde hair, Kelly narrowed her eyes thoughtfully at Robbie. "Who are you people? How do I know you?"

Robbie took in a deep breath, taking a quick glance at Danielle before turning back to Kelly. "That's Danielle, your sister. My name is Robbie, Robbie Anderson. I'm your... I'm your brother."

Chapter 42

Collinsville, California

Melanie opened her eyes to darkness, her body yearning for more sleep. She rolled over on her side to face Tyler, who was sleeping soundly next to her on his back. The clock on the stand next to the bed read five-forty-three, telling Melanie that she had seventeen minutes left to sleep if she wanted to make it to work on time. She couldn't sleep though, not when she felt nauseated and hungry at the same time.

Instead, she watched Tyler in the light of the clock as he slept, his head slightly turned with one hand on his stomach. She could just make out his profile, his closed eye with long lashes, his nose that had been broken at least four times. His mouth was average size, with full lips, and he had been lucky enough to never need braces, for only about three of his bottom teeth were slightly crooked. The ear she could see, his left ear, had two silver hoops pierced through.

The alarm went off before she realized that she had been staring at Tyler for so long, and she snapped it off in a hurry. Rising, she went into the bathroom, flicking on the light and grabbing a hair tie from the counter. She pulled back her long brown hair into a tight braid and clipped it up into a bun, not really in the mood to go through the trouble of washing her hair, and started for the shower, stopping and grabbing her stomach as a wave of queasiness raced through her. She felt a chill and fell down to the toilet as the nausea slammed against the back of her throat. Gripping the seat, she allowed it to take over her body.

A hand on her shoulder startled her, but Melanie couldn't raise her head. The nausea tightened in her stomach, and she was sick again. She sensed Tyler next to her as he kneeled down slowly, rubbing her back. She wanted to tell him to get back in bed, that he shouldn't be moving.

"Here," Tyler said softly as Melanie rose, handing her a small towel. She wiped her face, and he was glad that he could now talk without having to worry about his face splitting open again. "Are you okay?"

"I'm fine," Melanie answered hoarsely. "The things I go through for you."

He smiled faintly. "Take a shower. You'll feel better. I promise." He gently nudged Melanie after she had brushed her teeth.

"You shouldn't be up," Melanie protested as he massaged her shoulders. "You need your rest for everything to heal." She faced him, taking in the recovering wounds on his face. The scar across his cheek wasn't as bad as she'd feared it would be, and the cuts on his nose and eye were all but gone.

"I've been on my back for the past two weeks," Tyler argued, running a hand across her chin. "I think I deserve a little play time." He raised his eyebrows, and Melanie smiled when he pulled her closer to him.

"I have to get ready for work," she told him, returning the quick smile he gave her.

"Well then, I'll get you ready."

"Yeah?"

"Yeah. In more ways than one."

"O'Conner, I got the latest information on Jeffrey and Monica Ponder. And Kelly Mitchell was released from the hospital yesterday and went to live with the Andersons. Their number is next to your phone."

"Thanks, Hawkins," Melanie said as she walked into the main office of South Bay, trying to hide the smiles that were leftover from her morning rendezvous with the man who was determined to prove he was healed. Hawkins fell in step behind her, handing her the files. "What else have you got for me?"

"Well, a man named Zack Corwin called and asked for you to call him back as soon as you got in today. Actually, he demanded that you call back. Intimidated the secretary apparently. Friend of yours?" he asked when Melanie sighed and rolled her eyes.

"Not at all. He works for the F.B.I."

"The F.B.I.?" Hawkins repeated as they entered the empty break room. "What kind of trouble are you in now?"

Melanie lifted her eyes to meet his. "The kind that follows you around for the rest of your life. Now if you'll excuse me, I have work to do." She waited until he left before reading the files of Jeffrey and Monica Ponder. Jeffrey's trial was coming up, and as a key witness she was obligated to testify. She was supposed to go to court in a month, but the date had already been pushed back twice and she wouldn't have been the least bit surprised if it got rescheduled again.

Monica Ponder's trial had already taken place. Melanie had testified, but the real story had been from Robbie and Danielle. Monica, much to Melanie's surprise, hadn't been standing in a fit of rage, but instead stood weeping and screaming out claims that she was innocent. There had been many tears shed, and even more sobs choked out with pleas for the people to believe her, that she too had been a victim of Jeffrey Ponder's wrath. Melanie hadn't once felt any amount of sympathy for her.

Now, as she opened the files, she hoped with all her will that the woman would be spending her entire life in prison. She glanced through some information on the stepfather, noting the court date, before coming to the sentence.

"Monica Janice Ponder found guilty... Well, you deserve it," Melanie muttered, then continued to read. "Sentenced to three years' probation?!" She leapt to her feet. "One hundred community service hours and three years' probation after fulfillment, damn it, you miserable son-of-a-*bitch*!" She threw the file down, barely noticing that the papers fell to the floor as she punched the wall. "You should get *life*!"

"O'Conner?" a voice asked from outside her office door. "Are you alright?"

"I'm fine!" Melanie yelled back, not bothering to wonder who it was. Rummaging through the file, she found a small slip of paper with a phone number and the name *Anderson* on it. She dialed the number as fast as she could on her cell, waiting impatiently as it rang.

"Hello?"

"Is this Robbie?"

"Yeah. Who's this?"

"Melanie O'Conner." She was too angry to sit, so she paced the break room floor instead. "I heard Kelly was released. How is she?"

"She's better," Robbie replied, sounding grim.

"I was told about the amnesia. She doesn't remember anything?"

"Nothing." Robbie sighed. "We're not really sure what to do. The doctor says we should get her back into her old routine, but me and Danielle don't really want her to remember all that stuff that happened. You know, since she's been through so much and everything."

Melanie frowned and stopped her pacing. "If you didn't tell her what happened, what *did* you tell her?" She waited a moment, then listened impatiently while Robbie carefully outlined his plan for Kelly.

"So you're lying to her?" Melanie asked incredulously. "You're keeping everything from her, making her think she's someone she's not. Why would you do that?"

"If you had the chance to forget everything your father did to you, would you take it?"

The question hit Melanie hard and she felt a stab of cold pain pierce through her chest. She had to stop for a moment to realign her thoughts, and to keep the anger that had bubbled up under control. "What happened to me in my past has made me who I am today," she said as calmly as she could. "If you try to keep Kelly sheltered from the truth, what do you think is going to happen when her memory returns?"

"What's your problem?" Now Robbie sounded angry as well. "I thought you wanted to help Kelly!"

"I do, Robbie, but—"

"If you really wanted to help her, then you wouldn't be sitting here telling me that Kelly should know all about the days when her stepfather used to hit her with an iron wrench and leave her bleeding and crying while he went out and got drunk! I haven't known Kelly that long, but I'm pretty sure that's one of two thousand memories she doesn't want!"

Melanie took in a deep breath, calming herself again while rubbing her forehead. "Robbie Anderson, you listen to me. I realize you think that what you are doing for Kelly is good, but it isn't. She has to know her past, no matter how hard it hurts. Telling her that you're her brother and that your parents are her parents isn't going to make her life any easier! You—hello? Robbie? Oh, you little shit!" She nearly threw her phone out of frustration.

"Well," she said to herself, "I guess I'll be taking a trip to San Francisco." Opening the door, she headed for the counselors' building, where her office was located. She adjusted her dark green, army-style pants and walked towards the work station where the boys were sent to do their chores. As she approached it, she saw Drill Instructor Larry Harding yelling at one of the newest detainees, Charlie Knox.

Thirteen year-old Charlie had been brought after stealing his neighbor's car and smashing it into a guardrail, which was after assaulting a man who tried to stop the theft. Melanie knew that he was one stubborn hard-ass. Nearly the same, she mused as she stalked over, as she was at that age.

"What do we got here, Harding? All bark and no bite, is he?" She smirked at Charlie, whose face was red from anger.

"You want a bite, bitch, come and get it," Charlie retorted, holding out his arms. "You think you people can lock me up in here and order me around? Well, kiss my goddamn ass, bitch!"

"How long you in here for, Knox?" Melanie crossed her arms and peered over at the boy while he kicked at the dirt.

"Eighty days. But you can bet I'll be busting outta this shit-hole before my time's up, and there ain't a damn thing you can do about it! So ease up off my damn back before I pop you one and finish off what's left of that fucked-up face of yours."

Melanie's hand shot out and a second later she had grabbed hold of his wrist, twisting it sharply while sweeping a leg around his feet. Charlie fell to the ground, crying out in pain as Melanie grabbed hold of his neck with her free hand, pressing her thumb into the flesh between his neck and jaw. The arm she had grabbed before tripping him she held against the ground at an odd angle, careful not to snap the bone, though she could have done so with ease.

Charlie winced in pain, arching his neck to try and avoid Melanie's pressing thumb, but the more he squirmed, the worse it felt. "You bitch!" he yelled, catching a glimpse of Harding's smug face staring down at him.

Melanie leaned down close to Charlie, her eyes narrow. "You just got your ass kicked by a woman, Charlie. A *pregnant* woman, no less. Not so tough when you're the one pinned to the ground, are you?" She tightened her grip on his wrist. "If I can get you now, you better believe that I can get you tomorrow, or the day after that. You sleep on that for the next eighty days, and then we'll decide who has the bigger bite after all. You got me?"

Charlie managed a slight nod. "Yeah, I got it. Now get the hell off me." He started to shove Melanie away when she released him, then changed his mind and instead simply rose to his feet.

"Now, you're going to do your chores without complaining, or I will be back out here, and you can bet your sorry punk-ass that I will make you bleed from every hole in your scrawny body. Are we clear?" Melanie waited until Charlie nodded again to smile smugly. "Oh, and Charlie?" Charlie turned, his face a portrait of fury and embarrassment. "I'll see you in two hours, my office. I'm going to be your counselor."

Melanie left Harding to look after the rest of the boys as she headed into the counselors' building, still fuming over Robbie and his lies. Instead of an abusive stepfather, Kelly was now stuck with a head full of forgotten memories and a stubborn jack-ass of a friend. She couldn't get the girl out of her mind. She could replay every conversation they had, could remember the way Kelly had been determined, strong willed, full of fire.

Now, thanks to one man's abusive ways and a boy's stubborn desire to heal old wounds, the girl would never be the same.

She saved my life. Please, help me save her hers.

Danielle's plea rang though her head. Melanie knew she had to do something, and letting Kelly Mitchell go on thinking that the Andersons were her picture-perfect family would never make her life any easier. She had to keep her promise.

Or she would die trying.

Chapter 43

Two hours later, the door to Melanie's office swung open and an angry-looking teenager stomped in, followed by Sergeant Brian Hawkins. Hawkins said nothing as he released Charlie Knox and exited the office, pulling the door shut behind him while Charlie stood with his arms crossed. He stared over at Melanie, who was sitting on the edge of her desk, glancing through a file. She had looked up when he entered, but now she turned her eyes back to the file, his file.

"Mr. Knox, seems you did a lot of work to get yourself in here, huh?" she asked, turning a page of the folder. "You really know how to piss off the authorities."

"Bet I know how to piss you off too."

Melanie snapped the file shut and stood. She was nearly the same height as the boy, as he had only about an inch on her. "You probably could," she replied coolly, gesturing for him to sit. "Let's get right down to it, Charlie. Why'd you do it?"

Charlie shrugged lazily. "Just wanted too."

With a smirk, Melanie shook her head, wondering why the kids all seemed to use the same excuse. It was always a lie, a cover-up. "No one does stuff like that just because they want to. People do it for attention, or to make a point, or because they want to be villain of the year. Believe me, I know. I've done all that bullshit. So what's your excuse? Were you trying to impress a few friends, establish your turf, what? Or was this all some desperate cry for attention?"

"What do you care?"

His tone of voice told Melanie that she was getting closer, which pleased her, considering that she had been talking for less than ten minutes. "I care because I want to help you, but I can't unless you tell me something."

Charlie huffed and shook his head. "All you bastards here care about is punishing us. Even you kicked me to the ground."

"True, and I don't regret it, either," Melanie agreed. "But I did that to make a point."

"And what point is that? Never think twice about hitting a chick?"

Melanie suppressed a huff, allowing Charlie to believe that she had taken him down only because he had issues about hitting members of the opposite sex. Still, she shook her head, keeping her voice soft.

"There are some things in life you can't control, Charlie, but you being here isn't one of them."

"Screw you. You don't know anything."

"So tell me something." Melanie leaned back against her desk while Charlie glared at her with an intense hatred.

"I'm not telling you jack-shit, so just go to hell."

"Okay, I can see you want to play hardball." Melanie crossed her own arms and returned Charlie's glare. "For the next eighty days you will be in here twice a week for two hours. If, by the end of those eighty days, I don't think you're ready to be released, I'm going to write up your report saying that I recommend that your sentence is extended, in which case you will be here for at least another month, if not longer. And that's a promise." She bit back a smile when she saw a glimmer of displeasure run through the boy's eyes. "But that can be changed. You hold the keys to freedom here, Charlie. All you have to do is talk."

Charlie hesitated, squirming in the chair before replying. "About what?"

"About whatever you want. Movies, music, girls—"

"Pornos?" Charlie cut in, and Melanie was slightly taken aback by the sincerity in his question, although she didn't show it.

"If... that's what you want to talk about for the day, then fine. You pick the topic." She suppressed a smile when Charlie seemed to be considering what she was saying, knowing that she had to deal with him differently that she had with Kelly. Kelly had been easier to break, but that was because Kelly had something to lose for not talking – Danielle.

Charlie uncrossed his arms and folded his hands, narrowing his eyes suspiciously at his counselor. "Why would you let me pick all the topics? What do I gain out of all this?"

"Well, Charlie, as long as you promise to talk," Melanie shrugged, "then I promise to listen."

San Francisco, California

Lakeside High was calm and quiet, a contrast to the usual bustling cliques of teenagers that were always chattering loudly and quickly. The first bell was yet to ring, and the halls normally were crowded with students at their lockers or hanging out with their friends, but on this morning their usual shouts were not heard. Instead, they whispered amongst themselves, pointing and doing their best to be subtle about it. Some people turned away and headed for their classrooms, wanting to avoid a confrontation, while others simply stood and stared.

To Kelly Mitchell, nothing was out of the ordinary. As she walked down the halls on her first day back, she couldn't remember the school ever being a loud and rowdy place, couldn't even remember the school itself, but she did start to wonder why she was getting so many stares. Her arms were beginning to ache from the crutches and the skin beneath the cast was itching, but she ignored it. Robbie, at her side, carried her books as he brought her to her locker, trying to ignore the whispers.

Kelly looked around as she made her way through the crowds. She saw girls whispering to one another behind their hands and sympathetic smiles and frowns being cast towards her.

"Why are they staring at me?" Kelly whispered over to Robbie.

"Because, um, the car crash was a big deal. Everyone was really amazed that you survived," he lied, nodding to a few of his friends. He had made sure days earlier that as many people as possible in the school knew not to mention the real truth.

"So do I know all these people?"

170

"Most of them. You had a lot of friends." If he was going to give her a new past, he was going to make it a good one.

"Kelly, girl, you look great!" Natalie Weathers cried as she ran up, giving Kelly a big hug. "Welcome back!"

"Thanks..." Kelly shook her head as she struggled to remember the girl's name.

"Natalie."

"Natalie," Kelly repeated. "How, um... how do I know you?"

Natalie stole a quick look over at Robbie, who was staring at her expectantly. She knew what to do. She had been friends with Robbie for almost ten years and dated him briefly during their sophomore year, remaining friends after they had realized that they weren't meant to be anything more.

"We've been friends for years," she answered Kelly. "Since like the fifth grade. We do everything together. Come on, I'll fill you in on the way to class." She took Kelly's books from Robbie and started to lead her off down the hall to her first period classroom. They turned around a corner, bumping solidly into a person on the other side. He caught Kelly as she lost her balance, tripping over her crutches.

"Whoa," Matt Harper said as he helped Kelly gain her footing. He held on to her arms, staring down at her. It was the first time he had seen her since she was released from the hospital.

"Are you okay?" he asked as Kelly pulled back a bit.

"I'm fine," she said sharply, sighing when Matt took a step back. "Sorry. I'm just sick of everyone asking me if I'm okay."

"Hey, I completely understand. It's a tough time for you. If you want to talk, I'm here." Nodding at her, Matt offered a smile.

Kelly considered the comment. "You know, you're the first person that's said that to me. Everyone else is all, do you remember me and everything. It's really frustrating. My brother said—"

"Your brother?" Matt cut in, confused.

"Yeah, Robbie. He said that one day I'll remember again. I just have to give it time."

Matt raised his eyebrows, looking down at Natalie as she winced and bit her bottom lip. "I don't know what Robbie's been telling you, but—"

"Come on, Kelly. We're going to be late for class." Natalie grabbed Kelly's arm and started pulling her away. When they were out of range for Matt to hear them, she turned to Kelly. "Girl, you are so lucky. Matt Harper is only the hottest guy in the school, and he wants to talk to *you*."

Kelly craned her neck to see if Matt was still in view. "Did I know him before? He's cute." She was starting to like her old life, especially since it was filled with friends and Matt Harper.

Natalie searched her brain for a story, suddenly remembering that Kelly wasn't supposed to be talking to Matt. "Well... you two hung out in different crowds."

"What do you mean, different crowds?"

Shrugging, Natalie tossed her hair over her shoulders. "You're really popular, and Matt, well, he hangs out with what some people refer to as the bad kind of crowd." Robbie would want her to get Kelly to stay away from Matt. "But he's actually kind of dangerous. He steals and fights and stuff. He may be cute, but you might want to stay away from him."

Kelly couldn't see how someone who looked and dressed like Matt Harper could be dangerous, but then again, how was she to know? With a sigh, she looked down at the floor. "I guess so," she replied. "But if we're in different crowds, why did he talk to me just now?"

Natalie gestured to a classroom, escorting Kelly through the door. "You talked sometimes, but not all that much. Before the crash he was planning on asking you out."

"How do you know?"

"Hey, I got my sources." Natalie smiled. "But like I said, he's dangerous. Come on, class is about to start."

"Kelly, can I see you before you leave?" Daniel Fiesk asked as the bell rang and his chemistry class was released for the day. Kelly nodded and hobbled up to her teacher's desk, adjusting her arms on the crutches. She looked over her shoulder for Robbie, but he had already left, saying he had to do something right after class.

"Well, first I wanted to tell you that in order to make up your grade for this semester, you're going to have to do a lot of work." Mr. Fiesk gave a small smile when Kelly sighed. "But I know that all your teachers are saying that, and I always liked you, ever since you first came to my class. So I'm going to give you two worksheets to do. If you complete them, then you get the extra credit."

"Really?" Kelly's face brightened. "No tests or projects or anything?" She grinned when her teacher shook his head. "That's awesome. Thanks, Mr. Fiesk."

"Anytime. And one more thing." He took a stack of papers from his desk and handed them to Kelly. "These are some of the things I never got to return to you. There's some tests, quizzes, worksheets, essays. I thought you might want to see how good a chemistry student you were, and maybe it would help you move right along."

Kelly sifted through the papers. "Yeah, this is great. Anything that can help, right?" She was happy to see that at least she had gotten good grades before the car crash. But before she could enjoy her successes, a test she peered at brought forth a frown of perplexity. "Hey, what's this? I don't think this is my stuff." She held out the sheet of paper and pointed to a name. "That says Kelly Mitchell."

Mr. Fiesk smiled in confusion. "Which is why I'm giving you the papers." He sounded unsure, and Kelly noted that.

"But my name's Kelly Anderson." Her voice was convincing, and Mr. Fiesk wasn't sure if she was trying to persuade him or herself.

"Kelly, your last name is Mitchell."

After taking a moment to stare at her teacher as though she had all of a sudden forgotten where she was and who she was talking to, her mind desperately searching every crack and crevice as to who she really was, Kelly nodded quickly to try to brush off her puzzlement.

"Right, right. I still get confused with everything." She tried to play it off, then stopped when she remembered Matt Harper's confused face when she said she had a brother. "Thanks for the stuff, Mr. Fiesk," she said to her teacher, and exited the classroom as quickly as possible. She wanted to go home and sort out her things, do a little investigating on her past. She wanted to see the type of person she had been, what activities she had been involved in, what guys she may have liked or even dated.

More than anything, she wanted to know her name.

Chapter 44

Collinsville, California

Melanie entered her home angrily, tossing her jacket onto the chair by the front door and pounding up the stairs, her heavy black boots echoing off the walls. Once in her bedroom, she stripped off the camouflage shirt and pants, pulling on a pair of her usual baggy jeans and tank top. She slung her work clothes into the corner, whirling around and shoving the door to the bathroom open angrily. Tyler was still at work, and it was just as well. She wasn't in the mood to talk, and had no problem letting people know she was pissed off.

Her cell phone rang shrilly from the nightstand by the bed. Melanie took her time answering the call, catching it on its sixth ring.

"What?"

"Miss O'Conner?" The voice was hesitant, and Melanie knew instantly who it was.

"Danielle? What's wrong? Why are you calling?" Melanie didn't mean to sound as harsh as she did, but she was still angry with the Andersons and with Danielle.

"I wanted to talk to you about Kelly," Danielle replied. "Robbie told me that you called here earlier asking when you could come and see her, and that you were mad. I know that you don't agree with what we're doing, but—"

"You're damn right I don't agree!" Melanie cut in sharply. "You are *brainwashing* Kelly into thinking she's someone she's not. And that's not even the worst part! I called Robbie hoping I could see Kelly and help her, and you want to know what I found out? That you guys are sending her to live with Robbie's grandfather in New York for two months. My guess is, he's in on this whole bullshit plan and that Kelly's being sent away so people won't talk about the truth."

"That's not why," Danielle protested. "She's confused right now, and she needs some time to sort things out. Even the doctor says so!"

With a disgusted sigh, Melanie threw out her free hand and punched the wall. "You're damn right she's confused! She has no memory of who she is, Danielle! Why can't you understand that Kelly needs to know the truth? Why can't Robbie's parents see how wrong you guys are in doing this? Why the hell are they so supportive of this bullshit decision?"

"Because they know how horrible everything is, with what Kelly's gone through and all. And they understand why me and Robbie are trying to protect her from it all."

174

"That's bullshit, Danielle, and you know it," Melanie shot back at the reply. "When her memory comes back, how do you think she's going to feel about you guys lying to her?"

"I would think she'd feel grateful!" Danielle's voice got stronger, braver. "She always wished she could just erase everything that Jeffrey did to her, and now it's all gone! If her memory does come back, she'll thank us for wanting her to have a happy past instead of one full of abuse!"

"You just don't get it, do you?" Melanie sighed again and shook her head, lowering herself to the bed. "You are in no way, shape, or form helping your sister. If anything, you're destroying her. Kelly isn't Kelly Mitchell, sister to Danielle, friend to Robbie Anderson, anymore. Now she's a creation of you and Robbie's imagination. A character in some sick and twisted plot." She could only imagine what would happen when Kelly's memory returned and she found out that her new life was nothing more than a lie, a fantasy.

"Have fun with your story, kid."

Melanie hung up the phone before Danielle had a chance to reply. With a loud breath, she fell back onto the pillow and closed her eyes, running a hand over her stomach. She struggled to force Danielle into the back of her mind, let go of the stress like Tyler wanted her to.

Less than four more months, she thought, her mind going to Tyler. *What the fuck did we get ourselves into?* But she craved that unknown, needed it, needed her family. It had taken her too many years to discover, and not without surprise and bewilderment, that for the rest of her life she didn't want to be alone. She, the fiercely independent Hell Hound who had no fear in wandering dark streets at night, was ready to give up her wild past for the mere possibility of a future filled with structure instead of spontaneity.

And what a punch to the gut *that* was.

She hadn't planned on falling asleep, and it wasn't until she opened her eyes to see Tyler staring down at her that she realized she had just wasted the past two hours on sleep.

"Long day?" Tyler asked, kissing her on the cheek after slowly kneeling down at the side of the bed.

"And then some," Melanie replied. "What about you?"

Tyler shrugged and propped his head up on his hand. "Not much. It was pretty slow. Just did some paperwork and stuff. The boss doesn't want me going out to face the foster families with my ribs and all, so he gave me some files and shit to go through. What about you?"

"I had a kid try to show me up today." Melanie gave Tyler a detailed description of the teenager's attitude. "All talk and no walk. Not a lot of muscle. Nothing more than a high-school thug."

"Well, I hate to call you a hypocrite, but..." Tyler trailed off with a grin, laughing when Melanie shoved his shoulder lightly. He rubbed a hand over her stomach. "So, how's everything in here?"

"Fine. I'm ready to have the thing out of me, though. I'm getting tired of this nausea."

"Yeah, and plus with the whole mood swing thing—"

"I haven't had any mood swings," Melanie cut in with a frown. She made a face when she caught Tyler's playful grin.

"So I've been thinking, what are we going to name it... him... her?" Tyler looked down at her stomach. For over five months, she wasn't very big, but he had been told that some women stayed fairly small.

Melanie thought about the question. "Well, we don't know if it's going to be a boy or a girl, so we should come up with names for both. I think it's going to be a boy, though."

"Why?"

"Because the damn thing kicked me this morning, and scared the crap out of me. Far as I figure, only a guy wants so much attention that he has to kick me in order to get it." She raised her eyebrows pointedly and looked up at Tyler cocked his head to the side.

"So if I kick you, I'll get attention?"

"You'll get your own foot up your ass."

"Naturally." He kissed her again. "So back to names. How about... Seth?" Melanie shook her head after a brief pause to consider. "Dean? Michael?" Two more disagreements. "Well, what do you have in mind?"

Melanie hesitated before answering, wondering if Tyler would agree or not. She was sure he would, but was anxious because the answer would mean everything. Swallowing and breathing in again to steady her nerves, she gave a small smile.

"Josh." Her voice was quiet, sadly soft.

Tyler felt a wave of nostalgia run through him at the name, one that would always be in his memories. Melanie spoke of Josh Tucker, a forgotten name but not a forgotten friend. The person claiming that hidden name was a hero, was a legend. He was someone who meant the world to more than one hundred children, to four former Hell Hounds.

Josh Tucker was also known as Wess Porter.

Tyler grinned, wondering why he hadn't thought about using Wess's real name as he nodded down at Melanie. "I love it," he told her honestly, and he truly did. "Josh it is."

"You can pick the middle name," Melanie decided, and Tyler didn't hesitate to answer.

"Mathew. Joshua Mathew Scotford." When they got married it would have to be under the name Mel Scotford, since technically Tyler Mason didn't exist.

"Mathew for Mathew Harper." Melanie understood. The first child taken by the Helping Hands, the beginning of the legacy. "It's perfect."

Tyler sat down on the bed next to her, happy to finally have a name. He would feel even better when he told Melanie what he had also done with his slow day at work.

"I was talking with a co-worker today—"

"You? Talking small talk with a co-worker?"

"Yeah, well, I was bored," Tyler replied with an impatient shake of his head. "Anyway, he told me about this bed-and-breakfast a few towns over, like two hours away. It's like a marriage bed-and-breakfast. You go, get married, and stay the night. I thought you might want to know about it. I got some information online if you want to see it."

A bed-and-breakfast sounded surprisingly pleasing to Melanie. Neither she nor Tyler wanted a big wedding. They weren't even going to get dressed up, and the only people they wanted to invite were Taryn and Caleb, and, of course, Fred Kindle. Tyler had wanted Mickey to attend as well, but decided against it after considering the fact that it wasn't safe to start bringing in people from the past of the original Helping Hands, as well as the current benefactor for the newest branch.

"So we can get it done in a night? Just go and get married?" Melanie smiled. "No hassling with wedding plans, no uninvited guests showing up—"

"No reporters trying to find a story," Tyler finished. "Just us. And, we can go anytime we want, so long as we have a reservation."

Melanie felt a twinge of anticipation run through her stomach. "Maybe we should find out when the next opening is."

"Next Wednesday, seven PM. It's been a slow month and not many people get married during the week." Tyler grinned when Melanie rolled her eyes.

"So confident, you are," she teased, her face turning serious as the realization of it all set in, the fact that in less than a week she would be married. Her, Melanie O'Conner, former Helping Hand and convicted felon. Never had she imagined marriage, or even making it through life without being killed or locked away for good. She had come a long way, they all had, and she was happy.

For once in her life, she was happy, and that said something.

"So we're doing this, really doing this now? After all the bullshit—"

"We're finally getting married," Tyler finished her sentence again, and kissed her firmly. He had always loved her, ever since he met her at the age of eleven. It was one thing to be with her on a mental and emotional level, then a physical, and another to have her as a fiancée. But as a wife, and soon-to-be mother of his child, he knew he couldn't ever be happier.

"I'll call Taryn and Caleb."

Part Two

Chapter 1

Three Months Later

San Francisco, California

Kelly stepped out of the car and onto the sidewalk in front of her home, taking in the sight that was most familiar to her. It had been three long months since she'd been back, although spending the time in New York with her grandfather had been great. Days of shopping and exploring the sights, everything being new to her, nights of attending the theater, dining at elegant restaurants, or just relaxing in the penthouse her grandfather owned. She'd had a chance to clear her mind, and her wounds were healing nicely.

She still didn't remember anything, but there had been moments when it seemed like something was familiar or there was a memory trying to break through, and she had decided that in time it would all come back. Until that time came, she would wait patiently and enjoy the fact that the car crash hadn't killed her.

It seemed a little suspicious that she was sent to New York after only a week of being back in school, but she didn't question it because she wasn't all that sure she wanted to be around people. She got the impression that most of them were uncomfortable around her.

"So how's it feel to be back home?" Robbie asked as he closed the car door and took Kelly's bags from the trunk.

"Refreshing." Kelly turned about herself, staring down the street. "New York was nice, but I'd rather be home."

"Well, let's get you all unpacked." Danielle took Kelly's arm and began leading her up the front walk. Rachael and Adam were already inside getting dinner ready.

She was about to turn away from the street when a house a few doors down from her own caught her eye. Kelly stopped, staring at the pearl-white dwelling with dark blue shutters. Her eyes traveled up the trellis that led to the second floor. There was a window shaped like a dome, with white lace curtains.

"Have I... been there before?" Kelly pointed and asked Danielle, who hesitated before replying.

"One of your friends used to live there," Robbie replied with ease. It was a lie he had been preparing for. "She moved away when you were in eighth grade."

"So who lives there now?"

"Nobody," Danielle answered, glad that she wasn't lying to her sister. "It's been vacant for a few months now."

Kelly nodded, chewing on her bottom lip as she stared at the house. She felt something, almost like she was remembering, her mind was searching for a memory. She could *almost* figure out why the house seemed so familiar, and it was frustrating that she couldn't put the pieces together.

"I guess it just seems familiar," she said, then went into the house as her brother and sister ushered her inside.

Salem, Oregon

Fred Kindle's home was silent, the air tense and the atmosphere gloomy as the night progressed. The room was bright, but failed to lessen the sinking hearts of the three sitting around the dining room table.

Melanie picked at her food, pushing a bite of steak around the plate with her fork as she swallowed heavily. Tyler sat across from her, tapping his fingers on the tabletop while Fred watched the both of them silently, waiting for one of them to speak. He didn't think either of them would want to be the first to outwardly acknowledge what he had just told them.

Finally, Tyler took in a deep breath. He blinked to keep the tears from his eyes. "How much... um, how much time do you have?" he asked, his voice low, forehead creased with distress.

Fred gave a small shrug. "Three months, maybe five," he replied. "There's a doctor that I went to in Florida. Says that if the chemotherapy works, I might have at least six months." He knew that his last comment wouldn't make his nephew and niece-in-law feel any better. It certainly didn't make him feel better.

"So the trip to Florida wasn't for a woman," Melanie put in.

"No." Fred shook his head. "My doctor here recommended a specialist in Jacksonville. I couldn't tell you guys because I didn't know everything yet. But hey, on the bright side," he tapped Tyler's arm, getting his nephew to look at him, "at least I got to see the two of you get married. I had to live with you guys for over a year, always yelling and fighting. 'Bout drove me nuts with all your soap-opera drama." He smiled when the couple at the table looked at one another, sharing a small yet sad grin. "And if I'm lucky," he added, "I'll get to see the newest addition to the family."

Tyler looked over at Melanie, for a moment feeling a spout of joy before the reality hit him.

Lung cancer. Damn it, his uncle didn't even smoke. Fred Kindle had been a father to him, had taken him in when he was homeless, hungry, and a criminal on the run. He had supported the Helping Hands project and given Tyler an education.

And now, Tyler couldn't find a way to help Fred, to repay him for his kindness.

"Fred, I don't... I don't know what to say to all this," Tyler finally admitted. "I mean, what... where do we go from here?"

Fred glanced down at his plate before replying. He hadn't eaten much, and neither had Tyler or Melanie. "I guess all we can do is take care of one another. I'm leaving the garage to the both of you," he told them. "Maurice, the manager, can take charge when I'm... um... I trained him myself, so he'll do a good job. One of you guys will have to take a trip up here once or twice a month to check everything out, but you'll do fine. I'm also leaving you guys some money, and some for the baby as well." He gestured towards Melanie with his head. "Even after I'm gone, I'll be taking care of you."

"Fred, isn't there a chance that you can make it through this?" Melanie asked, trying to recall anything she'd ever heard about cancer. "I mean, can't we do something? Anything? Fred," she pleaded when he only shook his head at her questions, tears brimming in his eyes.

Tyler let out a deep breath and rose from the table slowly. He wrapped her arms around Fred, his only remaining blood relative. After a moment's hesitation, Melanie joined them, and the three hugged silently beneath the glimmering chandelier.

Chapter 2

Collinsville, California

Tyler sighed and lowered himself down onto the couch, staring at the blank television in front of him and not saying a word. He didn't spare a glance over at Melanie when she settled down next to him, nor did he respond when she took his hand.

They arrived home only an hour before, Tyler silent the entire ride. His thoughts and emotions were jumbled about, and he was perfectly content to remain in a state of clouded denial. It made things easier, less real. Fred would be fine, live for many more years still to come.

"It'll be okay, Tyler," Melanie said in a soft voice, a tone she hardly ever used with anyone other than the children she helped. "We'll make it through this."

Tyler swallowed heavily, moving his eyes from the television down to his hands. Leave it to Melanie to take him out of denial. "I don't want to get through this. I want it to not be real. He was like a father to me," he replied quietly. "He took me in and gave me a second chance. He protected me from the cops, supported the project, welcomed you into his home. And now all I can do to repay him is sit back and watch as he dies."

Gnawing on her bottom lip, Melanie gazed at Tyler's crestfallen face, searching for the right words to comfort him. "I don't know what to say." She lowered her eyes dejectedly. "What do you want me to do?"

"Tell me Fred will be fine," he replied, closing his eyes when she pressed her lips together sadly.

"I can't do that, Tyler."

He sighed and rubbed his eyes. "I know." He lifted a hand and let it drop back down to the couch. "I just... You know, in a few months we're going to have a lot on our hands." He traced a finger over Melanie's stomach. He was changing the subject and Melanie knew it, and obligingly let him. "I bet he'll be just like me."

"Great," Melanie replied sarcastically. "Another pain-in-the-ass hot-shot with an ego the size of Texas." She grinned as Tyler shrugged sheepishly.

"Hey, hot-shot or not, you married me."

"Yeah, well, I had to. You knocked me up."

Tyler raised his eyebrows playfully, doing his best to forget about his uncle for the moment as he looked down at the Melanie's swelling stomach. "Damn glad I did, too," he replied. "Otherwise you might be off running around with old man Casper making all sorts of crack head babies." He smiled when Melanie huffed and smacked his arm. Expression turning serious, he reached out to take her hand. "You know, I always wanted a kid of my own. I spent so much time helping others, I started wishing that one of them was mine. And I always hoped it would be with you."

Melanie toyed with a strand of hair. She didn't know how to reply, for she wasn't good with words. But she did know what she had thought as a teenager, and that she could tell without a problem. "When I was a kid, I never thought I'd make it to twenty-one. I always thought I'd end up dead or in prison. I guess one of those thoughts was right." She gave a small laugh, and when Tyler didn't reply, she frowned. "I never really thought about the future, because I knew I wouldn't have much of one."

"Then what did you think about?"

She shrugged. "The project, the kids, the gang. Where and with who I was going to spend the night." She nudged Tyler when she saw the disappointment in his eyes. "But if it makes you feel any better, I always wanted to spend the night with you."

"Yeah?" Tyler couldn't help but grin. "You know, if anyone ever heard you talk like this, they'd think you'd gone soft."

"Yeah, because you're so tough," Melanie shot back. "No one would be afraid of you if they knew *you* talked like this."

"True," Tyler agreed. "So it's our secret." He held out his right hand, and Melanie took it to seal the deal.

"You got it. Our secret."

San Francisco, California

Kelly toyed with her food, absently spreading the peas on her plate until they were surrounding the meatloaf. Danielle watched her closely, thinking to herself that her sister may not remember anything, but her tastes hadn't changed a bit. That much was comforting.

Adam and Rachael Anderson talked to one another about work, while Robbie conversed with Kelly about school. Every now and then he managed to get a smile out of her, and he answered all her questions about Lakeside and the students that attended it. He avoided some with ease, others having to hesitate before replying with a credible lie.

He had done all he could to give Kelly a good past. Surprisingly, Matt agreed to keep the secret when Robbie cornered him at school. There was a nagging thought in the back of his mind that perhaps the Treehouse kid had some ulterior motive, but as the days passed and Matt remained silent, the worry was beginning to fade.

"Kelly, honey, are you not hungry?" Rachael asked.

Kelly glanced up at the woman she thought was her mother and shrugged. "No, I was just thinking," she replied, her eyes scanning the scars on her arms. She figured that the car crash must have been serious to leave her with such marks.

"You should eat your vegetables," Adam piped up with a wink. "Help make you strong."

Nodding with a small smile, Kelly nudged some peas onto her fork. "I guess."

Robbie watched as she took in a mouthful of peas and chewed with a grimace. He couldn't stop the grin. "Go on, eat up," he said in a mocking tone much like his father's. "They're just little, green, mushy spheres. They won't kill you."

They won't kill you.

A deep, rough voice slammed through Kelly's ears. As her head shot up, Robbie's face changed into that of a tall, shady man with eyes glaring like fire and a snarl on his lips.

Her breath exploded out of her as the vision faded as quickly as it had come, and all that was left was Robbie, now looking concerned. "What did you just say?" she whispered.

Robbie's brow furrowed. "I said they won't kill you."

He straightened and reached out to try and comfort her, and Kelly's fork dropped to her plate with a clatter as she envisioned a hand flying out at her. She peered at Robbie to see that he had again been replaced by the terrifying older man with thick hair and a gruff, shadowed face.

It's time you learn to respect your elders, the man screamed, and slammed his fist at her face.

"Don't!" she cried out, pushing herself away from the table and nearly toppling over when the chair tipped backwards. As Danielle rushed to calm her sister, Robbie saw that Kelly was near tears.

"Kelly, what happened? What's wrong?" Danielle asked, worry in her voice.

"I… I don't know. It was Robbie, and then… then it wasn't," she stammered as Rachael rose from her chair.

"It's okay, it's okay." Rachael took Kelly's arm soothingly and led her away from the table. "Why don't you go upstairs and rest. I'll come up and check on you later."

"Yeah, that's sounds good." Kelly couldn't argue as she was brought up the stairs and to her room. Rachael didn't ask what had happened, for she had an idea of what Kelly saw. A vision, a picture.

A memory.

Kelly lay down on the bed, throwing her arm over her eyes as she tried to sort out the vision. *It had to be a memory*, she thought as Rachael left the room, pushing Robbie and Danielle out into the hall, *it must be something*.

But, she argued with herself, *what could it mean*? A man sitting across from her with angry eyes and a deep, threatening voice that sent chills down her spine when it ran through her ears again. Who was he? Why was he yelling at her?

Why did he hit me?

She had a thousand questions with no answers, and that frustrated her, really ticked her off. She wanted to ask Danielle or Robbie, or even her friends at school, about her past, but every time she did she always got the feeling they were lying to her.

Then there was Matt Harper, who she had seen arguing with Natalie and Robbie several times. But he always acted different around her, nice, and yet, like he knew things she didn't. Important things, about who she really was.

Also, she continued, there was Mr. Fiesk. She couldn't ignore the evidence he provided. The papers he handed back to her had the name Kelly Mitchell, and, as she'd discovered, had handwriting that matched her own. So who was Kelly Mitchell? And, for that matter, who was Kelly Anderson? She was starting to feel like she was losing her mind.

For weeks now she felt different, her mood swings taking her from shy and withdrawn to irritated and even a little arrogant. Now that she was back home, she was still feeling kind of… bitchy was the only term that came to mind. She had no idea how she was supposed to act.

Kelly didn't know if her confusion and frustration was normal or if there was something wrong with her, but whatever the cause, she was determined to discover her identity.

Chapter 3

Collinsville, California

Shuffling through a stack of papers, Tyler pulled out a file on Aneesa Watersby. He skimmed it briefly, already knowing most of it by heart. Eight year-old girl, put up for adoption at the age of six when her mother died and father skipped out on her, then a few weeks ago put in a foster home with the parents of Tori and Alan Ferral. He expected his home visit today to go smoothly, wouldn't have it any other way.

It was important to him that he succeed in providing loving homes for kids in need. Since he was thirteen he'd been doing just that, albeit illegally. Now, he had the law on his side, and there was a certain satisfaction in watching the bad guys being taken away in a squad car.

Tyler had to admit that had it not of been for Melanie, he never would have cared as much as he did. It had been her dream, her vision, that started it all. He and the others merely followed their leader.

It wasn't until they found their first child that he truly understood what it meant to help the helpless. Observing Mathew Harper, witnessing the abuse, made Tyler realize what Melanie truly went through and the significance of her project. The longer he was a Helping Hand, the more he understood, and the more it all meant to him, the more he believed in it.

"So you going to see the Watersby girl today?"

Disrupted from his thoughts, Tyler glanced up to see Annie Baker, another case worker, staring down at him, her curly hair falling across her shoulders. "Yeah. I'm just going to make sure everything's as it should be."

Annie smirked, knowing that when Tyler said he was just going to check up on things, it usually got physical. But, he did one hell of a job sniffing out shady foster families from a mile away.

"Well, just promise me you won't go bashing anyone's head into the wall." Tyler just shrugged, and so Annie handed him another file. "This came in earlier this morning. The boss wants you to take a look at it."

Tyler took the file. "What is it?"

"How should I know?" Annie shrugged. "He said something about you wanting some information on that Mitchell girl and her sister."

"Oh, right." Although he didn't agree with Melanie getting involved with the girl, he was going to do what he could to help. It was either fight her, or help her. "Well, thanks." Tyler gestured with the file and rose, catching Annie's grin as she took a step back from his desk. "What?"

"You just seem like too tough a guy to be wearing a ring. Just can't get over it, that's all." She laughed to herself and flounced away, while Tyler looked down at his ring.

"Neither can I," he murmured, then grabbed his keys from his desk and headed for his car.

The Ferral house was located inside a community filled with kids and families, which was one of the reasons why Tyler was sure Aneesa would love her new home. Pulling up next to the curb, he glanced out the window to see Aneesa playing on a tire hanging down from a rope that was attached to a massive tree in the front yard, clad in blue jeans and a sweater despite the warmth of the afternoon. He hung back at his car for a moment to watch her, always pleased to see a happy kid playing outside, before heading up the driveway. As Tyler approached, Aneesa looked up, her face immediately breaking out into a grin and her teeth flashing beneath the afternoon sun.

"Mel! Mel! You came to see me!" she squealed, jumping down from the tire so quickly that she tripped. She gave no care to falling and picked herself up with a smile, running over to Tyler.

"How you doin', kid?" Tyler laughed as he picked her up, smiling right back.

"I went to school today and got a hundred on my spelling test and got the best grade in the class because no one else got a hundred except me so that means I'm really smart," Aneesa answered, never taking a breath as the words spewed forth. "And my teacher told me I was smart and maybe I could enter the spelling bee because she thinks I can beat all the other kids from the classes and different schools 'cuz I got the best grade on the spelling test."

"That's great, Aneesa. And when you win first place, I'll be right there in the front row cheering for you." He grinned again as her eyes went wide.

"Really? You'll cheer for me and clap when the other kids lose? Really?"

"Really. And I'll bring you flowers. Big red ones." With a laugh, he set the girl down on her feet. 'How about a ride on the swing?" He started to guide her to the tire, but stopped when she flinched away from him. "Aneesa, are you okay?" he asked, concerned when she rubbed her shoulder with a child-like, over-exaggerated grimace. "Are you hurt?"

"No." Aneesa shook her head, her voice going soft.

"How did you hurt your shoulder?"

Aneesa paused, glancing down at the ground, then over at the tire. "I fell off the swing. But it doesn't hurt at all," she quickly told him. She could tell that he didn't believe her, and that scared her.

Gently, Tyler turned the girl around and pulled down the collar of her sweater. He swallowed hard when he saw the bruises, five finger marks against her dark bronze skin. And around them, he noticed with rage, were scratches, obviously caused by nails.

"Stay here," he ordered Aneesa, who nodded silently, her eyes wide as Tyler rose and stalked to the front door of her house.

Tyler didn't bother to knock. He shoved the door open and went in search of Tori Ferral, as her husband was out of town. He found her in the kitchen, knife in hand as she cut carrots for a salad. She spun around when she heard Tyler's footsteps, and let out a little cry when he grabbed her and slung her up against the wall. Her head connected with a thud.

On reflex, Tori reached out with the knife and felt the blade pierce the skin on his arm. Through wide and fearful eyes, she watched as blood began to fall, but the man in front of her seemed to register no pain at all. He had a crazed look on his face, one that took her breath away as her heart thudded against her chest. He pulled the knife from her trembling hand and threw it to the floor, taking her by the neck. She couldn't struggle, and was too afraid to scream.

"If you think you can hide those marks you put on her with turtlenecks and jackets, you better think again." He was all but growling as he leaned in close, eyes narrowed and teeth clenched. "You're lucky to get away with your life."

Fear welled up in her gut, but Tori could do nothing but quiver as he held her against the wall, hand tightening. "It would be so easy," he snarled. "You remember this moment, and know that I will always be watching you. *Always*."

With a final shove, he pushed away from her and stalked out of the house. Slamming the front door behind him, Tyler picked Aneesa up and brought her to his car, where he would bring her back to the agency.

Chapter 4

San Francisco, California

The day had come for Jeffrey Ponder's trial, after weeks of waiting and endless dates being cancelled and rescheduled. The hype had been established for the public, reporters and tabloids speculating about the case that brought the infamous Melanie O'Conner back to court, this time on the other side of the questioning.

Melanie was ready to testify, ready to get all the bullshit over with, and her attitude showed in her eyes when she strode up the steps to the courthouse, ignoring the reporters and flashing lights while Tyler, at her side, shoved people out of the way. They weren't there to appeal to the public or to appease the activists.

When she entered the courthouse, Melanie paused, for the first time experiencing the other side of the trial. But this one was more than drugs and kidnapping abused kids in order to save their lives. This time, the enemy would pay for what he did. She was fighting a monster, a beast, a disgusting excuse of a man.

Jeffrey Ponder was the enemy.

When he came in, taking his place behind the desk with his lawyer at his side, Melanie got her first real look at him, and she was momentarily taken aback. She knew he was a successful businessman, so she had been expecting a clean-cut, decent-looking man with good posture and short-cropped hair, like the picture she had seen in Kelly's file. Instead, she saw a tall, slightly stooping man with bulging veins and hair that fell across two dark, narrow eyes.

The truth was, he was intimidating, and Melanie could see why the two girls were so afraid of him.

The trial began, and with each person called up to testify, Melanie's thoughts began to drift. All of the memories were starting to come back, the fear of looking up at Judge William Foster, the lawyer accusing her of killing the kids, feeling as though these people were trapping her in the courtroom. She hadn't shown it then, but her mind had been racing with panic, sweating on the inside, fighting to keep from wringing her hands together.

"Miss O'Conner?"

Melanie snapped out of her daze. Tyler was nudging her arm, and she realized that she was being called up to testify. She cleared her throat and rose, ignoring the whispers that spread around her as she walked up to the stand, displaying her usual arrogant confidence. When she took her seat and was sworn in, she zeroed her glower in on the man seated across the floor. His dark eyes leered back.

"Miss O'Conner," Jeffrey's defending lawyer, Carson Darren, began, his words smug as he approached the bench. "Or should I address you as Mrs. Scotford?"

He sounded almost scornful, and she knew he was just trying to rile her up. "O'Conner is fine," she replied just as coolly.

"Miss O'Conner, you began work as a counselor at South Bay Juvenile Detention Camp earlier this year, correct?"

"Yeah."

"Yes," Darren corrected, not getting a reaction out of Melanie. "So then Kelly Mitchell was your first patient?"

"She was one of the first, yes."

"One of the first?"

"I have multiple kids coming to my office every day. When I was seeing Kelly I also had three other individuals that I was meeting with on different days."

"But you have no formal experience in counseling, correct?" Darren asked, pleased when Melanie frowned. "You never attended college, so you don't have a degree in psychiatry. Yet you work as a counselor. Is that not practicing without a license?"

She knew what he was trying to do, and it wouldn't work. "No, it's not," she answered calmly. "I have nothing to do with medication. My job is merely to encourage the kids to take a better path. My job is more along the lines of being a motivational speaker rather than a therapist. Don't need a license for that."

Darren thought about it, or pretended to, before replying. "So you encourage the kids. Does encouragement include getting a patient to lie about their home life?"

"Objection, your honor!"

"Your honor, it's a fair question, merely for curiosity's sake," Darren said before the judge could consider the objection.

After a moment of thinking, the judge nodded. "I'll allow it. Miss O'Conner, please answer."

Melanie narrowed her eyes, lifting a single brow. "And just what lie are you referring to?"

"The lie your patient spoke of her stepfather, Jeffrey Ponder, abusing her."

"The patient has a name, and it's Kelly," Melanie said, suddenly angry. "And she didn't lie. I saw the bruises. I saw her in the hospital. There is no doubt as to where the wounds came from."

"And where did they come from?"

Melanie scoffed and kept from rolling her eyes. "Where do you think? From your client, Jeffrey Ponder." A murmur worked its way throughout the crowd, along with nodding heads.

Darren waited through the talking, letting the judge take care of it. This was the moment he had been waiting for, the chance to take down the famous Melanie O'Conner. But he had to build up to it first, build up the drama and tension.

"So your patient, Kelly Mitchell, told you that Mr. Ponder physically abused her?" Melanie agreed. "Did you ever ask Mr. Ponder about this to get his side of the story?"

"I didn't need to ask his side of the story," Melanie growled. "I saw the bruises, and I heard the sound of her voice when she told me what kind of monster she'd been living with."

"Monster," Darren repeated quietly. "So you just believed what you were told? How do you know she wasn't lying?"

"I know."

"How?

"I just know." She couldn't say how she really knew, that Matt and his Helping Hand gang had been her scouts, and not being able to give away such information hurt her case.

And Darren knew it. "You just know. You just know that a man you've never met was the reason why an angry teenage girl was sent to a boot camp for drugs and auto theft." The courtroom was silent, everyone wondering what was going to happen next between the cocky lawyer and steaming former Helping Hand.

He decided to go in for the hit. "Miss O'Conner, do you think that your opinion and allegation against Mr. Ponder is augmented in, shall we say, severity due to your own personal past of domestic abuse?"

Melanie froze at the question, instantly furious. "Excuse me?" Her voice was hard, with the threat of death on the tip of her tongue.

"Calm down, calm down," Tyler, in the crowd, whispered worriedly, hoping she would keep her cool. Her father was the one subject that really set her off, and he had the feeling the lawyer knew that.

And he did. Carson Darren had done his research on the woman, and knew how to get her reeling.

"When you were arrested, it became public information that your adoptive father, Jerry Hunter, abused you for the duration of your stay with him. Correct?" He stared at Melanie, seeing the rising anger. "Is it possible that your idea of what happened in the Mitchell-Ponder household was, in fact, a manifestation of your own home life that you were never granted closure for?"

"Objection, your honor!"

"Overruled," the judge replied, holding up a hand. "Answer the question, please."

"Yes," Darren repeated smugly. "Answer the question."

And after she had swallowed back the threats and unclenched her fists, Melanie was ready to react. "How dare you," she growled, her voice low. "How dare you accuse me of being a person of weak judgment merely because of my past. I do *not* live my life by the memories of Jerry Hunter. Jeffrey Ponder abused Kelly Mitchell, attacked her, and it led to her being hospitalized, when it's not on the court's time, but as of right now we will discuss Kelly Mitchell and Kelly Mitchell alone."

"Oh, but Miss O'Conner, your past and Kelly Mitchell are one and the same. The anger you display here is only one more reason why your testimony is perhaps a bit corrupted." Darren raised his eyebrows. "As a counselor, you did your job of discovering the problem. But as a confidant, as someone who could supposedly relate to the victim's problem, you serve as a factor that creates a mountain out of a molehill. Which means," he said quickly before Melanie could interrupt, "that the statements made to Melanie O'Conner by Kelly Mitchell could have very easily been the creations of an exaggerated home life instilled by an older, influential role model for a young and impressionable girl. She—"

"Kelly developed amnesia after being thrown down the stairs by her stepfather!" Melanie shouted, leaping to her feet. "Jeffrey was arrested with Kelly's blood on his hands! What more do you want? That man is *guilty*!"

"Miss O'Conner, you will take your seat or I will have you removed from this courtroom and arrested for contempt!" the judge yelled, banging down the gavel.

Still reeling, Melanie dropped back down into the seat, biting her teeth together to keep from saying anything more. In front of her, Darren was gloating. He had gotten to her, and he was reveling in it.

She wouldn't give him the pleasure.

"Maybe you're right," she said, her voice soft enough to catch him off-guard. "Maybe my testimony means nothing. But I want to know if you can look at that girl over there," she gestured with her head to Danielle and was slightly surprised when the lawyer followed her gaze, "and imagine how it must have felt for her to watch her only sister tumble down the stairs in blood and broken bones and know deep down that she wouldn't be okay. And then to have to sit in court, watching the man who assaulted her be defended as though he couldn't hurt a fly."

Unable to help himself, Darren stared at Danielle, at the tears that stained her round cheeks, at the desperate pleading that shone in her fretful eyes. In those eyes he saw pain, he saw fear, he saw the love of one sister for another. Something in her spoke to him, spoke to the compassion he'd fought so hard to bury.

It was no longer about winning, but about justice. He swallowed hard, feeling his control slipping away. He had to save his reputation, and so he tore his eyes away and faced Melanie.

"Can you prove your accusations, Miss O'Conner?"

"Can you disprove them?" She waited for Darren to answer with a quick snap, but all he did was stare at her. Shaking her head, Melanie rose, sparing a quick look at the judge. "You don't have to remove me for contempt," she told him plainly. "I'm going to remove myself."

Melanie stomped off the bench, the thud of her boots echoing off the high ceiling, and strode for the door. Tyler, who had sensed what she was about to do, was already waiting for her in the hall, and they left without saying a word.

It wasn't until they were halfway through the silent car ride home that Tyler dared to speak. "So... you okay?"

"Yeah."

"Are you really, or are you just saying that?"

Melanie turned her eyes to her husband tiredly. "Why would I lie?"

Tyler shrugged. "I'm not saying you're lying. It's just that, what that lawyer did was sleazy, and you have every right to be pissed off at him. So be pissed. It's okay."

"I'm not mad at him." Melanie looked down at her hands, then let her head fall back against the headrest. "I'm mad at myself."

"What? Why?"

"Because what I did could have cost Kelly everything. I let him get to me, Tyler. I wasn't strong enough."

"Don't even start that," Tyler demanded. "Whatever happens isn't your fault."

"You say that because you don't know, Tyler," Melanie argued, crossing her arms. "I should have been strong enough to let his comments just roll off me, but I wasn't."

"Melanie—"

"No, Tyler, just let it go, okay? Just leave me alone."

Sighing in defeat, Tyler slammed a hand down on the steering wheel. "Fine."

"Fine."

After five minutes of submitting to her demand to leave her alone, Tyler decided he couldn't stand it anymore and pulled off the side of the road, putting the car into park and shifting so he was looking directly at his wife. Confused when Tyler turned off the road, Melanie sat up straighter.

"Tyler, what—"

"Melanie, there are some things in this world that you don't have to be strong for," he interrupted, his voice solid. "I know you want to help everyone you can, but it's not your job to be their backbone every single time." He gently took her chin in his hand and turned her face towards his, and saw the tears brimming in her eyes. "Whatever happens to Jeffrey Ponder, happens to him, and there will be justice. But do *not* let that goddamn lawyer make you feel like shit just because he knew a few superficial things about your past. You're better than that."

She knew he was right, and for once that fact didn't irritate her. "Thanks," she said quietly, fighting back her tears. "I can deal with the things that happened to me, but to have some stranger throw it all in my face like that... I got carried away, took it too personally."

"No, you did what you do best," Tyler disagreed. "You defended yourself, you proved that you're not going to take any shit. And that lawyer was speechless. So don't ever say you weren't strong enough."

Leaning over, he kissed her gently, lingering against her lips. When they parted, she kept her hands on his shoulders, savoring the moment. "You're too good for me, you know that?"

"Is that delirium from my amazing charm speaking or are you actually admitting that you need me?" Tyler grinned, kissing Melanie's cheek when she rolled her eyes.

"I admit to nothing, you arrogant bastard. Let's go home." She sat back, and Tyler did the same. Before putting the car back into drive, he paused, looking back over at her.

"Hey," he said, waiting until she had glanced over. "I need you too."

Melanie smiled to herself, all her worries and anger over the trial passing, if just for the time being. "Good," she answered. "I was kinda hoping you did."

Chapter 5

South Bay Juvenile Detention Camp

"Charlie Knox." Melanie lifted a brow, her hands on her hips. "I have to say, I'm proud of you."

Charlie nodded arrogantly. "I knew I'd get out of here."

Melanie huffed and shook her head. They had come a long way since she had thrown him to the ground. Sure, he made have had to stay past his eighty-day sentence due to a certain outrageous death threat made on his part to the Admiral, but the important thing was that he had turned his attitude around.

She'd finally gotten the truth out of him - his workaholic father was never home, his alcoholic mother was always passed out, his older brother was the star of the family with a football scholarship. The kid wanted attention, in any form.

And now, Melanie was ready to release Charlie Knox back into society as a reformed young man. She figured he'd slip up now and then, but was confident that he would do well.

"So what're you gonna do when you get home?" Melanie inquired.

Charlie shrugged, flicking back his hair and staring out the window of the office. "Go back to school," he said, almost indifferently. "Maybe... go apologize to that guy I beat up."

"Sounds like a plan. Just do me a favor when you get out." She waited until Charlie had looked up. "Don't do anything stupid. If I find out you're back in here, I'll pay you a visit and personally see to it that your ass is beaten to the ground. Got it?"

Although he could see that she was serious, Charlie couldn't help but laugh. "Yeah, I got it." He didn't know if he could be the person he was promising to be, but he was going to do all he could to try. One, because his old life would lead him to either prison or death or being a total loser; two, he really didn't want to be anywhere near Melanie O'Conner ever again.

When it came down to it, she scared the hell out of him.

"Charlie, are you ready?" Hawkins appeared in the doorway.

"Yeah." Charlie headed to the sergeant, stopping at the door and turning back to Melanie. He paused before giving her a small smile. "Thanks," he said quietly.

She didn't need to reply.

"So, you've been here for less than a year and already you've straightened out at least thirty of these kids," Hawkins, who had come into Melanie's office after seeing Charlie off, said with a shake of his head. "I have to hand it to you. You know your stuff."

"I know kids who think they're big and bad," Melanie corrected him, barely glancing up. Boss or not, he still irritated her. "Did you want something?"

"I came to ask what you're planning to do about the Mitchell girl. I know what the Andersons are doing. About lying and everything."

"You mean brainwashing," Melanie replied angrily. "I'm planning on going to San Francisco on Sunday. I'm going to talk to Kelly, see what's going on. And I have a few things I want to say to the Andersons."

"Well, try to keep your cool." Hawkins lifted his eyebrows, his expression serious. "They're only doing what they think is best."

"I know that," Melanie answered in a cool tone. "But so am I."

It was pointless to argue the case anymore, so he gave up, instead pulling out a folded piece of paper from his pocket. He stepped closer, bracing himself for a verbal attack. "You got a call while you were in the field. The secretary took a message. It's about Jeffrey Ponder's trial."

Melanie stared at Brian for a second, then took in a deep breath and nodded. "They reached a verdict?"

"Yeah." He hesitated. "He got five years' incarceration, three years' probation upon release."

Five years' incarceration. Three years' probation. Melanie could only accept the information in silence.

So there will be no justice, she thought grimly. Jeffrey deserved death, and nothing short of that. But she had lost it in court, let that damn lawyer get to her.

She failed Kelly. Nothing she would ever do could make amends for that.

Chapter 6

F.B.I. Headquarters

There was nothing more frustrating to Corwin than a case he couldn't solve. Everything about the Helping Hands had him stumped. How they worked, how they planned, the execution of those plans. And it should be so easy to figure out, he'd always thought.

It angered him just thinking about how many kids they had taken. He had no idea how many people not part of the actual group knew about the project, but was positive that Melanie O'Conner was one of them. It had to be some sort of pyramid scheme, with Melanie at the peak.

But, Corwin couldn't prove it; not with all the evidence and information he had spread across his desk and bulletin board could he offer even a modicum of a lead. Every piece of data, no matter how big or small, just led him in frustrating circles. Corwin was pissed, if not embarrassed, to think that he was a fifty-eight year-old veteran of the Bureau who couldn't take down a project created by an uneducated thirteen year-old girl living on the streets.

In one aspect, he hated the Helping Hands for doing what they did, for kidnapping and breaking the law, for frustrating him to no end. On the other hand, he had to admire them for their efforts and successes. The gangs had been alive for at least twelve years, and in those years only two members of the project had been caught, one being dead and the other working at a boot camp.

And the one that was alive would never talk.

His partner wasn't much help either. Corwin couldn't really blame him, though. Jay Neilson was new to the Bureau and still needed some experience to sharpen up all his book smarts and add a little of those from the street. He offered some good advice every now and then, Corwin considered, and when he did, it was usually just what they needed.

Which was what Neilson was doing that afternoon while Corwin pondered over the Helping Hands. He stood at the bulletin board, rubbing his chin thoughtfully as he read over the kidnapping reports.

"It's the Harper kid," Neilson said, nodding at his own words. Corwin turned slowly, seeing that his partner had dropped down in his leather chair, feet propped up on the desk as though he owned his boss's office. "It's gotta be. My gut says so."

"Oh, well so long as we have the word of your gut," Corwin retorted, glancing over the report on Mathew Harper. He had done his research on the teen. First child ever kidnapped by Melanie O'Conner, captain of the football team, good student, son of Janet Harper. Corwin knew all he needed to know.

"Who else would it be?" Neilson continued, running a pen through his fingers. "Think about it. He associates with O'Conner, takes up for her, gets twitchy when questioned. He's the first kid, so naturally he'd want to be a part of the project that saved his life." He stared up at the ceiling as if deep in thought. "Yeah, I have to go with my gut on this one. Harper's a part of the new gang. And I'll bet his entire gang is made up of Treehouse kids, if we go on the basis that he started his gang because the Helping Hands helped him."

"Even if you think that, we can't just go in and bust him," Corwin argued, seeing Neilson's point clearly. His partner was right, and he made a mental note to do a check on all the Treehouse kids, see where they were and what they were up to. "We'll have to watch him, and if and when he screws up, we'll be right there to catch him."

Six days later, Corwin peered through a pair of binoculars as the final bell to Lakeside High rang out. He kept his eyes trained on the front doors, watching as Mathew Harper exited, Leighann Cross at his side, the two hand-in-hand. Together they walked to his car and started out of the school parking lot.

Corwin followed Matt the entire way home. Matt knew what he looked like, so he kept his face hidden the best he could and stopped his car about seven houses down from the Harper residence. He was sure he would be waiting to see absolutely nothing, as he had done for the past week.

Every day, he thought glumly, *the kid does the same damn routine*. Woke up at six-thirty, went to school, went home, sometimes with his girlfriend, then left at precisely four-thirty to go to work until eleven. At times he came home at ten, and it was then that Corwin was wary that he might have a kidnapping planned. But so far, he saw nothing.

He was about to tell Neilson to forget the whole thing when a second car appeared in the driveway and a few moments later Isaac Davidson stepped out, pulling off his dark sunglasses and setting his jaw as if getting ready for a fight. Corwin was sure that was his normal expression, for he knew the nineteen year-old well. Beaten severely as a child by an ex-wrestler father, starved by a painkiller-and-alcohol-addicted mother, left to die with several lasting scars that made him look vicious and intimidating. Corwin couldn't ever remember seeing Isaac smile. It gave him all the more reason to believe Neilson's theory of the gang being made up of Treehouse kids, for after doing his research on the seventy-one children, Corwin had discovered a small group that was leading what could be considered suspicious lifestyles.

First, there was Isaac Davidson. The kid had skipped out on his home and worked odd jobs here and there until settling at a junkyard, with no known residence.

Next was a girl named Bonnie McGuire. No one had heard from her in years. From what Corwin could piece together, she had packed up and disappeared, and that was that. Either she was dead or keeping her identity a well-kept secret.

Then there was Jimmy Fencles. Not a bad kid, shy and quiet, very book smart and apparently street savvy, but what caught Corwin's attention was the discovery that he had quit his job at a restaurant just months before the first kidnapping of the San Francisco branch. Corwin had called the boy's boss, who informed him that Jimmy had left after 'some guy with a scar' walked in and 'had a little chat' with him.

Along with Jimmy were four other names: J.J. Silverton, a shady kid who dropped out of high school and was currently out of work; Robbie Newfield, attending a community college a few towns over from San Francisco; Carry Valentine, too sweet and innocent for her own good; and Mason White, just downright suspicious.

"Neilson, what do you think?" Corwin turned to his partner when the front door shut behind Isaac. "Planning a kidnapping?"

Neilson shrugged. It looked like a normal afternoon to him, with a friend going over to another friend's house to do whatever teenagers do. "Or maybe they're studying, or hanging out, or going out to eat. Hey," he nudged Corwin with a sly grin, "maybe they're hooking up for a threesome."

"Grow up," Corwin replied with a mutter, getting a twinge in his stomach that told him this was it, this was what he had been waiting for.

It was nightfall by the time Isaac came out of the house. He headed down the front walk carrying three black bags to his car. Corwin waited until he had driven to the end of the street to pursue.

By the time they hit the main road, Neilson was on edge. "So where's he going with all those bags?" he asked with a grin. "Destroying the evidence, maybe?"

Corwin didn't reply, but instead kept a watchful eye on Isaac's car. He knew that he could be going on a wild goose hunt, but he didn't care. Something told him he was getting closer to cracking his case.

Isaac led them straight to Mickey's Mechanics. Corwin knew something was up when he saw that the auto shop was closed and that all lights were off with the exception of one opaque window in the back. He watched as Isaac got the bags from the backseat and strode up to the shop, banging on one of the side doors and waiting impatiently until it opened. He disappeared into the shadows, and Corwin got out of the car, ordering Neilson to stay where he was.

Creeping up to the side door, Corwin waited, ducking behind a tree. It wasn't exactly by the book, hanging outside garages without backup, but he was tired of waiting around. It was time to take action. Before long, he heard voices from inside the shop, and soon after, the side door opened again.

"So I'll see you next Tuesday, right?" a husky voice asked.

"Yeah, we'll bring the rest of the stuff," another replied, a younger tone that Corwin identified as Isaac Davidson. "Thanks, Mick."

So Mickey from Mickey's Mechanics is a benefactor, Corwin thought. He didn't know for sure, but was ready to set the facts straight as the teenager walked out of the auto shop.

Stepping out from behind the tree, Corwin grabbed Isaac's shirt and pushed him up against the wall of the shop, holding him there with a strong arm. On reflex, Isaac reached out with a fist and slammed it into Corwin's shoulder, missing his face by inches.

"Easy, kid. I'm not going to hurt you," Corwin said to him in a quiet voice. "You can punch me again, but I'll only arrest you for assaulting an officer."

Anger overcame all senses. Isaac pushed against Corwin's grip, and the two grappled for a moment until the agent gained the upper hand and slammed the boy against a tree.

"Let me go, you fucking pig." Isaac shoved Corwin again.

"You listen to me," Corwin began, leaning in close, "I know who you are, and you won't get away with it. I know who your gang members are, and now I know one of your benefactors. Turn yourselves in and return the kids and you got a chance at not spending the rest of your life in prison. Keep this shit up and you risk it all. You screw up once, *once*, and I'll arrest your sorry punk ass so quick you won't have time to kiss it good-bye."

Isaac narrowed his eyes, not the least bit fazed. He knew how to handle threats, and didn't appreciate them being made against his gang. And there was no way in hell he was going to stand there, shoved up against a tree by an over-the-hill cop who was threatening to shut down his gang, without fighting back.

"Well, you're right about one thing, old timer," he replied through clenched teeth.

Raising his eyebrows, Corwin leaned closer and sneered. "Yeah, what's that?"

"You're gonna have to arrest me for assaulting an officer."

With the skill and violence he had learned for all the wrong reasons, Isaac slammed his head into Corwin's, connecting with his brow. Corwin muttered a sharp cry and fell back as Isaac lashed out with his foot and kicked him hard in the gut. Neilson jumped from the car and ran over to help, while Isaac raced to his car, the tires screaming against the pavement as he sped away from the auto shop.

Chapter 7

Melanie tried not to feel any pity for the girl she saw sitting on the curb, staring out into space. She was sympathetic for her nonetheless, understanding that she was going through a hard time.

"Kelly Mitchell?" Melanie asked, wasting no time in introducing herself. "My name is Melanie O'Conner."

Kelly glanced up, shading her eyes from the sun. This stranger had just used the same last name as her teacher. For weeks now, months really, the name had been lost, forgotten, as though she had heard it only in a dream. Dreams seemed to be coming so frequently these days.

"Melanie O'Conner?" she repeated, saying the name again and again in her mind as she searched for a memory, finding only a shimmer of a picture before it faded back into darkness. "That sounds familiar. Have we met before?"

Nodding, Melanie squatted down next to her, deciding that the best approach would be the direct one. "Yeah, actually, we have. I met you at boot camp."

"Oh." Kelly nodded, frowning when the answer sunk in. "Wait a minute. Boot camp?"

Melanie wasn't surprised by the dumbfounded shock in Kelly's voice. But, the girl deserved to know the truth, no matter the consequences, and Melanie was going to give it to her. "That's right, boot camp. You were sent there."

Kelly didn't know whether to be surprised, disappointed, or wary. "Why was I sent to a boot camp? What did I do?" When the woman in front of her took in a deep breath, Kelly felt her hopes rise at the possibilities of the reply. "Do you know who I am, like who I *really* am?"

Melanie observed Kelly for a moment before answering. Curiously, she edged closer to her. "Who do you think you are?"

"I don't know." Kelly turned to gaze down at the house that looked so familiar, for some odd reason feeling as though she could trust the woman who called herself Melanie O'Conner. Maybe, she considered, it was the way she had simply come up and told her more about her past that she actually believed in one sentence than she had ever gotten from Robbie or Danielle. She was learning to trust her instincts, since they were all she had to guide her now that she was positive she couldn't depend on anything else in her mixed-up life.

"I keep getting the flashbacks of a house, of this man who hit me at the dinner table, of Danielle having a cast on her leg. It's all these little pictures that I can barely even see, but I can't put the pieces together. It's so frustrating, you know?" She looked down at her hands while Melanie listened patiently. "Sometimes I feel like I'm about to remember something, then... nothing. But when I'm around certain people I feel like I might know them, and I trust them more than others." *Like you*, she silently added. "So I talk to them more even though I'm not sure if I really know them."

"That sounds like good progress." Melanie was pleased that her memory was returning.

"Yeah, I know. But I still can't piece it together. I just get these pictures and mood swings and this feeling like I'm supposed to be protecting someone." The teenager flung out her hands in frustration, exasperated with the situation. "It's just a bunch of stupid goddamn *feelings* and it totally fucking sucks!" Kelly paused as if surprised at what she said. "You see?" she asked, staring at Melanie. "Where did that come from? That keeps happening. I just all of a sudden say things like that without meaning to. What kind of person was I? Why do I feel like I should be protecting someone?"

"You used to protect your sister, Danielle."

"From what?"

"From Jeffrey, your stepfather." Melanie turned to Kelly when the girl questioned her reply, seeing that her eyes were narrow and her mouth set in a frown. "Your stepfather abused you."

Her shock was smothered by anger. "No. No, I don't know what you're talking about." Kelly leapt to her feet, shaking her head defiantly. "I don't have a stepfather. I live here, with my parents, and Robbie, and—"

"Those people are not who you think they are," Melanie cut in, lifting herself to Kelly's level. She observed the girl for a moment and was unable to keep herself from sighing and giving in to the guilt that had overcome her heart the past few weeks.

"Look Kelly, whether you remember me or not, whether or not you believe me, I came here to apologize."

"For what?"

"For letting you down." Melanie blew out a breath dejectedly, pushing back her long hair. They stood face-to-face, Kelly's eyes filled with confusion and Melanie's reflecting remorse. "I told you that I would do everything I could to make sure things worked out the way they were supposed to, and I didn't do it. I couldn't help you."

Kelly frowned, licking her lips nervously. "Um... I don't understand. Let me down with what? Help with what?"

"They've been lying to you, your so-called family," Melanie said bluntly. She had promised to help, and brutal honesty was the only way she knew how. "You are not an Anderson. Your name is Kelly Mitchell."

Kelly stopped shaking her head when she heard the name. "Mitchell," she whispered, the word ringing through her ears.

"Danielle is your sister, but Robbie and his parents are people you met when you moved here from Florida last fall," Melanie continued, afraid that if she stopped Kelly would turn away from her. Pointing to Kelly's old house, she went on. "You used to live there, in that house. And those scars aren't from a car crash. Jeffrey attacked you and threw you down the stairs. You went into a coma and ended up with amnesia. All those visions you're having are of your past. Your *real* past."

It was too much to take in all at once. Kelly shook her head, fighting tears. She no longer knew what was real and was beginning to feel afraid. "No, you're the one that's lying. My family would never lie to me." She made her voice convincing and sharp, but Melanie could see right through it.

"I know it's hard to accept. But you can't let them lie to you any longer." Melanie looked up sharply when she heard a shout and saw Robbie emerging from the house. She turned back to Kelly. "Look through their old photo albums, see what you find. You have to trust me, Kelly."

"Hey! What the hell do you think you're doing?" Robbie shouted as he ran up.

"I'm not doing a damn thing, you two-faced liar," she retorted, taking pleasure in the fact that Robbie's face reddened with anger.

"Get out of here or I swear I'll call the cops."

"Ooh, the cops. Never had to face them before," Melanie mocked, then stepped back when Robbie stepped forward. "Relax, kid. I'm leaving. Just remember, *someone* is going to pay for all of this." Turning on her heel, she strode back to her car and left.

After the car disappeared around the corner, Robbie turned to Kelly. "What did she tell you?" he asked carefully, frowning when Kelly looked at him with a shrug after watching Melanie drive away.

"Nothing, really. Just asked who I was and if I remembered her. I didn't, of course," she added when Robbie sighed.

"Okay, but listen. That woman is dangerous. She's always getting into trouble with the law. Not too long ago, before the accident, Dad tried to have her put in prison and she decided to take her revenge out on him by stalking him. We had to get a restraining order. Stay away from her. She's dangerous," he repeated sternly. He put an arm around Kelly's shoulders and began leading her up the driveway. He turned back in slight confusion when she stopped, peering at him thoughtfully. "What?"

"Robbie, you wouldn't ever lie to me, would you?"

He felt a slight hitch in his stomach. "I'm your brother," he replied with an uneasy laugh. "What do you think?"

Kelly watched him walk away, a little too quickly. "I think you didn't answer the question."

Chapter 8

Tulsa, Oklahoma

George Livingston paced his living room floor, cursing beneath his breath as he stared at the carpet, his hands clasped tightly behind his back. On the couch, his wife sat perfectly still, the three dogs sitting at her feet. In front of him stood the sheriff of Tulsa, clutching his brown hat as he shook his head.

"I'm sorry, Mr. Mayor, but there's nothing more we can do," he said apologetically, fully expecting the icy glare he got in return.

"What do you mean, nothing more you can do?" the mayor snapped at his face. "You're the goddamn sheriff of this goddamn town. If you can't find my daughter, then tell me who the hell can!"

Shaking his head again, Sheriff Westerlund sighed deeply. "With all due respect, Mr. Mayor, Emily's been gone for over two months. I can't keep my guys out there much longer, and since y'all refuse to have the F.B.I. help, like I said, I can't do much more." He refrained from glancing at Mrs. Livingston, who was in tears. "Mr. Mayor, I'll keep looking, I promise. I gotta get back to the station right now. If I hear anything, I'll be sure to give ya a holler."

"Fine," Livingston spat out, running a hand through his thick brown hair. He watched as the sheriff left, mumbling another apology. "Good-for-nothing K-nine cop."

Turning to his wife, he shook his head. "I'm going to work." He left her there on the couch, dogs at her feet, while she wiped her tears with a tissue.

When he got to the den, he entered and locked the door behind him. He headed over to his desk, where he pulled out a small leather box engraved with his name, a gift from his running mate for the position of mayor. He took out a key from his pocket and shoved it into the lock. The top snapped open, and the mayor slowly reached inside and grasped a small, folded slip of paper. Tension curled in his fingers as he gripped it, his breath shuddering when he read the words.

That was way too easy.

The message put him in a blind rage. He wanted desperately to find the filthy bastards, those gang members who were foolish and arrogant enough to call themselves the Helping Hands. Who were they to come into *his* house, kidnap *his* daughter, dishonor *his* pride? They would pay for this.

He hadn't shown the note to his wife or to the police, not even when the kidnapping went public. He couldn't risk anyone investigating him. His career would be over and he would be thrown in jail, after which he knew his money-hungry wife would divorce him and take the millions he had stashed away along with her.

So he lied, claiming that Emily had been kidnapped, simple as that. No anti-child-abuse gangs watching him, harboring his daughter, making a fool out of him. And if the police couldn't find Emily, then she was as good as gone. Sure, he made a few tearful pleas to have his daughter returned back to him so the press and public would be satisfied, but only he knew that his heart was hard as stone. The kid was an inconvenience, always asking for this and that, nagging him when he was trying to write a speech, crying every single night over whatever her latest problem was.

He never wanted to be a father anyway.

So it wasn't the fact that she was kidnapped that made him angry. It was knowing that he had been outsmarted and that now the thugs were most likely out having a drink and laughing at how stupid they thought he was that really ticked him off.

He felt the fury rising again, but shoved it back down when he heard his wife call out to him from the bottom of the stairs. Rolling his eyes, Livingston tried his best to drown out his wife's nagging voice, a voice that made him cringe and consider giving her a lobotomy in the middle of the night.

Yanking open the door to the den, Livingston allowed it to slam back and barely noticed that the doorknob crushed against the wall.

"*What?*" he shouted, his voice echoing down the stairs.

"There are two men here to see you!"

Sighing heavily, Livingston threw the message back in the box, locked it, and set it on his desk behind a stack of files. He strode down the stairs, his heavy footsteps making dull thuds until he reached the landing base. Going to the door, he glanced out at the figures that were standing on the front porch, not able to keep back the here-we-go-again snarl that formed from the sight of the two uniformed men.

Chapter 9

San Francisco, California

Matt glanced around as he exited the pizza parlor after work. It was late, and the dark night gave him the creeps. Shadows hid strange things, the noises around him were unfamiliar, and there was the never-ending possibility that someone was watching.

He had always been afraid of the dark. It wasn't something he was ashamed of or embarrassed about, because he had good reasons for the fear. The night, always the night, was when he would hear his father's footsteps in the hall, when he would see his shadow beneath the door, and to the day he refused to go to sleep with the hall light on.

And now he had even more reason to worry. Isaac had informed the gang of his encounter with the F.B.I. agent, and added to his own run-in at the school, Matt was starting to plan for the worst. He couldn't put off any kidnappings because he would never, absolutely never, sit back and let innocent children suffer, so it all meant that now he had to be more careful.

And more importantly, become a better liar.

A shout to his right made him jump. Reflexively, he glanced down the sidewalk on the way to his car, seeing a man and child no older than eleven dressed in ragged clothes and looking as though he hadn't bathed in a week. He made a mental note to keep an eye out for them when he saw the father slap his son sharply across the face.

"You don't question me when I tell you to do something, you hear me?" the man was shouting, the little boy nodding solemnly. "I swear to God, it was because of your goddamn stupidity that your mother left you. No good whore is what she is. Let's go!" He grabbed the boy's shoulder brusquely, and Matt saw him wince.

"Ow!" the boy cried out suddenly. "Dad, that hurts!"

Matt's mouth dropped open when the father spun around and shoved his son hard to the ground. The man pointed at the child. "I told you to shut the hell up! You better thank your lucky stars I'm going out tonight, or I swear this would be the end of you!"

On instinct, Matt followed the two home. They lived only about ten minutes away in an old apartment building that Matt had passed a few times before. It was run-down and nearly abandoned.

Observing the apartment, he saw that there was one window, but it was boarded up. The wood looked as though it had rotted years ago, but he eyed it critically and decided that it was probably still habitable, and most likely provided for easy access. And if the father was going out like he claimed, then the front door would be wide open.

Making up his mind, Matt reached for his cell phone to call his friends.

It was one in the morning before everyone managed to sneak out and meet Matt in front of the pizza parlor. All looked tired and slightly irritated, with the exception of Isaac, who was bright-eyed and ready to roll. He loved a midnight kidnapping.

Matt quickly told them what happened and his plan. He knew it was dangerous, doing a kidnapping on impulse, but he couldn't let that child live another day with a man like that. He led his friends back to the apartment complex.

There were no streetlights, no glow from a lamp or candle to light their way. Matt glanced around when he approached the door, peering through the darkness and seeing nothing but the shadows of the night. He had watched the tall man with matted blonde hair and rough beard leave just before his friends arrived, but even so he pressed his ear against the door and listened for any sounds.

Hearing none, he grasped the doorknob with a gloved hand and turned it slowly, not surprised to find that it was unlocked. He pushed the door open, the light on the inside of the apartment barely better than a dim glow emitted from a weak lamp resting in the corner atop an ancient plastic table. His eyes took a moment to adjust as they scanned their surroundings.

As he entered, his friends close behind, Matt saw a small shadow perched rigidly on the end of a tattered bed. The boy's position was strange, oddly curious, but they gave it no further thought.

"We're not here to hurt you," Matt said carefully as he knelt down in front of the boy, who barely even glanced at him and instead kept his features blank. "We can help you."

The child turned his eyes from the wall to Matt, then glanced over the rest of the gang indifferently. He looked bored. "I don't need any help," he replied, his voice emotionless.

Matt heard Leighann sigh, and he refrained from doing the same. "What's your name, buddy?"

"Mike."

"Well, Mike, my name is Matt. Listen close, okay? We know that your father hits you. If you want to go, I can take you somewhere where you'll never be hit again."

The boy shook his head, staring at Matt through the darkness. "What are you talking about?" he asked. "I'm just here 'cuz some guy gave me two hundred bucks."

Matt's eyes widened with both confusion and dread. Leighann's hand, on his shoulder, dug into his flesh as his throat tightened. "What... what do you mean?"

"*Freeze! Don't move! Put your hands where I can see them!*"

The night became alive with shouts, and the Helping Hands spun around to see two men bursting through the doorway of the small apartment, wood splintering and exploding across the floor. Behind them was the tall, blonde man.

Carry cried out and tried to run as she was grabbed from the side, only to be spun back around violently and wrestled to the floor, a knee shoved in her back. "F.B.I., you are under arrest!" Corwin yelled at her, cuffing her wrists behind her back while Neilson went for the others. Matt stood frozen by the bed, knowing he was caught and not being able to do a thing about it. A movement to his right caught his eye, and Matt glanced over to see the father reach up and pull off the blonde wig he was wearing to reveal short, dark brown hair.

It was a set-up, he realized, fear eating up his guts. Lights flashed against the walls and shone in eyes that were glittered with terror. He watched Leighann struggle helplessly against Neilson, one wrist slapped with metal. Isaac and Jimmy had fallen back into the shadows, and the boy on the bed already fled from the apartment. Carry, cuffed and against the wall, moved her eyes to meet Matt's in a silent message filled with distress. The darkness of the room closed in on them, and Matt shook his head, watching as Corwin headed his way, knowing that it was all over.

But then he saw the agent's eyes go wide. Matt followed his gaze to see the man posing as the father pull a gun from behind his back, the barrel a gaping hole that swallowed up all his reflexes and instincts. Corwin had only just started to shout when it happened.

The shot went off before anyone could stop it. The men attacked one another, curses and fists flying. Carry dodged out of the way while Isaac fought against the urge to join in on the fight.

"Who the hell is that?" Leighann whispered, clutching Matt's arm, shaking him when he didn't answer. "Matt? Matt, what's wrong?"

Matt was oblivious to Leighann, to the yelling and struggling, to the confusion, for he saw where the bullet landed.

Jimmy's hands clutched his stomach, blood streaming between his fingers as his knees hit the floor. He sucked in a single deep breath, lips trembling, throat managing an eerie gurgling sound. Leighann scrambled to catch him before he fell to the floor, while Carry, still cuffed, stumbled across the small room. She reached him just in time to see his eyes roll back into his head.

"Livingston! What the hell are you doing?" Corwin shouted as he grabbed for the gun. "Are you crazy?" He went for his second pair of handcuffs, ready to arrest the mayor who had been all too eager to help him and Neilson. For a second Corwin wished he had requested back-up, but he had been foolish and arrogant enough to think he could handle it alone, wanting all the glory for himself for his last bust before retirement.

Livingston leapt back as Corwin came to him, waving the gun menacingly. "I'll do what the hell I want! These bastards took my kid and if you stand with them, then you deserve to die too!"

With that, he aimed the gun at Neilson, not hesitating in pulling the trigger.

Matt didn't know what to do when Neilson fell to the floor and Corwin began wrestling over the gun with Livingston. He and Isaac glanced at one another, then at Jimmy, blood trickling from the corners of his mouth as Leighann held her hands over the wound. The floor around them had already formed a large crimson pool that was quickly spreading across the wood.

Corwin grabbed Livingston's wrist, slamming his knee into the man's stomach, but the other man only rammed the agent against the wall, snarling and shouting and cursing. Isaac stood watching, entranced by the brawl, fear keeping his feet in place. Despite the chaos around him, all he could do was watch as everything he cared most about went up in flames.

The third gunshot snapped Isaac out of his terrified and frozen stance, and he saw the second agent's eyes go wide as his back hit the wall and he slid to the floor, leaving a thin red trail down the fake paneling. Lunging for the man, Isaac took Livingston by surprise and punched him hard in the jaw. When the mayor's head snapped back, he grabbed the gun and wasted no time or thought in burying the rest of the bullets into the man's chest, a long, furious shout filled with desperation piercing the air.

As Livingston let out a groan that signified his death, Isaac went to Jimmy and the girls while Matt headed for the agents. He reached Neilson first, and was terrified to see that the bullet had lodged itself in his stomach. On the floor, Neilson stared up at him, unable to talk. Matt had the distinct feeling that he wouldn't make it and the thought both terrified and satisfied him.

Corwin was a different story. Matt saw that he had been shot in the shoulder, right above the lung, and that the bullet had gone straight through. He didn't know if that was good or bad, or what would happen with the agent. For a second he thought of Melanie.

She would know what to do.

She always knew what to do.

She had warned him that this would happen.

Poor planning, spontaneous kidnappings.

She would never forgive him.

Doing the best he could, Matt grabbed the cell phone he saw on Corwin's belt with a gloved hand and called for an ambulance. After telling the woman on the other end what happened, he turned to his friends. "We have to go! *Now!*"

"Come on, Jimmy," Isaac said gently as he lifted Jimmy from the floor. Jimmy, sobbing and gasping for air, barely felt himself being carried as he drifted in and out of consciousness. Leighann and Carry followed, their eyes wet with tears and their faces stained with blood.

"You made a bad decision, Corwin!" Isaac shouted over his shoulder as he left the apartment. "A *bad* goddamn decision!"

As his friends left, Matt turned back to Corwin quickly, seeing that his face was pale and his chest was shuddering. "We're not the bad guys you think we are," he said softly, leaning close. "I didn't have to call anyone. We could have let you die."

Rising, Matt turned away from the three men lying bleeding on the floor, stepping over George Livingston's dead body as he ran after his gang.

Mickey Wraling gasped when the back door to his auto shop burst open and he saw Jimmy collapsed in Isaac's arms, bleeding and choking on his own blood. The rest of the gang was painted red as well, and although she had managed to get her arms in front of her, the cuffs were still wrapped tightly around Carry's wrists.

"What the hell happened? Why is he bleeding? Who shot him? Answer me! *What the hell is going on*?" Mickey shouted as Isaac lowered Jimmy to the floor, his cheeks crimson and his shirt soaked with blood.

"He was shot, Mickey! We were set up and he was shot!" Matt answered, his eyes filling with tears of panic as he felt himself losing control. "Oh, God, is he going to be okay?"

Mickey leaned over Jimmy, grasping the boy's chin. "Jimmy? Jimmy!" he yelled, taking a towel from Isaac when he offered it. Pressing it against the wound, he shook his head. "I don't know. I... God, Matt, do the cops know you're here?"

Trying to figure out the question in his head, Matt stuttered out a response. "Um... I-no. They... they, no, they couldn't. We... we were-Mickey, what's going to happen to Jimmy?"

Mickey didn't want to say what he was sure was inevitable. The boy that lay shaking uncontrollably at his feet was far past the possibility of hope. "He needs to go to the hospital."

"No!" The reply was cracked with sobs as Jimmy fought to shake his head. He couldn't go to a hospital. He couldn't have a doctor and files and people asking too many questions. Then the cops would come, and then he would be revealed, and if he was, then his friends would be exposed as well. He had to protect the Helping Hands.

Even if that meant sacrificing himself.

"Jimmy, you have to go!" Leighann cried, dropping to her knees. She ran a hand through his hair when he shook his head again. "Please, Jimmy, please. You have to go."

Matt, who couldn't find the energy to comfort his girlfriend, felt a chill run through his bones when Jimmy turned his eyes, teary and red, to meet his own.

"We... were great," Jimmy choked out, a convulsion of pain slamming against his chest as he cringed. He could feel the hot metal of the bullet searing his insides, could imagine his flesh slowly tearing a gaping hole down his stomach.

He knew he wasn't going to make it.

Matt forced a smile as he nodded. "We did all that we could, and it was great."

"O'Conner is so proud of you guys," Mickey said to Jimmy, his hand still covering the bullet wound and his face and arms soaked with blood. He saw the glint in Jimmy's eyes that made his own water, and he realized then that Jimmy hadn't been a part of the Helping Hands just for the kids, or for himself, or to be a part of the legend. He was repaying Melanie for all she had done, thanking her, and knowing that, Mickey smiled down at the dying teenager in front of him.

"She thinks you're a hero. She's proud of you."

It was all Jimmy needed to hear before he gave in to the darkness.

Chapter 10

An hour later, the rest of his gang having gone home after Mickey picked the locks on the cuffs for Carry and Leighann and Isaac washed up in the bathroom, Matt paced in the office of the auto shop, cursing himself silently. He kept his head down, his hands behind his back, as he struggled to sort out his thoughts.

It all happened so fast, he thought. *What was I supposed to do? Where did I go wrong?*

What would Melanie have done?

There had been no warning. He'd thought he was doing a good thing, helping that bastard kid get away from his bastard father. Just because the boy wanted to earn a few bucks, Matt's best friend had to die. Not to mention that two agents had been shot. Matt didn't know if they would live or not, but honestly, he wanted them to die. That way, they couldn't tell anyone who the Helping Hands of San Francisco were.

And that way, they would pay for the death they had caused.

Mickey had come up with their cover story. He would bring Jimmy's body to an alley, one that only he knew about, and make the death look like a drive-by murder. It both disgusted and shamed Matt that his friend would be forced to endure such a death.

He deserved better.

A knock on the office door made him jump. Spinning around, he saw Mickey entering slowly, his hands and face freshly scrubbed of Jimmy's blood. He came to the teenager and put an arm around his shoulder.

"It's not your fault," he offered his solace, but Matt shook his head.

"I should have listened to O'Conner," he replied with a sob. "She didn't want us to do this because she thought it was too dangerous and that we weren't ready, and I just brushed her off like she didn't know anything."

Mickey took hold of Matt's shoulders and stared straight in the eye. "Mathew Harper, this is not your fault," he repeated firmly. "You can't blame yourself for any of this." He waited for Matt to reply, and when he didn't, he took a step back. "You need to call her. She needs to hear what happened from you, not from the reporter that will be talking about it tomorrow morning on the news."

Matt swallowed heavily and glanced down at his cell phone. It seemed like such a hard thing to do, to pick up the phone and dial. He wasn't sure he wanted to tell her, because she had told him this would happen. He didn't know how Melanie would react.

In fact, he was terrified of what her reaction might be.

Collinsville, California

Melanie reached up with a tired arm and flicked on the light by her bed. Next to her, Tyler grumbled in his sleep and covered his head with a pillow. Wishing she could do the same, Melanie grabbed her cell and held it to her ear, silent for a moment until she found the energy to talk.

"What?"

"Um... O'Conner?"

She would know the voice anywhere, even if it were choked with tears and whispered with hesitance. Sitting up straighter, she ran a hand through her hair, feeling Tyler stirring next to her. Worry flooded through her and was enhanced by the fact that the caller addressed her as O'Conner and not Miss Melanie.

"It's like three-thirty in the morning. What's going on?"

"Who is it?" Tyler asked groggily. She mouthed Matt's name to him, and he felt concern take weight in his chest.

"O'Conner, something happened," Matt answered after taking in a deep breath.

"Matt, it's okay," she said when she heard him on the verge of breaking down. "Just tell me what happened."

He did, giving every gruesome detail with a sob or a sigh, pausing here and there to gasp out a few tears, not caring that it wasn't safe to discuss such details over the phone. When he finished, Melanie rose from the bed, rubbing her temple with a shaking hand. The line went silent, and she took a moment to collect herself and to make sure that when she spoke she would sound in control. It took several deep breaths before she could manage it.

"Where... Where's Jimmy?" She could only manage two words, and those two were strained as it was.

"He's here," Matt sobbed. "He's still here. But what if the cops are looking for us? What if Corwin doesn't die and he starts talking? It just happened so fast, I couldn't stop it! I don't know what to do, O'Conner! *I don't know how to handle this!*"

"Matt! Matt, relax," Melanie said, struggling to keep her voice even. "I want you to go home and try to get some sleep, and let me deal with it."

"I can't, O'Conner. I don't know what to do about this! I'm totally over my head here! I—"

"I'll take care of it," she cut in, no longer tired. "I want you to go home and sleep. Stay home from school, do whatever you have to do. Tell the others not to say anything to anyone. I promise you that I will take care of this."

Ending the phone call, Melanie stared down at the receiver, imagining her fingers smeared in blood, knowing that soon her hands would be covered with it, if not literally then figuratively. Either way, the blood was shed and she had to clean it up.

Just like she predicted.

She didn't want to get involved. She told Matt if he screwed up it would be up to him to sort things out; it would be his mistake, his problem, his fucking screw-up. But goddamn it, she couldn't turn her back on him, not when he called her in the middle of the night, terrified, weeping, grieving. Not when he had the death of a gang member on his hands would she cast him aside.

Jimmy Fencles, the boy she had nursed back to health for six long months. The child that nearly died in her arms. The one kid who had always told her his dreams and goals, always been so bright and helpful, so full of life, was gone.

Dead. Forever.

Murdered in cold blood.

Just like Wess.

The thought forced up a fire from deep in her soul and she drew back her arm, throwing the phone across the room with a furious scream. It crashed into a picture of her and Tyler, falling to the floor as the glass shattered. Tyler jumped up from the bed as Melanie sank to the carpet, a grieving tremble working its way through her body.

"Melanie? Mel, what's wrong? What happened with Harper?" His face was filled with concern, and he rubbed her back as she cried. When she wrapped her arms around his neck and buried her head in his shoulder, voluntarily surrendering to his solace, he held her tight, trying to suppress her shudders while healing a hurt he did not yet understand.

Chapter 11

Gregson, Oklahoma

Caleb sighed as he hung up the phone, turning to Taryn. She sat at the table in the kitchen of their Helping Hand hideaway, anxiously awaiting information. Her hands were wringing together, her knuckles white.

"Well, Tyler says that Jimmy was buried yesterday morning," Caleb informed his best friend, joining her at the table. "Ceremony was short. I asked if I could talk to O'Conner, see how she's doing, but Tyler said she refuses to talk about it and is doing her usual thing. You know, where she ignores the real problem and just gets mad when someone tries to help."

"And lets the problem eat at her until there's nothing left but the thirst for revenge."

He knew it was true, for he had seen it all happen before. When O'Conner got to that point, to the point to where she could no longer see clearly, the entire world became her enemy. Tyler was the same way, which was probably why the two bonded the way they did as kids. One of the things Caleb liked about Taryn was that she was a lot mellower than his other two best friends. Anger and grief didn't have the same effect on her, and he found her easier to live with, even despite the fact that they argued day in and day out because she was so goddamn hardheaded.

"Yeah, O'Conner is still real broken up about it."

"Who can blame her? She nursed Jimmy back to health. She hardly left his side for the entire six months he was healing," Taryn replied, remembering the night they had taken Jimmy. Only Melanie believed he would live, and had never given up hope. For Taryn, that had been the kidnapping that cleared the fog, and she saw, for the first time, life through Melanie O'Conner's eyes.

"I still can't believe Livingston would do something like that," she said, and Caleb nodded, getting a chill when he thought about what could have happened if he and Taryn had been caught in Livingston's house.

It had been six days since the attack. An immediate investigation began upon discovering the two wounded F.B.I. agents and dead mayor. Police determined that a fourth person was injured based on the blood, but except for a few footprints in the blood, no fingerprints had shown up except for those accounted for at the scene of the crime.

The police bought the story Corwin told them about he and Neilson chasing Livingston into the apartment after seeing him selling drugs to a couple teenagers, especially since his past cocaine charges in his early twenties added plausibility to the story. Corwin, feeling as though he owed his life to Mathew Harper, was willing to lie to save the teenager from prison. Neilson hadn't made it through the ambulance ride to the hospital, and his death was hard on Corwin. He could only surmise that it was his fault that his partner died.

Jimmy had been found just hours after Mickey left the alley, almost a full day after the cops arrived at the apartment. Police ruled it just another alley drive-by, and hadn't bothered to put a connection to Jimmy's murder and the F.B.I. agents because as far as they knew, Livingston was a dealer and not a child abuser, and Jimmy wasn't a Helping Hand but an unfortunate victim. It was a story with a lot of loose ends and left many questions to be answered, but it all made for an appealing media story and public sympathy.

And that was, after all, the name of the game.

Sighing again after giving Taryn's hands a reassuring squeeze, Caleb sat back in his chair. "Tyler said that the F.B.I. agent called O'Conner from the hospital. He's not going to say anything. Apparently he had a major change of heart after everything went down. He won't turn in Matt and his gang because, according to Corwin, they saved his life when they could have let him die, and that says something to him."

"Well, it better," Taryn huffed. "I mean, look at what he caused. It was all his fault to begin with."

The two fell silent for a moment, staring at everything but one another. The thought of never seeing Jimmy again depressed Taryn. She did her best to focus on the good memories, but losing him really made her think about the Helping Hands and how being one meant accepting the fact that every day was a risk.

It was amazing and fulfilling and exhilarating, saving the kids, but there were times when Taryn felt overwhelmed by all that had happened in her life. Surely, she thought, no woman in her mid-twenties should have to worry about her best friends dying, where each day meant having to look over her shoulder for cops or vengeful parents. It was one thing when she was seventeen, without a care in the world or a penny to her name, but now she was an adult, and as much as she loved being a Helping Hand, there were times when she yearned to lead a normal life.

She deserved normal, whatever normal was. They all did.

After considering her thoughts, Taryn sat up straighter and breathed in deeply. "Caleb, enough is enough. This has gone too far." She glanced up to see him staring at her, his expression not saying whether he agreed or disagreed. "We've been doing this for like twelve years, and look at what's happened. Wess died, Jimmy died, that Evan guy was murdered. Not to mention O'Conner getting arrested and all of us getting split up. We've gone through so much. I just want a normal life."

"I know what you mean," Caleb agreed. "I know we mentioned it before, but never talked about it seriously. I was talking to Brayden earlier and he was saying that he thought he was ready to be on his own. Aaron said that if Brayden went anywhere, he'd go with him. But Paige and Dawn said they weren't ready. So I bet they'd stay here and care for the kids. I mean, we have seventy. It's not like we need any more."

The possibility of having a normal life was becoming more and more appealing to Taryn. No more hiding, no more looking over her shoulder for vengeful enemies.

No more friends dying.

With a smile, Taryn nodded. "Then let's do it. Let's retire. Maybe we can get a place near O'Conner and Tyler. Maybe even on the same street. Remember they were telling us that some family moved out a few weeks ago and is still trying to sell their house?"

"Yeah." Caleb remembered the conversation. It had been a casual one, with the comment about the house being made nonchalantly, but now it served a purpose. "It would be nice to settle down and not have to worry about all this anymore." He waved his hand and glanced around him. "I mean, I'll always love the Helping Hands, and I'll always help out with the kids and everything, but I think that for a while I'd like to watch it from the outside."

Leaning close to one another, the two friends began discussing their plans for retirement from the Helping Hands.

Chapter 13

South Bay Juvenile Detention Camp

The sun was high and the air warm and breezeless, making every teenager at the boot camp wish they were home swimming in pools or at the beach instead of suffering in the sweltering heat. They carried out their chores, attended their classes and counseling sessions, and argued with the drill sergeants whenever and wherever they could.

Sitting inside in the cool air-conditioning and cushioned chairs were Melanie O'Conner and Brian Hawkins. They sat in his office, going over the file of Riley Beach, their newest detainee. The fourteen year-old delinquent was scrawny, obnoxious, and an overall nuisance. Hawkins was sure he could break him through rigorous training and discipline, while Melanie warned him of the possibilities.

"Fourteen year-olds are different," she told him. "Not yet an adult, no longer a child. They're trying to make a name for themselves, impress the older guys so they can fit in. They have to prove themselves. I don't think he'll be an easy case at all." She sat back, raising her eyebrows.

Hawkins knew the challenging expression well, for she used it often. "O'Conner, we're talking a rich, spoiled little boy craving for some attention. He wants to make a name, fine. But he won't do it on my time. I don't waste a single minute on kids like him by letting them give me any attitude. The second he shows his, I'm going after him."

Melanie smiled, and Brian knew it was her way of telling him that she was betting against him. "Fine. Have it your way. I'm only counseling him. What could I possibly know about being a fourteen year-old who does drugs and is committed to a life of crime?"

Noting the sarcasm in her voice, Brian shook his head and adjusted his hat. "I never said you couldn't relate to him. I'm just saying that—"

"That if I had been sent to your camp when I was a teenager that you would have been able to break me," Melanie finished for him. "Don't be so goddamn cocky, Hawkins. It's bound to get you in trouble."

"So's that mouth of yours," Brian warned. "Just because we came to you for this position doesn't mean you can talk to your superiors the way you do."

Melanie enjoyed the irritation that was quickly spreading across her boss's face. The satisfaction she felt helped to drown out both the misery of the Ponder case. "So tell me, Hawkins, just how *am* I supposed to talk to you?"

"With respect."

"Respect?" Melanie scoffed, the disgust obvious in her voice. She would have leapt to her feet if she could have. Instead she glowered at him from across the desk. "You want me to talk to you with respect? Why the hell should I? You don't treat any of the kids here with respect. You act like you're better than them."

"Tell me, what have they done to prove themselves otherwise?"

"They're *kids*, Hawkins!" Melanie cried, more and more frustrated by the second. "Each and every one of them, just scared kids begging for attention. It's not about proving that they're good enough to be treated with respect. In order to get it, you have to *give* it. All you do is strut around here like you're God's goddamn gift to saving kids—"

"Oh no, O'Conner, that's your specialty."

"Fuck you, Hawkins."

"Now you listen here, and you listen damn close." Hawkins sat forward, pointing at Melanie with a furious scowl. "You've been all pissy ever since you got word on the Ponder verdict, picking fights with everyone who works here and being a major pain-in-the-ass. Now I understand that you're upset, but you leave your baggage at home when you're here. It's time you got over yourself and start focusing on the kids here that still have a goddamn shot. You hear me?" He slammed a hand down on the table, pausing when Melanie flinched suddenly and grabbed her stomach as if she had just been socked hard. "O'Conner? O'Conner, what's wrong?"

Melanie couldn't reply at first, for when she opened her mouth to do so, she could focus on nothing other than what her body was telling her. The tight jaws clamped hard in her gut. "I think... I think I'm going into labor," she managed to tell him.

Momentarily at a loss, Hawkins fought to clear his thoughts so he could figure out just what the hell he was supposed to do. "Oh, shit," he muttered, grabbing for the phone and fumbling it a bit as he dialed the number for the hospital, telling the receptionist that he would soon be in with a pregnant woman. Then he helped Melanie to her feet and half-carried her out to his car.

Melanie grabbed the nurse's arm when another contraction pulled at her stomach, beads of sweat forming along her brow. She fought the urge to scream out in pain, and instead dug her fingers into the arm she had taken hold of. The nurse clamped his teeth together, amazed at how strong such a small woman could be. He silently prayed for her husband to get there soon so *he* could be the one getting his arm bruised.

"You're going to have to breathe!" another nurse ordered, her mouth covered with a mask. She demonstrated, and Melanie felt mildly ridiculous. Her hand clutched the sheets as she felt the child inside of her fighting to be free, demanding it, not taking no for an answer.

It was her kid all right.

"Any minute now," Doctor Ron Dodds said with a smile, although she couldn't see his mouth.

Melanie ground her teeth together, determined not to be the crazy screaming woman in a hospital bed always portrayed on TV. But when the doctor told her again that it would be any minute, she shook her head fiercely.

"I am *not* having this kid without Mel!" she shouted, convinced that she could wait and determined to do so. But she didn't have to, for Tyler burst through the doors, clothed in dark green scrubs and a white surgical mask hanging around his neck. He strutted up to her, smiling with a glint that lit up his eyes.

"Hey, babe. How's it goin'?" he asked casually, knowing that Melanie would have punched him had a contraction not gotten in the way. He tried to act relaxed, otherwise his nerves would cause him to stumble over his words and make him sound like a fool. The fact that his child was about to be born, that it was all really happening *now*, made him feel sick with anticipation and apprehension.

Sensing another bout of pain beforehand, the nurse gestured to Tyler. "You take her. Give my arm a rest."

Tyler laughed, kneeling down and gripping Melanie's sweaty hand, immediately jerking back up when she squeezed so hard that she crushed his fingers together unmercifully to the point that he swore he heard cracking.

"Ow! Ow, Melanie, *damn it*, that *hurts*!" he cried as she tightened her grip. He clenched his jaw when she squeezed harder, bending bones that weren't supposed to bend, then finally, *finally* let go when the contraction passed. Instantly he pulled back his hand. "Holy *shit*, Melanie! What the *hell* was that all about?"

"Tyler, I swear to God I'll kill you for doing this to me," Melanie snapped back, not caring that she had said Tyler instead of Mel in front of a bunch of strangers. "You think that hurts? Wait until you got a goddamn body coming out of your—" She bit back her words when pain lanced through her stomach, swallowing a shout.

"It's crowning." The doctor positioned himself at Melanie's feet while Tyler unwillingly gave his hand back to Melanie after biting back a snarl, though he couldn't keep his upper lip from curling with regret. "Melanie, on the next contraction, I want you to push."

It took an hour, and with a final push and burst of searing pain, Doctor Dodds was holding a screaming baby boy in his arms. The nurses took no time at all in cleaning him up and handing him to Melanie, who was damp with sweat and exhausted from the effort.

Melanie took her new son in her arms, holding him against her chest. Her breath was taken away as she held her child, her mind, for once, cleared of any worries. Complete amazement taking him over, Tyler hovered over her, running his hands over the baby's hands, his breath taken away as well. With a smile, Melanie looked up at Tyler.

"Joshua Mathew Scotford," she said quietly, and Tyler grinned back, thrilled that for once, she was finally letting herself be happy.

When she held up the baby, Tyler took his son in his own arms. It felt so odd to be holding such a small thing, so delicate and fragile. He saw ten perfect fingers and ten perfect toes, a perfect son.

His son.

Melanie watched Tyler with the baby. It was a real sight to her, a man nearly six-three, somewhere around two-hundred-and-ten pounds of pure muscle, holding a newborn of seven pounds, eight ounces against his chest. Her eyes widened a bit when she saw the tears that had formed. She had never, not once in the thirteen years she'd known him, seen him cry.

Tyler knelt down and handed baby Josh back to Melanie. The two were oblivious to the nurses around them as they stared at one another, Melanie's face glistened with sweat but still managing to shine with radiance, Tyler's eyes soft and filled with warmth. Tyler leaned over and kissed his wife lovingly, thinking to himself that *this* was the day he had always waited for.

"Hey, Melanie?"

"Yeah?"

"We've been through a lot together, seen and done a lot of shit in our lives. Blood, guts, drugs."

"Yeah. So?"

Taking in a deep breath as his mind replayed the last ten minutes, Tyler swallowed heavily. "So, you have no idea what childbirth looks like from the other end. I think that was the most nauseating thing I've ever seen."

A laugh burst out of her at the sight of his pale face, a laugh that was pure, heartfelt. It had been so long since she laughed, and it felt both foreign and familiar.

Pulling Tyler up onto the bed with her, Melanie kissed the father of her son, one hand on his shoulder and the other grasping their newborn child while she could think of nothing but the fact that now, after so many years of being alone, she finally had a family.

Chapter 12

San Francisco, California

She was told all she needed to know by the pictures in the photo albums. Or rather, the lack of them. She searched through every one she could find, starting with the photos hanging on the walls and lining tabletops, then combing the house for any more that may be stored away. There were endless photos in cabinets, books, files, dressers, but no matter where she looked, she found not one picture of herself or her sister. She had even glanced through one of Robbie's old yearbooks, also not finding anyone who had her name.

Kelly Anderson did not exist.

Ever since Melanie O'Conner's visit, Kelly had been unable to forget her visions, or her suspicions. They were there at the back of her mind, willingly suppressed, eventually creeping up until she could hear herself screaming at something as a dark shadow crashed down upon her. She didn't know what her visions meant.

But there was one way to find out.

It took her until nightfall to get out of the house. There was always something or some*one* in the way. First Danielle stopped her in the hall to ask for help with her homework, then Robbie wanted to talk about school and other unimportant details of her supposedly real life, and then Rachael asked her to do the dishes. It was as if fate was working against her, urging her to remain locked in her state of unawareness.

But now she was free to escape.

Stepping out onto the front porch, she glanced around tentatively, half-expecting to see Robbie appear from around the corner to stop her. He always seemed to be there, in the way as she tried to find out anything about her past. But at the moment he was up in his room with his stereo nearly blasting away the windows as he did his homework.

She walked down the sidewalk, never taking her eyes from the house down the street. It was burned in her memory, and yet, so strange. She could picture herself climbing down the trellis at night. Robbie said she had always had an active imagination, said she loved to make up stories.

Robbie said a lot of things.

Nerves ran through her stomach as she reached the house and strode up to the door. Twisting the knob and finding that it was locked, she took a frustrated step back, pacing for a moment. She was about to turn back and give up the search she hadn't even yet begun when the anger of not knowing who she was took hold of her emotions and she spun around, sending her elbow into the thin glass window next to the door, ignoring the pain. As it shattered, she brushed away the shards and stepped through, barely noticing that her elbow was bleeding. The house was dark, lit only by the fading sun that peeked through the closed blinds. She stood in the foyer, taking in her surroundings with unease.

Here, oddly, she felt at home, and that scared her. She wasn't supposed to know any place except the one she was being told should be the most familiar to her. Stepping from the foyer, she somehow knew that to her right would be the kitchen, complete with a tall white refrigerator and wraparound counter. Glancing that way, she saw that she was right. As she stared at the light-blue tile and ashen cabinets, a woman flashed through her mind, a woman with straight blonde hair neatly brushed and a face covered with makeup. She turned to the teenager, a dreamy smile playing across full red lips.

"Make sure the living room's clean. I'm having visitors tomorrow."

Kelly blinked the picture away and pushed herself from the doorway, then headed into the dining room. Instantly she was hit with an invisible wall of dread. Fighting against it, Kelly turned away and pounded up the stairs, sobs forming in her throat as her mind pleaded for answers. She burst through a bedroom door, and the first thing she saw was a picture. Her feet stumbled to a halt, her lips parting as her pace slowed from a frantic run to a worried crawl. Her eyes remained on the photo, and she crept closer, closer, until she could take in with disbelief every detail of her and Danielle hugging a woman in a bridal gown.

A wedding, she thought, *but whose? Is that my mother?*

Another picture to the left was of her and a man she didn't recognize, but in the background was a yellow house surrounded by flowers. That house, that house she knew. Florida, two years ago, down the street from her grandfather. 1742 Wicker Street. The day after her birthday.

"What the hell is going on?" she asked aloud, not wanting to believe that Robbie really had lied to her.

She was about to make her way down the stairs and back to Robbie, but when she reached the top landing she froze. Her breath shook, her eyes watered, and she could do absolutely nothing as it all came back.

There was blood, bright red blood on the walls, on the terrifying man's hands, on the floor. There was a wrench, an iron wrench that attacked her late in the night as the moonlight caught the metal gleam and sent the glow deep into her child eyes. Her mother, striding down the aisle in a brilliantly white gown, a grin on her face and tears in her eyes as she married the groom she loved and the man her children feared. Running away, more than once, and each time being brought back by the police only to receive harsh, blood-spattered punishments from her stepfather. The disappointing move from Florida to California, and her sister breaking her leg when she tripped over a box that she had packed all her books into. Brittle bone disease, which was why Kelly had been so intent on protecting her.

Stepping in front of the fist.

Taking the hit herself.

Kelly gasped when the pain of the blows came back all at once. All over again she was a child cowering in sweat-and-blood-soaked sheets from the iron fist. She was the teenager trying to be rough and tough and scare away the guys so she would never have to face the touch of another man. Then she was seventeen year-old Kelly Mitchell, weary of the game and letting herself fall for the guy who had been lying to her all along.

"Oh, *God*," she choked out as she sank to the floor, tears streaming down her cheeks when she remembered Jeffrey Ponder, his angered face red and snarling, his fist ramming into her stomach and her back hitting the wall, head slamming back with a thud. Her hand slipping on the banister and the pain of hitting each solid step with a dull thump, ribs cracking, bones snapping, bright lights flashing, eventually landing on the base of the stairs only to glance up through a red haze at a glowering, furious man.

The pain, so much of it. The blood, so red, so thick as it dripped off the white-painted walls. She saw it, saw the red stains against the white of the walls where someone had attempted to wipe it away but failed miserably. Then came the thought of death, the wish for it, the silent pleading for it all to end and to escape the Hell that had become her life. Flesh ripped, blood poured, bones pierced skin and liquid-choked gurgles bubbled up from bruised organs.

Hysteria from the horrible memories breaking through her emotions, Kelly picked herself up from the floor and fled the house.

Chapter 14

Music blared as Robbie stared at his chemistry book, his eyes reading the equations but his brain refusing to comprehend them. Closing the book and tossing it to the floor, Robbie got up and headed for the door. He wanted to see Kelly.

Knocking on her bedroom door and not getting a reply, he entered to see that the room was empty. For a second he thought that she might have gone out to dinner with his parents, but he didn't want to call his parents because then they would worry and come home early.

Robbie felt a little concerned when he looked out the window and saw that his car was gone. Kelly must have taken it, he figured, but he hadn't even heard it start.

But where would she go without telling me?

The phone rang before he had a chance to work up a major fret. He answered it, concentrating hard when he heard the sniffling voice on the other end. "Kelly?" he asked hesitantly, concentrating on the background noises. "What's the matter? Where are you?"

"I know!" Kelly cried back, her voice raked with sobs. "I know *everything*!"

Robbie sucked in a deep breath and raised a hand to his eyes. In the background he could hear Kelly crying, the sounds of other vehicles on the road.

"Kelly, it's okay," he tried to calm her as he began to pace. "Just tell me where you are, or where you're going, and I'll come and get you."

"I can't!" she yelled back. "It's too much! I can't *handle* these memories, Robbie! He hit me! He tried to *kill* me!"

Robbie jumped when he heard a car horn blast through the phone line and the sound of tires skidding met his ears. "Kelly, are you all right? Are you okay?"

"It's all too real."

"Kelly, listen to me. You have to stop the car and wait for me. Where are you going?"

On the other end of the phone, Kelly shook her head and gripped the steering wheel, her eyes blurred from tears. "I don't know. The school. It's all so much." Her voice got tougher now. "Why, Robbie? *Why did you have to lie to me*? All this time, all this *goddamn* time I've been trying to remember a life that never even existed! I was so lost! And you knew! You knew why I was confused, and you still *lied* to me!"

She heard him hesitate. "Kelly, I'm sorry. Just please, whatever you're doing, stop!"

Shaking her head again and bursting into another fit of tears, Kelly pressed hard on the accelerator. She knew she was hysterical, but something inside told her to keep going, to go faster. After all, what did it matter? What did any of it matter now that her life was a lie? Her own sister lied to her, the guy she fell for betrayed her trust, and her mother… she no longer had one.

She was alone.

There was nothing left worth living for.

She ran a red light and barely missed a collision with a small pick-up truck. She could hear Robbie screaming at her from the phone, but her mind ceased to decipher his deceitful words. Her eyes no longer saw the road as they were taken over by visions of Jeffrey Ponder raising his fist at her, shouting at her, threatening to kill her. The pain came back bit by bit, and she relived each blow as it was lashed out. The pain, the blood, the endless fear of what the night would hold.

The wish, the pleading, the desperate desire, for death.

She didn't see the car that was pulling out of a gas station, and she crashed into it before she could slam on the brakes. Her car skidded across the road, slamming into the guardrail. She didn't feel the impact of hitting the steering wheel and didn't realize that her lips were busted and two teeth cracked. Looking out her window, Kelly saw a dark truck headed right for her, headlights glaring, brakes unable to stop in time. Her face held no emotion as her hands dropped listlessly to her lap.

Her eyes went blank while her body sat limp, motionless, and without the protection of a seatbelt.

Her heart pounded, not in fear, but with anticipation.

Her mind shut down, no longer caring, no longer able to function.

She blinked, eyelids heavy as her jaw fixed her mouth in a position of indifference.

In those two seconds before the collision, as she watched the truck's shining chrome grill become larger and larger to her tired eyes, Kelly could think of nothing but the fact that soon, so very soon, all her pain would end.

And so she sat back, blank and defeated, and she waited to die.

Chapter 15

"*Kelly!*"

Robbie grabbed at his hair when all he could hear was glass shattering and the sounds of metal being twisted and torn. A horn blasted, and a second later, the line went dead.

"God*damn* it!" He grabbed his jacket and raced from the house. The school, she said. He would go to the school. She had to be there. *She* would *be there*, he told himself. His feet pounded on the sidewalk as he ran faster than he had ever run before. His breath became heavier as he panted, praying that Kelly was alive. He could think of nothing else, nothing other than to wish for her life.

Pictures began to form in front of his eyes as his feet started to cramp, visions of Kelly. How her face had been scared and worried and indifferent all at the same time when he introduced himself that very first time they met. The anger in her eyes when she slammed the locker door on his fingers, then the sadness that replaced it when they talked in the library.

"*It's all a game with you guys,*" he could hear her saying, in her voice so soft. "*Fighting, seeing how long you can go before your opponent breaks down, before you win and the other guy loses.*"

"*You can only lose if you let yourself lose. So don't let the other guy win.*"

Robbie could replay the entire conversation in his mind, could picture Kelly's face, so sad yet so determined.

"*Sometimes I wish I could just be normal, you know?*" she said to him on that night when they snuck out for the party, the night before Jeffrey sent her away. She had been so free, so careless, dancing as though only she and Robbie existed, laughing like nothing in the world had ever made her as happy as she was lying in the grass with the stars overhead.

He could still feel her lips against his, could still smell her shampoo, could still imagine the touch of her skin beneath his hand. The party had been more than a night of escape. It had been about freedom, about trust, a trust that Robbie had thrown thoughtlessly into the gutter.

The first things Robbie saw when he came to the street just a block from his school were flashing lights. He ducked under the police tape, shoving away an officer.

"You can't go back there!" the officer yelled, tightening his grip on the struggling teenager. "Hold still!"

"*That's my sister!*" Robbie shouted back, his voice frantic as the gathered crowd whispered to one another. "You have to let me see her! I *have* to see her!"

224

"There's nothing to see, son. She's gone." The officer steadied Robbie and shook his head. "There was nothing anyone could do. She wasn't wearing her seatbelt, and went through the other side of the car."

"Where is she?" Robbie spun around, searching the road. *Tell me where she is!*"

The officer took in a deep breath and gestured with his head to a form lying next to Robbie's shattered Mustang. It was covered by a blanket, and took a few shaky steps towards it before the policeman grabbed his arm.

"I wouldn't look, son," he gently advised with a shake of his head, but Robbie ignored the warning.

"You have to have someone identify her, don't you?" he asked, his voice sharp. He didn't know why he wanted to see her, just that he needed to. "You can't just assume who she is."

With reluctant agreement, the officer, Danny Kells, knelt down and pulled back the cover, revealing Kelly's head and upper body. Robbie didn't know what he had been expecting, but the gruesome sight in front of his eyes certainly wasn't it.

Blood was smeared across Kelly's cold flesh, some of it dried, some still leaking from the gashes across her nose and forehead. Glass shards were cut deep into her skin, and her lower lip was sliced in half, revealing her bottom teeth, three of which were missing. The skin on the right side of her head was peeled back, showing a bloody mess of bone and tissue.

A bitter bile taste hit the back of Robbie's throat and his body shook at the sight as he fought against the urge to vomit, losing the battle quickly and painfully.

Officer Kells, seeing the boy's struggle, covered Kelly's body back up while fighting back tears of his own. He had a daughter that would be seventeen in a few years, and the thought of his only little girl ending up like the one in front of him was too much to bear.

"I'm sorry this happened," he said softly, knowing that there were no words that could make up for the horrible accident. "You shouldn't be here. I can get someone to take you home."

Robbie shook his head. His breath gone and his mind shutting down, he glanced around, seeing the road covered in glass, metal, and car parts. The debris led to a black truck, the front of which was mashed nearly up to the windshield, which had all but fallen out. Next to the truck was the guardrail, bent in and coated with the black paint of his once-whole Mustang.

He finally saw his car and was shocked, not at its damage but at the fact that Kelly had been in it when the collision occurred. The driver's side was punched in and the seat was nearly folded on top of the passenger side. The back tire had popped off and all the windows on the driver's side were shattered. Edging closer, Robbie saw blood on the seats, on the road, smeared across the beige interior as if someone had taken a can of red paint and dumped it inside the car. The passenger door was open, and he saw that on the window was a circular hole with cracks around its edge, where her head likely struck the glass.

Robbie's knees gave out, but Kells was right behind to catch him before he hit the pavement. He held Robbie by the shoulders as the sickness overwhelmed him and he vomited again, burning tears forming as he squeezed his eyes shut. The officer helped him over to his squad car, bracing the teenager on the seat.

"It's okay, son. What's your name?"

"Robbie," he replied numbly,. "How… how long has she been here?"

"Not too long." This was the hardest part of his job, facing the family of the victim and having to work through the grief and shock. Kneeling down, he met Robbie's eyes. "The driver of the truck said that it all happened too fast for anyone to stop it. Other witnesses said the same thing. The truck driver was injured, but other than that, I don't know what happened. Investigations are being done. I'm very sorry for this."

Nodding, Robbie felt a tear run down his cheek. "I know what happened," he whispered, his chin quivering. "He won."

Chapter 16

Collinsville, California

Joshua Mathew Scotford gave a small cry of delight as he was passed to Taryn, who cuddled him tight against her chest. A spitting image of her two friends combined into one, the little boy was destined to be the next street-roaming bad-ass with a big heart and an equally big mouth.

"He's such a happy kid," she said to Melanie, who was sitting on the couch next to Tyler. "He hardly ever cries."

"Give 'em another week with these two," Caleb piped up from his spot on the floor and gestured to the couple. "Seven more days with them and the kid's bound to get fed up. Who knows what he'll do to them in the middle of the night."

"Watch it, Brinson," Melanie warned. Caleb only glanced at her with a smirk. "He turns out anything like me and you're gonna have to be watching your ass until the day you die."

"Ah, so all beware the spawn of Satan."

"I'd take Satan over the two of them any day," Taryn put in, and the group laughed while Melanie kicked at Caleb and missed when he dodged to the side.

"You just wait. You'll get what's coming to you."

It had been just over a week since her son's birth, a week that had given Melanie a release from the stress of "real life" as she cared for Josh at home and spent as much time as possible with Tyler. As they rejoiced in their family, and how far they had come since their early years, they realized that everything they'd been through had been worth it, all leading up to this moment.

For the first time, Melanie was happy, and was afraid of losing the life that made it all worthwhile.

"Yo Jones, you gonna pass the kid up or hog him all day?" Caleb asked, gesturing for Taryn to hand Josh over to him. She did so with an unwilling frown. Observing the baby, Caleb couldn't help but grin. There wasn't a doubt in his mind that Josh had the two greatest parents in the world. He would live the life none of them ever had, and would be given more love than he knew what to do with.

"Maybe one day he'll do something great, like we did," he said to Melanie and Tyler. "Who knows, maybe he'll be the founder of a new branch of Helping Hands."

"Not if I have anything to do with it." Tyler shook his head and put his arm around Melanie. "No way am I putting my son at risk of being arrested or killed." He looked over at Melanie to see her nod in agreement.

With a shrug, Taryn slapped Caleb's back. "Well, Brinson, looks like it's up to us to bring a new heir to the project into this world." She laughed when Caleb punched her shoulder with his free hand. Tyler, sensing a possible wrestling match, leaned over and took his son from Caleb. As soon as his arms were free, Caleb grabbed Taryn and held her in a headlock.

"You just wait till we get a place and start working like normal people," he told her, barely having to put forth any effort to control Taryn's struggling. "Doing things the legal way, you'll be so damn tired, you won't ever want to have a kid."

"I don't know about that," Melanie said after allowing Josh to take her finger, watching him gnaw on it. "I think you two would make one hell of a couple." She took them both by surprise, as she knew she would. Caleb released Taryn with playful abhorrence while Tyler nodded.

"Totally. I mean, you've known each other practically all your lives. And after all, me and Melanie got together, so it's only natural that you guys will do the same."

"Yeah right," Taryn scoffed. "The day I hook up with that arrogant bastard is the day I become a stripper and Brinson admits he's a pansy." She dodged another punch from Caleb and looked at Melanie. "I still don't know how you can put up with that one," she pointed to Tyler, "seeing as how they both act the same exact way."

Melanie shrugged. "I guess I have a higher tolerance level." She glanced over at Tyler when he replied with a biting remark loud enough for only her to hear and made a face at him.

A knock at the front door made all four of the former Hell Hounds glance over their shoulders. With a sigh, Melanie hoisted herself up from the couch and Tyler handed Josh back to Taryn, following Melanie. He frowned when the person knocked again, this time more urgently.

Melanie opened the front door to see Matt Harper standing on her front porch, his hands in the pockets of his navy blue jacket, his head hung low, and his eyes red. When the door opened, he raised his head and stared at Melanie with sorrow. He didn't say anything, nor did Melanie, for she was surprised at how bad he looked.

Melanie started to ask him what was wrong when Matt shook his head suddenly and let out a sob. "I'm sorry, Miss Melanie, I'm so sorry."

As his tears overcame him, Matt grabbed Melanie into a hug, and after a moment of stunned hesitation she wrapped her arms around him. She felt his hands clutch the back of her shirt as he buried his head in her shoulder.

"Matt, it's okay," Melanie soothed, tightening her grip while Tyler and the others hung back. "It's okay. What happened?"

Matt pulled away after a moment, wiping his eyes with his hands. "I... I couldn't help it. It all happened so fast that I didn't know what was going on until it was all... all over."

Melanie led Matt to the couch, taking his hands as she knelt down in front of him. "Matt, is this about Jimmy? I told you, that wasn't your fault. And you don't have to worry about the F.B.I. agent, because he—"

"Kelly's dead!" Matt cried, his voice full of tears.

The words felt like a ball of fire in her stomach, climbing up her chest and clamping down on her heart. "No. No, Matt, she can't be dead. What happened?"

"She remembered everything, and she lost it," Matt replied, pushing back his hair. Tyler sucked in a deep breath and closed his eyes. "She just lost it, stole Robbie's car and freaked out. She ran a red light and was hit by a truck. It happened a few days ago, but I couldn't tell you then. With everything that happened, I just couldn't. Don't you ever watch the news? The story was all over the media."

Melanie sensed the anger and pain running through her blood before it actually hit. She hadn't watched any television since her son was born. She hadn't had the time or desire. But now she cursed herself for shutting herself away from the world because it prevented her from hearing the news when it actually happened, when maybe she could have done something.

Rising to her feet and shaking her head again, Melanie left the room, heading for the kitchen. With Taryn still holding Josh and Caleb taking a seat next to Matt to comfort him, Tyler turned and followed.

"Mel?" He came to a stop a few feet behind her, unsure if she would erupt into a fit of rage or just the opposite, one of grief. And grief was harder for her, and him, to deal with. With anger she could rant and rave, go after the first thing that crossed her path and pummel it to death. She could punish something for the way she was feeling.

But grief, grief she didn't know what to do with.

He stared at her back, and when she didn't reply, he came to her side. He saw that she had one hand covering her face, the other across her stomach as though in pain. When he put a hand on her shoulder, she flinched, but he didn't pull back.

"Melanie, look at me," he said to her gently.

"Tyler, leave me alone."

Although her voice was quietly commanding, Tyler saw her throat tighten as she swallowed hard and fought against tears. A year ago, he would have followed her order and walked away without ever even trying to comfort her. He would have let her sort out her issues alone, and let her deal with them in her own way. But now she was his wife, and the mother of his son, and there wasn't a power in any street, alley, or Helping Hand force that could make him turn away now.

Tyler took hold of her shoulders and drew her back against him. She resisted, but he didn't let go.

"Tyler, stop it." Her words were sharp and bitter, and she tried to yank her arm from his hand. "I said let go!"

"Melanie, you can't turn away from me," Tyler replied as he tightened his grip on her arms. "You need me." He could have yelled, but it would have been pointless. Instead, he let her struggle against him, never letting her go as she cursed. He kept his stare trained on her face, catching the sorrow, the guilt, the shock.

Melanie stopped fighting when a sudden wave of exhaustion overcame her and she stared up at her husband. "Please don't do this, Tyler. Just let me go."

Still holding her by the arms, Tyler gently shook his head, not saying a word. Words weren't what she needed. They stared at one another for a moment, until, with a sigh, Melanie relented and lowered her head. "I let her die, Tyler," she confessed, tears in her eyes. "I walked away when Robbie told me to. I didn't go back even though I knew I should have. I wasn't there for her when she needed me the most."

"My God, Melanie." Tyler sighed as well and stepped back. "You can't keep blaming yourself for this!"

"I promised her that she would be safe!" Melanie felt rage in her blood as she listened to Tyler's words. "I told her I would watch out for her and make all the bullshit she's been through go away! But I didn't. I made the wrong choice. I was too wrapped up in my *own* goddamn life and now she's *dead*!"

Tyler grabbed her again when she started to walk away. He didn't let go when she fought him, nor did he say anything to try and calm her down. Melanie put her hands on his chest and pushed, but as always, he was strong. He saw the way her face was held in a visage of barely-controlled rage and angst, and could feel her muscles at work as she tried to free herself.

"It'll be okay, Melanie," Tyler soothed, whispering in her ear when he felt her finally give in to his hug. She covered her face with her hands and rested her head against his chest, tears starting to fall. She was overwhelmed, and with that he could empathize.

Kissing her forehead, Tyler placed his cheek on the top of her head and held her tightly against him. "You'll be okay. We'll get through this together."

Chapter 17

Melanie held her child close as she entered the church, creeped out by the statues with eyes that followed her every move. She could feel Tyler's hand on her back as he led her to a seat in the back.

Settling down, Melanie glanced around and saw a large group of high school students, their eyes red. Voices were whispered through tears and sniffling sobs, and the sounds brought her back to her feet.

"I'll be right back," she told Tyler, handing Josh over. Tyler took the baby without a word and watched as Melanie walked down the aisle and up to the closed casket.

Approaching the casket, the former Hell Hound and Helping Hand shook her head. The lid was layered with flowers and pictures, as well as a few items that she was sure had meant something to the teenager at one point in her life: a dark red pen, a chemistry flask, and a guitar pick, among other things.

Melanie wondered how Kelly felt before the truck hit, what she had seen, or thought. Had she been afraid? Brave? Indifferent? Did she even care about living? She could only wonder.

"I'm sorry, Kelly," she whispered. "I should have been there. I never wanted this to happen. I chose my life over yours, and I was wrong." It was hard to accept the fact that Kelly's death was the result of her own selfishness. After so many years of running the Helping Hands, of creating it and leading it and helping the project grow, she had deserted everything for her own greedy desire for some degree of normalcy. If she had chosen the Helping Hands, Kelly would still be alive. Perhaps Josh wouldn't have been born and she and Tyler would still only be friends, but at least with that choice, no one would have ended up in a casket.

But it was too late to change things, and so with a heavy sigh, Melanie ran her hand along the edge of the casket and then returned to her place next to Tyler. She didn't glance around at the people sitting in the first pew. If she had, she would have seen Robbie Anderson watching her every move.

Turning to Danielle, Robbie frowned and gestured towards Melanie. "Can you believe she showed up? I mean, the woman is practically responsible for this, sending her home from South Bay and letting Jeffrey get to her."

Danielle shrugged, her eyes puffy. She had cried all she could in the past few days. She cried over the loss of her sister, over the loneliness she would forever feel, over the blame she knew she had to accept. There was nothing she could do to make things right again, and she was relieved that she would be leaving soon, going back to Florida to live with her grandfather. Her mother had lost custody, Jeffrey was in prison, and she wasn't left with a whole lot of options. But she didn't want to live with the Andersons anymore.

In fact, she never wanted to see any of them ever again.

"Kelly liked her," Danielle replied in a detached voice. "Maybe she's just paying her respects."

Melanie O'Conner tried to do the right thing, Danielle thought, and when the name ran through her mind, she glanced over her shoulder. Sitting in the last row, she saw Melanie, who was whispering something to a muscular, blonde man next to her holding a baby. As if sensing the stare, Melanie's eyes shifted to Danielle's. Danielle pursed her lips when Melanie gave her a nod, her features soft. For a brief moment Danielle felt slightly comforted.

When the minister called his name, Robbie sighed and stood up slowly, Danielle's eyes watering despite the fact that she thought she could cry no more. The walk to the podium seemed miles away, and Robbie took each step carefully, swallowing heavily as he passed the casket.

He stood at the podium, staring out at the sea of faces. Most he recognized, some he didn't, like the man sitting next to Melanie O'Conner. Then again, they all were strangers to Kelly.

"I'm not... I'm not going to stand up here and say what a great girl Kelly was, or how she always got good grades in school, because we all know that," he began, his hands gripping the sides of the podium tightly. "What I want to say has more to do with how Kelly changed my life." For once, he was going to speak the truth, and though it would be a blow to his pride, he didn't really care anymore.

"I've always been a fighter. Ever since I was a kid I loved getting into fights, and making people afraid of me. I thought it made me look tough and cool. I was wrong."

"Kelly told me something once that at the time didn't make any sense, but now I finally get it." He was surprised at how badly his voice was shaking. "She told me, it's not *who* you fight that matters, but *how* you fight. When she said that, I thought she meant that I should only fight people I knew I could beat, but now I realize that she was saying that I shouldn't hurt people. Ever, even if they are wrong, or if I'm wrong, it doesn't matter. She taught me that a hand should never be raised to anyone under any circumstance."

Breathing deeply, Robbie shook his head and sniffed. "Kelly was stronger than she thought. She was a hero. She *is* a hero," he corrected himself, his lips trembling when he felt the tears coming to his eyes.

Robbie stared dismally at the headstone, his eyes barely reading Kelly's name. The air was thick and heavy, filled with tears and darkness. Hundreds of flowers, all different colors and sizes, were placed around the grave, showing to the world just how much Kelly Mitchell had been loved. But despite everyone's love and affection, the cemetery had emptied out long ago. The casket had been lowered and he'd come back an hour after, once everyone had gone home.

Everyone except for Robbie.

He didn't know if he stayed to be alone, or because he was afraid of how he might act in the company of others, but nevertheless, there he was, hands in his pockets as he stood in front of Kelly's grave. He shook his head as his thoughts swarmed inside his mind. He heard accusations, pleas, angered shouts, whimpering apologies, and he couldn't figure out what any of it meant.

He thought about the viewing, how all those people he knew had been there, but not really for Kelly. They didn't know her, and that was his fault. But, he tried to argue with himself, it was *Kelly's* fault that she was dead. He told her to stop the car, to talk to him. She hadn't listened. She ignored him, brushed him off, just like always. If she hadn't been so stubborn, she would have heard his side of the story, would have understood why he lied.

He had almost convinced himself of that when he realized that a tear had fallen down his cheek. He wiped it away angrily as he stared at the gray stone. It seemed so distant, so detached from everything. Just like Kelly had been.

Cold.

Indifferent.

Cared only about what was best for *her*.

"Shit, Kelly," he whispered. "Why? What the hell were you doing?" Relenting to his feelings, he kneeled down and reached out to touch the headstone. He sniffed and held back a sob, tracing his finger over Kelly's name. "You let him win, Kelly. You let the bastard win."

"She was an incredibly brave girl."

Robbie straightened quickly, his face hardening when he saw Melanie O'Conner standing behind him. With a scowl, he faced Kelly's grave again. "She ran from her problems," he replied coldly. "That's hardly brave."

Melanie walked to Robbie's side, her hands in her pockets. "Maybe she knew where she was running to."

"It doesn't matter where she ran," Robbie argued. He despised this woman, the convict who claimed to help people but let them die instead. "Running is still running, no matter what you call it."

Melanie inhaled deeply, silently reading Kelly's name on the stone. She recalled doing the same in Denver when she visited Wess's grave. "You can't blame Kelly for what happened. You don't know what it's like to have to live with all that pain."

"That still doesn't make for a good excuse to kill yourself," Robbie answered spitefully. "I tried to talk to her, but she refused to listen. It was her own selfishness that killed her."

Normally she would have reacted with rage, but Melanie was so over death and so tired of fighting with the boy that she merely sighed. It didn't surprise her that Robbie was so angry. He loved Kelly, missed her, and needed someone to blame for her death other than himself.

But just because he couldn't handle the blame didn't mean she would let him condemn Kelly. There were a lot of people Melanie didn't like, and she absolutely loathed Robbie Anderson.

"Robbie, I wouldn't expect you to understand. You can't even face the fact that you had something to do with her death. Someone like you would never willingly take any sort of blame because according to you, *you* never do anything wrong." When Robbie didn't respond, she continued. "She only lived for one thing, Robbie. One thing, and nothing more, and believe it or not, that one thing wasn't you and your bullshit idea that all girls are supposed to fall madly in love with you. She lived to protect Danielle, give her sister an escape. If she got to enjoy life while she was at it, then she'd take advantage of it. You said it yourself. She was, is, a hero."

"Yeah." It came out as more of a scoff than an agreement. He had been thinking a lot about that comment, wondering what could have possessed him to say such a stupid thing. "A hero. What is a hero anyway."

"A hero is someone who does the right thing, even when the right thing means risking it all for someone other than yourself."

The two were quiet for a moment, Robbie swaying from foot to foot and Melanie standing still as a rock. She knew the teenager next to her wanted to say something from the way he kept stealing sideways glances at her, but she didn't initiate the conversation.

He wondered if she would say something, so he wouldn't have to. *Maybe*, he thought, *she's one of those people who don't need to hear the other person say they were sorry in order for the apology to be accepted.* He didn't really think so, because he had heard the anger and disappointment in her voice, and he knew that she didn't like him. Hated him, most likely, thought he was a loser. So why should he talk to her? He didn't owe her anything. What did she ever do for him?

Tried to stop me before it was too late, he answered his own question. *And I was dumb enough not to listen.*

No, he argued silently, refusing to accept his answer. *No, I tried to help Kelly. She's the one who didn't listen.*

Because I never gave her the chance to.

"You know, I um... I was wrong," he admitted. "With Kelly, you know, and... lying to her about her past. I've had time to think about it, and me and Danielle and my parents talked it over, and I was wrong." Kicking the ground, he glanced up at Melanie, who was watching him wordlessly. "This is mostly my fault, I know that. I lied to her, and she died because... because she couldn't handle the truth when it all came back. I should have listened to you. You were right all along."

Melanie accepted his apology silently, her jaw set. She was sympathetic, but at the same time, she was also furious. It had been his stupidity and stubbornness that led to this.

And besides that, Melanie silently cursed, *it doesn't take a fucking lie-detector test to figure out that the kid's apologetic guilt-trip is all an act.* He wanted her to think that he wasn't a complete bastard.

"Robbie," she began, raising her head and squinting in the sun, "I'm not going to tell you that you only did what you thought best. Saying you're sorry doesn't make what you did okay and sure as hell doesn't change anything, especially since you're not being sincere. Yes, you were wrong, and I'm not sure I'm ever going to forgive you." She sighed heavily and looked over at Robbie, waiting until he returned her stare. "But for Kelly's sake, I'm going to try."

Robbie watched her go, knowing that nothing would ever be the same again. He lost the most amazing person he had ever known, and also the respect of the most influential person he'd ever met. He didn't know what would happen tomorrow, or a few weeks down the road, but he did know that the impact Kelly Mitchell made on his life was something he had never felt before. She made him see the foolishness in fighting, in taking joy at other people's pain. Even now that she was gone, he wanted to be a better person. If not for her, then for himself. His only wish was that he could have found a way to thank her for all she had given him.

Saying a silent good-bye to his departed friend, Robbie Anderson wiped away his tears and turned from the grave.

Chapter 18

California State Penitentiary

As he made his way down the hall and into the sweltering laundry room, Jeffrey Ponder let loose a stream of profanity that echoed off the corridor walls. His words were bitter, his eyes narrow, his body itching from the hideous brown uniform. When the cursing stopped, he resorted to muttering under his breath, talking meaningless threats of what he planned to do with that bitch once he got out of jail. Big plans, bloody plans.

Jeffrey was pissed. More than pissed, he was livid, infuriated, and each day was spent mentally planning his attack. He wouldn't be in jail forever, and when he got out, those traitorous bitches would pay. Melanie O'Conner would pay. Monica would pay. Danielle would pay. Kelly was already dead, but he knew exactly where she was buried.

Her body would burn.

The wheels to the laundry bin squeaked as he came to a stop next to the washing machines. What a joke, he scoffed, the idea of him actually doing laundry the right way, sorting colors and dumping in the proper amounts of detergent, then folding the shirts and pants and towels for distribution. Like he was some kind of housewife or something. No, he would show everyone that Jeffrey Ponder didn't do anyone else's dirty work, and he had just the plan.

After much consideration and preparation he still wasn't entirely sure that his scheme was going to work, but as far as he was concerned he had nothing to lose. It was just something he had seen on a B-list movie that he always wanted to test just to see if it really worked or if it was a mere manifestation created in the mind of the director.

His plan came into the laundry room just minutes after he had arrived. "You got it?" Jeffrey asked, holding out a hand expectantly. He dropped his arm when the man simply stared over at him. "What? You got a problem with this? Your shit ain't in this load."

"No, no problem. It ain't like it's some big scam or anything," the man, Ripley Baxter, replied. "Itching powder and crushed glass. I'm so scared."

Ripley's bored tone annoyed Jeffrey. "Whatever. Just give it to me." Once again he held out a hand, and then drew it back after Ripley dropped a box into his palm. Satisfaction and demented pleasure ran through him when he imagined how the inmates would feel once they put on their new 'clean' clothes. Their flesh would bleed for weeks, for he knew exactly what he was doing. Or at least, he knew what he had watched during the ninety-minutes-too-long horror flick.

Nothing but sand stared up at him when he opened the box, gray sand from the exercise yard in the back of the prison. "What the hell is this?"

"An excuse to get you down here," Ripley answered, crossing his arms and leaning against the wall. His voice was rough, a tone acquired through years of smoking and drinking nothing but hard liquor. One of these days his bad habits would kill him, but he thrived on his addictions nearly as much as he did his love of treachery, larceny, and cold-blooded murder.

"Me and the boys wanted to have a private word with you."

"The boys?"

Jeffrey's eyes widened slightly as two other men entered the laundry room, shutting the door behind them. It was three on one, and his odds weren't looking good. He knew some of the inmates were after him, not being fans of a man hauled in for domestic and child abuse. Apparently he had misjudged Ripley Baxter's open attempts to form an alliance with him, however superficial it was.

"What the hell is going on?"

"You got a score to settle with O'Conner, right?" Ripley asked. "I heard you got your lawyer to bring the bitch down in court."

A smirk worked its way across Jeffrey's rough face as a twinge of relief fluttered in his gut. "Yeah. But it ain't over yet. I've got my plans. You want in on them?" When Ripley and his friends smiled, he took a curious step closer. "What's your score with her?"

"Street business," one of the men, known only as Banx, answered sternly.

"The bitch deserves some vengeance," Ripley put in, his voice cruel. "One person fucks with another, heads start to roll. So what are you planning?"

It seemed too good to be true, that he would have the help of three men who knew O'Conner on a personal level. "I've got this, shall we say, lawyer friend from DC who dug up some dirt on her father, and has a way to get him out of jail. He wants some money out of the deal and who can blame him, so all I gotta do is have the funds transferred from my account to his and Jerry Hunter is home free."

"And when the father gets out?" Banx inquired as Ripley nodded along with the information. "Then what?"

"Hunter wants her dead," Jeffrey answered. "But he wants her to suffer first, so he's going after her family. Husband, kid, other gang members. He wants her to beg for her life, for her kid's life. Show her what happens when she fucks with the wrong people."

Ripley thought about it, finding it somewhat amusing that the self-loving former lawyer or manager or whatever the hell he was actually thought he was dealing in the big leagues. Crushed glass, paying people to get an enemy's father out of prison, who did this guy think he was?

"So where do you come in? What's your part in all this?"

Jeffrey held out his arms as though the answer should have been obvious. "I'm the treasury department. The guy won't free Hunter unless he gets some big bucks. He doesn't care half as much about bringing O'Conner down as he does about being richer than he already is. So I have the funds transferred, my friend gets the cash, he pays off a judge to release Hunter, and O'Conner gets paid back for all the trouble she's caused."

Fingertips tapping together, Ripley cocked his head to the side. "Now you see, that's where the problem is. You know, the whole paying-O'Conner-back thing."

Jeffrey glared over at the three men. "What? I thought you wanted O'Conner dead."

"When did I say that?"

"What about deserving some vengeance? You just called her a bitch not five minutes ago."

"I always call O'Conner a bitch, ever since I met her. I call her a bitch, she calls me a self-righteous fucker, and we go about our business." Ripley shrugged, a hint of a smile tugging at his lips when he saw the worry in Jeffrey's eyes.

Banx stepped forward then, lifting a finger to point at the man. "You see, we all knew you got yourself in here for beating your wife and step-kids. That alone is enough to get you all sorts of fucked up. But then we heard that you messed with O'Conner in the process, and Melanie O'Conner is a very good friend of ours."

"You mess with O'Conner, you mess with her friends."

"And she has many, many friends," Ripley continued after the third man, Nick, had put in his comment. "You screwed up, because we're in good old San Fran, and O'Conner spent a lot of time here. You might have friends in the government who can get people out of jail, but she has friends from the street who will fuck you up all the way back to Hell, and she doesn't have to pay them. In fact, she doesn't even have to ask."

He took a step closer, and another when Jeffrey started to back away. "Rule number one of revenge, pal, is to know exactly who you're messing with, because that certain someone might have an entire army backing her up. Maybe someone owes her a favor, maybe they're just a good friend." He stared plainly at his next target. "What I'm saying, tough guy, is you're not going to be making that transfer."

The men faced off for a moment, three against one. The tension built quickly, and Jeffrey's breath came out short when he realized what the three were planning on doing. Before he could even attempt a fight, Jeffrey was thrown into one of the washing machines, Banx throwing him to the floor and holding him there.

Ripley pulled out a small box from his pocket, gesturing with his head to Nick. "Hold his head."

"Motherfuckers. Get the hell off of me!" Jeffrey shouted. He let out a furious growl when Nick gripped his chin and pried his mouth open, fingers digging painfully into his jaw. Jeffrey twisted his head, but the man was too strong. Ripley lowered himself until his knee was braced against his victim's cheek.

"You wanted crushed glass, you fucking bastard, you got it."

With that, Ripley dumped the contents of the box into Jeffrey's mouth, letting the shards pour down the man's throat. Instantly Jeffrey started to choke, tears forming as Nick held his mouth closed and forced him to swallow. Jeffrey could feel the tiny glass bits slicing into his throat and he tasted bitter blood, his eyes bulging when he felt the jagged bites of razors eating at his insides.

"That's for the girl," Ripley whispered into his ear, then hauled the man to his feet. "*This* is for O'Conner."

Prison warden Bob Daffney made his rounds that night as he usually did, starting with the courtyard and ending in the basement laundry room. He half-heartedly looked around corners and in small spaces, watching out for the prisoner who hadn't been in his cell that night at bed check. Daffney figured the guy, Jeffrey Ponder, was most likely hiding out somewhere, waiting for his chance to run. It happened all the time, and the prisoners were always caught.

Daffney frowned when he heard the sound of a dryer running. He headed closer, annoyed that an inmate had undoubtedly screwed up a load. Reaching out to turn the dryer off, the guard grimaced at the strange stench coming from the inside compartment. "Damn," he muttered in disgust. "Didn't know they stank *that* bad."

A clunk that sounded when the machine stopped had Daffney slowly turning back around. He eyed the machine, trying to remember if it had been clothes or shoes that were being washed that day. Carefully, he lifted a hand to the dryer door and yanked it open.

"Oh, holy *fuck*!" Daffney shouted, stumbling back until he bounced off the opposite wall. A searing sickness slammed against the back of his throat, yet he was unable to tear his eyes away from the gruesome sight before him.

The man, unrecognizable as his flesh melted like candle wax off his bones, was bent backwards in the cycle, his broken arms twisted into a knot behind his back, his heels shoved over his shoulders, blood caked from two gaping holes where his eyes used to be. Spine snapped in two, the man's back was nearly folded in half. The hair on the corpse had fallen out in chunks, the jumpsuit twisted enough to reveal a chest of snapped, jagged ribs breaking through skin, and blood was splattered everywhere.

With fumbling hands Daffney grabbed the walkie-talkie on his belt. "Sampson," he called for one of the wardens on duty. "Sampson, get to the laundry room. We have a situation. I think… I think I found Ponder."

Fighting to keep from vomiting, Daffney kicked the dryer door shut and turned away from the sickening sight.

Chapter 19

Collinsville, California

Tyler was in the shower when the phone rang. Melanie, alone in the kitchen after having put her son to bed, took her time in answering, not really caring who it was or what they wanted. Tossing a spoon into the sink, she lifted the receiver to her ear. "Yeah?" she said, tired, then woke up when the person identified himself. "Darren? What the fuck do *you* want?"

She said nothing as the lawyer told her what happened, that Jeffrey Ponder had been found broken and baking in the prison dryer, identifiable only through DNA testing. She hung up on the man after he finished his story, lowering the phone and gripping the counter as emotion overwhelmed her. Her mind fought to comprehend the new reality, that the iron-fisted bastard had been murdered in cold blood. There were no suspects, Darren said, not yet. No one knew because no one would talk, no one would rat out the men who had done Jeffrey in because that was how things worked and everyone followed that code or else there would be more than just Hell to pay.

But there was only one man at the prison who had a penchant for removing eyes.

Ripley Baxter. It had to be Ripley, and possibly Banx. She had known them since she was thirteen, met them in San Francisco through a mutual friend. She and Ripley hadn't been the best of friends at first, but eventually they warmed up to one another. Regardless of time or place or circumstance, there was a bond, an 'always got your back' agreement between the three of them. Now they were lifers, triple sentences for serial killing. They had nothing to lose with an inmate murder, and they had always promised to watch out for her best interests.

And right now, her best interest was the murder of one specific bastard who deserved it the most.

Jeffrey Ponder was dead. The words made her breathless. He would never again lift a hand to another woman, would never again be the cause of an innocent girl's death. If only she could have had one minute alone with him, sixty seconds to wrap her hands around his throat, to feel his blood on her hands. He made her want to kill, and for that she hated him.

Melanie sank down to a squat, her back braced against the counter. Her hands clutched the phone tightly, resting it against her head. Tears came from an unknown place, sobs from a wound deep in her heart. She rocked gently, holding back a whimper.

It was over. He was dead, and she no longer had to feel the desires of murder. Her throat tightened, her teeth clenched together, her knuckles white by her tight grip, and her mind raced with questions as to why she was so upset. Then she realized that it wasn't grief at all.

She was relieved.

She was thankful.

There was justice in the world after all.

Later that night, Melanie stood by the bed while pulling her long hair back into a loose braid. As she ribboned strands of hair around one another, she thought about the past year-and-a-half. Things had happened that she never thought possible. She had a legal job she actually enjoyed, a husband who was also her best friend, a newborn son, a life with people who cared about her and would risk their own heads in order to save hers. She lost a best friend to a man with a vengeful heart, and had to say good-bye to two teenagers whom she cared deeply about.

She still had her worries, of course. Her father was in jail and would one day be released. Wilson Winbaker, the father of Teresa Winbaker who had attacked Taryn and threatened to expose them a year ago, was getting out in three months. Then they would have to face the possibility of the man attempting to reveal their identities. Thirdly there was Matt and his new gang, and Taryn and Caleb's decision to retire. And not to forget, she silently added, the F.B.I. agent who had promised not to talk. The media was still hot on the mysterious shooting and death of Mayor George Livingston.

But through it all - the murders, the confusing messes, the parents who sought revenge, her closest friends retiring from the Helping Hands - Melanie knew one thing was certain. She had a legacy she was leaving behind.

Matt was that legacy, her legacy. Dylan and Shane were Wess's legacy. Caleb and Taryn's retirement from the project would create their own branches, three to be exact. All of them, the original four, were leaving their mark on the world.

Melanie lifted the heavy comforter and lay down next to Tyler, who was already in bed. He positioned himself so that he was leaning over her, one arm on either side of her slender figure. "It's all okay," he said quietly, and Melanie nodded.

"It's all okay," she repeated.

Tyler brushed back her hair from her face with his fingers, lowering himself enough to kiss her softly. She responded by wrapping her arms around his neck and holding him to her, their foreheads gently touching.

Yeah, Melanie thought, feeling it deep down when Tyler kissed her again, *it's all okay*.

As she settled onto her side and pulled the blanket to her chest, Tyler reached over and put his arm around her stomach, pulling her against him as he said a quiet goodnight.

Here, Melanie thought as she felt the well-defined muscles of Tyler's chest against her back, *is where it all makes sense*.

Epilogue

The auditorium was packed, two children sitting anxiously up on stage, the last of what had been a group of twenty. The announcer stood at the podium, her hair tied back in a tight bun at the nape of her neck and her dark blue suit neatly pressed. In her hands were cards with the words on it, and silently she guessed who she thought would be the winner. Her money was on the second child, as was her preference.

"Miranda," she said to the first little girl, "the word is 'exhaustion.'"

"Exhaustion," Miranda repeated, her young face twisted into an expression of deep thought. It was a hard one, and she hesitated before replying, quietly sounding out the word syllable by syllable. "Exhaustion. E-x-a-u-s-t-i-o-n."

"I'm sorry, Miranda, that's incorrect." The announcer shook her head sympathetically and Miranda's shoulders slumped. Turning to the second child, the woman gave a small smile. "Aneesa, if you spell this word right, you will be the winner of this tournament. Please spell, 'exhaustion.'"

Aneesa thought about the word, saying it in her head as many times as she could before visualizing it. Her deep brown eyes scanned the crowd, and she smiled a tremendous smile when she saw Mel Scotford sitting in the first row, just like he promised.

Turning to the announcer, Aneesa took in a deep breath. "Exhaustion. E-x-h-a-u-s-t-i-o-n. Exhaustion."

"That is correct," the woman at the podium said over the thundering applause. Aneesa jumped up and down as a man came from the side of the stage and placed a medal over her head. He shook her hand, congratulating her, and told her with a laugh to go tell all her friends. Then she ran to the edge of the stage where her parents, her new, loving parents, came to greet her.

"Congratulations, honey!" Toya Baglin hugged her daughter fiercely. "You were so great up there!"

"I knew you could do it!" Dwight Baglin hugged Aneesa as well, affectionately messing up her hair. "First place and a gold medal! Looks like we got a genius in the family, huh?"

"And a very pretty genius at that."

"Mel!" Aneesa squealed when Tyler appeared from behind her parents. She hugged him hard, then gasped when she saw the huge bouquet of roses in his hand. "Are those for me?"

Tyler laughed at her astonishment. "Who else would they be for? Didn't I promise to be here in the front row with big red flowers when you won the spelling bee?" He chuckled when she grabbed at the flowers, cradling them against her chest.

"She talks about you nonstop, you know," Toya informed Tyler, nudging him playfully. "She got rather jealous when I mentioned you had a wife."

Tyler laughed, watching the girl show off her flowers. "She's quite a kid."

"That she is," Toya agreed. "So where's yours?"

"Around here somewhere." He gestured with a wave of his hand. "Some woman wanted to talk to the infamous Helping Hand. She should, oh, there she is." When Melanie appeared at his side, Tyler put an arm around her shoulder and faced the two parents. "Mr. and Mrs. Baglin," he said, "I'd like you to meet my wife, Melanie, and our son, Josh. Melanie, this is Toya and Dwight Baglin."

"Hey," Melanie said, shifting and hiding a scowl when Tyler nudged her in the side with a discreet elbow. "Uh… nice to meet you."

"You too, dear." Toya smiled at the woman's discomfort. She obviously wasn't used to being around large groups of people, and for some reason, she found that charming. "I have to say, you are one lucky woman. Mel is a great guy. After all, he gave us our little ball of sunshine."

"Daddy, Daddy! Can we go out to eat? Please, please, please!" Aneesa asked excitedly as she ran up to the small group, her small body wriggling as she poked Dwight's left shoulder repeatedly, then ran around to his other side and began jabbing her finger at his right one instead. "Ice cream! Ice cream for the winner!"

Dwight laughed and scooped Aneesa into his arms. "Anything you want. You're the champ." He turned to Melanie and Tyler. "Guess we better get goin'. Maybe if we eat now she'll be asleep by midnight."

After they had gotten into the car and were heading away from the spelling bee tournament, Melanie turned to Tyler. "She's got great parents."

"Yeah, she does. I'm really glad they decided to adopt her." He had done a lot of research to find the perfect home for Aneesa, and the Baglins were just the couple. Happy, incredibly generous, and fully able and willing to spoil Aneesa for the rest of her life.

Tyler glanced in the rearview mirror, seeing Josh gnawing on his fingers, drool dribbling down his chin in the careless indifference all babies had. With a grin, he reached over and took Melanie's hand. In their quest for a normal life, they could only hope that no one was following as they made the journey home, where their family would continue to grow with all the love and happiness the two former Helping Hands had to offer.

But there was always someone watching.

There was always someone waiting for the perfect moment to strike.

Little did they know, that moment was rapidly approaching.

ABOUT THE AUTHOR

A friend to the written word since the time she first picked up a pen, Kristina Circelli shares her passion for fiction in her multi-genre novels.

Circelli is the author of several fiction books, including <u>The Sour Orange Derby</u>, a young adult novel about family and childhood imagination steeped in southern traditions; <u>Beyond the Western Sun</u> and <u>Walk the Red Road</u> of The Whisper Legacy, which centers on Native American cultures and the legends that come to life in the spirit realm; and <u>The Helping Hands,</u> a book that follows a gang of friends who rescue abused children.

The Whisper Legacy melds fantasy and legend in an epic quest that brings to life the stories and creatures of Native American lore. These novels feature Whisper, a Cherokee woman following her destiny to defeat the evil Raven-Eater and restore balance to the spirit realms. Circelli's latest 7-book series, The Helping Hands, features the reprint of her first published novels, <u>The Helping Hands</u> and <u>The Iron Fist: Legacy of the Helping Hands</u>. This series places readers in the middle of a fight against child abuse as Melanie O'Conner and friends kidnap abused children and bring them to a secluded hideaway, caring for them while struggling with their own personal demons of addiction and loss.

From her extraordinary ability to vividly create heretofore-unknown worlds to her engaging prose, Circelli's landmark novels signify the emergence of an important voice in American literature. As a young author navigating the indie publishing route, she has been invited to participate in several author and school literacy events, including book signings, panel presentations, and introducing best-selling author Carl Hiaasen at a college presidential lecture. She also speaks in front of young writers' groups for kids passionate about writing, as her novel <u>Beyond the Western Sun</u> is being taught in middle school classes.

Currently, Circelli works full-time as a copywriter and part-time as a creative writing professor at the University of North Florida, where she received her Bachelor's and Master's degrees in English. She resides in Jacksonville, Florida with her husband, Seth, and cat, Sir Whisky Sour.

Contact Information:

Email: kristina@circelli.info
Website: www.circelli.info
Twitter: @KCircelli
Blog: http://anawfullybigadventure-kc.blogspot.com/
Books Found at: Amazon.com, BN.com, & www.circelli.info

www.ingramcontent.com/pod-product-compliance
Lightning Source LLC
Chambersburg PA
CBHW072217170626
46813CB00003B/981